A PARADOX OF DREAMS

BOOK 3 OF THE *HAVELI* SERIES

HARSHALI SINGH

Readomania

Readomania
An imprint of Kurious Kind Media Private Limited
readomania.com
contact@readomania.com | Facebook: @iamreadomania |
X: @iamreadomania | Instagram: @iamreadomania

First Published in 2022 by Readomania. Reprinted in 2026.

Edited by Indrani Ganguly

ISBN: 978-93-91800-16-1

Typeset in Palatino Linotype by Shine Graphics
Printed in Delhi

Prologue

'Do you think when terrible things happen, it leaves a stain on the place where they occur?' she asks me, touching my stone-cold heart, warming it with her cheek. 'Why do I feel it has left one on me?' she questions.

I am not at liberty to disclose the cause of her pain, even to her. The dreams that haunt her, the otherness she feels, all stem from her past. A past she has misplaced, suppressed. I wish I could hold her, wrap my arms around her, a gesture she rarely allows. I yearn for my inanimate self to...only for a moment, become alive. Not because I want to experience touch, but so I can give her a moment of respite from the nightmares that haunt her on some nights.

She is Charu, the third daughter of the large Sharma family that inhabits me now. I am Anwar Haveli—the Haveli with hundred doors.

A solemn baby, she was born with eyes too old in her infant face. I knew then that she was an old soul who had chosen to be reborn. She was special. The quietest of the siblings, she held my stone-heart in her palms since she lost her sight at nine years of age. It was sudden. The devastation her parents underwent was nothing compared to what the little girl had to come to terms with. Her confusion, helplessness, and anguish on sensing her parents' inability to handle the irreversible change in her circumstances were agonising to watch. They tried to do the best they could, but sometimes our best is not enough.

I have weathered the storms of progress in this old colony of Naugraha. In the last 150 years, I have seen old Delhi's lanes grow narrower; the outcrops and illegal constructions almost choke the streets. Once, horse carriages rode regally here. Large water fountains stood resplendent in every courtyard the trickling water, perfumed with ittar, attracting a hoard of butterflies fluttering around the flowers. Art and culture were celebrated through the lively mehfils and mushairas. Such happy days they were, yet so short-lived.

We used to be nine Havelis once. Soon the loneliness, the ignominy of the lives that surrounded me, usurped me. The new era shook me to my very foundations and obliterated many of my counterparts. Slowly, the families moved away, but the nostalgia lingered, haunting the sprawling mansions, reminding us of the changing dynamics of time.

The grandeur faded, and so did we. The sepia hue took over all the facets of our existence and, like the gauzy film of dust that lies unmoving, we watched silently as the world continued its rotation.

I wonder what would have become of me had the Sharma family not moved in. The head of the Sharma family, Arun, came as a young boy brimming with promise and ambition. His father's heavy-handedness and Arun's unfulfilled dreams made him into the man he is today—passive and resigned.

His half-brother Varun also grew up in my rooms. Two brothers separated by warring mothers.

Arun's wife, the devout Uma, who walks with a limp due to a past illness, joined this dysfunctional family. Full of gumption and emotional strength, she resolved to find a peaceful solution to the constant unpleasantness.

She reinstated Arun's mother as the matriarch and set up Varun's mother and her son in a modest house in another part of the city. This small victory instituted by handing over her gold and appealing to the lady's vanity, Uma was able to weed out the chaos from their lives.

It was my Uma who shook away my malaise. Airing out my shuttered rooms, she let in the sun and restored my pride with a quick coat of paint. The glass panes shone again, and the lattice jalis were scrubbed clean of cobwebs. The gardens flourished, the fountain gurgled, and I felt revived...rescued.

The children came within a few years of each other. Aruna, the eldest, then Bhavya and, finally, Charu, my sweet sunflower. I had thought they had given up having more children after Charu, but Uma had always wanted a son. Maybe, it was to save her crumbling marriage that she decided to try one more time. This time she was successful in bearing a male child, the heir.

The pride of this achievement shone on Uma's face for many years. Women crave to give their families a male child. And so, Dheeraj became the heir apparent, set to inherit the saree shop his father had been gifted.

The children grew up together, loved and happy. The parents masked their personal struggles as best as possible and tried to present a united front.

After a few years, Arun mollified his panicked wife when they found out the cause of her morning sickness was not one child but three. Etti came first; a second later, it was Fanny, and then came Gina. And, so, the already big family became enormous.

Despite the love that surrounds me, it was only when Charu started calling me by my name, Anwar, did I truly become a part of their life. How easily she made me tangible. Maybe I am biased, but I am allowed to play favourites at my age, I suppose. And, she is that, the most beloved out of the seven children.

When Charu was nine years old, she told her mother that she could smell the grass, feel the hot sun, and sense her mother's fear, but could not see anything. The doctors confirmed that she had suffered from a condition as a result of her untreated eye problems. It had caused her to go blind.

It was an arrow into the heart of the family's happiness. Uma took the news to heart, blaming herself for delaying Charu's treatment. Arun fell into a strange melancholy and became estranged from his wife and children—a chasm that kept growing.

Uma was caught between a mother's guilt and the constant problem of not knowing what to do to help her daughter who was disabled and would always be treated as a lesser being in this world just as she had been regarded. Her fear of repeating her own mother's mistakes kept her at arm's length from her daughter.

My Uma staggered under the weight of being strong and buckled under the pressure of taking care of her seven children and me. Suresh, Arun's best friend, helped with Charu and her special needs like a surrogate father.

The little girl became more subdued as the days passed. She had to unlearn everything, acquire new skills to survive. Joy seemed to drip out of her one day at a time. Uma had always been fearful of the heightened intuition that was a part of Charu's personality. She found it growing stronger when Charu lost her vision.

After trying to manage on her own for almost two years, Uma decided to send Charu to her mother in Surat to be home-schooled. Though she knew her mother was stiff and cold, she also knew if someone could give Charu the skills to stand tall in this challenging world, it was her.

Charu was heartbroken when the news was shared with her. I heard her weeping the night before she was to leave, repeatedly asking her sisters what she had done wrong.

As time passed, I saw Charu change. The bond had broken. She blamed her mother for not wanting her enough. The silences grew sharper, the distance between them longer. The loss of her vision augmented her ability to sense people's feelings and thoughts, isolating her further, for no one wants to be read like a book. But, this ability also allowed her to find her calling.

Oh, Charu has had a difficult life. Every bruise she carries inside and out is a consequence of my presence in her life. She still suffers and fears being abandoned and displaced because no one addresses the hurt that still throbs inside her. She dreams again, not the restful dreams of the future but nightmares that lead to a reality that is best left buried.

This is Charu's story…

1. Charu

4:30 am, Wednesday

The girl gagged, pushed back, ready to vomit the meagre contents in her diminished stomach. The large hand in her hair tightened, punishingly keeping her in place. Her head was throbbing since she had hit it on the pillar after he had pushed her. She didn't remember what happened after that except that she had woken up with a pain so intense she wanted him to hit her just so she could replace this nauseating pain.

'Yes, you'll fetch me a good sum at the mandi,' said the mocking voice she had come to hate in the last three days. 'You will come to like it...make a good student. And, I will enjoy teaching you,' the slurred voice said.

Wh...w...why me...the little girl thought again, hoping for a miracle. Knowing there would be none today. Again. She squeezed her eyes closed, the rancid odour making her heave again. This time the overweight man belched loudly before pushing her away in agitation. He spat at her as she scampered back until her back hit the wall. The girl felt his angry eyes on her. Popping her thumb in her mouth, whimpering, she curled on her side facing the wall, rocking herself, foetus like.

The frustration and anger burning inside the man twisted as he watched the little girl crying. He found his release savouring the anticipated pleasure her screams would bring on the day her training would begin. He spilled his seed on the packed dirt floor with a satisfied grunt. The intent in his fetid thoughts frightened the girl even though she couldn't make sense of them yet. Leaning back on his cane mudda, his back against the uncemented wall, he lit a bidi and watched as the girl mumbled something. She seemed to say 'help me' again and again. He smiled, wanting to tell her there was no help for children like her. She would be a rag doll from now on, going from hand to hand until she either died or killed herself. Picking up the end of the dog chain he had tied around her neck, he yanked it hard. She stopped.

Smiling, he went back to smoking, wondering what more he could do to her before they moved her across the state lines. A gift had fallen into his hands when he had been asked to hide her for a few days. From the corner of his eye, he saw the girl's head lift, tilt. Suddenly, there was commotion above. Flicking his lit bidi at the girl, he quickly tied his pyjama over his yellowing vest and ran towards the familiar panicked tread clattering down the stairs.

'What's happening?' he shouted, making the girl flinch.

'Bhaiyaji...jaldi...it's the police,' the other man called out.

The heavy-set man turned his eyes scorching with frustration and stalked menacingly towards the girl lying wilting behind her knees. She felt the coarse hands grip her arm, jerking her up making the carousal in her head spin faster. As she surrendered to the whirlwind, she heard someone shout a name...

'NO,' Charu sat bolt upright on her bed, the bedsheet twisted underneath her quaking body. Her sudden movement woke the man beside her. He instantly switched on the bedside lamp and held her clawing fingers away from her neck's translucent skin, watching the red scratches she had already inflicted. She pushed him away, panting in distress. Charu ran her hands on the wiry headboard, the white stick that leaned against it clattered to the ground, confirming that she was in her small room in the haveli, safe.

'Hey! It's okay, Charu, I'm here. It's Ravi,' he said, taking her hands and placing them on his face. Her panicked fingers traced his familiar face, the long-broken nose, the broad forehead, the bushy eyebrows, the edgy jawline, and the curly hair. Ravi kept talking to her in a low voice while she reaffirmed his presence. In the last two years, he had become adept at calming her every time she woke from her dreams, if one could call them that. He felt her breathing equalize before she pulled away. Her sightless, mocha-coloured eyes were enormous in her lean face.

'Sorry, Ravi, I woke you again,' Charu said, looking away.

'Tell me...what did you see? Was it a murder...a gruesome attack?' Ravi asked, looking at the fear that swam helplessly in the woody depths of her eyes.

'It is another version of the dreams that started when we solved the last case,' Charu murmured.

'The one with the small girl?'

Charu nodded, drawing up her knees and hugging them.

'Until now, I had seen her being slapped and pushed around. But today...was so much worse. Ravi, I don't think she's going to survive this torture...mentally,' she said, stopping when her voice wanted to break. 'Somewhere in a basement with uncemented, red brick walls is a small girl suffering. I couldn't see the faces, and I pulled out of the dream a minute before a name was called. If only I had waited...I could have...we could have narrowed a location...,' she said.

'You know the dreams don't follow a pattern, and you have no control over them. You say they come with no forewarning, and I have seen they are usually a premonition. And, since they started after the last case, they could be pointing to a new case coming our way,' Ravi said, getting up to wear his clothes.

'Ravi, if these dreams are a precursor of things to come... I... I...don't think I am equipped to handle a case with a small child,' she said.

'Charu, listen, we won't take the case if this turns out to be one with a small child, okay. I won't let them push you to work on a case you are not comfortable with.'

'I...no it...isn't that...well, maybe. I don't remember anything about my own kidnapping, but I know I am uncomfortable dealing with traumatized children. I can't anymore.'

'Then, don't give it another thought. I will not take this case. Okay,' Ravi said, placing his rimless spectacles on his nose, frustrated at his inability to allay Charu's fear.

These new dreams of the little girl are shaking her up. I've seen her worried but never scared like this; Ravi stood thinking, watching Charu's mind work.

Her softly rounded face was stretched tight in worry, and her slanted eyes that saw too much had a faraway look. Her bare shoulders were rigid over the sheet that covered her body that he had explored passionately last night.

Her mind full of the sickness she had witnessed, Charu rubbed her sweaty forehead, repulsed by the images that seemed to be burned in her brain. *Who is this little girl? Why am I seeing her and the man, the devil who is hurting her*? Charu wondered.

She wanted to find answers, but the revulsion that came naturally when a small child was traumatized made her unsure of her ability to begin. Used to seeing adults create or bear the consequences of destruction, Charu's brain scampered to make sense of the images she had seen.

The vibrating phone startled Charu. 'Unknown number,' the accented voice on her mobile intoned. As soon as her fingers curled around the phone, Charu froze. She knew who it was.

'Hello, Prithvi.' Her pale fingers tightened around her mobile. The voice at the other end pulled her into a past she had long kept buried.

'Chumki, you knew it was me? Your ability never fails to amaze me. I am sorry to wake you up so early in the morning, and I know I have a lot to explain, but I need you...I mean, I need your help.' The deep voice at the other end of the line she would recognize anywhere sounded tense.

Hearing Prithvi call her by the name he had coined for her almost a decade and a half ago felt surreal. 'How can I possibly help you, Prithvi?' she said, hesitantly. 'And calling me after almost...what...fifteen years!'

'I know I have a lot of explaining to do, Chumki, and I will. I just took the easy path... There is no excuse. But, right now, I need you to help me find my little daughter. She is missing... someone has taken her. You have to be the bigger person and look beyond the hurt I caused you, dear, as you always did,' he pleaded.

Missing...little daughter, Charu froze reminded of the little girl in her dream. *Did I dream about his child? Why now? Why her?*

'How old...is your daughter, Prithvi?'

'She is eighteen months old.'

The girl in my dream is older, around eight or nine maybe... so it can't be Prithvi's daughter. 'No, Prithvi,' she answered, curtly. 'You have the whole country at your beck and call. I should congratulate you on achieving what you always said you would. Power. Please approach someone else. Prithvi, whenever we come together, something bad happens.'.

'Once...it happened once, and it was my fault. I paid for it; I am still paying for it. Chumki, please...I don't trust anyone else. Please don't say no. *Please.*' His voice deepened again.

'Where are you?'

'I am close to you, Chumki. Very close.' His words gave her goosebumps. 'I am in the havcli three doors down from you. I bought it when I shifted to Delhi from Hisar after I won the ticket. We shifted into it two months ago after Anumita, my wife, had it renovated. I do have a bungalow in Delhi, but the family lives here.'

'This is quite a coincidence.'

Alerted by Charu's tone, Ravi watched her as she rubbed her arms. He opened the back door and leaned against the doorframe, breathing in the fragrant dawn. He eavesdropped on Charu's conversation as the light began peeking out from the horizon. Ravi's robust frame was warrior-like, a result of diligent exercise and discipline. Cinnamon skin, dark eyes, a broad nose, and curly hair. His above-average height had helped him clear the Indian Police Service (IPS) exam, for which he thanked his mother's side of the family. Charu, aware of Ravi's presence nearby, went on.

'Prithvi, I am a part of a semi-government funded Special Investigative Team; I'm not a private detective. I don't understand how you want me to help you. The cases are given to us by Commissioner Bakshi. We have no say in what comes our way.'

'I know that. Look, come to me. I will explain everything. Chumki, I need not tell you we are short of time. My younger daughter was kidnapped yesterday afternoon from my house. Please don't let the past come in the way of what you can do. I will send a car. Come as soon as you can, please.'

How can this be real? Prithvi Chauhan, the minister, calling me after fifteen years of silence, Charu thought, her heart beating in fear and anticipation.

'Also...um...Chumki...I need to keep...'

'Yes, yes, I know, you want to keep this quiet. Even if I take on your case, I will have to inform Bakshi Uncle. I mean, Police Commissioner Bakshi,' she said. Ravi had been listening to her voice rise and dip with emotion, with growing trepidation. He turned at the mention of the commissioner.

'I spoke to Bakshi Uncle last night, and he has okayed it.'

Charu could almost see Prithvi's smile. Her irritation grew.

'I know you cannot say no when it comes to children,' he continued, softly. 'I know you are annoyed about my leaving Surat the way I did. But, there was too much going on at that time. Even though I left, I never forgot you—or what we once shared.'

Charu had had enough. 'All that was a long time ago, Prithvi,' she said, firmly. 'I understand you are married and have kids—one of whom, you say, has been kidnapped. I feel for you, Prithvi, but I don't think I should be a part of this.'

'I always believed you and I were meant to be together, Chumki.' He exhaled loudly as if trying hard to control his emotions. 'Look, it's almost 5 am. At least, come and speak to me. I'm at my wits' end. I need someone I can trust...someone who doesn't need anything from me. Please, Chumki. For old times' sake.'

'Let me talk to Commissioner Bakshi.'

'Listen, I will send a car to fetch you. My security officer will pick you up.'

Charu ended the call, and her shoulders drooped.

Ravi waited for her to explain, the rising October sun at his back. 'Charu, who is Prithvi?' he asked.

His question startled her. Ravi watched her unmasked face. The fight she was having with herself was visible in her gluey, unbaked, clay-like gaze.

God, she is beautiful! he thought. Her heart-shaped face was pensive as she filtered her thoughts. Her hair had come undone and fell down her back. The first rays of the sun made her bare skin glow.

Charu hesitated. 'Prithvi was a schoolmate, senior by five years. I met him the first day I landed at Girija Devi Vidyalaya, the school my Nani ran in Surat. I was eleven. He found me confused and alone, unable to understand why my parents had sent me there. I confessed everything to him: my doubts, fears, my anger... He answered all my questions. We...I...spent my growing-up years with him. He was the only one I trusted. We were inseparable for five years. Then, one day, he just left the school without a word...and never came back.'

Left you shattered, your trust and your heart broken, Charu's inner voice interrupted her thoughts.

'And, now he wants my help. He is Prithvi Chauhan, the minister from Haryana. His younger daughter has been kidnapped. Apparently, he has already taken the go-ahead from Commissioner Bakshi for our team to work on his case. He wants me...us...to meet him as soon as possible at his haveli. I can't believe he found me after so many years.'

'Well, what is worrying you?' Ravi asked. The knowledge that Prithvi had been more than a friend to Charu bothered him.

Charu knew Ravi was upset, and she didn't want to tell him she wanted to stay away because a small part of her still yearned for Prithvi, even after so many years.

'Wait. Don't overthink this. We can't do anything until we get direct orders. And, I haven't received a call from...' Ravi's phone began to ring. 'Sir,' he said.

Charu knew it was the commissioner. She heard the one-sided conversation as she slipped into a t-shirt.

Ravi heard Commissioner Bakshi before he answered, 'Right, sir. Sir, Charu may not be comfortable with...um... Sir...' Ravi faltered when Charu waved to him not to refuse. 'Yes, sir, sorry, please continue. How would you like us to proceed?'

Ravi turned away from her listening to his superior. Charu's room was small but, for some reason, her parents had wallpapered it to depict a luminous forest. They said Charu had wanted to bring the outside into her room. Ravi always found it overwhelming: the flimsy, white wrought-iron bed, the cerulean blue furniture, the transparent curtains at the window and a back door that opened into the thriving backyard. It was a room from a fairy-tale.

Yet, the room did not suit Charu's personality, at least not the Charu he had come to know during the last six years. She was a strong, independent woman who faced the worst kinds of human behaviour. Her dreams or premonitions were full of blood and gore, of murderers and rapists. She could wake up from one of her dreams and tell him exactly what had happened without batting an eyelid. *But, this Prithvi has her flustered. Who is he*? Ravi thought.

Charu heard Ravi note down the basic details of the case.

'Well, Charu, we are officially on the case,' Ravi said. 'Commissioner Bakshi has asked us to look for Myra Chauhan, the younger daughter of Prithvi Chauhan, the minister. Myra is almost two years old and was kidnapped from her home yesterday afternoon. This is a quasi-official assignment, a favour to Commissioner Bakshi. Which means fewer resources. I'll call Reeti and tell her that her station leave has been cancelled. Until further instructions, this stays under the radar. Let's get ready and meet near the portico in an hour. Did Prithvi say what time we have to meet him? Where? And how do we get there?'

'He is in the haveli that was rebuilt recently. It's just a couple of doors down from ours. He said he'd send his car over to pick us up.'

'Oh. Okay.'

Charu bent down, trying to locate her white stick. Ravi walked over and handed it to her. She went to her cupboard and started pulling out her clothes, her back to Ravi, putting some distance between them. It didn't go unnoticed by him.

2. Ravi

5 am, Wednesday

'Charu, this may not be the right time to ask, but have you given any thought to my marriage proposal?' Ravi asked, tentatively.

He saw her fidget. 'Ravi, let's not talk about this now. I… you sprang it upon me unexpectedly. I'm not ready. We have a good relationship. We work together. We are practically living together. Why spoil a good thing?'

'I want to make it official. I don't like this sneaking around. I don't understand your hesitation, Charu. I am a thirty-five-year-old Assistant Commissioner of Police. I don't want to behave like a skulking teenager. I love you and want to marry you. What is the problem?'

'Ravi, I don't want to tie myself to anyone, be responsible for anyone. I can barely manage to take care of myself. YOU can't handle the burden that comes with a *blind* person,' she paused, 'especially one who can sometimes hear your thoughts and with whom you will always have to be on guard. You will come to resent me, eventually, just like everyone else—including my parents.'

The constant need to know where I am, the inability to appreciate beauty, the sameness of my existence sometimes grates on me. How can I expect Ravi to share that prison? There was no adventure, no spontaneity and a million rules. Love will not grow in the shadow of my perpetual need.

'This is unfair. You cannot paint me with such broad strokes. I don't know your parents' reasons for sending you to your Nani's house when you were eleven. Maybe, they thought she was better equipped to take care of you. And, look how you've turned out. But, you need to resolve this anger against your parents.'

Charu turned her face away.

'Are you saying no?' Ravi asked.

Charu's heart trembled. 'I am saying...don't rush me. Let me think about it.'

'And, Prithvi?' he asked.

'What about him?'

'He is your first love, the one who broke your heart, isn't he?'

'We moved on,' Charu said, calmly.

'Somehow, I don't think this was just a teenage affair that fizzled out, as you would like me to believe. But, I get your point,' said Ravi, as he slipped out of the door.

Charu heard his soft tread in the hall, the creak of the stairs he took to go to his room on the first floor of the haveli.

This room was her space, a *kothri* at the back of the haveli, a storeroom to stock baggage.

Apt, Charu laughed, humourlessly.

Her father had converted it into a room for her and her attendant when they had won the case for the haveli. Charu knew that the back door and the window beside it opened into the backyard where her mother diligently grew the seasonal flowers and vegetables so that her room always smelled of the outdoors.

Charu stood at the open window, giving herself a moment to hear the birdsong, to breathe in the clean smell of dew on the *nargis* her mother had planted. She knew one would have an unrestricted view of Noorie's tomb from where she stood. Aruna had elucidated it's unique beauty on a full moon night, the shiny Opal stone whispering of a long-lost love.

I'll never know what it looks like.

But, she knew of other things. Secrets that remained between her and Anwar Haveli like the door behind the almirah in her room. She knew her father used it to visit the mausoleum when it called to him. The *kothri* in Aruna and Bhavya's bedroom where she had found the green wooden chest. A part of the treasure of that chest had paid for her freedom.

She knew of all the hidden and back staircases that felt like a magical world that lay behind the realm that everyone existed in. It was used at one time by the servants of the kings and nobles who lived in the haveli. That spectral world had been a lonely girl's playground while growing up.

Her mother never understood why she preferred scraping her knees and dirtying her clothes in these passages rather than playing with her sisters.

'They are always in a hurry,' she had once tried to explain.

Shaking away the memories, Charu turned to her almirah. She pulled out a silk *kurta,* a dupatta and a pair of blue jeans from the three neat piles she had stacked the last time she was home. Charu heard the creak of footsteps, doors opening, the haveli waking up in anticipation of a new day.

As she stood under the shower, her thoughts kept returning to Prithvi, the boy she had once trusted implicitly. *Why am I still conflicted about him, even after all these years?* Charu mused. She couldn't help whispering his name. 'Prithvi, Prithvi, I loved you with everything I had.'

Chumki, small like a jhumki, Prithvi's Chumki—she recalled the song Prithvi used to sing. She squeezed her eyes closed, wanting to erase the teasing voice echoing within her.

As Ravi climbed the steps soundlessly to the first floor, he found himself fretting about this omission about Prithvi from the account of Charu's past. He wasn't even sure if they had had a serious relationship. They had been children, after all. But, something told him it had been significant—at least for Charu.

He walked over to the glass windows and drew the curtains back to stare at the rising sun. The sky before him was a canvas of brilliant colours, unsullied for now by the haze of the pollution-belching city. The excitement on Charu's face at the prospect of this new case was not the same as what he had seen when she first joined his team as a consultant empath. He remembered his irritation when he had first been introduced to her. He had known he would become the joke of the department along with his team.

He had taken one look at her unconventionally beautiful face, her long brown plait, frail body, Velcro shoes, and white stick, before dismissing her as an indulgence. He barely interacted with her in the initial weeks but, slowly, in her quiet way, Charu became a valuable asset with her ability to sense the details the team sometimes missed.

Often, she alerted them when a suspect's thoughts didn't match with their words or if a room had been scrubbed clean after violence. She could tell if some evidence had been tampered with or if a smell was misplaced. Her observations worked as a lead to follow, and most times, they had led to cases being solved faster. Over time, he became more comfortable with her and her way of helping the team.

As more cases started coming their way, they started travelling together as a team. He saw her for the woman she was—someone who had to jump hurdles every day to live a life of dignity. They soon developed a rhythm, and one day he found himself asking her opinion on a lead. She, too, started sharing with him what she felt when she stepped into a crime scene. It wasn't necessarily about the cases alone, but what she felt personally. He knew she had started trusting him, even if the feeling was still tentative, and he soon realized the trust was mutual. They became friends.

Charu knew about his family, his ancestors, his dreams and desires, and he knew she was lonely. But, he had to be mindful of tectonic shifts in her. He was moderately extrovert, while she would retreat behind a wall of silence. Their relationship had seen many milestones. The biggest being her confession about how, as a child, she had been kidnapped from her school for money. She didn't remember those three days. She only remembered that her parents sent her to live with her grandmother after a few weeks of coming home from the hospital. The reason her mother gave was that she needed constant supervision after she lost her sight. Charu still carried an unspoken grudge against her parents for this abandonment.

He wished she would talk to her parents about this issue. He also knew he had no right to push her until she was ready. Over the last two years, once they became intimate, he had thought they were building something together. He was wrong.

'Maybe if I had more time with her, I could convince her. But now, with this new variable, Prithvi, I have no option but to wait,' he muttered.

Ravi called the third team member, Reeti, and brought her up to speed. Reeti Gaur, ACP Cyber-crime, their tech support and also a brilliant conversationalist. Both Charu and he lacked what Reeti brought to the table. Building bridges. With the families and with the government. She was a hardy woman from Haryana who lived for her job, despite her parents pushing her to get married. As he spoke to her, he could see the middle-aged woman in his mind's eyes. Her robust laugh at something he said made his lips curve upwards.

The door of Ravi's room was slightly ajar. Charu's mother, Uma, eavesdropped when she heard a familiar name. He had been telling his teammate about the case.

Prithvi Chauhan. Could it be the same boy? But, that would be too big a coincidence, she thought nervously. Uma knocked on the door and pushed it open further. 'Ravi, are you and Charu already on a new case?'

'Aunty, nothing to worry about. It is close by, actually. May I leave my suitcase here for a few days?' He stood up.

'You don't have to ask, Ravi. You are a part of our family. Has something happened nearby? I ask because I heard the name Prithvi. Is it the minister Prithvi Chauhan, whose family lives in the renovated haveli nearby?'

'Yes, Aunty. Why do you ask?' Ravi noticed Uma's nervous habit of twisting the edge of her saree with her fingers.

'That man is trouble, Ravi,' she uttered scathingly before leaving his room.

In the room below where Ravi stood wondering about Uma's abrupt comment, Charu checked the time on her Braille watch, with her fingers. It was a graduation gift from her grandmother.

Picking up her bag, Charu checked her ID badge. Their Special Investigative Team worked in the background, trying to find people who were absconding, murdered, kidnapped, or dead.

Charu was aware that she was an experiment, a trial run to see if her heightened intuition, and other senses, could be used to solve cases faster. Once the mother of a man, who had disappeared, kept saying she was worried about her depressed son. She said he was capable of ending his life. But, Charu found her instincts contradicting the mother's fears. It had taken her a few hours with his things before Charu informed the team that he was alive and in a cold place. All his winter clothes were missing. They found him in far-flung Nova Scotia. He had wanted to live off his insurance payout. So far, Charu had been worth the money being spent on her. But, Charu knew this could change at the first misstep.

Her Nani's close confidant, Bakshi Uncle, an Additional Commissioner of Police at the time, had given her the first puzzle to solve, a case study. Her interest instantly piqued; she worked at the puzzle until the pieces aligned to her satisfaction. The story of a kidnapping emerged, and Charu was promptly hooked. After that case was solved, Bakshi Uncle would leave her with hints about other cases, and Charu spent her time drawing up questions pertaining to those hints. She gave him a detailed scenario that he could look into with his team. Sometimes her questions helped.

Charu was fifteen years of age when she helped solve a murder case. Helping Bakshi Uncle gave her a feeling of achievement like nothing else had before. Going to his office, joining the strategy meetings for a case, touching the evidence made her feel important and needed.

Helping people, reuniting families, finding answers made her feel powerful in a positive way. It freed her from the burden of always being the needy one.

'I will go to Prithvi, confident about my own place in this world,' she said to herself. Extending her hand to find the white stick, she opened the door of her room and stepped into her battlefield.

Charu didn't need to count her steps to reach where she was going. She had, after all, spent the first eleven years of her life here, learning to walk and then run in these very corridors. Twelve steps to reach the living room...

Suresh Uncle, her father's best friend who lived with their family, had painstakingly created a blueprint of the haveli by poking holes in a flattened carton. She was still getting lost in the haveli, banging into walls where she thought a door had been. It had been his way to help her make a map of her home in her mind. It had worked.

Charu turned left, and twenty-five steps later, she entered the proverbial centre of the haveli, the kitchen.

She crossed the threshold and moved towards the gas stove to touch the knobs, feel their presence, the newness. Her heart beat, accelerated as she moved her hands across the granite top. Bending down, she found the handles of the wooden cupboards.

One... Two... Three... Charu counted before she opened it to reach for the pan. The plastic handle felt familiar. She pulled on it victorious, and out came all the smaller bowls crashing onto the floor.

The sound was jarring, vulgar in its suddenness, making her and every other person in the house freeze. Everyone waited for the small steel bowl to finish its clattering spin on the floor before rushing to the kitchen as if suddenly realizing that SHE was in the house.

Running, striding, limping, her family reached the kitchen in several stages of disarray.

Charu squeezed her eyes closed, cursing silently, before turning around with a sheepish smile, holding the pan aloft.

'Anyone for tea?'

'Charu, are you going somewhere?' Back from his morning walk Arun, Charu's father, asked as Uma took the pan from her.

'Yes, I am going to meet a client. We've got a new case,' she replied. Turning to her mother, she said, 'I'm sorry, Ma. I didn't mean to disturb everyone.'

'Don't be silly. I was already up. Go, I'll make the tea,' Uma gestured to her son. Dheeraj led his sister out of the kitchen.

I wish she would talk to me like the other children, demand things like they do. Maybe, she feels I won't understand...since I stay at home. I wish I could just hold her tight and tell her that she doesn't have to tell me big things. Small things will be enough. Things that make her smile, things that upset her, what vegetables she likes to eat now...anything. I wish she would complain, throw a tantrum, be less formal; Uma thought, her eyes on Charu's stiff shoulders.

'But...you just came back from a case recently,' Arun mumbled as he watched Ravi coming down the stairs. 'Are you also going with her, Ravi?'

'Yes, sir,' Ravi answered.

'Oh, okay then. Take care.' Arun nodded, relieved and went into his room.

'The world will keep spinning into new centuries, but my father will still feel that a male protector is needed to accompany his daughters everywhere,' Charu scoffed.

'He is just looking out for you, Charu. I don't blame him. It is difficult to be a father these days with the kinds of crime around. Case in point, where we are going,' replied Ravi.

Charu heard her sisters yawn and tell their mother that they were going back to sleep before ambling back into their shared room. She listened to the banter of her siblings, felt her mother's affection as she asked them to have something to eat before they left. But, the warmth didn't seep into her heart. She wanted it to, had hoped it would for many years. But her heart remained split, never whole, just parted.

Charu knew she was socially awkward. She had friends but not an intimate circle. She wanted to experience unrestrained love and marriage, too, but her rational brain had accepted that with her blindness, maybe that was not something she should wait for. She was happy that she got to live a slice of that love with Ravi for the last two years. But, since she had rejected his proposal before coming home, that too was a thing of the past.

How can I worry about my inconsequential issues when a little girl is suffering somewhere? Charu shook herself out of her thoughts.

'Are you okay, Charu di? You seem preoccupied...is something bothering you?' Gina, her youngest sister, asked, coming towards her.

'Yes, I'm all right,' Charu replied. 'I'll wait outside, Ravi,' she called out before walking towards the main door.

Gina walked beside her, 'Charu di, I've always wanted to know...when did you know that you were special?'

'Special as in...do you mean blind?' Charu asked with a knowing smile.

'And...intuitive...an empath, is that what you would call yourself?' Gina clarified.

'Well, you know I wasn't born blind. The realization that my circumstance had changed irrevocably seeped in, like grief... I suppose...it is the "normal" I had to learn to accept. There was no other choice.'

'But, how do you accept it? I ask because no one ever talks about it,' she said.

'Initially, you try to fight it, get better, and when everything fails, you explain it away as destiny. Ma and Papa took me to many doctors. When they realized it was pointless, they made sure I had the tools to live around it. About being an empath, I think Ma knew before I did. She told me not to say things that made people feel uncomfortable. I couldn't help reading minds. Aruna used to get angry since I would tell everyone when she was lying, and Bee used to laugh it off,' Charu remembered, chuckling.

'Some days it feels like I am a fraud who is not particularly lucky either. And, then there are days when I help solve a case, I feel so powerful like I could change the world.'

'But, everyone else believes that you solve the crimes all by yourself,' Gina said.

'I think people like to believe in miracles. But, the truth is that I can't do this alone. The team does the work, and I help where I can. I am just an ordinary girl who talks to the family, collects information, writes reports on most days. Some days, I just follow the team around, filling in the gaps.'

'Your sister is downplaying her role. She is an important member of our small team,' Ravi interjected from behind.

'How does it feel when you read people?' Gina asked, leaning closer.

'Sometimes other people's thoughts and emotions are exceptionally intense, and I perceive or sense what they are feeling instantaneously. Sometimes, I get pictures connected to a person. Or, I will see an object that should not have been there, a pull, a vibe. It is like having an open line to the ether around me. Think radio. The thoughts people broadcast are sometimes so loud that I can't help receiving them. I can't tell the number you think of, but I can tell if it makes you excited or hurt or confident.' Charu tried to explain.

Uma called out to Gina, who pranced away, hastily saying goodbye. Ravi came and stood next to her. 'Ready?' he said. Charu nodded.

While they silently waited for the car, Charu's thoughts returned to Prithvi. A tragic incident involving another boy had made him leave abruptly, either due to guilt or to save himself. But, Prithvi had never looked back, never gave her another thought. And, that had hurt. Despite her intention to merge into the background, the last two years in school after Prithvi left had been excruciating. She had waited for a call, an explanation, something to keep her hopes alive but, after six months passed without a word from Prithvi, she had allowed the flame of love to rest.

Charu knew she had changed in that time, hardened, become more focused. She had unlearnt that a man would give her security and made sure she never depended on one again.

And, yet, Prithvi only had to call you once, and here you are, sitting at your doorstep, ready to dance to his tune, her inner voice scolded her.

3. Prithvi

7:30 am, Wednesday

A car honked as it turned towards the haveli. Charu stood up and felt Ravi rise to his feet beside her. It took them only 700 heartbeats, or ten minutes in the car, to reach Prithvi's house. She knew it would have taken them half of that time on foot. She had been keeping track of the distance with a finger on her pulse, as was her habit. The overcrowded streets, suffocating fumes from the roads' increasing traffic, and incessant honking meant the car moved slowly. The sounds and smells were painfully nostalgic to her. She felt as if she had never really left.

The early morning sounds reminded her of going to school in a cramped van. The smells of bread pakora, omelette, and parathas wafting in from the window made her wonder why Prithvi had come to live in this part of Delhi. He could have housed his family in the pristine bungalow he had been assigned by the government in the heart of the city.

'I've always wondered, why does your Nani take in kids who need...help?' Ravi asked, treading carefully.

'Ma had an autistic sister, and Nani started the school for her, taking in troubled children initially for her daughter. When my aunt died, she already had the infrastructure, so she took in more children to forget. All the children were from families that had money but no time for their children. In the years I spent there, I don't remember any child from a middle-class background. Well, except me.' Charu answered. *Why is he asking me about Surat?*

As soon as she started talking, Ravi observed that the driver's head tilted towards them. It was a subtle shift, but working closely with Charu had made him attuned to these small changes.

'We'll talk more later...,' he whispered, grabbing her hand in his big calloused one.

As the car made its way to Prithvi's haveli, Charu focused on what Prithvi had told her about his daughter's abduction. The way he had sounded on the phone in the morning confused her. She could understand his need to rush things, but why was he bringing up their past?

Maybe it is our shared past that makes me distrust him. It would be better to just say no politely and leave, Charu decided, feeling boxed into a corner. *Is that why I am going to meet him...to see what is driving me forward? The dreams that I have been having could be consistent with this case. But, Prithvi said his daughter is not yet two years old...a baby. Oh, God! I have to find her. What if it is her future I am dreaming about?*

'Chauhan Haveli,' Ravi announced, reading the ostentatious stone plaque beside the large iron gate as they drove in.

Cold air snuck underneath Charu's stole as she stepped out. It made her shiver. She stood silently for a minute, feeling the haveli before her. Charu sensed melancholy settling around her.

A dreary sadness clings to Chauhan Haveli unlike my Anwar Haveli, Charu thought.

As the driver guided them towards the main door, she ran her hands over the lock hanging from the latch. It was a simple pull-and-rotate padlock. She knew how to work it.

'Still feeling the locks? Some things never change,' a deep voice teased her.

Her back straightened. With a neutral expression, Charu turned towards Prithvi. 'You were the one who drilled it into me, taught me to pick most locks too,' Charu replied.

'I remember how you hated confined spaces. It gave you a sense of power like nothing else.'

'And, I've always been grateful for that particular skill.'

'We never did rob that bank, did we?' he said with a smile.

'No, you left before we could get to that.'

Charu heard his embarrassed cough. 'You look good, Chumki. It is great to see you again.' He turned towards the man who stood beside her.

'Sir, ACP M. Ravi Nair.' Charu heard the click of his heels, the snap of his salute. She felt the two men sizing each other up in the moment of silence that followed.

'ACP Nair,' Prithvi extended his hand, 'Prithvi Chauhan. Please join us.'

Ravi watched him take Charu's hand and lead her into his house.

Unsettled at Prithvi's closeness, Charu pulled her arm away almost twisting her ankle, as the tiled floor made way for a soft carpet. Prithvi's hand was immediately at her waist. With his right arm supporting her, he began walking towards the glass doors, to the sunny lawn outside. Ravi found Charu's disconcerted behaviour troubling. She was not a woman who was rattled easily, and yet here she was—unable to find firm footing. He wondered, again, at her feelings for Prithvi. He saw Charu stop mid-sentence, and knew she had sensed his thoughts.

It was a small, square lawn, well-manicured—a private sanctuary for Prithvi's close friends and family. A few cane chairs and a lounger were arranged around a glass table, with fashion magazines on top. A jug of juice stood in the centre. They made themselves comfortable. Prithvi asked someone to bring in tea.

'So, Charu, you are doing exciting work—leading a team and all,' said Prithvi.

'Excitement is the last thing I do it for. I can't find any thrill in knowing that someone is suffering.' Charu corrected her posture, crossed her ankles, and folded her hands in her lap, feeling his eyes weighing her every move.

'I hear you are in Anwar Haveli these days. How is that going for you? Living with the ones who abandoned you?' Prithvi asked, leaning back into the chair.

'Prithvi, I...whatever I said to you in Surat was not fair to my parents. I was young. But now, in hindsight, I'm sure they had a reason for what they did.'

'You mean you still haven't asked them why they sent you away to live with your grandmother?' Prithvi sounded surprised.

Ravi looked away, feeling like an intruder in their midst.

'Before we start, Prithvi, I must mention that we have never taken such a young child's case before, and you are very high-profile. I am not sure...'

'Chumki, why do you underestimate yourself? I have asked around; you are one of the best teams. Please, help me look for my daughter.'

Charu took a deep breath and nodded her acceptance. 'Tell me about your daughter.' She heard the rustle of a small writing pad opening. Ravi would meticulously jot down everything he observed.

'My daughter Myra has been missing since yesterday afternoon,' Prithvi began.

Charu closed her eyes and said, 'Tell me how the day went.'

'I left for work in the morning as usual. Anumita, my wife, dropped Sia to her school. Later, at around 1 pm, she picked Sia up from school and brought her home. She looked in on Myra, who was napping. The nanny was there. Anu left for a meeting with a prospective client around 2 pm. The nanny, Gita, found Myra's cot empty when she came up to check on her after lunch. They searched the grounds, but couldn't find anything. So they called me after half an hour.'

'Why after half an hour?' Ravi spoke up.

'I didn't ask. The guards said they looked around the grounds on their own once.'

'I am sorry, but...can you trust your wife to be telling the truth? And, the driver?'

'What kind of question...? Yes, she can be trusted. She is Myra's mother. Why would she lie?'

Charu knew Prithvi would accept the magnifying glass his life was going to be put under, grudgingly.

'Is there an initial FIR we can see?' asked Ravi.

'There isn't any,' Prithvi replied, coolly.

'Sir?'

'Why haven't you called the police, Prithvi?' asked Charu.

'In my position, I need to keep this quiet. I don't want undue publicity. The police may not be working on this case actively, but they'll lend you all the support you may need. If the news is leaked, the press and the opposition will have a field day. As soon as we realized Myra was missing, I knew I needed you to find her. Please help me.' Prithvi grabbed Charu's hands. Immediately, she felt the tremor in his heart, and the dread of a scared parent. He was pulsing with anxiety and fear.

'Chumki, you have to find her.' He brought her hands to his forehead.

Charu wanted to wrap her arms around him and comfort him. She also felt Ravi's piercing gaze on her. She extracted her hands from Prithvi's and sat back, reminding herself that she was here to do a job.

'Do you suspect anyone?' she inquired, clearing her throat. 'Anyone who could have a motive, in the house or outside?'

'No, no, I trust my family. It has to be an outsider.'

'Sir, how many people live in your house?' asked Ravi.

'There is Myra, and Sia—my elder daughter—and myself. There's my wife, Anumita, and Swami Ram Vilas Ji, my spiritual guru. Also, my mother-in-law, Malti Devi. The nanny, Gita, and a few servants and drivers live close by. You can ask my wife for their details.'

'What about your parents?' asked Ravi.

'They live in our hometown.'

'Sirsa?' Charu raised her head.

'Yes, but they are unaware of this and out of the picture. I don't want to involve them unnecessarily. You can concentrate on the people here.'

'Is there any reason for the kidnapping you can think of?'

'Look, ideally, I would like you to investigate all angles, but I have a feeling it is someone who wants revenge or money. I don't want to influence you in any way,' said Prithvi.

Charu leaned forward. 'How many people were in the house when Myra was kidnapped?'

'I was at the party office, along with Swamiji. Anu was out for a meeting with her client. My mother-in-law said she was sleeping. Gita was having lunch. And, Sia was studying with Manik, her tutor.'

'What about the staff?'

'The cook and the maids were in the kitchen. The drivers were out with us, and the guards were at their posts.'

'How are you so sure of this?'

'When we were getting Chauhan Haveli renovated, Anu had security cameras installed everywhere. I didn't think we needed so many, but she said she felt safer with them, so I gave in. I checked the feed from the cameras.'

'That is good news, sir. I will have Reeti, our expert, take a look at the security footage immediately,' said Ravi.

'Have you received a ransom note, a phone call...anything?' asked Charu.

'Nothing, as of now. We kept waiting by the phone last night, but nobody called.' Prithvi rubbed his eyes.

'Is everyone at home now?'

'No, Swamiji and my mother-in-law have gone to his ashram in Sirsa.'

'What! Why? Why did they go at this time?' Both Charu and Ravi were surprised.

'They wanted to do a special puja for Myra. I saw them off myself. Oh...no, no, you don't have to worry about them,' he said, looking at their suspicious expressions. 'One is Myra's grandmother, and the other has been my mentor forever. He is the reason why I am here today. They have no cause to even think of something like this.' Prithvi waved his hand.

'What about your wife?'

'Anumita and Sia are asleep. Listen, I want to warn you. Anu is slightly high-strung, and Myra's kidnapping has made her all the more...anxious. She can be a bit harsh sometimes. Please, don't let it affect you.'

'What about Manik, the tutor?' asked Charu.

'Manik is my cousin from Sirsa. He teaches in a government school here. He came to Delhi around three years ago. His father, my *tayaji*, has a carpentry shop in the village. He requested me to find Manik a job. I also got him a job at the club as a cricket coach in the evening. And, he also helps out with Sia's studies.'

Just as Charu was about to ask him about his mentor, Ram Vilas, she heard a high-pitched voice.

4. Anumita

9 am, Wednesday

'Prithvi? Prithvi! Where have you been all morning? I've been trying to call you, but you didn't pick up. I didn't know where you were. What if I had had an emergency?'

Instinctively, Ravi placed himself between Charu and the source of the voice. He saw a dishevelled woman, in a long gown, striding towards them. Her slippers slapped on the tiled floor loudly.

Prithvi moved towards the woman, his lips pressed together in anger. 'Anu, calm down. I told you I had to brief the investigation team we are putting together to find Myra. Now, *calm down*.'

Ravi noticed the way Prithvi held his wife's arms, tighter than he would have expected.

'This is Charu, and this is Ravi...and another team member, Reeti, will be joining them in a while. Have you made sure the servants have cleaned the back rooms for them?'

Ravi knew the woman before him was fighting inner demons to stay afloat. Her trembling hands, agitated speech, the tic that she couldn't control, told him the story of a severely distressed woman. Under the circumstances, he found it natural.

Anumita's wide eyes, fixated on Charu, were strangely hostile. 'She doesn't look blind,' she said, condescendingly.

'Hello, Anumita,' Charu offered in return.

'Hello. The backroom, yes, I think it's done,' Anumita replied to Prithvi, collecting herself.

'Sir, I will call my forensic expert to do a sweep of the house,' said Ravi in a low voice, as he watched Prithvi walk past him. Prithvi almost hauled his wife up the stairs, talking to her in a quiet but firm voice.

'Oh my,' Charu gasped. 'She doesn't like me or trust me. I felt her burning anger towards me, which is strange because I have never met her before in my life.'

'And Prithvi? Wasn't he a bit harsh towards her?'

'Hmm. What does Anumita look like?' Charu asked, frowning.

'Looks-wise, she is pretty, brittle, like glass collectables in a living room. She looks disturbed and scared, Charu. I don't know how else to describe her. Dark, shoulder-length hair, thin face, haunted eyes. She's slender, not athletically, though. Think trophy wife.'

'She must be worried about her daughter.'

'Did you sense anything in the house?'

'The house is like a swamp of emotions. Prithvi is locked tight. I cannot access his inner thoughts or feelings. Anumita...,' Charu sighed. 'I felt her distress, guilt, hope, suspicion.'

What she didn't share with Ravi was how having Prithvi close by all the time was like standing next to a roaring fire. The warmth was just short of a burn.

Unaware of Charu's thoughts, Ravi continued, 'Why would anyone go for a puja at this time? I wish we could get started. Draw up a strategy. Reeti should reach here anytime.'

He saw the minister walking towards them, dressed in a freshly starched kurta-pyjama. He noticed how Prithvi bent before Charu to whisper something into her ear, his hand cupping her blushing cheek.

'Ravi, they are setting up the room. Please give them a few more minutes,' Prithvi said to him.

'We could have done that on our own, sir.'

'No, no, it is *my* daughter you are looking for. You will find the best audio recorders, sample collection kits, cameras, fingerprint pads, evidence bags, forensic light source, everything Bakshi Uncle normally sends along with you. I took the liberty of procuring the best. It is all ready and waiting.'

He checked his watch. 'I am leaving now. I must behave and work normally. I'll meet you in the evening.' Prithvi turned towards Charu as if he wanted to add something, but he decided against it and left.

Charu felt Ravi's eyes on her. She knew he had questions, but she also knew he wouldn't ask, at least for now.

Ravi looked at her expressive face as she sat resplendent in the morning sun. Charu was his unmitigated longing. So beautiful, it sometimes hurt just to look at her. Fragile to the point of breakable, no one could gauge the inner strength she hid within. Just as no one could imagine the layers she hid her true self behind.

Her external beauty had stopped affecting him after the first couple of months. It wasn't the sexy, sultry beauty. Rather, a delicate princess in an ivory tower kind of mystical beauty. It made every man want to become her knight.

'Why does he call you Chumki?' Ravi couldn't help asking Charu.

'Hmm, it's my nickname.'

'But no one in Anwar Haveli calls you by this name.'

'My schoolmates gave it to me, and it stuck. The family doesn't know.'

'Prithvi gave it to you?'

'How does it matter who gave it to me? I am not having this conversation.'

Ravi lowered his voice. 'He is very suave, trying to look the part.'

'What does that mean?'

'You know—an older version of Ranbir Kapoor. Fair, good looking, Nehru jacket, impressive oratory skills, a lost man-child. The works. Groomed to take the top slot.'

'Don't be silly. I wonder how long Anumita will take to meet us.'

'I am going to have a look around. Will you be all right on your own?' Ravi noticed the tense horizontal lines on her forehead, her thumbnail scratching at her index finger, all signs of worry. He walked away, when Charu nodded leaving her to mull over everything she had absorbed.

He walked to where the car had left them at the covered driveway. Ravi noticed the four-armed sentries at their posts. There was a wicket gate that stood locked along the sidewall. The green cover of the thorny bougainvillaea bushes around the boundary wall served as a privacy screen, making it difficult to scale the wall. With gardens circling the house, it was prime property in a cluttered city.

Unlike Anwar Haveli, Chauhan Haveli was squat, two-storeyed, and looked relatively modern. The walls were made of Lakhori bricks, whereas Charu's home was mainly marble and lime mortar. The restored teal main door, screen or *jaal, chhatri,* and the pillars had been left intact to remind one of the architectural style of the Mughal times. This was one of the nine havelis of Naugraha.

This haveli must have cost Prithvi a substantial amount. But, why stay here when he could have a modern mansion in central Delhi? Ravi mused.

Walking sedately along the corridor, he found himself in a large living room. It looked like an exhibition hall with expensive crystal figurines and large, breakable vases bursting with artificial flowers in pastel shades. Hookahs and antique brass-and-marble decorative pieces dotted the room. The theme of a restored haveli was kept alive in the deep beige couches, an expensive looking silk carpet, and a massive painting made with geometrical designs in primary colours. Ravi could see corridors with rooms on either side. A staircase to his right led up to the floor above. The security cameras gave it a feel of a heritage hotel rather than a home.

He was pulled out of his contemplations by the sound of running feet. A small girl of about seven years sauntered down the steps, her ponytail waving behind her, badminton racquets in hand. She came to an abrupt halt when she saw him. Rather than shrink away, she stood scrutinising him through her pink-rimmed glasses. The shiny lights on her sneakers made him smile.

'Wow, even I want those sneakers,' Ravi waved at her. A shy smile curled her lips.

'Sia, let's play in the room.' The young woman, beside the little girl, said softly. 'Sorry, sir, I will take her away.'

Her north-eastern accent was almost non-existent. She was short and had an earnest, round face. She was dressed in jeans and a branded t-shirt that looked like hand-me-downs.

'And you are...?'

'Gita, sir, the children's nanny,' the young woman answered confidently, holding the girl's hand protectively in hers.

'Did you know we were coming?' Ravi asked, gently.

The direct question seemed to have made her uncomfortable. 'I...no.'

'It's okay,' Ravi said, smiling at Sia. 'Let her play here.'

Charu heard Ravi's voice from inside and stood up to join him.

'Why are you here?' Sia asked him. 'Are they here to look for...'

'Sia...shh...,' Gita's voice was firm. Ravi saw her give the child a stern look.

Ravi noticed Charu walking towards him. Her head shot up at Sia's voice, her eyes scared, she went completely still.

She leaned forward, her eyes lowered, and asked, 'How old is she?'

'Around five or six years.'

They heard the sound of heels, not flimsy stilettos but robust, comfortable wedges, the shoes of a woman who was on her feet for a better part of the day. They were climbing down the steps hurriedly.

Charu heard a refined voice. 'Sia, please go to your room.'

Why is mummy so angry all the time? Does she blame me for Myra getting lost? Charu felt the pang of the young heart nearby. The shuffling of retreating sneakers made her feel for the little girl.

'Sorry, Sia, but we need to talk to your mother,' Charu couldn't help saying out aloud.

'Let me add my sorry to Charu Aunty's for having kept you from your badminton game,' Ravi added. 'May I request a match later on? You seem to know the game.'

'Really? Will you have the time?' Sia said with a smile.

'I will make time for this. I want to improve my skills. So, is it all right?'

'Is that all right, Gita Didi...Mummy?' Sia asked, hesitantly.

'Yes, of course, we will see,' her mother answered. Her voice was firm, without any anxiety or nervousness they had witnessed earlier with Prithvi. Sia and Gita resumed their trek up the steps.

Somehow, Ravi always catches on. How does one push away a man who will go the extra mile to ease a troubled child? Charu thought.

Meanwhile, Anumita waved at the large living room, maybe one of several in the haveli, with a careless air. 'Sit, sit, please. Don't worry, Gita will take care of her. She is great at keeping Sia entertained and, if nothing else works, there's always TV. First of all, thank you so much for coming here at such short notice.' Anumita sat down next to Charu.

Charu could feel the waves of rigidity and animosity from her. *She is clearly unhappy I'm here but pretends not to mind. Why?*

'Let me first apologize for my appearance in the morning. I barely got any sleep, and then, when I woke up, I...' Anumita couldn't finish her sentence.

'Please, ma'am, we understand,' Ravi interrupted her.

'Are you okay?' Charu asked, tentatively.

'I'm sorry. Keeping up appearances in front of Sia is exhausting. Myra has been missing since yesterday, and it feels like someone has pulled my heart out of my body. Prithvi told me you can help find her faster. That is why he does not want to involve the police at this stage. I just hope his confidence is not misplaced.' She touched Charu's elbow, seeking comfort. Charu took her hands in her own. As soon as Anumita placed her hands in hers, Charu saw flashes of her crouching in a pink room, crying with a little rag doll held close to her chest. Charu squeezed Anumita's delicate hands in sympathy and drew a breath. Her throbbing heart pulsed with regret and sorrow. Charu was familiar with this pulse. It rang in most parents and echoed in the air long after they had left.

'It will be all right. Don't think about anything right now,' Charu said. She sensed raw icy fear in every cell of Anumita's body.

Why is she so scared?

Warmth emanated from Charu and slowly engulfed the cold terror, raising goosebumps on Anumita's arms. She felt Anumita's stiff shoulders gradually relax.

After a while Anumita asked, 'Prithvi told me you have some special ability. How does it work if you can't see?'

Charu sensed the sarcasm behind her words.

'Well, I wasn't born blind, so that is the easy bit. I lost my eyesight at around nine years of age. Retinal detachment due to severe myopia. It happened suddenly. It is the "normal" I've learnt to live with,' Charu explained in brief.

'And, your skill as an empath... Was that always there, or did it develop later?'

'Well, strong emotions like anger, love, hate, pain are especially easy to catch. But mostly, they are like shadows, like jigsaw pieces. Sometimes I get pictures—snapshots of things that have had an impact. Or sometimes, I see an object that should not be where it is. Sometimes, I can only sense a place or people connected to a person—whether they are in a comfortable environment, sitting in a stuffy dungeon, or freezing in the cold out in the street. Sometimes, I hear sounds. It takes team effort to form the big picture with these pieces. It is not something I can control. But, when something clicks, all I can do is hold on until I find something that helps the case.'

'Can you read my thoughts?' Anumita seemed to mock Charu. She was obviously not convinced, but she was also worried and uncertain.

'Sometimes. But, trust me, I don't go meddling with anyone's mind. So, you have nothing to worry about. I don't enjoy looking into other people's thoughts all day. It is tiring and quickly becomes tedious.'

There was a tense silence after Charu finished.

'Hmm...very interesting.'

Charu couldn't fault Anumita for the slight distance she could feel between them. It is not easy opening yourself to a stranger. And, though she didn't find the questions offensive, Anumita's tone felt fake.

5. Ravi

10:45 am, Wednesday

Ravi watched Charu explain her situation to Anumita and was again reminded of why he had fallen in love with her. One only had to close their eyes, and try and walk across a familiar room, to understand her world. He had tried it and been defeated by the loss of control.

'Right, ma'am. So, please tell us about your day...your routine,' he said.

'What does that have to do with what you are here to do? I thought you would touch Myra's things and tell me where she is or who took her.' Anumita turned towards Charu.

'It doesn't work that way, Anumita. I, too, need a bit of background, and it is the team that looks for the child. I am only a part of the whole.'

'Oh, so it is an investigation. But, Prithvi said...' She stopped herself.

'Is it a problem?' Ravi's voice was an octave lower.

'No, not a problem. Usually, I wake up early, do yoga, or spend time at our personal gym. Then I wake Sia, get her ready for school. Sometimes, I go to drop her at school, or she goes with Gita and the driver. I wake up Myra and oversee her morning routine till Gita comes back and takes over. By noon, I am ready to step out for an afternoon engagement, a coffee date with friends, a movie, or lunch. It's my "me-time", you could say. I pick up Sia and bring her back home. We schedule everything a day in advance. Evenings are for Sia's homework.'

'And, Myra?' Charu interrupted her.

'She goes to the park with Gita in my absence. In the evening, I usually have an early dinner with the family or, if there is an official engagement, I go out with Prithvi—if he wants me to. If not, I put the kids to bed, and go to sleep early myself.'

'I will need information about the entire staff, their details, place of hiring, residence, family background, etc.'

'Sure. I hired Gita myself. The files are with my mother. But, they all come with proper background checks. Do you think it could be Gita or one of the drivers?' Anumita's eyes were troubled.

'Let's study the details first. It is routine to ask for details of all the people who were in contact with the child,' Ravi went on scribbling in his notebook.

'Her name is Myra,' Anumita's voice broke.

'Yes, of course. Myra, sorry.' Ravi looked at her apologetically. 'We will be doing a preliminary interview with everyone, including your support staff. We would have liked to talk to your mother first if that was possible, but Prithvi sir told us she and Ram Vilas Ji...um...left for some puja immediately after the incident.'

'Yes, they have gone to Ram Vilas Ji's ashram in Hisar to pray for Myra's safe return. He said he would perform the puja.'

'Why did they want to leave immediately?'

'When Mummy decides to do something, no one can stop her,' Anumita laughed nervously.

'Tomorrow, then?'

'Yes, they should be back tonight. It's not far.'

'What about Mr Ram Vilas? Does he live here?' Charu asked.

'He sleeps in his own government flat, near the bungalow on Ashoka Road. But, he has an office here in the haveli. Prithvi insisted on it. They spend most days together there, discussing the next strategy. Oh...you mean when he will get back? I wouldn't know. You will have to talk to Prithvi about his whereabouts. I am not sure he would know either. Swamiji has the greatest freedom out of us all.'

Charu detected a trace of bitterness lacing Anumita's carefully moderated words. 'Prithvi told us you were at a meeting when Myra was kidnapped,' she said.

'Yes, the work I did in this haveli has landed me several projects. I was at a meeting with a prospective client when I received Mummy's call. She asked me to come home immediately. I rushed back.'

'We will need the details of this client. What did you find when you came home?'

'Sure. When I got back, Mummy told me Myra was nowhere to be found. Prithvi looked at the security cameras. Manik, Sia's tutor, searched everywhere, along with the guards. We didn't find her. Then Prithvi and Swamiji shut themselves in his office, and we were left to wonder what they were discussing. A little later, Prithvi told us he would call you to look for Myra, that it was all arranged.'

'Arranged?'

'I asked him what he meant. We should call the police, do something, I said, but Prithvi dug his heels in, and Swamiji supported him. Mummy followed suit because Swamiji can do no wrong in her eyes. Obviously, I was left alone again. Prithvi explained that you lived close by. How convenient, no? He was sure you would come.'

Charu couldn't help but notice the insinuation in her words. She wondered if she knew about their history. Maybe, Prithvi had told her. After all, she was his wife. She would have had the right to know everything before they were married.

'What happened next?'

'Since Swamiji had forbidden it, we couldn't raise an alarm. Maybe, if we had, we could have—someone would have prevented it. I keep cursing myself for attending the meeting that day. I don't know where my poor baby is. She is so young. She doesn't even know what is happening or why.' Anumita broke down.

Charu let her cry. She heard Ravi pour a glass of water for her. She could feel Anumita's desperation for her daughter come at her in waves. When Anumita regained her composure somewhat, Charu said, 'Do you suspect anyone?'

'I...I don't think so. We shifted here because Prithvi wanted to pretend to be from a royal family, I think. I begged him to let us stay at the government bungalow, but he dragged us all here. He said it was a gift, that he wanted me to renovate it and showcase it to my clients. I am an interior designer. But, living here comes with its set of problems. It is not the life I envisioned for myself when I married him. We are hidden away in this fortress while he roams outside freely. Had we been at the bungalow and not in this massive haveli, maybe my Myra wouldn't have been kidnapped. And keeping us locked away didn't help, did it?' she sniffed.

'You didn't answer my question, ma'am. Do you think...?'

'No...I don't know,' she said too quickly before turning away. Then she looked Ravi in the eye. 'Does Prithvi have enemies? Of course, he does. He is in politics. Someone always wants to throw him off the next election. There can be no other reason. It must be someone from the opposition party, or maybe from his own...someone who is jealous of his meteoric rise, and wants him to step down. It could be enmity or revenge.'

'Or money?' Charu added.

'It usually is, isn't it? But, if someone took away Myra for money, they should have asked for ransom by now,' Ravi reasoned.

'Why would someone do such a horrible thing to a child? I can't wrap my head around it,' Anumita cried.

'Do you want to go into her room now?' Anumita asked Charu. Charu hesitated. She knew that despite everything she had told Anumita, she still wanted her to touch Myra's things and tell her where she was. She had faced this, enough times to know that people were disenchanted with the process very fast.

'Yes, we can go now.' Charu stood up. They went through the lobby, up the broad wooden stairs, to the first-floor landing. A few steps away was Myra's room.

Entering a room where a crime had been committed, always proved to be the most challenging part for her. She usually worked with adults who had faced some kind of violence. It always affected her intrinsically, even physically, but she could handle it. She was confident in her ability to find the balance in the most gruesome of situations, past the pain. But now, standing at the threshold of Myra's room, Charu wondered what this first step into a little child's world would uncover.

What is making me so nervous?

Kidnappers used their victims as pawns in disputes, a bargaining chip to settle a personal score, for perverted sexual fulfilment, or just to manifest their idea of love. If the victim resisted or struggled, the remnants of the assault were sometimes left behind. Violence or evil thoughts were like sticky black tar that clung to the corners of a room, taking a long time to fade. When she walked in, they became attuned to her receptiveness, and throbbed with renewed vigour. She knew it was the unexplained debilitating fear of walking into an unknown room. She always felt trapped, like she would not be able to get out. Like no one would know she was inside.

Ravi is inside, she reminded herself.

She took the first step into Myra's room. It was the smells that inundated her senses first: Ravi's soap, a strong perfume—probably what Anumita wore. Right now, she was saying something to Ravi. Charu ignored her and took a deep breath, absorbing the air in the room. Her stick struck the crib. She took a step closer, leaned forward, and inhaled. Under the adult perfumes were softer baby smells, not the ones that Aruna, her elder sister, used for her children. Aruna used the fragrance of violets, readily available in India. The strongest scent here was different, buttery—with a hint of honeysuckle. It was not overpowering but gentle. Sweet. There was no cloying incense smell as compared to the ground floor. As Charu sifted through the odours, she found what she had been searching for—another faint smell—not in keeping with a child's room. It was acrid and stale.

The crib was next to an open window. Charu could hear the traffic, the flimsy curtains swooshing at the window, and Sia's voice further down the hall. She could feel the wind blowing towards her.

'Ravi, can you describe the layout?' she asked.

'You are standing before Myra's crib. It is next to a large window. We are on the first floor, so there is nothing in front. The trees are far away. There is a ledge, but it is too thin. There is no way to climb in from outside except with a ladder. That would attract the guard's attention at the corner of the outer wall. The terrace is too far up,' Ravi answered, leaning out of the window to check.

'One wall has almirahs and the changing station that holds Myra's toys and books. The opposite wall has a plush sofa upholstered in velvet. The door to the room, with an attached bathroom, is a few steps apart. Barring one empty square space high up, all the other racks over the changing table are filled with soft toys, books, nappies, and baby products.'

Closing her eyes, Charu put her hands on the crib. She knew she wouldn't remain unaffected if the child had been hurt here. Pink-hued images appeared in her head: *a toddler standing in the cot, gurgling, calling out, smiling happily. She heard a faint sound of a zipper closing, a lullaby, and men's voices. She saw a colourful rotating mobile, picture books, and the child being fed by an unknown hand.*

'She is a fussy eater,' Charu said out aloud.

She heard Anumita gasp at her comment, and wondered if she had been right to allow her to stay. Letting a family member remain in the room while she read it was not her usual practice. Their emotions were always close to the surface, and Charu felt their distress interfered with her work. She focused on the task at hand.

Ravi observed her. He knew she was pushing herself to remain impervious to the images and sensations. Her brow was smooth, her shoulders stiff—but not ominously so. She began to run her fingers over the cabinets in the room. She felt Myra's clothes. She sat on the sofa, staring at the walls, her head tilted.

Ravi and Anumita stood silently, watching her stand up and repeat the same things again. Then again. She crouched, always touching something: the carpet, the bassinet, the knobs. A soft cloth-doll held wonder and love. There was a rattle, more soft toys, the crackling-bath book.

There was not an inch of the room she did not feel with her hands. If Charu got a sense of something, she would go still. Wait. Push. Go deeper. Ravi was used to watching her, but he could see how fascinating it was for Anumita. Charu asked questions when needed.

'Who gives her a bath?' she asked from the bathroom, her hands on the lip of the bathtub. She touched the bath toys and the bottles that lined the sides.

'Gita does it in the morning, and I do it at night,' Anumita answered.

'Does Prithvi?'

'He comes to say bye to Myra sometimes, while she is having a bath, but he has never made an effort to give her a bath himself.'

'Who visits the room regularly?'

'We all do. But, it's mostly Gita, Sia, and I. Sometimes my mother. I don't allow any other staff to come to the first floor. Gita is the only one.'

'Why?'

'I find it safer. My girls are young; I have to be careful. Gita and the other staff are aware of this rule. I've never had any problem…I mean until now.' Anumita looked dejected.

'What about at night? Does anyone check on Myra?'

'Of course not. Prithvi comes sometimes but, usually, one of us is here. What are you getting at, Charu?' Anumita seemed offended.

'Nothing. I sense a male presence in the room. I am trying to find out who has access to Myra.' Charu continued to question Anumita, who answered her with a trembling voice.

While following Charu's conversation, Ravi explored all possible ways to enter and leave the room without being seen on the camera over the door. With only the window as the other possible entry point, Ravi found himself wondering how the kidnapper could have let themselves in. He stood in the middle of the room and turned around slowly. Everything was within an arm's reach. His watch beeped. He wondered how Reeti was doing with the preliminary interviews of the servants. He watched carefully as Charu and Anumita walked out of the bathroom.

Charu had told him once that sometimes the initial silence was a smokescreen, and she could be bombarded with excruciating images of an assault just as she began to relax. Ravi had seen it first-hand and always made it a point to be around her when she entered a room. Once, she had felt a man who had been stabbed fifteen times being killed. Charu had felt the knife go into her back. The shock and the disbelief had made her lose her balance and fall. He had failed to catch her then. Her cries had left him shaken. He stepped closer when she raised her head.

'Someone's outside,' she said.

'It's only Gita.' Anumita turned towards the door. Ravi watched Gita's eyes searching the room for something when Anumita asked her to enter.

'Did you want something, Gita?' Ravi asked her.

'No,' Anumita answered instead. 'I asked her to check on us. I didn't realize it's been more than two hours since we came up. Lunch must be ready. We can go down now.'

Charu could feel the sorrow in Gita's heart. She stretched her hands towards her. Immediately, Gita took them in hers.

'I shouldn't have gone to have lunch for so long. I am so sorry,' Gita cried.

'It's natural to feel responsible for the incident, Gita. If you haven't done anything, you have nothing to worry about,' Anumita said, dismissively.

Why did I have to open my mouth in front of Aunty Ji? Charu heard the thought in Gita's head.

'Anumita, would it be possible to arrange for something to eat for Charu right here?' asked Ravi.

'Yes, of course. Gita, please arrange for lunch to be served here.'

The girl almost ran out of the room.

'So, what do you think? What did you see? Do you think it could be Gita?' Anumita clasped Charu's shoulder as soon as Gita was gone.

'We are just starting out, Anumita. Please let us finish our full investigation,' said Ravi.

'No, I want to know now,' she said, stubbornly. Turning to Charu, she continued, 'Don't treat me like a damn fool. I know who you are, Charu. I know why Prithvi called you. I come from an equally well-connected family. Do you think I didn't know about your sleazy affair at school? Or, why he has called you in now? Do you think I am that blind? I knew there was someone. But you...you can't even *SEE* Prithvi, but then that is the novelty, I suppose. He does not need to wear a mask with you.'

'Mrs Chauhan...' Ravi cautioned her.

'Do you want me to leave?' Charu asked, solemnly.

'It's strange. A part of me wants you out of the door right now, consequences be damned. And, then another part wants to say you are welcome to take Prithvi. I don't want him; he is good for nothing. For all you know, he could be the one who...' Anumita stopped abruptly and audibly gulped down the rest of her words.

'Just find my daughter,' she said, composing herself as suddenly as she had let her emotions loose, like a flipped switch. Then she stood up and went out.

'Damn.' Ravi rubbed his face. *Did she just accuse her husband in front of us?* he thought.

'She clearly does not like me. She is looking for answers—someone to hold accountable for Myra's kidnapping. All these things are acceptable because she is the mother of a young girl who has been kidnapped. Ravi, there may be something Gita has told Malti Devi about Anumita that she regrets. You need to look into that. Interview her immediately,' said Charu.

'I saw her scanning the room to see if everything was in place. All right, I will be on this right away. Did you pick up anything else?'

'No violence, no blood. There was no lingering fear or confusion.'

Why is Charu not talking about Anumita's suspicion, about Prithvi being a possible suspect?

Charu waited for a moment and spoke up again. 'Ravi, please take out the mattress from the crib and shake it on the sofa. See if anything falls out.'

She heard him do what she had asked. 'No, nothing,' he said.

'Is there nothing shiny, sparkly?'

Ravi crawled under the crib. He found a small cluster of crystal gems stuck between the wooden leg and the wall. Picking it up with a pair of tweezers, he held it up.

'Charu, there is a small crystal flower, like you would find on clothes.'

'I saw a point of light that wasn't supposed to be there. It could just be something that fell off a dress and may have nothing to do with Myra's kidnapping.'

Ravi placed the cluster of crystals in a small Ziplock and sealed it. 'Done,' he said. Then, referring to the kidnapping, he continued, 'It is probably someone Myra knows. Most probably an inside job. Do you need to stay on a while?'

Charu nodded.

'What else is bothering you, Charu?' Ravi asked, watching her closely.

'Ravi, could the horrid dream about the girl and this case be *connected?*'

'But, Myra is too young compared to the girl in your dream. And, Sia does not seem to be in danger.'

'You are right. It's nothing. We will talk about it later,' Charu retreated, looking away.

'Are you sure?' He knew he would watch Charu closely for any conflict of interest. He hoped he wouldn't be disappointed.

'Yes, go now.'

Ravi hesitated; he knew she was fretting about the girl in her dream. 'I will map this floor, and the terrace, and circle back to you. We need to figure out how Myra was taken out of the house.' Ravi walked out slowly, glancing at her worriedly and closed the door behind him.

The click of the door latch falling in place sounded ominous to his ears.

6. Charu

12:30 pm, Wednesday

Charu could clearly picture the room she was in. Ravi had described it to her, and she herself had touched every crevice. She held on to Myra's cloth doll and focused her mind on the missing toddler. Abruptly, a child's face appeared before her only to disappear in a flash. She breathed deeply and tried to concentrate on that innocent face again. The same thing happened. This time for longer—long enough for her to see the child's face and the pacifier she was sucking on. She tried to hold on to the image.

The sound of a moving train nearby distracted the child. She turned her face and looked out of the open square window. The fluttering flag atop the illuminated temple dome and the decorative moving lights held the child transfixed. In the process, the pacifier slipped from her mouth. The little girl realized its absence and began to cry. Then she grabbed hold of a clump of her own hair pulled it. Snivels turned into loud bawling before someone cooed close to her.

Charu felt no fear in her, just anger at the delay in being attended to.

Feminine hands replaced the pacifier in the little mouth that latched on to it instantly. Long fingers with painted nails opened the child's fist to retrieve a small clip, then pinned her hair back while talking to her gently. The sound of bhajans over the loudspeaker was close. The woman sang a few lines for the child. An elliptical gold ring shone on her index finger. A black birthmark was visible at the bottom of the hand, near the wrist.

The walls were old and peeling behind the single bed covered with a floral bedsheet. The laughing baby turned her face to look directly at Charu. She frowned at her in confusion, her chubby hand reaching out as if to touch her.

Charu pulled back, breathless. This had never happened before. Until now, she had always been the observer in her visions. No one knew she was watching.

Did the baby see me? Was it possible? How had the baby looked at me directly, reached out to me? A sudden headache overwhelmed her, and she allowed herself to be pulled into the black hole.

'Charu, Charu...wake up,' she heard Ravi's deep baritone calling her out of the comfortable darkness. Charu wanted to resist but opened her eyes when he shook her gently.

'I'm fine. Stop tapping my cheek,' she grumbled. 'Who else is here?'

'It's Gita. She came with your lunch, found you on the floor passed out, and ran to fetch me,' he told her.

'Are you all right, Didi? It seemed as if you were...I tried to wake you but...'

'Yes...yes. I must have fainted. Thank you for bringing Ravi here. Gita, can you take the food downstairs? I will have it later.' Charu hoped Gita would be discreet about the scene she had witnessed.

Ravi waited for the girl to leave. Then he turned to Charu. 'What happened?'

Before Charu could respond, Anumita rushed into the room, her eyes taking in the couple sitting close together. Charu moved away, trying to look nonchalant, wiping her anguished, wet eyes.

'Anumita,' she said, 'does Myra suck on a purple pacifier? A pacifier with a broken ring on top?'

'What! You saw Myra? Oh my God, is she...is she all right?' For the first time, Anumita sounded impressed. 'But how do you know it was Myra?'

'She's small for her age, reed-thin with chubby cheeks. She wears her hair in two small ponytails. Yesterday, she wore clips in her hair and pink nylon bands.'

'Yes, yes...' Anumita's hands were icy cold on Charu's flushed skin.

'We will call the forensic artist to sketch what Charu saw and confirm it,' said Ravi.

'Did you see anything else? Was there someone else with her? Was she crying? She does suck on a pacifier, but her pacifier is here, see, Ravi ji. Was she all right?' Anumita broke into sobs again, holding on to Myra's soother.

'Anu, she was upset her pacifier fell down from her mouth, but she looks all right. She is unharmed, even comfortable,' Charu reassured her.

Ravi helped Charu up. Anumita backed away. As he turned to close the door behind him, he saw her standing at the window of her daughter's room dialling a number. At that moment, the yellow bird in the clock chirped two times, making Anumita jump. She noticed Ravi watching her.

'I was just calling...um...Prithvi...to tell him to hurry home,' she explained in a rush. Ravi nodded and shut the door. They walked towards the rooms cleared for them on the ground floor. Charu could hear Reeti talking to someone on the phone. Their unit consisted of five members, if she counted herself as part of the core team. For this case, they had to do with three. She didn't know if that was a good omen or bad.

'This is where we have set up the command centre,' Ravi murmured to her as they entered. He looked around at the large suite divided into two parts by a wooden panel. Everything Prithvi had promised them stood in shiny cases. Reeti already had a head start. The computer screens now were a latticework of security camera footage accessed from various sources. A number of cameras were faulty, with distorted images or interrupted and flickering feed. Ravi found it odd that Prithvi had not mentioned it.

They had several phone lines and tables and chairs scattered around. An old couch had been pushed against a wall, and next to it were Reeti's bags. On the other side of the panel was the recording equipment.

Reeti looked up.

'Hi, Charu. Thanks, Boss, for calling me in. My parents had been planning to parade me before prospective grooms. At this age, can you imagine? And worse, I would have let them. They were put out, to say the least, but I am glad to be out of the house. And, for such a high-profile case, Prithvi Chauhan, the handsome minister. Wow!'

Reeti, the IT expert and government liaison, was the bridge between their team and the power corridors.

Charu smiled in response to Reeti's light-hearted banter.

'Reeti, call the forensic artist in, please. Charu will have to describe what she saw in her dream,' Ravi said, feeling a twinge of anger at the way first Charu and now Reeti had reacted to Prithvi.

'You already had a vision, Charu? Oh my, fast work. What did you see?' Reeti turned to Charu in awe, letting Ravi's irritation slide. She was used to his surliness. Her fingers moved undeterred on her cell phone to send out a message to the sketch artist.

Charu repeated her account. 'I am pretty confident it was Myra, but best to have corroboration. Another thing, is it Diwali yet?'

'No, we are in the middle of October. Why do you ask?'

'The temple was illuminated with the lights that moved in a linear manner, as if for an occasion. There were bhajans on the loudspeaker.'

'Charu, it's Navratri. Most temples in north India must be decorated with such lights. Could you describe the temple, or the surroundings, a bit more?'

'There's a train track nearby. I heard the sound of a train crossing, but not the regular train. It was faster, smoother.'

'Good, we map out all the temples near the new tracks. This gives us a place to begin. What about the hand?'

Charu described it in detail. 'Not a woman of means. I only saw the lower half of her face, maybe because the baby was focused on that. She had soft skin, and she was young. The pacifier was not expensive. One we would find in any chemist shop. The ring on top was broken, so well-used. Even the cartoon print was wearing off.'

'Reeti has done some preliminary interviews of the staff since she arrived. But, first things first. Let's collate our findings.' Ravi leaned against the table while Charu and Reeti moved closer. This was their routine method. Everyone would do their digging through the day, and brief each other at the end of the day. Full disclosure.

'Prithvi Chauhan lives in this house with his family, extended family, and mentor/guru,' Reeti began. 'His security and support staff have the run of the place. He also holds a government bungalow, as a sitting MP of the party, where he stays over when he is out too late. His eighteen-month-old daughter was kidnapped yesterday, allegedly between 1:30 pm and 4:30 pm. No ransom calls, no notes, as yet...and we are nearing the twenty-hour mark.

There were three people on the first floor at that time. Anumita's mother, Malti Devi, was apparently sleeping in her room. The tutor, Manik Chauhan, and Sia, the elder daughter, were studying in her room—as verified by the camera in the corridor. However, the nanny cam in Myra's bedroom was not working and was due to be replaced. It was put in the teddy bear on one of the square racks.'

Convenient and explains the empty rack, thought Charu.

'No FIR yet, but our team was contacted and asked to convene here ASAP,' Reeti went on. 'This VIP investigation is under the radar for now. Gita took the child for her nap around 1:30 pm. Anumita checked on the sleeping Myra around that time before she left for her meeting. Gita went for lunch, returned to check on Myra at 3:30 pm, found her missing, and raised an alarm. Manik, along with the guards and the other staff, searched the grounds. This took about thirty minutes. Then they called Prithvi Chauhan and Anumita around 4 pm.'

'What about everyone's whereabouts? Have we been able to cross-check those?' asked Ravi.

'Prithvi Chauhan was in a meeting with the party president and members. He came home with Ram Vilas as soon as he was told about the crisis. I still have to interview Ram Vilas's driver,' Reeti replied.

Charu smelt the marker on the glossy surface of the whiteboard when Ravi started the list.

'Anumita was in a meeting with a prospective client for her interior decorating business. She, too, came home immediately. Malti Devi was sleeping and was woken up by Gita. She was the one who called her daughter and her son-in-law. She left with Ram Vilas for some Kul Devi mandir puja. Utter crap, if you ask me. It makes no sense. Plus, didn't her daughter Anumita need her?' Ravi combed his hair with his fingers.

'What could have prompted them to leave for the ashram at this time?' Charu wondered.

'It is odd that both Ram Vilas and Malti Devi left only a few hours after they discovered Myra had been kidnapped. That's what Prithvi said. What strikes me as more surprising is that Prithvi didn't find that either disturbing or questionable. But, no conjecture for now; let's stick to the facts,' Ravi continued.

'Gita is completely shattered. She's a young girl and has been with the family since Sia was born and took care of the children like her own. She was having lunch in the kitchen with the other staff who, by the way, are each other's alibis,' Reeti said.

'While we were talking to her earlier, Gita was guilt-ridden. She thought she shouldn't have said something to Aunty Ji,' Charu added. 'I wonder what she knows.'

Ravi added Gita's name to the list in red.

'Let's shake her up and see what falls out.' Reeti's voice rang with excitement.

'Anumita worries me too. When we met her later in the day, she had changed completely from what she was in the morning. Like there were two women—one who was all over the place, desolate and broken, and the other calm and collected, softly despairing, talking in a very cultured manner about her grief. The lady of the manor. Even her physical appearance underwent a drastic change. I trust the one I saw in the morning more.' Ravi added Anumita's name to the board.

'Moving on, Sia was studying with her tutor, Manik Chauhan. He's a teacher and also Prithvi's cousin from Sirsa.

Pity job, I think. I haven't spoken to Sia yet,' Reeti continued. 'I spoke to Manik over the phone. I've asked him to come over for an interview. He says he was with Sia. Gita came in after her lunch asking if he had Myra. He didn't. Manik then ran to check Myra's room for himself, found her missing, and searched the grounds. He left when Prithvi and Anumita came back. Before that, he stepped out of the room twice, according to the surveillance camera, apparently to use the bathroom. Once at 2 pm, and the second time at 3:05 pm, which falls within the time frame of the kidnapping. He left at 4:30 pm on his bike, which is his routine. It's all on the cameras, so there are no gaps. Malti Devi and Ram Vilas's interviews, remain pending. First thing, once they come back.'

'We need to grill each of them separately and establish a timeline. This takes care of the main family members. Is there a list of outsiders we can go through? We need to dig deeper for political rivalries, fanaticism, or personal agenda. If Prithvi feels the opposition party may have something to gain from this personal attack, let's look at that angle. He said as much, right?' Charu voiced her thoughts.

'Reeti, will you find out from your contacts on the opposite side? I don't have to tell you to keep it low-key,' said Ravi.

'Did that already on the way to this place since it was taking so long. I tried to unearth Prithvi's background. After he left Surat, he's been a fairly straightforward guy, liked by everyone on both sides of the divide—except for his anger issues. He was pulled up by his party president for slapping a peon and manhandling a party worker. He rose to power based on his work at the ground level and contacts with the right people. The other side is, prima facie, unaware of the kidnapping and unlikely to try this stunt, so close to the elections. But, I will dig deeper. Of course, if we knew more about his earlier years, it would help,' Reeti concluded. Charu knew they were looking at her.

'Parents?' asked Ravi.

'In Sirsa and unaware of this development. Not too much contact with their son. Prithvi's father was a sarpanch in the

Panchayat Samiti and seems to have retired from public life. This Ram Vilas hails from the same place. He was the guru who rose to power along with Prithvi. He introduced Prithvi to politics after he left school in Surat mid-year in class twelve.'

Reeti outlined Prithvi's work in the party as the youth-wing *karyakarta.*

How strange it is to hear about Prithvi from people who know him only through newspapers and articles, Charu thought.

'Have you interviewed the staff?' asked Ravi.

'The first round, yes. I interviewed all the support staff, drivers, maids, security personnel while you were in Myra's room and, so far, I have no leads. They all have an alibi, and nothing seems out of place. I will get in touch with their families and interview any floating staff first thing tomorrow morning. The house has been combed. But, why were we called in so late? All the evidence has probably been walked over and destroyed.' Reeti, being a stickler for rules, found this unofficial favour very shady.

'Anyway, so no physical evidence of any foul play. Phone records are next on the agenda.'

'Where are we on the security footage?'

'I will scan the security footage after we are done with this meeting.'

'Would you like to add anything to this assessment, Charu?' Ravi asked, politely. Too politely.

Charu took some time to answer Ravi's question. 'First, Anumita is scared of something, maybe someone. I know that's to be expected in the circumstances, but there's more to it. When we were sitting together, the impression of the fear was pretty deep. It wasn't for Myra alone.

'Along with a mother's worry, there was an overwhelming dread. It was like she existed with a sense of horror every day. She is deathly scared of something or someone. I will spend more time with her and try and find out,' Charu concluded.

'It could explain the added security measures, her anxiety, the way she panicked in the morning when Prithvi was not around. But, that does not explain the magnitude of the fear you are talking about,' Ravi observed.

'She is like a bird in a golden cage. She can't go anywhere without it being recorded in some form. The gym trainer is female. The driver is Prithvi's trusted guy, who has been with the family for years. Her phones, and all other communication devices, are synced with either the home systems or those in Prithvi's office.' Reeti scrunched her nose in distaste.

'But, why so much surveillance? It's weird. And, why has she not objected?' Charu weighed in with her thoughts.

'I asked her about the cameras while checking out the first floor,' answered Ravi. 'She said she was the one who had them installed. The synced devices make it easier for them to keep track of each other's schedules. She also said she had nothing to hide and she preferred it this way.'

'More than half of the cameras don't work, by the way.'

'Anything else?'

There was nothing else with which Charu could delay the inevitable. Charu knew she would have to take the step voluntarily. She hesitated, maybe because she had to tell her current lover about a past relationship that had impacted her deeply enough to change her. There had been no closure, and Prithvi's presence still confused her.

'First, I don't know if this has any bearing on the case. But, I don't want to hold on to anything that may come to light later,' Charu said, hesitating. Slowly but clearly, Charu related the relevant details. In the utter silence that followed, Charu began in a soft voice, explaining what she had barely understood at the time.

7. Prithvi

3:30 pm, Wednesday

'Prithvi and I met when I was eleven years old, and he was around sixteen. I reached Surat after my parents decided that they could not take care of my special needs. Their words, not mine. My father and his brother were also fighting a case in the courts for Anwar Haveli. Though I vaguely recall having a caretaker, I don't have any clear memories of that time. I never questioned why until now, actually.'

'You have shared stories from your childhood with your sisters?' said Reeti.

'No, I do have memories till about ten years. There is a small gap, and then I am in Surat. I think after this case is over, I will ask my parents to fill that gap. Anyway, coming back. I met Prithvi in my grandmother's school in Surat. We became friends. He took me under his wing, so to say. He was always the ring leader. And, truth be told, it was really a zoo. And, we were all strange, defective animals whose parents didn't know what to do with them anymore. So, we found ourselves at Girija Devi Vidya Mandir in Surat as a last resort.'

'Was the school residential, like a hostel? Having a unisex hostel in Surat, a second-tier small town, is progressive,' said Reeti.

'Yes, you could say that. In reality, it was just an old bungalow. We were never more than twenty at a time, so it was a very closed group. The children were from affluent families. Difficult children. I know Prithvi was there because he had caused some trouble back home with his unruly behaviour. He had a temper and was always fighting. His parents were overly stringent; I remember him telling everyone. His father was a big shot in his village, so he was sent to my grandmother's school to be disciplined,' Charu laughed, nervously.

'Was it like a home-school?' Reeti asked.

'It was, in the morning. In the evening, we all trained in hypnotherapy, astrology, numerology…not your regular curriculum. My Nani believes in all forms of healing. So, from crystal healing to past life regression, we were taught everything.'

'This is surreal. So, Prithvi is also like you?'

'I…no, Prithvi is very persuasive, and he can be extremely manipulative and a little cruel. I am not surprised at the aggressiveness you told us about, Reeti. That was his way. He had a dormant streak of violence most of us could sense. He once threw a brick at another boy, slapped and kicked one, beat up the chowkidar. Every child there was troubled, sent there to be either hidden away or punished. Some children had been abused in ways you cannot even imagine because they were more than what was normal.'

'What does that mean? That Prithvi can coax you to do something against your will?'

'Not coax but suggest, and if you are so inclined, you will follow the direction he shows you. '

'Wait a minute, are you saying that Prithvi can convince anyone to do what he wants…incredulous, seeing that he is in politics, so ethical.' Ravi quipped, sarcastically. 'What proof do you have?' Ravi asked.

'None…we didn't need one there. I… I know it all sounds too far-fetched when you say it out aloud. I am only telling you facts about my interactions with Prithvi when I was a young girl,' Charu clarified.

When no one said anything to contradict her, Charu continued. 'The problem with people who have led normal lives is that they think the world is a bubble of happy childhood memories. For us, our childhood was the worst time of our lives. And, that bonded us like inmates in an asylum. We were just grateful that Nani made us feel like we belonged.'

'Why did Prithvi leave?' Ravi asked, abruptly.

'In his senior year, he became exceptionally challenging to handle. He started acting strange, misbehaving with the mentors, taking on dangerous dares. He bullied younger kids, disrespected teachers, bunked classes. One night we sneaked out into the grounds. Sitting on the fresh, sweet-smelling grass the boys had spent the afternoon mowing, we stared at the constellations in the sky, discussing our future. We teased each other. We were being silly and young. *Happy*.

A few young boys had climbed up on the tree while Prithvi and his friends watched and egged them on. I don't remember who began the game of Truth and Dare. The dares had up until then been simple: sing a song, do a handstand. But then the boys started pushing each other's limits. Prithvi's friend dared him to make the younger boys jump from the top branches instead of climbing down.

Most of us took it as a joke and laughed at him. The joke quickly turned serious when Prithvi began to act upon it. I asked him to let it go, told him it would lead to trouble, but he grew more obstinate. I couldn't pull him back like usual. They didn't have to convince Prithvi for too long. He enjoyed twisting the knife. Despite our misgivings, he raised his voice and asked the young boys to jump. When they laughed, he became angry, threatened to tie them to the tree. It became about his ego now. He asked them to jump a second time, and a few boys started climbing down, probably sensing something was amiss.' She could still hear their nervous laughter.

'Prithvi stood next to me shouting, threatening, pushing. One boy, who had just returned to school a few days back, still stood on the branch, looking down. The other senior boys and girls cheered him on. That was when Prithvi took his name and asked him to jump.' Charu gulped. Even today, she could hear the air parting when the boy took that step into nothingness.

'I don't know why he did it. We found out later that he came from an abusive family. Maybe, he was depressed. He was on medication, that much we knew. Whatever it was, no one expected him to leap from the branch.'

'What happened to him?' Reeti asked.

'He broke his leg in two places, fractured his spine.'

'Thank God, I feared the worst,' Reeti sighed.

Charu didn't tell her she had knelt next to the boy, touched him, experienced the excruciating pain. She had felt him drifting away and whispered to him to come back. She had held his hand until her grandmother arrived with the ambulance.

'Prithvi changed after that night. As the boy recovered, Prithvi deteriorated. He blamed everybody, including himself. His friends showed him the boy's file, said he was taking medication for depression, so the suicide attempt had nothing to do with him. But, Prithvi wouldn't listen. He left for Sirsa, took his exams there, and I never heard from him again. Until today, when he called in the morning.'

'The boy—the one who jumped—what happened to him?' Reeti asked.

'He was paralyzed from the waist down,' Charu answered. They were silent after she finished, processing what seemed unbelievable.

'So, now we know,' Ravi concluded, walking back to the board decisively. He had taken a few steps away to detach himself from the pained voice with which Charu had spoken about Prithvi. Ravi was now aware of why Prithvi bothered him. The woman he wanted to marry still hadn't got over her first love.

'Also,' Charu whispered, 'we were romantically involved... or I was.'

'What, you must have been all of...' Reeti broke off.

'Fifteen,' Ravi finished.

'Um...yes. Well, I just wanted you to stop speculating. It was a long time ago.' Charu wanted to change the subject now.

A knock at the door revealed the forensic artist, ready to draw the likeness of whatever Charu could tell him of her vision. She took him to the corner of the room where they settled themselves around a desk. She began to describe the temple top, the child, the pacifier, the hands, the pin, acutely aware of the hurt in Ravi's heart.

It didn't take long for the forensic artist to finish his work. Charu gave detailed descriptions of all she had seen, down to the faded print on the pacifier. Just as she began describing the pin on the child's head, the door opened, and Prithvi walked in. Ravi watched the two from a distance. He observed the way Prithvi's eyes searched the room for Charu before he rushed to her. He didn't acknowledge Reeti's greeting or the artist who was looking at him in surprise.

'What happened? I heard you fainted,' Prithvi took her by her arms and stared at her pale face.

'Occupational hazard, Prithvi. Yes, I did, but now I am all right. You didn't need to come back,' Charu murmured.

'Sir, we have everything under control. I should have asked Anumita ma'am not to call you,' said Ravi walking towards Prithvi and Charu.

'Anu? She didn't call me. I couldn't concentrate in the office, so I thought it was best to return and stay close to all of you, to help where I could. Are you okay, Chumki? You seem warm.' His hand was still on her forehead when his eyes fell on the sketches lying on the desk. He picked up the pages.

'This is Myra.' Prithvi's voice was heavy with emotion. He took Charu's face in his hands. 'You found her! I knew only you could. You found her! Is she all right?'

'Yes, in my vision, she looked unharmed. Don't worry, we will find her.' Charu was moved by his proximity, his trust in her abilities.

'Sir, why don't you take a seat? Charu is just finishing up,' Ravi interrupted, loudly.

'Yes, of course. You did well, Chumki. Sorry, please continue.' He picked up all the sketches and took them to the sofa, where he sat down, looking at them carefully.

Ravi joined Prithvi. He noticed the shock in Prithvi's eyes as he stared at Charu, describing the pin on Myra's head. He saw the frown lines deepen on her forehead. She shifted on the chair and rotated it so that her back was turned towards them...which meant she could feel Prithvi's eyes on her, and it was affecting her concentration. Ravi set about to distract Prithvi. Charu needed to work in peace.

'Sir,' he said, calling for Prithvi's attention. 'We will be conducting interviews with everyone in a graded manner. I would request you to tell all the staff members to make themselves available when we need them. We have already asked Manik to come in, but...'

'You can tell Anu to do all that; it is her department,' Prithvi cut Ravi's attempt short.

'Sir.'

'What can *you* tell me, Ravi? What did she see? What did the room look like? Do we know what the woman looks like?' Prithvi's agitation seemed to increase with each question.

How does he know about the woman? Ravi took Prithvi through Charu's vision step by step.

'The sound of a train—that's pretty specific. And, the top of the temple, the arrangement of the lights, give some clue. A mark on the hand is something we can work with, but half a face is useless.' Prithvi looked down at the sketch of the smiling woman.

'Sir, it's been barely eight hours since we got here. I have shared whatever she said with you. When will your mother-in-law and Ram Vilas Ji be arriving?'

'Late in the night, I suppose. The puja will be held at the Sirsa ashram, where our Kul Devi mandir is also located. They will be back soon, don't worry. You are stressing yourself out for no reason. Focus on my enemies, the opposition. It may be one of the drivers or the servants. Who knows what they can do if tempted?'

'We will be looking at all the angles, sir. You said you saw them off...I mean, your Swamiji and Malti Devi. Did they carry any bags with them?'

'Of course, they carried bags with them. They carried a bag of food and a couple of others that had clothes and other things.'

'Sir, were the bags small or big?'

'Ravi, I know what you're thinking, but, trust me, we take bags of clothes for the poor every time we go to the ashram. Malti Devi packs them herself. It is nothing out of the ordinary,' Prithvi insisted. Then lowering his voice he further said, 'You see, she comes from a destitute family. Her parents left her nothing. Sometimes, such people are over-enthusiastic about helping the less fortunate.'

'So, she has no other source of income?'

'No. My mother-in-law was livid when she found out that her husband had made me his heir.'

'There are no other children?'

'No.'

'Ravi sir, I am done,' the forensic artist called out, picking up his bag. He nodded to Prithvi, waved at Reeti, and left.

'Prithvi? Sorry to disturb all of you, but I just wanted to know if everything is all right.' Anumita peeped in from the door.

'Oh yes. Come and have a look. You didn't believe me when I told you Chumki could find her. Look, she has already declared her safe—within a couple of hours of arrival. Now, what do you say? Had we called her in sooner, last night, as I wanted, we could have been much closer to whoever took her. But, you wouldn't listen...' Prithvi trailed off.

Anumita walked up to him and took the sketches, her tears flowing freely. Her fingers caressed the face on the paper, and her eyes were full of regret. She looked keenly at the hands and the clip before putting them aside.

'This isn't a competition, Prithvi. I am worried about our daughter as much as you. You could simply have given Myra's recent photo to the police. But, you chose to call an empath. Your old...friend. You say you allow her to look into our lives for Myra, doing all this voodoo stuff for your daughter, but I, for one, don't believe you. Prithvi, we are losing time!'

'I will handle this my way, Anu. You should worry only about the house, all right?' Prithvi brushed her off with deliberate brusqueness.

'Yes, of course.' Anumita left the room, her eyes looking at Charu's bent head with implacable hatred. Ravi and Reeti exchanged a glance at the minister's conduct.

'Stop it, Prithvi. You may be tense about Myra, but you can't behave in this manner with Anumita. What is the matter with you?' Charu, too, was taken aback at his behaviour.

'You were the only one who could keep me in check. I am sorry. Now that you are here, I will be better,' Prithvi said, tucking a lock of hair behind her ear.

Charu went red with embarrassment and pulled herself away.

'I need to hear what you saw, Charu, from your own lips. Ravi, I am borrowing this girl for some time.' Prithvi's words reeked of a sense of entitlement. She could sense Ravi's agitation towards Prithvi like needles and pins on her skin. And, it was growing steadily.

Prithvi took Charu's hand and stepped out into the corridor. Charu had assumed they would be going out into the garden. Prithvi, however, pulled her into another room a few steps away from the control room, shouting distance away from Ravi and Reeti.

'I wanted us to talk without an audience,' he told her, shutting the door.

Charu moved away from his disturbed and animated aura. She didn't fear him, but there was an underlying discomfort when she sensed his thoughts. He still remembered their stolen moments behind closed doors ages ago. It unnerved her that he was recollecting them at this time. It opened the door she had firmly shut, triggering a slew of memories she didn't want to return to. It also made her wonder about the kind of man Prithvi had grown into.

'You aren't scared to be alone with me, are you, Chumki?' he asked, snidely.

Charu shook her head as she felt the room around her. The room made her uneasy. It was as if she had been pushed into a sulphurous hell. Something toxic and evil had taken place here, in this room. Something precious had been violated, like trust.

Charu wheezed, choking on the smell of incense and ash. She found the window and made her way towards it, guided by the clatter of the blinds and the fresh air flowing into the room. She fought hard to calm the turbulence within her.

A study, but not Prithvi's. There is too much clutter. Leather sofas, glass tables, dhoop batti. Bookcases with old books, rotting, unopened. A room that isn't aired too often. And, he wouldn't smoke this, whatever this smell is, she thought.

Prithvi watched her as she moved around, breathing deeply.

'Whose office is this?' she rasped.

'Swamiji's. He uses it when we work here. Initially, he used to stay over. He and I would do our *havans* and pujas together. Malti Devi and Anu would join us. But, then Anu found out she was pregnant, and suddenly she couldn't stand the smell of the *havan kund*. We had to stop. I think it was just an excuse. She hardly had time for taking part in any pujas after that,' he scowled.

'Do you feel Anumita does not like your way of life? I didn't know you were this religious...at least you weren't when we were in school.'

'When I met Swamiji, he taught me all about our ancient history. How forward-thinking and scientific we were in our approach. But, we lost everything during the invasions—first by the Mughals and then by the British. Swamiji taught me how important it is to make our country great again. We have to bring back the old times, the times when sages were revered like Gods.

Charu, don't take Anumita's words to heart. She is not an easy person to live with. She has chronic anxiety. We were married because our parents and Swamiji arranged it. She was all right for a few years, but of late has become paranoid. I gave her this haveli to occupy her mind and give her business a start, but instead of being appreciative, she became all the more distant. I am happy that her talent is being appreciated, but she can't neglect her other duties. Tell me, does being a working woman supersede your duty as a wife and mother?'

'What do you mean?'

'She has no interest in me or what I do: my work, my *puja-paath*. She stopped accompanying us to the ashrams. You can be what you want outside, but you have to obey your husband once you're inside the house, right? Truth be told, I am at the end of my tether.'

Charu was surprised to hear his thoughts and wondered how deeply his mentor had affected his thinking. She wanted to argue, but chose not to contradict him on his beliefs. It was not her place to do so. What stood out was that Anumita had undergone a change during her pregnancy that did not sit well with Prithvi.

'Where is my daughter, Charu?' Prithvi enquired again.

'I don't know, yet.'

'We don't have much time. You know better than me that the chances of finding a kidnapped child dwindle after seventy-two hours, and we are fast approaching that number. A little while ago, I pushed Anumita away for you, for talking down to you, but she wasn't wrong about losing time.'

'I know. But, you know as well as I do, I can't control the visions. They can't be manipulated.'

'A decade back, you would have added "the way you are manipulating the police" to that sentence.'

'We have changed, Prithvi. What we shared in school is long gone. I don't need a saviour anymore. And, you...you are someone I don't recognize now.'

'This is the Chumki I remember. The feisty yet soft-hearted girl. I miss you—your sharp tongue, your prickly nature, the quietly disapproving way you used to hold me accountable for my actions...' Prithvi smiled at her solemn face.

'Why haven't you called the police in yet, Prithvi?'

'Involving the police will spread the word around. I want to handle this quietly for as long as I can. You are my best shot. Besides, having you here is something I have imagined for a long time.'

'Do you realize how unconcerned you sound?'

'Charu, would it be better if I cried and convulsed in grief to show I am broken? You know me. I will prepare for the worst but hope for the best. I know all of you will do your best to find Myra. The police are my Plan B, but I am hoping it won't come to that. I have full faith in you. You are what I have been missing in my life. Won't you say it back?'

'Look, Prithvi, you are a married man now.'

'So, does being married mean I don't need support, someone to listen to my troubles, a warm body to lose myself in? Don't you remember anything?' Prithvi whispered into her ear.

Charu wanted to be drawn into what he was proposing. But, his voice reminded her of the night she had described to her colleagues a few minutes back. It was difficult to claw her way out of the miasma.

'You were better than this, Prithvi. I came as a friend, not... This is inappropriate.' Suddenly she changed tack. 'Did you keep in touch with Bilal, that boy from school who jumped from the tree at your words?'

'Bilal? Yes. He is a successful industrialist now. He lives here in Delhi and opposes all my work. He is a big donor to the party fund, so he has a lot of say within the ranks. He hates me. Charu...my God, you are a genius. Yes. He could be involved. Please look at him. He has had it in for me from the beginning because of what I...what he went through. Maybe, Swamiji was right all along. He said it was some usurper trying to sabotage my position in the party. See, what a good team we make!'

Charu was still processing his words when someone knocked on the door.

'Sorry, but we need to have that interview now, sir.' Ravi walked in and looked around the room where Charu and Prithvi had been talking for the last fifteen minutes. It would have been a luxurious study, except for the overwhelming presence of idols and pictures of various deities. The small silver bell in the large mandir in one corner of the room looked modest by comparison.

Ravi spied a life-size cut-out of a man in a white dress. He studied the smiling man. The man's hand was raised in blessing. His salt-and-pepper hair, long and loose, was combed away from his forehead. The big *tilak* in the middle of his broad forehead looked impressive. His beard and moustache were trimmed and well-groomed.

'Isn't Swamiji splendid?' Prithvi joined his palms and bowed before the cut-out. 'I had this made, so he would always be near me whenever I needed him. He finds it embarrassing, but I said I needed his guidance.'

'It's very different from his TV appearances with you,' Ravi nodded. 'I have always seen him in finely-tailored suits, carrying a briefcase. His hair is always pulled back and tied in a knot. Only the *tilak* is the same. It is like he is a different person here. Now I can't wait to meet him. Should we proceed?'

'Yes, yes, of course.' Charu moved towards him hurriedly.

She could still feel Prithvi's gaze. It made her uncomfortable. Anything less than complete surrender would result in harsh consequences. She remembered how vengeful he could be.

'I will join you in a while. Charu, we will talk again but, for now, let us follow Ravi's lead. I want my daughter found.' Prithvi walked away.

'He isn't happy. What did he want?' Ravi asked.

'Only news about his daughter. Remember that boy I told you about who jumped from the tree? Bilal? He could have a possible motive; we will have to talk to him. He's a big industrialist now and involved in politics. He lives in Delhi. He is against Prithvi, naturally. Also, this Swamiji needs to be questioned as soon as possible. His room has been used for something wrong. And, what is that smell?' she asked. The question had been bothering her since she had entered.

'What? The incense?' Ravi sniffed.

'No, it is sharper near the window.'

Ravi walked towards the window, sniffing. 'Wait. It smells like a bidi. It's peculiar, actually, maybe a joint, the kind you would smoke in a village. Why do you ask?'

'This smell was there in Myra's room too.'

'What!'

'Under the talcum powder and the washing liquid, there were traces of this odour.'

'Come on.' Ravi rushed out of the study and made his way into the back room. 'We need to look at the people who smoke a bidi,' he said. Leading Charu to a chair, he put her hand on its backrest and moved away.

'Why?' Reeti asked. Charu told her the reason.

'Smoking is not a crime.'

'I found traces of the odour in Myra's room. If the house help is smoking it, we will know they went up. And, I gathered from Anumita that she is strict about whom she allows into Myra's room.'

'Ram Vilas himself could have visited Myra. He is in the house often and knows the family well,' Reeti observed.

'Prithvi said the opposite. He said he only comes to the house with him. Since Anumita couldn't stand the vapours of the *havan* when she was pregnant, he hasn't been here so often.'

'According to Gita, she put the child to bed and left the door ajar when she went down for lunch so that if she woke up, her crying would alert her,' Reeti reminded them.

'So, whoever took the child is either a part of the household or someone within helped them. There are too many cameras for the snatcher to go undetected,' Ravi thought aloud.

'But, you said that some cameras are not functioning properly. Is there a possibility someone could go undetected?'

'There is always that possibility.'

'Which simply means we cannot see who went into Myra's room. Or Malti Devi's.'

'I don't believe in coincidences,' said Ravi.

'How would Gita hear the child crying from the floor above? And, isn't the kitchen at the other corner of the house?' Charu said. While the others were pondering over that question, she remembered the plug points over the changing table. 'Was there a baby monitor in the room when you swept Myra's room, Ravi?'

'Yes.' Ravi walked out of the room to fetch Gita.

Reeti turned to Charu, now that they were alone. She knew Ravi and Charu were in a relationship, just as she knew that the relationship was strained at the moment.

'Charu, are you...um...too close to this case? I mean...' she hesitated.

'I know what you mean and, no, it won't be a problem. If I feel Prithvi may be involved in any way, I will let you know,' Charu said through clenched teeth, aware that Reeti was right to ask. Her history with Prithvi, her feelings for Ravi, and the nature of the case, had created a murky cesspool inside her.

8. Gita

5:30 pm, Wednesday

After about fifteen minutes, Ravi walked back towards the back room, with a visibly nervous Gita following. He found Charu standing in the dimly lit corridor.

Charu had been trying not to think about the little girl in her dreams. She couldn't, for the life of her, find a connection between Prithvi's daughters and that little girl.

Charu heard Gita's nervous footsteps next to Ravi's heavy footfall. She could sense Gita's overwhelming fear as she neared. Prithvi stopped before Charu and asked Gita to continue inside.

Something about Charu standing in the dark hallway pulled at him. He knew she only wanted to keep their relationship as before, on her terms but sometimes in moments that he could not explain he found himself unable to control himself. He wanted to grab her, hold her tight, and never let her go. He wanted forever while she was happy with the present.

Taking a deep breath instead, he started walking away.

'Ravi…,' she called out.

'What?'

'Don't be angry with me. I know you want something from me that I am unable to give you, but can we not go back to the way things were?'

'Friends? You want to be friends with me?' he felt himself rip. 'How many friends do you know who sleep together? Who do things to each other that one would do only to and with their spouse? You can use me, Charu, but don't insult my intelligence by calling me a friend. Friends don't keep a big chunk of themselves hidden from each other, they don't lie…'

'I never lied to you.'

'Yes, you did. You made me believe that there was hope of tomorrow. You know I am a straight arrow; you know I don't do things impulsively in my personal life. So, you knew that when you chose to sleep with me, I would be committing myself to this relationship. It's not only a woman's prerogative to feel used in a relationship, Charu. And, at this moment I feel cheated...cheated out of a future with you. I know you will say that you didn't spell out anything, promised nothing. I know all that, but some things aren't necessarily said. They are understood in my world.'

'What are you saying?'

'That either you find the courage to be with me or this sleeping around, sneaking around...stops. We will go back to being colleagues and nothing else. You decide.'

His heart hammering, Ravi walked away, knowing he had played the biggest gamble of his life. 'We start Gita's interview in five,' he said before closing the door.

'Gita, don't worry. We will ask you a couple of questions. If you remember anything later, you can find one of us and tell us, okay?' Ravi said, calmly.

Gita nodded. Charu sat down opposite her, next to Ravi. Reeti sat down next to the recorder on the side.

'For the record, I, ACP M. Ravi Nair, am conducting this interview in the presence of Ms Reeti Gaur, ACP Cyber-crime, and Ms Charu Sharma, independent consultant. Her presence has been requested by Mr Prithvi Chauhan, the father of the kidnapped victim, Myra. This interview is of Gita Kire, the child's nanny. She has agreed to do this interview voluntarily, as stated by her. Please state your name and say if you are willingly cooperating with us,' Ravi leaned forward to speak into the small mike and nodded to Gita.

'I...I am Gita Kire, and, yes, I am doing this interview willingly,' Gita stammered, looking at the three attentive faces before her.

'That's good, Gita. Can you tell us where you were between 1:30 pm and 4:30 pm on the day Myra was kidnapped?' Ravi went on.

'I was playing with Myra. Then I put her down for her afternoon nap. I don't know the exact time, but...Myra... What do I say? I don't think I....'

Gita's disjointed sentences indicated her overwhelming fear. Charu leaned forward and held out her hand in silence. After some initial hesitation, she felt Gita place her hand in hers. Charu covered it with her other palm.

'Gita, it's okay. We simply want to know how your day went,' Charu said, gently.

Gita began to tell them about her day. 'I sleep in Myra's room if Anu ma'am does not take her to her room at night. Yesterday, when I woke up, Myra was already awake, gurgling, standing in her cot.'

Charu remembered the picture in her mind when she had touched the rails of the crib that morning. *So, the memory was from the morning before,* she thought. Charu sensed Ravi and Reeti's surprise. It made her smile.

'As usual, Anu ma'am woke up Sia. She came into the room to be with Myra while I got Sia ready for school. She then took Sia for her breakfast while I gave Myra her milk and a bath. Sia and Anu ma'am left for the day. So did Prithvi sir. Auntyji played with Myra after she had finished breakfast. I had my bath and breakfast. I think it was around 10:30 am. After that, I took Myra to the garden to play. Then we had lunch. It took a long time because she doesn't like mashed vegetable-khichri. Later, I took her for her nap; she usually falls asleep easily, as she is tired by then. Anu ma'am came to check on her and then left for her meeting.'

'How did she look?' asked Reeti.

'What do you mean? She looked nice; she was going to meet a client. Oh, you mean...she looked like she always does, nothing different.' Gita's voice was defensive.

'Where was Sia?' asked Ravi.

'I could hear Sia in her room. Anu ma'am had served her lunch before the TV.'

'What about Malti Devi?'

'She was arg...I mean, talking to Anu ma'am.' Gita cleared her throat.

Should I tell them what they were arguing about? I should not have said anything to Auntyji that day. Why did I think she would want Anu ma'am to be happy? A stepmother is always a stepmother; Charu heard Gita's repentant thoughts. She took a sip of water, a signal to the others that she had caught on to something. Reeti marked the number on the recorder.

'What were they talking about?' Ravi leaned forward, his knee touching Charu's, a silent acknowledgement.

'I...I don't know. I couldn't hear them clearly. The door was closed.' Gita lowered her eyes.

After a moment, she went on. 'I heard Auntyji go back into her room and close her door. She, too, usually takes a nap after lunch. After Myra fell asleep, I put her in the crib, drew the curtains, and went to check on Sia. Manik sir had already started the class. I asked him if I should wait to have my lunch after the class. He asked me to go ahead and have it right away. He said he would tell me if he needed anything. When I came out of the room, Auntyji was outside listening. She must have come back to check on Myra. Because she didn't find me with her, she was angry. Also, she doesn't like it when I talk to Manik sir.'

'Why?'

'I don't know. She's like that with Anu ma'am too. She can be very...sarcastic and insulting. Please, don't tell her I said this. She won't ask about Sia, but she has a strange fascination with Myra...maybe because she was here when Myra was born,' Gita replied.

'What happened next?'

'I went to the kitchen. When I came back after lunch, I went to check on Myra. The cot was...empty. I thought maybe she was making a fuss, and Manik sir had picked her up. He does that sometimes. He puts a sleepy Myra upon his shoulder in case she is fussy. It allows me to have my lunch break.'

'That's sweet of him,' Charu smiled.

'Yes, Manik sir does not mind holding her. But, yesterday, she didn't cry at all. I asked Manik sir if he had Myra. He said no, and he hadn't heard her cry. I told him she wasn't in her cot. We all ran back to the room to check again. He asked me to wake Auntyji up. She took her time to open the door. She was very angry with us, especially with Manik sir. She is always rude to him, always saying mean things. He never answers back. We know he is Prithvi sir's poor relation, but she doesn't have to rub it in every time.

I asked her if Myra was with her. She didn't have her either. We panicked. Manik sir called the guards, and they looked around the house and the grounds. Auntyji was ready to kill me, but Manik sir asked her to call Prithvi sir and Anu ma'am. Myra seemed to have vanished. How could someone have taken her when there were so many of us in the house?'

'What happened after Malti Devi called Myra's parents?'

'Anu ma'am and Prithvi Sir returned. They looked at the security footage but found nothing to suggest that an unknown person had come in or gone out. The staff is not allowed on the first floor either.'

'So, who has access to the floor?'

'Only Prithvi sir, Anu ma'am, Sia, Auntyji, Manik sir, and I do. Anu ma'am is very cautious about who is allowed around the girls. It is better to be safe than sorry, she says. I don't think she is wrong.'

'Were you there with the family when they watched the footage?'

'No, I was with Sia. Manik sir asked me to stay with her in her room. We watched them all from Sia's window. The guards ran all around, searching the place. Then Prithvi sir came up after some time and asked me to bring dinner for Sia. In the kitchen, the staff told me how Anu ma'am had fainted. Someone mentioned Malti Devi and Swamiji were off to the ashram in Sirsa to do a puja. I waited for the police to come, but Prithvi sir told me he had called a special team to look for her. I slept in Sia's room yesterday. She was scared. We both were.'

'When did Manik leave?' asked Ravi.

'When Prithvi sir and Anu ma'am came back.'

'Excellent, Gita. You have detailed everything very well. But, why did you leave the door of Myra's room open when you left for lunch since you take the baby monitor with you?' asked Charu.

'I...I normally leave it open now because once I left it closed, and Myra woke up and started howling. Auntyji was very angry with me. She asked me to leave it open so that I could hear her cry if Myra woke up. I didn't want to argue with her. She probably meant someone would hear her and inform me.'

'Gita, did you go out of the house yesterday at all?

'No, no. I didn't. I was inside the whole time.'

'Do you have a husband or a boyfriend?' Reeti spoke up.

'No.'

'Any family that lives in Delhi?'

'No, my family lives in Nagaland.'

'Who are your friends here?' Ravi asked.

'Since I am an in-house help, I have very few friends outside. Some friends from the village keep in touch with me via the phone. And, I meet some maids in the park, that's all.'

'Gita, is it possible you mentioned to someone that the family could pay a lot of money?' asked Reeti.

'N...no, why would I? We aren't supposed to talk about our employers.'

'Could it be that you left the door open for someone to...'

'No, never. I love Myra more than anybody. I would never do something like this. We are poor but hard-working people. What would I gain by spoiling my work record? I have been with this family since Sia was born. And, Anu ma'am has promised me I can stay with them as long as I want to.'

'Do you go to your village every year?'

'Yes, for a month in June.'

'Did you, by chance, discuss the family there?'

'Never.'

Charu drank another sip of water, and Reeti wrote down the number. They had developed this silent mode of communication, so the person being interrogated was utterly unaware that Charu was picking up their loudest thoughts.

'Did you see anything odd or feel something was not right? Maybe, someone was not behaving well with either Prithvi or Anumita? Even if it seems inconsequential, it could make a difference,' Charu tried to be more tactful.

'No, but...there is one thing—but I may be mistaken. It sounds silly, but I thought I heard the sound of a zip on the baby monitor. But, then I looked up and saw the cook closing her bag. Since there was a crackling sound after that, I didn't pay any more attention to it.'

'Gita, if anything comes to mind, you must find one of us and let us know,' said Charu.

'I will, Didi. You don't have to tell me twice. Can I go now?'

Ravi must have nodded because she started to pull her hand back.

'One more thing. Do you smoke, Gita?'

'No, Didi, I don't. But, everyone else does,' Gita smiled conspiratorially, relieved that the spotlight had been taken away from her.

'What do they smoke?' Reeti asked.

'Prithvi sir smokes cigars, the thin ones that come from abroad. Auntyji smokes a bidi, though she thinks no one knows. So does Swamiji, but he doesn't hide it like her. Anu ma'am smells of cigarette smoke, but I have never seen her smoke at home.'

Once Gita had left, the team switched off the recorder and relaxed.

'We need to find out more about Malti Devi and Anumita's relationship. They don't seem to have a cordial bond,' said

Charu. 'Is Malti Devi Anumita's stepmother, as Gita's thoughts revealed? She was also thinking about someone called Mavu. She feels duty-bound to take care of him. I think he may be her brother. We need to find out about her family. And, she felt guilty about of having said something to Malti Devi she shouldn't have.'

'Any other thoughts?' Ravi looked at her. 'Do either of you see any holes in her story?'

'Not really. If you have a baby monitor with loose or faulty wiring, you only notice when the baby starts crying. Actually, the static is like white noise. I have a device at home, and we rarely pay attention to all the static. We run when we hear my nephew cry,' Reeti answered.

'I think she knows something. She had access to Myra, and money could be a motive. We should look at her family in the village and any possible romantic liaisons,' said Charu.

'What about the bidi?' asked Reeti.

'If Malti Devi smokes it, then it is likely that she visits Myra's room, and hence there is a smell. But, Ram Vilas also smokes it, and that complicates the situation for me. It may be nothing, but I want to check it out,' Charu replied.

'Reeti, can you find out when Malti Devi and Ram Vilas are returning home?' Ravi nodded to her. 'Also, send someone to check her family in Nagaland.'

'On it. After which, I will see the security footage.'

'I'll talk to the guards. Charu, find Anumita again but prepare the report of whatever we have from Gita first. I promised Sia a badminton game; I must go. Let's regroup in a while,' said Ravi as the fax machine started whirring with the details of the call records. Everyone moved in tandem to start on their tasks.

9. Sia

6:45 pm, Wednesday

Ravi circled the gardens outside the bungalow. He wanted to find Sia and fulfil his promise to the little girl. He noticed the guards in their wooden towers, watching the road in front of Chauhan Haveli. They turned around to nod at him. He beckoned to the one watching him from the gate.

'Jai Hind, sir ji,' the thin, middle-aged man said, saluting him. His white hair was neatly combed back, and his shoes were polished, even if his shirt was creased.

'Jai Hind. I am ACP Ravi Nair. When will your shift end? I want to talk to you,' Ravi said, respectfully.

'Sir, my replacement will be here at 7 pm, but Reeti Madam has already spoken to me,' the guard answered. The worry lines on his forehead eased a little.

'Never mind that. We can have another chat. You are Arjun, right? Since when have you been working here?'

'Sir ji, it has been over three years. Prithvi sahib and Anu madam are very nice people. I have worked for many families, but here they give all the guards lunch and tea. *Aajkal*, this is difficult to find. These small things make us indebted.'

'That is true, Arjun,' Ravi smiled. 'Can you tell me how many entry points there are in this haveli?'

'Sir, originally there were three, but Anumita madam had all the gates locked, except for this one when she renovated the place. It is safer now.'

'Can you repeat to me what happened that day? How many people came in and went out?'

'Sir ji, I came for duty at 7 am to replace Ramu, the night guard. He is my brother. Prithvi sahib went for a jog. Then

Anu madam left with Sia Baby for school in her car. After a while, Prithvi sahib also left for work in his car. Madam came back with Sia Baby from school at the usual time and then left for some meeting. In the meantime, Manik Bhaiya came. After that, Swamiji came with a guest. Then he left again in a little while after the guest had gone. Later, when we heard the shouts, we all rushed to the house.'

'You left the gate unattended?'

'Sir, I thought something had happened when Maaji started shouting. Because of the security camera there,' he said, pointing, 'it is not a problem. We searched the grounds. The gate was closed and, as you can see, they are so high and heavy, no one can jump inside. I opened it when Prithvi sahib and Anu madam came back. Swamiji also came back with Prithvi sahib. He must have turned back halfway from his destination. Then I opened it again for Manik Bhaiya when he left for the cricket academy. After that, no one left until Swamiji and Maaji left for the ashram.'

'What time did they leave?'

'Around 8:30 pm.'

'Hmm. Were you here when they left?

'I was about to leave for home when Prithvi sahib called me to help put their bags in the car.'

'How big were the bags?'

The guard stared at Ravi. Realization dawned in his eyes. 'Sir ji, they were big—made of cloth. Usually, every two or three months, Maaji takes such bags to the ashram. They're filled with things they want to distribute there. She got them specially made out of old sarees. Prithvi sahib was standing there when I put them in the car.'

'When did you leave?'

'I left after a while. We...I told Ramu what had happened. I instructed him to keep even the wicket gate shut from then on.'

'This side entrance, you mean? Do you usually keep it open?'

'Yes, sir, during the day, we sit in the cabin and keep a watch on it.'

'What about when you go for a restroom break?'

'Sir, security camera *hai*. It records everything...and *woh toh zaroori hai na*. It is important.'

'Do you remember if you closed the wicket gate when you left your cabin to go to the bathroom?'

'No, sir ji, I don't remember. Usually, we close the gate, but maybe I was in a hurry. Anyway, if someone did come in through it, it would have been captured in the footage. *Aap woh check kar lijiye*,' the guard stammered, trying to remember how many times he had left the gate unattended the day before.

'Did Prithvi sir check the security footage?'

'Sir ji...I don't know but I suppose so. He receives the feed on his laptop and also on his phone. When the cameras were installed, I heard sahib could see the camera screens from anywhere. Anu madam too.'

'Arjun, do you recall anything odd thing that day at all?'

'Nothing out of the ordinary, sir ji, except that Swamiji and Maaji rushed off to the ashram. Please don't take this the wrong way. *Bhagwan dil mein hota hai*. We can pray from anywhere. I know all the old staff, Gita, Maitri ji—the cook, we have all been here for some years. I don't think we would do something this horrible to Myra Baby.' Arjun shrugged his thin shoulders. His gaze was evaluating how Ravi had received his opinion. His white stubble made him look older than his age.

'That's all for now, Arjun. Please send your brother to me when he comes.' Ravi made a move to leave.

'Sir ji, my brother—he is not involved. He came at his duty hour and wasn't there when Myra Baby was kidnapped. Please ask me anything you like. Anyway, he wasn't feeling well, so he may not come today,' he croaked, looking away.

'Hmm. But, why is Ramu suddenly feeling unwell?' Ravi looked at the guard with piercing eyes.

'No, no, sir ji, he may come in. I will call and check.' He smiled, unable to hide the panic in his eyes.

'Let me know as soon as you find out.' Ravi walked away. He knew he had to talk to Ramu, even if it meant involving another team member to go out into the field and interrogate him. He also needed to see the security footage immediately.

Ravi spoke to all the PSOs (Personal Security Officers) and received similar versions of the facts. All of them had heard the commotion. They had seen a guard run into the house. Soon, they came to know what had happened. They had followed the protocol and not left their posts. They had become extra vigilant and checked the perimeter walls for intruders. Only the first security guard and Manik had run all around, looking for Myra.

No one could have taken the child out of the haveli without the guards noticing. How did the kidnapper take Myra out? So far, only Malti Devi's bags look suspicious. Ravi thought.

He circled the perimeter until he reached the Champa trees at the back of the house. He spoke to the lone sentry, who watched the back alley through the hole in the bamboo screen. The wall here was taller due to the privacy screen covering the whole back wall. The trees stood closer together.

Ravi heard the soft giggle of a young girl before he spotted her on the swing, her eyes shining behind the glasses. She was now in track pants and a t-shirt, with the same pair of shoes on her feet he had seen earlier. Her hair was tied in two small plaits that flew as Gita pushed her higher to make her smile. Though Sia let out a small giggle now and then, Ravi could see she was unhappy. Gita stopped the swing when Ravi called out. She looked uncomfortable at his presence.

'Hello, may I join you?'

'Hello, sir, did we disturb you?' asked Gita as Sia climbed off the swing.

'No, no. I came to play a game with the young girl, who promised to help me improve my badminton skills.' Ravi smiled at Sia.

'Are you sure you have the time?' Sia asked.

Ravi found her directness unsettling. He knew this child would respect plain-speaking, and any standoffishness would be perceived as a weakness. 'Yes. I delegated all my work to other people, and now I have time to play. I also need some exercise. It's going to be dark soon. Would you rather talk or play?' He imitated her tone.

'Play,' she said after a thoughtful moment, handing him a racquet.

The tall, dark man and the small, bespectacled girl played a few games. Gradually, they slowed down and started talking about mundane things. After a while, twilight crept in on silent feet. Gita watched them from a distance as they fell on the fragrant grass, laughing. Finally, Ravi accepted defeat as the lights came on inside the house.

'You let me win, Ravi Uncle,' said Sia with a knowing smile.

'No, I am out of practice. Please don't tell anyone you defeated me.'

'Why, will they laugh at you too?'

'Laugh at me? Who will laugh at me? Does someone laugh at you?'

'No.' Sia's eyes found Gita standing at the back.

'If anyone laughs at you, all you need to do is find me,' Ravi told her in all seriousness. 'I will give you my phone number. If you ever need my help, just call me. I will come and get you.'

'Okay,' she said, quietly as she scratched her legs. Ravi noticed the small scars on her calves.

'What happened? How did you get these?'

'I fell and broke a mirror. The glass cut into my skin. It was before my last birthday. It was an accident, but it's okay now. These things happen; we have to move on and not think about them.' Myra was obviously repeating the words that had been repeated to her several times.

Ravi felt a strange pain lance his heart. He pinched his nose, displacing his spectacles, then smiled when he saw Sia imitate his action. They watched the house from outside. Sitting on the grass, surrounded by the grandeur of the bungalow with the flowers on the trellis climbing up in the corner, he appreciated the beauty money and power could buy. He could look into the living room from where he sat. The shiny crystals, the exotic flowers, the servants setting up the tea service. He shook his head at the fluidity of what was called success. He knew Myra's room was right above on the first floor. He stood up to walk closer to the plastered wall. The tall windows shone bright, and the greenery outside would be a pleasant view from inside.

Something nagged at him. He raised his hand to wave at the guard, who was watching him from near the wall. He saw Gita was picking out some yellow leaves from the climbing vine. And, he suddenly knew what troubled him.

'This is beautiful. My Amma would love this reclaimed wood design,' he remarked, moving closer to the bush.

'We all like it a lot. It was a good idea, and I helped in planting it,' Sia told him with pride, bounding to the wooden planks over which the vine had climbed up.

'Wow, that's something. Who built this?' he asked. Ravi admired how the planks were nailed one over the other, some distance away from the wall, like a ladder hanging from the terrace.

'Manik Chachu,' she answered, promptly.

'Madam was getting some renovation done in the house last year, and the carpenters would leave the wood around. One day we were playing here, and Manik sir saw the wood. He said he could build this support for the climbing vine. So, he did all the work and also planted the vine. He let all of us help. Right, Sia?' Gita said.

Now comfortable with Ravi, Sia began to explain how Manik found ways to make learning fun. They did many things together: experiments with water and soap that made bubbles, finding bugs with a magnifying glass, and small treasure hunts. She happily told him they had picnics and celebrations here in the back garden. This was their place.

'He sounds like a great teacher, Sia. Does your father also join in the fun?'

'No, Papa does not have the time. Sometimes Mummy does, but Nani is always angry when we make a noise, so it is usually just us,' Sia sighed.

Ravi examined the foot-long wooden strips that had been nailed horizontally to the wall at different heights. It was not a design one saw often. It showed presence of mind and an eye for simple, practical beauty.

Very easy to climb up except for the thorns, of course, Ravi thought. He grabbed a thin plank closest to him and yanked it to see how durable the wood was. It was flimsy and slight and almost broke under his pull.

No, it wouldn't hold any weight, he realized. He tried another couple of planks but found them similarly weak in strength.

'What's up there?' Ravi raised his head. The creeper ran between two windows.

'That is the bathroom on the first floor, and then it goes right up to the terrace,' Gita explained.

'Well, it is ingenious. But, I should get back ow. I hope we will play together again,' Ravi said to Sia.

'Thank you, Ravi Uncle. I enjoyed it,' Sia replied in a poised manner. Ravi bowed, making her giggle again, then went straight to the back room. Ravi was smiling when he heard the crying. He ran and pushed open the door to find Reeti trying to wake a shrieking Charu.

10. Prithvi

7:30 pm, Wednesday

When Ravi stepped out to find Sia, a wave of exhaustion hit Charu. Her eyes refused to stay open as she dictated the report on the speech to text program on her laptop. Informing Reeti that she was going to catch a power nap, Charu lay down on the couch. A few minutes later, Charu felt the pull of the whirlwind that signalled a vision. Charu recognized and even welcomed it. She knew Myra had gone happily…sleepy…with whoever had taken her and was in no danger…for now. But what Charu had thought would be further clues to Myra's whereabouts turned out to be a recurring hell that was getting more insistent for her attention.

The light was like feeble rays of the sun that made mild circles on the dusty floor.

The girl could not see all this but knew of the room below the fifteen stairs. Lying face down, hands tied over her head, back bare, the girl waited for whatever was in store for today. The old wounds had healed in a stairway of scabs. The stairway to hell, he had called them when he had nursed her injuries, she recalled. At this moment, she wished him dead with every fibre of her being.

Her senses were heightened due to the sack on her head tied loosely.

Just a bit of fun, or maybe her face made him feel guilty. Did it make him face the reality of his actions? The girl wondered, wishing she could wipe the snot that was running down along with her tears. Her arms were numb. The pain receding to some dark place in her mind. Sweat streamed down her shivering body.

She tried to distract herself from the pain by wondering what was in store for her today. Another patch of beatings or just endless abuses over her birth, her greedy family.

Scurrying sounds arose from the dark corners making her shift. She knew that they hid creatures that could bite and nip with relish at exposed skin. The sound had goosebumps rising on her skin.

The girl whimpered, wanting to cry out but didn't know if someone was listening. She gulped down her choking dread and readied herself for whatever would come next. Letting her mind go blank, she allowed herself to hide in the labyrinth of passages in her mind. She imagined herself perched on the precipice, talons shining and sharp, taking off to the open skies at will.

Her concentration was so profound that she missed the shuffling footsteps, the slap of the flip flops, the drag of his step, and the rasp of his laboured breath. Her flight of fancy was broken...as she too would eventually...with the clawing bite of a thorny switch on her back.

Her day had just begun.

'Come back...come back to me, Charu... You are safe.'

Charu heard Ravi's voice—a voice that was panicked but trying to seem controlled. She sat up. 'Ravi...'

'I have you. You are fine here, with me. Should I hold you or stay away?'

Charu opened her arms and let him hold her. Ravi pulled Charu close wrapping his quivering arms around her body. He sat embracing her, patting her back, oscillating gently until her breathing levelled.

'I tried to shake her awake, Ravi, but she was crying out like someone was hitting her and wouldn't wake up.'

'I know. It's all right.'

'Is it Myra? Is something bad...' Reeti stopped mid-sentence.

'No, this isn't about Myra, at least I don't think so,' said Charu, exhaling loudly. With one last caress on her cheek, Ravi disengaged and stood up. Charu immediately felt bereft, missing his protective strength.

'Charu, we need to get to the bottom of these dreams. I just hope your instincts are correct. Let's find Myra so that this dream of yours remains only that, a bad dream,' he said.

'Reeti, tell me what you found in the security footage of the main gate,' Ravi said, watching the images on the screen. He was still looking at them when she played the camera recordings of the main gate.

'No unknown person came in. The rest matches what the guard, Arjun, told me about everyone's movement in and out of the haveli. As you can see here,' she said, turning the laptop towards Ravi, 'the gate is visible. The wicket gate too. But, he left it open when he went to the washroom. Here you see Gita going out. And, then everyone coming in. Finally, Manik going out on his bike.'

'Wait, why did Gita go out?' asked Charu.

'She seems to be pushing something. I can only see a long handle. It looks like some sort of trolley,' Reeti told her.

'Rewind it. Let's watch it again,' said Ravi, alert. They saw Gita pushing something in front of her and returning within ten minutes while the guard was not at the gate. 'Why can we only see the top half? Is there another angle?'

'What time did she take the thing out?' asked Charu.

'Don't know. Are you suggesting someone carried Myra out from the main gate in broad daylight?' Reeti checked the live feed.

'More likely than not. How do you think they carried the child out? Gita said she did not go out, while here she is clearly hurrying out with some sort of trolley. Where is the forensic expert? Has he finished?' Ravi snapped.

'Yes, he will be sending us the report soon. He said there was nothing to suggest this was an outsider's job. So, it ties in with your theory that someone either helped in the kidnapping from within the household, or it was a very professional job,' Reeti agreed.

'Anything from the cameras within the house?' asked Charu.

'Yes, look at this. This is from the camera at the main door. I have matched the footage to what everyone said they were doing between 1 pm and 4:45pm. I guess Prithvi forgot to tell us about Bilal Siddiqui, which is pretty dumb considering that we would see the security footage in any case.' Reeti played another clip. Ravi recognized Ram Vilas from the cut-out in his office, walking into the house smiling, followed by Bilal in his wheelchair.

'They went into Ram Vilas's office at 2:15 pm. After twenty minutes, Bilal left. A few minutes later, Ram Vilas came out and left too. It was 2:45 pm. This places him in the house at the time Myra was taken. Well, he was in the premises if not on the same floor.'

'Why didn't Prithvi tell us about Bilal? He had seen the footage and obviously knew he had come into his house with Ram Vilas. When we asked him about all the people in the house when Myra disappeared, he did not once mention him,' Charu wondered aloud. *Why did Prithvi pretend that looking into Bilal was a great idea that I had chanced upon when he knew Bilal had come into the house with his mentor? What is Prithvi playing at?*

'Another thing—this is Manik. It seems he is usually here for about an hour. And, in that one hour yesterday, he spent half the time in the washroom. Here, look at the time stamp. He comes in at 1:40 pm, then goes to the bathroom at 2:05... and again at 3 pm. I can't believe I am looking at someone's bathroom habits so closely,' said Reeti.

'Great job. I'm adding Manik and Ram Vilas to the board,' said Ravi. 'Charu, find the cook and have a word. See what you can pick up. I have called Ramu, Arjun's brother, who does the night duty here. If he doesn't turn up, ask one of the boys at the police station to pick him up and interrogate him at the station.' Together they went over what Ravi had added to the preliminary interviews.

As they discussed their theories and possibilities, Charu let her mind wander. The questions were piling up: Why? Who? How? What worried her was the absence of the family. It felt as if they were detached from whatever was happening in the room. The house seemed disjointed; the synergy disrupted.

'Good evening. I am all done for the day and thought you might want to talk to me.' Prithvi walked into the room flamboyantly as if he was late for a get together with friends.

'Chumki, how are you? Do you need anything?' He knelt before her, running his fingers on her cheek. Ravi glared at this show of affection.

'We can talk now. Let's move to the other room, sir,' Reeti interjected.

'Yes, let's begin.' Ravi set the camera rolling and started speaking into the recorder professionally. 'Interview of Mr Prithvi Chauhan, Myra's father. Please tell us about the day Myra was taken.'

'I woke up, as usual, had my breakfast, went to office. I was in a party meeting. I received a call in the afternoon that Myra was missing, after which I came back. We searched the house and the grounds, asked who had seen what, and then called Commissioner Bakshi. At his suggestion, I called Chumki and met her and Ravi the next day.'

'Do you suspect anyone who would want to hurt you or your family?' asked Reeti.

'I am a politician; everyone wants to bring me down.'

'We would like a list of people you think are likely to or capable of doing something like this.'

'Sure, but it's going to be a long list.'

'Are you worried about your daughter?' Ravi asked, suddenly.

'Of course. I have made the best possible arrangements I could under the circumstances. My advisers have asked me to keep this under wraps, and so I gave you three days. After that, I go public. Panicking won't help Myra, me, or my career.'

'Have you made any other arrangements to look for your daughter?'

'No. I am confident Chumki will be able to find her,' Prithvi said.

Charu knew everyone was looking at her. 'Prithvi, did you leave the meeting or step out at all during the afternoon before you received the call from home?' she asked.

'No,' Prithvi hesitated, but only for a moment. 'Why would I?'

'Are you quite sure?'

'Of course, I'm sure!' He sounded offended.

'And, you were not anywhere around your haveli during that time?'

Prithvi gazed at her silently for a minute. 'No,' he replied, acidly. 'Anything else?'

'Where was your mentor while you were in the office?' Charu continued.

'Swamiji was with me.'

'Throughout the day?'

'Yes. Why do you keep insisting he's involved? Swamiji is not to be… Listen, Chumki, he is not that kind of person. He is responsible for my entry into politics. He is my mentor. Why would he…?' He stopped suddenly and shook his head.

'Tell them what you remembered, Prithvi.' Charu sensed his irritation.

'Chumki, stop looking into my thoughts,' Prithvi warned her.

'You brought me here for this. And, don't call me that. My name is Charu.'

'Sir, you need to be honest with us because your daughter's life depends on it. The more time we waste…' Reeti left Prithvi to deduce the rest from her unspoken words.

'Swamiji left the office for an hour for lunch around 1:30 pm. I sent him out. Does that make me a suspect? Tell them,

Chumki, he would never do this. He loves the girls. We may not see eye to eye these days, but he would lay down his life for me and I for him.'

'What do you mean by "don't see eye to eye"?' asked Ravi.

'We had a tiff, and I asked him not to sit in on the meeting with the party president and me. He left in a huff. He has been saying that my approval ratings have been decreasing for the past several months. You see, he belongs to the old school of thought. He comes from a generation when you could win votes based on your caste or religion. But now, there is a shift in the youth's perception. I wanted to focus on the development in our state. I wanted our PR team to highlight the charity work, the changes we have made at ground level, the schools, hospitals, shelters we have built for women. He wants to project me as an alpha family man, with a wife and two daughters in the background. He wishes I would have a son. At one time, that might have worked, but now...who knows? He fears that people will reject our good work. And, we disagree on the way forward for now. But, we have been discussing how to find a middle ground.'

'What kind of middle ground?'

'He suggested we try to garner sympathy votes.'

'Sympathy votes? How would you get those unless a tragedy struck?' Charu spoke up.

Prithvi paused, assessing the situation. He had said too much, but he couldn't backtrack. He sighed. 'This stays confidential because he suggested it as a strategy, and I know he did not mean it...or want to fool the public. He suggested that I, or someone in the family, have an accident or something that would make people want to side with me. It was said in passing; he didn't mean it. I told him point blank I wouldn't do anything like that; it would be too drastic. He was the one who asked me to keep Myra's disappearance under wraps. He knew that even our own party people would try and pull me down if they came to know. We have to find Myra. He wouldn't hurt my daughters. He wants me to try for a son.

He was the one who solemnized my marriage to Anumita in the first place.' Prithvi leaned forward to take Charu's hand in his. 'Believe me, Chumki, I would not allow anyone to harm my family. You know how territorial I am.'

'I think you'd better start from the beginning. How did you meet Ram Vilasji?' Ravi stretched his legs. This was going to take some time.

'Bauji, my father, was the sarpanch in our Panchayat Samiti. He introduced me to Swamiji. I had come back from Surat and decided to take my exams without going to regular school. Swamiji had a small ashram in our village, built on the land given to him by my father. He had a considerable following. He used to run the school for the nearby villages too: teach, give sermons, and help people. Initially, he involved me with his school. I would spend mornings teaching the young kids. We would spend the afternoons in his rooms talking, discussing the world. He is very learned. In the evening, we would play, or I would go to his sermons, see him motivate the local people, do charity work. It was a time of self-realization for me. He tamed my wildness.'

He turned towards Ravi. 'I am sure Chumki told you why I left Surat. Bilal's accident hit me hard. I couldn't stay there. I...I felt guilty and responsible. I was depressed and would stay in my room all day long. Swamiji helped me forgive myself, give up my pride, and made me help others as a way to get over it. I realized I enjoyed doing social work and wanted to help people do better for themselves. He introduced me to a few of his followers, who had some political clout. That was my initiation into youth politics.'

'Who were the people at his ashram?' Charu asked. 'About how many?'

'A couple of *sadhvis* and him. I started living there after about a year. He mentored me through college, showed me the light through spiritual texts. His interpretations made sense. When I was elected, he chose to stay with me to guide me. He isn't just my mentor, but everything. I know he would never do what you are suggesting. Why would he?'

'What about his ashram?' asked Ravi.

'That is still active in Sirsa. Swamiji visits when he can. It is a well-oiled, self-sustaining machine. My mother-in-law goes there regularly to do puja, distribute clothes, and help where she can. Trust me, this house is a much quieter place when she is there,' he laughed. 'Look, I don't want you to get the wrong idea about him. Swamiji does not need me. I need him. I cannot think of functioning without him. Today, if he asks me for all my wealth, which is way less than his, I would gladly hand him the keys to my coffers. All he wants is to see me rise.'

Charu heard the conviction in his voice.

'Tell us a little bit about your marriage,' Reeti asked.

'Anu...she is the mother of my children. After so many years of marriage, we have our own lives. I support her. She does what she wants.'

'Any other relationships where jealousy could be a problem? There are several news items on your women....'

'No, no, what is there to be jealous about? Reeti Ji, this arena is so cutthroat that if I talk to a woman at a party, she is my mistress the next day. I can't help that the media wants to paint every man as a philanderer. But, recently, I have tried to stay far away from women and their drama. Anu doesn't cooperate, you see. If I ask her to come to these political parties and marriages, she refuses. If I invite her for the *aartis* and pujas, she refuses. She wants nothing to do with my career but enjoy everything my profession provides. Swamiji has to accompany me everywhere. People talk if my wife is never with me. But, what can I do?

Actually, I don't know what to do about her anymore. She has increasingly become more and more detached. Her mother has tried to make her see sense, Swamiji has tried, but she just...I don't know what she wants. I am sorry I am saying all this about her, but I am tired,' he sighed.

'What is your relationship with Bilal Siddiqui?'

'Oh...he is a snake. I was shocked to see him when he came to a party event a few years ago. He started donating money heavily to the party to gain power. His backroom dealings are legendary. He opposes me on everything. I understand he is angry about the accident, but that was about fifteen years ago. He should get over it.'

'This morning, when I asked you if he could be involved in Myra's kidnapping, you said it was likely. Why do you think he would do something like this now, after so long?'

'Because, he can. He would derive pleasure in seeing me suffer. These people have no values. Last week, Bilal and I had a very public row in the party office, where he hurled abuses at me. All because I made sure that the company that deserved the tender for the flyovers got it. He said I was a bigot and whatnot and that I would regret my decision. He is simply a sore loser. I have no proof, of course, but it could well be him. Chumki, do you remember how strange he was even in school?' Prithvi tightened their fingers locked together. Charu didn't say anything.

'Did you see the security footage of the main door, sir?'

'Yes.'

'So, you know that Bilal came into the house with Ram Vilas Ji?'

'I have to ask Swamiji why he invited him into my house. I am sure there is a logical explanation, but I'll wait for my anger to subside before asking him why. I was hoping you people would do it for me.'

'Why didn't you tell us?'

'As I said, Chumki, he would have had a pertinent reason to allow Bilal into my house, knowing how much I dislike him. And, you can tell me why so I don't have to,' Prithvi said.

'Sir, do you smoke?' Reeti ventured.

'Yes, a cigar. Occasionally.'

'What about a bidi?'

'No, I don't like it. But, Swamiji does. Why?'

'Prithvi, does Ram Vilas Ji ever go up to Myra's room?' Charu asked, gently.

'He. . .he goes with me sometimes to say good night, but not alone and hasn't recently. At least, I don't think so. Anumita does not let anyone go up the stairs. She has resolved that the first floor is off-limits to everyone except the immediate family. Gita is always there. What did she say? Wait. I have also seen Malti Devi smoking bidis once or twice.' Prithvi stared at the serious faces before him. 'He wouldn't harm the girls. I can bet my life on it. Dig into my mother-in-law if this is an important lead. And, Bilal for sure.'

'That's it for now. Interview terminated,' said Ravi before Charu heard the final click.

'I will ask Anumita to organize dinner for all of you.' Prithvi rose from his chair.

11. Ramu

8:45 pm, Wednesday

Charu sensed the turmoil created by their questions within Prithvi as he walked away. This was another downside of this profession, besides feeling the victim's pain of separation. The questions they asked introduced cracks and doubts in relationships where there had been none before. When they left, she knew most families found it challenging to carry on. The secret lives, and the small lies people told each other to get through the day, became insurmountable when revealed. She wanted to tell Prithvi not to fret, but the way he had spoken about Bilal made her uncomfortable. She had listened to him silently. His devotion towards his mentor was impressive and perhaps the only genuine emotion she perceived in him. But, he was a narcissist who could mistreat anyone if they came in the way of his success.

'All right, everyone, I am going to start with Charu here. What did you catch?'

'Nothing much. Prithvi's faith in Ram Vilas is the truest feeling as of now.'

'What do you mean? Didn't you pick up anything at all? The guy was sweating.' The disbelief in Ravi's voice hurt her pride.

'Ravi, he knows me, knows why I am here. He won't let anything slip. I just picked up what he wanted me to. He has his…shields. I didn't catch anything that would lead us anywhere. He was pushing us to put Bilal and Anumita under the scanner—and he did.'

Ravi looked at Charu doubtfully. *Is she trying to protect Prithvi? He had meant a lot to her, obviously, being her first love.*

It would not be a far-fetched idea that she may be trying to protect him out of a misplaced sense of loyalty. Did she participate in the incident with Bilal all those years ago? Ravi thought.

He saw Charu turn pale and realized his mistake. Turning away, he berated himself. 'Let's break this up for now,' he said. 'There is no need to discuss this outside this room. Get back to work. I am going to meet Ramu, the night guard.' Slamming the door, he walked out.

Charu sat still. The shards of his suspicion lodged deep within her heart. She closed her eyes. A picture flashed in her mind.

A woman stood in a busy street, her head covered. Myra's face was now nestled against her chest. She was in a light blue kurta. They stood near a red brick building with a big, open gate. It looked like a school. The words written on the black, rectangular board were unreadable. They went in the opposite direction, into a narrow lane. Myra looked up and saw multiple clotheslines crossing each other. A woman was drying clothes in her balcony. And, though she tried, Myra's eyes wouldn't stay open. She fell asleep with the temple bell clanging loudly nearby.

'Charu? Charu...where are you?' Reeti's hand was on her shoulder.

'Myra went past a red brick school with a black, rectangular board. I couldn't read the name. It was evening, and the temple bell was ringing like it does for the *aarti*. Myra could see clotheslines, or maybe electrical wires, crossing overhead. There were flats at four levels, constructed with narrow lanes separating them,' Charu told Reeti as soon as she had caught her breath. Reeti asked Charu to repeat what she had seen, recording it on her phone.

After leaving the room brusquely, Ravi stood at the end of the corridor, cursing himself. He closed his eyes and banged his head against the wall, hoping to dislodge the image of the devastated face of the woman he loved from his mind.

She sensed my doubt, was hurt by it, and yet she will do whatever is necessary to find Myra. And, here I am, letting my feelings of insecurity get in the way.

Ravi heard Charu and Reeti's voices behind the closed door. He wanted to beg Charu for forgiveness and tell her that he believed her. But, she had put herself in danger by telling them everything she suspected in a house that was under constant surveillance, authorized and unauthorized. The fact that Prithvi could access the camera feed on their phones meant they, too, were being watched.

When Ravi stepped out into the night, he saw the two guards arguing. He rushed forward when one pulled at the other's shirt.

'Stop. Stop! What happened?' he yelled.

'Nothing, sir ji. He is as usual late and...drunk.' Arjun pushed the younger man away. Ravi caught him before he could fall down.

'Don't try to paint me as the trouble maker...I am not drunk, sir,' the other man said, belligerently.

Ravi watched the brothers glare at each other. This was obviously Ramu, a man who did not warrant another look. His uniform had sweat patches, and his shirt buttons were open at the neck to show his vest. He smelt unwashed and hungover.

'Have you come on duty drunk, Ramu?' Ravi's face hardened.

'No...no, sir. I am not drunk.' The man wilted under Ravi's gaze.

'Sir ji, this is my brother Ramu. He is careless, but he wouldn't harm a fly. Ramu, tell sir ji what you know about yesterday.'

'You can stop trying to act all concerned now. You must have told him lies about me. But, you won't say anything about your friends, will you?' Ramu shot back.

'*Chup kar...nikamma kahin ka...*' Arjun raised his hand to shut him up.

'Stop this, both of you! I want you to report for duty on time tomorrow. Arjun, is that understood?' Ravi said, sternly.

'I will, sir ji,' Arjun scowled at his brother, who smiled mockingly. Ramu locked the gate behind Arjun.

'What did you mean, Ramu, when you said Arjun would not tell on his friends?' Ravi lit a cigarette and offered one to him. He knew how to make the man feel comfortable.

'Sir, I am not drunkard like Gita's brother. But, I am sure Arjun mustn't have told you that. Yes, I drink, but never on duty. My brother likes to show me in a bad light at every chance.' He took a deep puff.

'Gita's brother? He lives in Delhi, does he?'

'Yes, sir. He has been here for some months. He came to Chauhan Haveli and started fighting with Arjun. I was there. He shouted *gaalis* at Gita and gambolled around like a madman. He even broke all the pots outside until I gave him a good beating. He was in the hospital for a few days. I don't remember what happened to him after that. Must have gone back home, I suppose.'

'Which hospital?'

'It's the one on the roundabout. Gita used to go there every day to meet him.'

'Isn't that a private hospital?'

'*Wohi to*. Where did she get the money? When I asked Arjun, he told me to mind my own business.'

'What do you mean?' Ravi looked at Ramu suspiciously.

'Sir, one day, when I came for duty, Gita was talking to her brother on the phone. He has a strange name. She was telling him that Anu madam had refused to give her the money he had asked for, and she couldn't ask her again. He shouldn't have lost the money she had given him already. She said she would have to work for a very long time as it was—to compensate for the money she had already taken as advance. She was very apologetic.' Ramu looked around surreptitiously.

'If anything else comes to mind, you will find me and tell me. And, you will stay away from Gita. Is that understood,

Ramu?' Ravi didn't threaten or shout. It was the soft, dulcet tone that made Ramu believe him capable of dispensing harsh punishment.

'What did you see when you came on duty?'

'I didn't see anything. Mata Ji and Swamiji had gone to Sirsa. Arjun told me what had happened before they left. The lights were on in the haveli for a long time. Prithvi sir was in Swamiji's study, pacing and talking on the phone. In the morning, Arjun came for duty on time.'

'How do you know what Prithvi sir was doing?'

'You can see the window of the study from inside the guard's room,' Ramu clarified.

Ravi went into the guard's cabin. He could see the bookcases, and a part of the desk, through the study window.

'I don't want you to leave town, Ramu. I want you to report for duty on time. Is that clear?'

'Ji, sir, but I didn't do anything.'

Ravi closed the notebook in which he had been writing Ramu's statement, and walked away. He wanted to think. They had explicitly asked Gita about her family. She had not told them about her brother, a drunkard, who was in Delhi, or had been around the family recently. Also, the altercation that led to a hospital admission was reason enough to have informed them.

'Money is a powerful motivation,' he murmured. He liked Gita and the way she protected Sia, but he wasn't happy now.

Meanwhile, Charu climbed the stairs to Myra's room, feeling the residual ache of Ravi's thoughts in her bones. She opened the door and walked in. It was still and quiet. She could hear muffled voices coming out of Sia's room across the hallway. Small details that filled her subconscious were best explored in solitude. An important clue one missed at a cursory glance became the fulcrum upon which the whole case hinged. Charu didn't feel any urgency in the room.

I'll talk to Sia soon, she thought, shutting the door behind her. She could also hear the sounds from outside—the passing cars, the insects, the hum of the street light.

I need to refocus now and maybe think of stepping away from Ravi after we've found Myra, she thought. She stretched her arm and felt the curve of the rocking chair. She sat down on it and closed her eyes, rocking it gently. She leaned her head against the backrest, wishing she could stop her mind for some time. Pictures of Anumita feeding Myra sitting on the same chair formed in her mind. The image was so full of love, Charu felt her eyes fill with tears.

How wonderful it must be to feel this kind of unconditional love. Things with Prithvi must have been good at this time.

Her body jerked as the door opened suddenly.

'It's me.'

'Prithvi? What are you doing here?'

'I had to talk to you, away from all your sentries. We both had an exhausting day. I wish we were far away. This house is like a twenty-four-hour news channel. Someone is always looking at the monitors,' he said, walking towards her. 'Do you seriously think Swamiji could have had something to do with this?'

'I haven't met him yet.'

'Listen, I have been mulling over your questions since we spoke. I think my mother-in-law is more suspect. I am telling you because you are my friend, and because we share a history. She was the one who insisted on going to the Kul Devi temple within a couple of hours of Myra's disappearance. Who does that?' he said, rhetorically. 'She just wouldn't listen. Surprisingly, Anu, too, said it was better she went, that she would just get in the way—blaming everyone.'

'Why didn't you tell me this on record when I asked if you suspected anyone?'

'I started thinking after you all started putting these thoughts in my mind. They don't get along at all, you know.

Sometimes, I wish I hadn't let Anu's mother come and stay with us. She never left. But, Anu was having such a hard time with her pregnancy. Then they came up with a word for her melancholy—postpartum depression. But, she was always moping about even before Myra was born.' Prithvi started pacing the floor.

Charu wondered if it was the depression that had made Anumita cry earlier.

'My mother-in-law was the one who insisted that Swamiji should do the puja. I found that so odd. But, then Anu said yes, and the temple was close enough, so I didn't object. But, I found it very strange, to tell you the truth. Could she have had a hand in snatching away my sweet Myra? Charu, at least tell me this—is Myra alive?' Prithvi knelt in front of her.

'Prithvi, there is no way…'

'I know, I know, but I thought you might have sensed something. I am sorry. I know you will never do anything to hurt me. But, you told them about the school and about why I left. What else have you told Ravi? Did you tell him what we shared? Our dreams, the first kiss, our first…'

'Prithvi, that's enough.' Charu was angry at the way he was constantly bringing up their past to influence her.

'Why? What did I say? I am not the one who opened the door to our past. You did that. And, why are you sitting here in the dark? You could have called me. My room is just next door.'

Charu detected childish irritability in his tone, an adamant compulsiveness that she recognized from their schooldays. She remembered how his insistence could turn into hostility and, eventually, violence when he didn't get his way.

'I wanted to think in silence,' she tried to pacify him.

'You can come, you know. Anu and I have different rooms.' Prithvi let that statement hang between them.

'Prithvi, what are you saying?'

'Chumki, do you remember how we used to believe you and I were destined to be together? I agree I made a wrong decision—I let you go then. But, now that fate has brought you to me again, we have to be together. You are as incomplete as I am.' He grabbed her arms.

'You are not making any sense, Prithvi! You are a married man. Please stop this. Our priority should be your daughter.'

'I may be married, but I've never loved Anu. Ours is a marriage of convenience. And, I am stuck in it.' Prithvi sat down.

'Then get a divorce.' Charu was tired.

'And say goodbye to my career?' Prithvi scoffed at the idea. 'We might be living in the twentieth century, but a politician is still seen as the *adarsh* husband, son, and father in our country. Swamiji says divorce is for the weak. A widower is the next best thing, but the people of our country will never accept a divorced man sitting at the top. Already things are challenging. Swamiji is always on my case. A politician's young son thinks he can cut in line for the CM's seat. No, I can never get a divorce. But a paper does not draw a line around your heart, does it?' He stood up again to resume his agitated walk across the room.

'Prithvi,' Charu was exasperated, 'what is it that you want from me? I will always be your friend.'

'That's not what I want from you; don't you get it?' Prithvi jerked his head.

'Prithvi, I am here to look for your daughter and nothing else.'

'I refuse to accept that. And, I want to prove that I trust you more than anyone else in this whole world, so I will tell you something.' He waited for his words to have an effect. 'Do you remember I told you Bilal and I have had problems? Well, they started when I outbid him at an auction in Mumbai, about two years ago. I knew he was keen on these jade wine cups that dated back to the court of Shah Jahan. Bilal had traced his ancestry back to the people who crafted those cups for Shah Jahan. Anyway, I found out that he was desperate to buy them.

So, I outbid him. You should have seen his face when the sellers handed those cups to me,' he laughed, proudly.

'But, they must have been horribly expensive. How did you get the money?'

'That is the brilliance of being in politics. There is always some billionaire industrialist willing to put in the money for future favours.'

'So, you took those cups just to spite him?'

'He was becoming a nuisance, and I needed him to know his place. Anyway, I didn't tell you this to hear you lecture me. I want to tell you that, right now, you are standing in the room where I have hidden those cups from the Mughal court. They date back to the seventeenth century. I wish I could show them to you, Charu. They are an exquisite piece of history. I am telling you this because they remind me of you. Priceless and delicate.'

It was strange. Charu had always assumed that when she met her schoolmates, they would be different people—grown up and successful, but she had repeatedly found that they were mostly the same, with the same insecurities, the same baggage they had lugged around when they were kids. This story he had cooked up was too ludicrous to believe.

'Prithvi, your sole aim in life, for the moment, should be to find your daughter.' Charu stood up, wanting to get away from Prithvi's cloying obsessiveness.

'Why won't you believe me?' Prithvi sounded sulky. 'I could show them to you right now, but it'll take a while to unpack them and pack them up again. I'm not the right person to do all that. I have neither time nor patience for that kind of thing. Women are good at that, but even Anu doesn't know they're here. But, would you like to touch history, Charu? Do you remember how we used to talk into the night for hours on end? I miss that.'

Prithvi's hands gripped her arms, and he pulled her closer. Before she could push him away, she heard the sound of footsteps. Prithvi heard them too and quickly moved away. The door to the room was shoved open by Anumita. She looked almost thunderous.

'Prithvi, Charu...what are you doing in the dark?' she said accusingly, switching on the light. She looked at Charu's stillness, and Prithvi's guilty eyes and made her deductions, as did Ravi, who stood right behind her. He felt as if someone had sucker-punched him.

'Nothing. I came to call her for dinner. Come on. Ravi, will you bring her?' Prithvi walked away without another glance in her direction.

'Sure,' Ravi replied, his eyes meeting Anumita's. She glanced at Charu before slipping out of the room. Charu felt the animosity cut across her senses. She was exhausted with the men pushing at each other. She knew she was the reason, and she hated it.

'Hey, what happened? Are you all right?' Ravi shook her gently.

'Yes.' She nodded shakily after a moment. 'Why did you come? Did you forget some accusation you didn't think of before?'

'I am going to hold you now,' he said.

'Ravi...'

'You may not need it, but I do, just for a minute...please.'

Just for a moment, she told herself and nodded. Ravi's long arms went around her, and he leaned closer, loosely holding her in his arms. Charu tried desperately to stand straighter. His hand moved in circles on her back as if collecting all the pockets of stress from her muscles, new and old. 'For a psychic, you aren't quick on the uptake,' he whispered. After a moment of reflection, Charu murmured, 'He knew I told you and Reeti about Surat and our relationship in school? Prithvi was... listening to everything.'

'Yes, throughout—and we don't know who else. The house is brimming with spy cams and bugs. Why do you think we keep going to the lawn to talk?'

'Why didn't you tell me?'

'I thought I would when I could get a moment with you, but you…' Ravi knew there were no cameras in Myra's room. But, he was still wary of talking inside the house.

'He is not okay. He is not himself. Ravi, there is something wrong with him,' she said, raising her head.

'Shh…it's all right; we will get there,' he said. Charu pulled his head towards herself, her lips near his ear. 'Prithvi's marriage is not stable,' she whispered. 'Anumita had postpartum depression after Myra was born, but she'd been sad even earlier. Malti Devi came to live here to take care of her.'

Ravi took a deep breath. 'Gita, too, lied to us. She has a brother who is a drunkard. She asked Anumita for money and was refused. It seems it's time for another chat with both of them.'

Desperate for tenderness, Charu leaned closer to him. His heart, beating in her small ear, sounded steady. His hands stilled after some time, and they stood holding each other, breathing in the mystical perfume of the night. The moon hid behind some clouds, diffusing the light, giving them some privacy or just feeling shy at this innocent expression of love. *I should let her go,* Ravi tried to convince himself.

'Please don't, just a minute more,' Charu murmured tiredly, her words muddled in his shirt.

He went still before leaning down to her waiting lips.

12. Anumita

9:35 pm, Wednesday

Reeti, Anumita, Sia, and Prithvi were waiting silently when Ravi entered the dining room with Charu. The squarish room was situated between the kitchen and the stairs that curved towards the floor above. It was dominated by sideboards filled with crockery and a mahogany dining table that shone under the bright chandelier.

Reeti raised her eyebrows, communicating the awkward silence she had been forced to bear in their absence. Ravi noticed that the husband and wife looked at Charu with different emotions. Prithvi's eyes were measuring, while Anumita's held spite. The stiffness in their posture heralded trouble. Ravi glanced at Sia, who sat between her parents, with her head bowed, playing with the fork. She looked miserable.

'Anything you can tell us, Ravi? It has been a whole day since you came.' Prithvi leaned towards him, away from his wife.

'We are on it, sir. Anumita ma'am, there are some follow-up questions. Also, Manik was asked to be present today. Should I have him picked up from his address?'

He saw Sia look up at Manik's name.

'Why, he called to say he is unwell and will be there tomorrow morning. I forgot. Sorry,' said Anumita.

'Anu, you can't forget things at this time, for God's sake. What happened? Why didn't he come? This is the least he can do after all I have done for him.' Prithvi banged his fist on the table, making Anumita and Sia jump. Sia's eyes filled with fear; her lips trembled.

'He told you about his upset stomach yesterday. It has worsened. He said he didn't go to the academy either, he just went home from here. I told him to rest,' Anumita replied, watching her daughter.

'Oh. Don't worry, Ravi. He'll come.' Prithvi waved his hand.

Prithvi's intimidation of his wife did not sit well with Ravi. He hoped he wouldn't be faced with a situation where he would have to choose between doing the right thing and respecting his subordinate status to the minister. Charu, too, was disturbed by Prithvi's behaviour. She realized Sia was aware of the tension between her parents, and was suffering for it.

Prithvi began to talk. 'It's all right. Manik will be here tomorrow if my dear wife has ordered him to come.' He grinned cruelly, with his arm around his wife. Anumita looked down at her plate in embarrassment. 'Who else are you looking at?'

'Your party members and donors, the opposition party, the staff. Everyone is a suspect until we find the person, or people, who kidnapped Myra,' Ravi replied.

Please bring my sister back. I will never wish for her to go away again, Charu heard Sia pray. She realized Sia was blaming herself for her sister's disappearance. *But, what if she had had a hand in...?*

Charu didn't want to think on those lines. It was natural to feel jealous of one's younger sibling. She, too, had disliked Dheeraj for a long time. He had been allowed to stay with her parents while she had been thrown away. He was the perfect son, while she was the defective child.

'The staff? Our staff is reliable. They have been with us for more than a year—some even longer than that. They came with us when we moved into this haveli. They wouldn't do something so horrible.' Anumita defended her support staff.

'Don't be naïve, Anu. Who knows what someone is going through? Let these guys do their job,' Prithvi admonished his wife again.

Sia went rigid, expecting her parents to start fighting once again.

'Sia, would you like to have your dinner in your room?' Charu asked, loudly.

'Yes, please. Can I, Mummy?' she asked in a small voice.

'Go, but watch TV only until you've finished dinner. Gita... GITA, take her!' Anumita shouted.

'Charu wanted to hug Sia and tell her she would find her sister if that was the last thing she did, but she held her tongue. Instead, she turned towards Anumita. 'Anumita, I want to know what happened to the camera in Myra's room. In fact, several cameras are not working. Can you tell us why?'

'The cameras were faulty,' Prithvi answered. 'I was the one who told Anu that. I usually check the camera feed on my phone when I can. She called the company that had installed them, and asked them to replace them immediately. They said it would take a couple of days. Ours were a high-end model, and they didn't have spares lying around.

Anu asked me to buy new ones from somewhere else, but I thought she was being paranoid. Our cameras were still under the warranty period. Wasting money on new ones made no sense; the waiting time would have been the same. But, now I wish I had listened to you, Anu. We still haven't heard back from the guy, have we?'

'No,' Anumita snapped back.

The fact that Myra's room had a faulty spy camera troubled Ravi. He looked at Anumita and wondered if she had a role to play in it. But then, she was the one who had had the cameras installed in the first place. In fact, she had insisted upon them.

The woman before them sat stiff and edgy, her hair escaping from her clip, her eyes anxious. Her fingers quivered. This woman was different from the Anumita, who had asked her husband to call the police and not waste time with their team. That woman had been composed, in control of herself, and even haughty. Very much a minister's wife.

What triggered her? Was it finding Prithvi and Charu together in a dark room? Ravi wondered.

Prithvi sat eating his lavish dinner as if he didn't have a care in the world. He looked right through his wife's sadness. It didn't seem that his young daughter had been missing for more than twenty-four hours.

Ravi pushed his plate away. Just as he was about to excuse himself, he felt Charu's hand clutch his thigh. He looked at her, wondering what she was doing. She had been pushing her food around on her plate for the last ten minutes.

What is she waiting for? Ravi wondered and then heard a car in the driveway. He saw her sit up.

A nasal female voice, and a musical laugh of a man, reached the people in the dining room. Ravi watched, surprised, as a wiry, saree-clad woman entered the hall. Malti Devi, whom they had expected to be greying and old, was actually a young woman in her middle or late forties. She couldn't have been more than a few years older than Anumita. She was completely different from what they had imagined. It was late, and she had travelled the whole day, but dressed in a floral chiffon saree, pearls around her slender neck and with not a hair out of place, Malti Devi looked simple, elegant, and unapproachable—like royalty. She was followed by a tall man in a white gown with a broad forehead and a flowing mane of white hair. Ram Vilas.

Charu froze beside Ravi, her nails digging into his arm. Ravi watched Prithvi jump out of his chair to touch his mentor's feet. Malti Devi gave Charu a once-over before patting her daughter's head, admonishing her for her unkempt appearance. Anumita looked sick.

The necessary introductions were made. Ram Vilas joined his palms in a namaste, and Ravi followed suit. The long, loose hair caught him off guard. Though he had seen it in the cut-out, coming face-to-face with the tall, robust man, his hair flowing down to his waist, was unnerving. The vermillion *tilak* between his brows reached his hairline. It looked like a glowing liquid flame.

Charu spoke haltingly with Ram Vilas, her eyes lowered, another first for the confident woman Ravi knew her to be.

Charu's face was expressionless as she felt a piercing gaze take her in. The hair on the back of her neck stood up. She could only see a grey haze where she knew a man stood towering over her.

'You must be Charu, the seer, as Prithvi mentioned,' said the soft voice, drawing everyone's attention.

Charu raised her hand for a handshake towards the voice.

'So sorry, I always join my palms together in a namaste while greeting someone. This is our *sanskriti,* our tradition, after all.' The contempt in his eyes was unmistakable.

Charu joined her palms together as if at a command.

'Yes, our very own namaste is going global. Everyone is adopting it, and here we are, trying to shake hands with the opposite sex. Women hugging men without any *lajja,* any shame. The youth does not understand the effect it has on our energies. But, they will in time.' He addressed his words to Ravi, dismissing Charu as irrelevant.

'I know both of you must be tired, but we would like to talk to you immediately. Maybe, you can rest for a bit and then come back?' said Ravi.

'We have been on the road for five hours. How do you expect us to sit for anything? I am going to bed, and so should Swamiji,' Malti Devi made her displeasure clear.

'Mummy...why don't you rest for a while? And, then maybe you can talk to them?' Anumita came and stood next to her. She put a hand on her mother's shoulder.

'What do you mean, Anu? Don't you care how tired we are? We went to do puja for *your* daughter—and this is how you repay us? By being adamant?'

Anumita took a step back.

'Malti Ji, don't lose your temper. Today's children don't know how to respect their elders and the sacrifices they make for them,' Ram Vilas added, self-righteously.

'See, Swamiji is so kind to us. You should be more thankful to him, Anu,' Malti Devi scolded her daughter in front of everyone. Anumita looked down, embarrassed. Ravi saw her hunched shoulders as she cleared her throat and offered her a glass of water. Anumita's hand shook slightly when she lifted it to her dry lips.

'Prithvi *beta,* this man cannot be serious. Why does he want to question us? What could we possibly...?'

'Mummyji, Anu and I have already spoken to them, and so will you,' Prithvi said sternly before walking out of the room to answer his ringing phone. Ravi found the whole 'Beta' and 'Mummyji' affair weird since they were most likely the same age. His eyes met Reeti's. She looked equally perturbed.

'Malti Ji, we are duty-bound to help. Don't worry.' Ram Vilas put his hand on her head. Malti Devi bowed, her palms joined together before Ram Vilas. A look of utter devotion appeared on her face.

'Ma'am, we will send for you in an hour,' said Ravi. Then he heard her muttering angrily as he walked out of the dining hall with Charu and Reeti.

'What is that blind girl doing in your house, Anu? You better keep an eye on Prithvi.'

Ravi wanted to carry Charu away from the viciousness they could still hear Malti Devi spewing at her daughter.

'Unbelievable. It feels like I have jumped into a rabbit hole,' Reeti grumbled.

'What are you talking about?' Charu sensed that something had left both Ravi and Reeti astonished.

'Malti Devi is a young woman, not as old as expected,' Reeti told Charu.

'Oh, a stepmother! Of course. Anumita's father married a young girl. It explains why I sensed her feeling of competition and dislike towards Anumita.' Charu shook her head.

'We should check for bugs in the room,' Ravi whispered as they reached the door of their den.

'I already did; found two. I've removed them. We are in the clear for now. No cameras or listening devices inside anymore,' Reeti said, happily. Charu felt embarrassed that Prithvi had tried to keep tabs on their meetings. It was not a sensible thing to do. He should have known they would find out. *But, why am I feeling embarrassed for him? It is his doing, his responsibility,* she reasoned with herself.

'Why are you so quiet? Malti Devi is probably like this with everyone,' Reeti commented, linking her arm with Charu's, as they walked into their den.

'No, I am used to that, but I think she knows about my past with Prithvi...maybe, everyone does.' Charu pondered about what they must be whispering amongst themselves.

'Maybe. Does it even matter now? Unless...Charu, tell me if you feel you can't handle Prithvi,' said Reeti.

Charu hesitated, wanting to confide in Reeti about the pull she felt whenever she was near Prithvi, even though she knew he was married. But, as usual, Charu just said, 'I'm fine.'

'Ram Vilas needs to be looked at properly...in-depth.'

'Why do you say that?' Ravi said from the door.

Charu recounted what she had experienced. She knew they would listen to her without dismissing her opinion outright. 'As soon as Ram Vilas and Malti Devi entered, my insides started screaming, telling me to run. Ram Vilas was a dense haze, almost opaque. I felt suffocated by his presence. He did not want Prithvi to bring me here. They had a tiff, most likely regarding his raking up of our past. On the other hand, Prithvi wants me to feel grateful for this opportunity to show my skills.'

'Do you think Prithvi will elaborate on his mentor's objections if you ask him?' said Ravi.

'I could ask.'

'What about Malti Devi?'

'I didn't even register her presence. Ram Vilas sucks out the oxygen in the room. His energy saps everyone else's. He is one of those people around whom others feel subdued. He overwhelms everyone with his presence,' Charu answered. Ravi and Reeti considered Charu's impression of the man.

'After you do Malti Devi's background check, I want you to use all your sources to find out whatever you can about Ram Vilas,' Ravi said to Reeti. 'Look for whatever is not out there in the public domain.'

Ravi told them about Gita's brother Mavu. 'I will go to the hospital tomorrow and find out the details of his discharge. Where are we on the call logs? And, on Bilal?'

Reeti took out her notebook and read out whatever she had jotted down. 'Call logs checked. Most are pretty straightforward, but there is something I am still looking at. Let me get back to you when I get to the bottom of it. And, I spoke to the cook about Gita going out with that trolley we saw on the security camera. She said a carpenter had been called to fix the tea trolley that day. This is the interesting part. According to her, the trolley had been fine, but she saw one side of it breaking away two weeks ago.'

'Who called the carpenter?'

'Prithvi. Apparently, Gita told the cook Prithvi had asked her to take the trolley to the carpenter, waiting outside,' Reeti answered.

Charu sensed her excitement. Reeti was tight-lipped until she could back up her words with hard evidence.

'I will check out the carpenter tomorrow. Charu, anything you'd like to add?' Ravi enquired.

'Bilal was not in Delhi. I asked him about Prithvi and his grouse with his politics. I know Prithvi was overly critical of him, but Bilal wouldn't do such a ghastly thing as kidnapping a toddler. If he wants to hurt you, he will strike at your business, your career, but never your family,' she told them.

'He has filed his nomination for the same post as Prithvi, however,' Reeti added.

'How can you say this with such certainty, Charu? I mean, did you sense this when you spoke to him?' asked Ravi.

Charu shook her head. She could feel him doubting her every word. After six years, she had thought they were past that stage. The deep gash that his distrust left on her heart did not find reflection in her next words. 'All of us are capable of doing the unthinkable. But, whoever did it, most likely, either hates Prithvi or…'

'…or they want to hurt him politically, as he says. I am sorry, we stay on Bilal. He suffered a serious accident at Prithvi's hands, became a donor in the same party, and now he's filed his papers for nomination. All these things spell a motive to me,' Ravi replied.

'Guys, I am more concerned about no ransom call or note. If the motive is money, there should have been a ransom call. In its absence, it could be a crime of passion, obsession, or something related to attention,' said Reeti.

'Oh, hello, Mrs Chauhan,' Reeti called out when she saw Anumita had entered the room.

'Hello, I…I wanted to ask if you needed anything for the night. My mother will be coming in a while,' said Anumita, twisting her fingers.

'No, we are good, thanks. If you have some time, we would like to ask…'

'I have a splitting headache right now. Can we do this tomorrow?' she said, looking seriously unwell. She quickly slipped away before Reeti could answer.

13. Malti Devi

12:30 am, Thursday

It was after midnight when Anumita heard her mother arguing loudly with someone and ran downstairs. She found her mother standing near the staircase, facing Ravi. He was trying his best to remain calm in the face of her tantrums.

'How dare you grab me! You have mistreated me! I will not forget this!' Malti Devi wagged a knobby finger in Ravi's direction, trying to intimidate him.

'Ma'am, this is evidence. You cannot take it away with you,' said Ravi, retrieving the cluster of crystals from the sole of her slipper.

'I…I didn't know they got stuck to my slipper. You should have taken care of it. How was I supposed to know it was on the floor?'

Ravi handed the tiny crystal flower to Reeti.

'What happened?' asked Anumita, stopping next to Malti Devi.

'*Uff!* Nothing happened. They showed me this stupid crystal flower, the kind we stick on our clothes. It must have fallen on the ground, and I must have stepped on it. That is why it got embedded in my heel. And, they think I was trying to steal their precious evidence.'

'Mummy, come, let's go and rest,' Anumita pulled at her mother's wrist.

'No. Call Prithvi. I want them arrested,' her mother said, crossly.

'He is at the other house,' Anumita said as if that explained everything. Malti Devi glared accusingly at her daughter, then harrumphed and stomped upstairs.

'What is she talking about…what crystal flower?' Anumita asked Ravi.

'We found this in Myra's room, near her crib.' Ravi held the tiny cluster up.

'Are you sure this was in Myra's crib?' she asked.

'Have you seen them before?'

'Ram Vilas Ji has a pocket square with these crystal flowers. But, he isn't allowed—I mean, he hasn't gone up to Myra's room. How is this possible? It would have been captured by the camera.'

'All the cameras weren't working,' Reeti answered.

'How are you so sure the crystal flower belongs to Ram Vilas?' asked Charu.

'Because I bought the pocket square for him. Prithvi asked me to buy something for his mentor on a special occasion. That is why I am sure,' she snapped at Charu, and then she was immediately repentant. 'Sorry, I shouldn't have been so rude.'

Then she followed her mother up the stairs.

Ravi returned to the back room with his colleagues, where they had just finished the interview with Malti Devi. He looked at the paint, starting to peel at the corners of the ceiling. Ravi hadn't noticed the damp walls earlier. He straightened the chair upended by Malti Devi's angry departure.

'Sometimes, I wonder why we do this.' Reeti shook her head, flinging herself onto the chair. 'First, she comes in late, then she has the gall to shout at us. Look at the nerve of this woman, trying to conceal the crystals in her slipper. I don't believe a word she said.'

'Reeti, we will need to check everyone's wardrobes first thing tomorrow. She was obviously trying to remove the crystals. Also, check who was wearing what the day Myra was kidnapped.'

'Ravi, the possibility that she and Ram Vilas could be in this together is very real. Malti Devi was on the same floor. Ram Vilas and she went out with some bags right after Myra disappeared,' said Charu.

'But, why would they do this? Motive?'

'To get even with Anumita; to help Prithvi's career; to get Ram Vilas back into the Prithvi's inner circle. She's thick with him, anyone can see.'

'It is probable. We need to find evidence first,' Ravi agreed.

'I'd like to listen to her interview again. Both the women talk in riddles. What did Anumita mean when she referred to the "other house"? The government bungalow? Or, does he have another house? Why did he leave without telling anyone that he would be late?' Charu sat down. Prithvi was behaving so strangely. Now that his mother-in-law and his mentor had arrived, he had disappeared. After dinner, Ram Vilas had left for his flat, and Prithvi had left on the pretext of dropping him off.

'Okay, let's listen to it together.' Ravi switched on the recorder, then sat down next to Charu. He let his eyes wander, taking in the tube light, the intricate spider's web, the dirty window grille. The backroom seemed to be an eyesore compared to the rest of the haveli. Sitting on a stool near the recorder, Reeti swung her legs as they heard Malti Devi's voice through the speaker.

'This interview is being conducted by Ms Reeti Gaur, in the presence of M. Ravi Nair and Ms Charu Sharma. The time is 11:15 pm. The interviewee is Malti Devi, Myra's maternal grandmother.'

'Give my full introduction. My name is Malti Devi, wife of late Sri Ratan Lal, mother of Anumita Chauhan and grandmother of Myra Chauhan,' the nasal voice said, sullenly. Ravi watched Reeti roll her eyes and smiled.

'I am from Hisar, Haryana, and married Anu's father right after graduation. My husband was a great politician. I have only one daughter—my husband's daughter, that is—Anumita. She's married to Prithvi, the son of a family friend. Anu, being the daughter of a prominent politician, understood the demands of marriage to a politician.'

'What do you mean? What demands?' asked Reeti. Charu had felt Malti Devi's exasperation at being asked such silly questions at this point.

'A politician's wife needs to be like Gandhiji's three monkeys for most of her life. Do you understand? No? *Tsk*. Now, look at this blind girl. Don't mind. My Anu knows she was Prithvi's girlfriend in school,' the voice continued. 'Which wife would allow such a woman to enter her home? But, Anu...my Anu did not say anything. She is more concerned that her husband should not be dissatisfied with her. The husband should be taken care of at all times—if not by her, then by whoever he wants.'

'Ma'am, let's move on,' Reeti interrupted her.

'Yes, but why did you bring her? Was there no other member who could have looked for Myra? I am telling you... like I told Anu...it is a way to get...'

The desk creaked under Malti Devi's weight. Charu realized she had been leaning on it, trying to get her point across.

'Ma'am, how did you come to live in Delhi?' Ravi interrupted her opinion of Prithvi's decision.

'Swamiji has been our guru for a long time. We knew him from his Sirsa ashram days. He asked for Anu's hand in marriage for Prithvi. He got Prithvi involved in my husband's party work. And, look where we are now.' Malti Devi allowed Ravi to shift the focus from Charu to herself. Charu had sensed the pride in her voice as she spoke about her status as the minister's mother-in-law.

'After her father died, I was lonely, with nothing to do. When Anu developed problems, Swamiji asked me to come to Delhi to take care of her. He requested me, you see. Anu started having trouble sleeping about two years ago. We took her to the best and the most discreet doctors. They treated her for depression.'

'When you say discreet, what do you mean?' asked Charu.

'I...I mean...people in our position...we can't afford the tabloids finding out we have health issues. The stigma regarding mental health—I mean, we go to our family doctors if we have a problem.' Malti Devi had adjusted her saree, a nervous tic visible near her eye.

'So, your family doctor will be able to give us the details of Anumita's medical history?' Ravi's voice came through the recorder.

'Anu went to a new doctor at that time. I can't say.'

Charu had sensed Malti Devi freeze, calculating how she could backpedal from the tight spot where she had landed herself.

'Malti Ji, we will find out. You should tell us now because if we enquire around, people will start asking uncomfortable questions. And, you know better than anyone else that once people start that, it becomes difficult to control,' Reeti warned her politely.

Malti Devi had scowled at her before letting out a haughty sniff.

'Don't think I will let your threats go unpunished. I could have you out of here at one phone call. But, since it is the matter of my granddaughter, I will tell you. Anu gets anxious, has panic attacks. I think she does it for attention, but these new doctors want to give medicines for everything. After Myra's birth, Anu became almost suicidal. Happy now?'

Charu sat back and crossed her arms, listening to Malti Devi talk about Anumita as if she was speaking about a spoilt, particularly difficult child she didn't really like but had sacrificed a lot for.

'Ma'am, we are only doing our job. Sorry to ask, but you are Anumita's stepmother. Was it difficult to play mother to a grown-up girl, only a few years younger to you?' Charu asked.

'It is common knowledge. And, why should I find it difficult? She was the daughter of the house, and I was the stepmother. Our roles were clearly defined. My daughter is suffering—and you think it matters if I gave birth to her? I always have her best interests at heart, even if she can't see it. I have taken care of her since I got married.'

'You have no other children?'

'No, this was the promise her father took from me before marriage—that we wouldn't have children. You see, he thought if there were more children, my attention would be diverted from Anu.'

'Why didn't you refuse this unfairness?'

'Hmph...there is so much you young people will never understand. Marriages are contracts. You give something... you get something. I gave away the right to be a mother and got status, money, and every privilege you can think of. I have no complaints.'

'Please tell us where you were the day your granddaughter was abducted,' Ravi changed the subject.

'I was at home. I oversaw her morning routine. Myra's maid, Gita, takes care of her. When Myra took her nap, I, too, slept like I usually do. After that, Gita came to wake me up, banging on my door like there was no tomorrow. She was crying like a banshee—along with that Manik. Anyway, we looked for her everywhere, then called Prithvi and Anu.'

'How far is your room from Myra's?'

'It is the last room in the corridor, just above Swamiji's study.'

'Do you leave your door open when you take your nap?'

'Why would I do that? I am a respectable woman, and there are cameras and intercoms in every room. Someone is always watching. Not that I have anything to hide. If they need me, they knock on my door. I am a light sleeper.'

'A couple of days ago, you instructed Gita to leave Myra's door open when she went to take her meals. Was there a reason for this?'

'Well, obviously. I did that so that if Myra cried, I could hear her. What kind of *behuda* questions are you asking me?'

'Just a moment, ma'am. Please explain why you told Gita to leave Myra's door open two weeks before your granddaughter was kidnapped. If there was no one on the floor, and your door is usually closed, what was the need?'

'What are you suggesting? You stupid people, do you even know who I am?' Malti Devi was livid at, what she felt, was a pointed attack on her. 'I…I could destroy your career with a snap of my fingers. All I have to do is tell Swamiji, and he will do as I say. He can control Prithvi. Do you people think I don't see what Prithvi is up to? And, who said there was no one on the floor? Wasn't Sia studying with that Manik at the time? Did you question him?'

'Yes, ma'am, he has been questioned—and he is also being called for an interview in person,' said Ravi.

There was stony silence, during which Reeti and Ravi remembered how Malti Devi had glowered at them, pulling her saree's *pallu* tighter around her shoulders.

'How was your puja?' Charu heard Reeti ask.

'It went off very well. Swamiji even offered to perform the *yagna* himself. How many times does one receive such an offer?'

'So, he suggested the puja? But, why within two hours of Myra's disappearance?' Ravi asked her.

'When Swamiji suggested it, how could I say no? You won't understand.'

'Did you perform the puja at the ashram, ma'am?'

'Yes, of course. At the Sirsa ashram. Our Kul Devi temple is there. This is how it has been done for generations,' she said, watching their faces.

'You took a few big bags with you to the ashram. We were told you packed them with clothes yourself for donating.'

'Yes, I do that every two–three months. So?' Malti Devi scraped her nail on the tablecloth.

'Can you tell us where those bags are?'

'I left them there…at the ashram. The caretaker will return them to me the next time I visit after donating everything I took. I got six bags made out of my old sarees for this purpose. I will fill the others and take them with me the next time I go. He will return the empty ones to me. It is a system I have worked out.'

'But, why Hisar? Why not Sirsa—where you performed the puja? I mean, it must have been a detour.'

'It was the same route we always take. Why should we not do the same this time? How is that important? Why...what does that have anything to do with Myra?' Malti Devi had seemed confused and put out.

'If she could have shot someone with her eyes, I think it would have been me,' Reeti said, pausing the recording. Then she played the rest.

'Do the bags have a zipper?' It was Charu. She had remembered the sound Gita had heard—the sound of a zipper closing—over the baby monitor.

'Yes, obviously.'

'Do you also remember what clothes you took with you this time? How many?'

'Yes, I have made a list. I always do; otherwise, these supervisors will take the best clothes away and sell them—and then tell me they donated them. I always make it a point to ask them to whom they donated the clothes on my next visit. I am very meticulous that way.'

'Thank you for clarifying that. Ma'am, do you smoke?' Reeti spoke up.

'What! How dare you! I am held up as an example of good values,' Malti Devi sputtered, furious.

'Ma'am, please answer the question. For Myra's sake,' Reeti tried to cajole her.

The woman relented hesitantly. 'I have an occasional one, but never in the house—before the children.'

'Bidi?'

'Hmm...sometimes, when I miss my old life. I borrow the masala from Swamiji...,' Malti Devi admitted in a low voice.

'Do you visit Myra's room after smoking it?'

'No, no, Prithvi doesn't know, and you won't tell him. It is a small secret Swamiji and I share. I usually take it with me when I go out for the day.'

'Is there anything you would like to tell us?'

'About what?'

'Anyone you suspect—who could have kidnapped Myra.'

Malti Devi had opened her mouth to say something, then thought the better of it. She had frowned and shaken her head.

'Can you tell us if you recognize this?' Reeti recalled how Malti Devi's eyes had widened when she held up the small Ziplock bag with the cluster of crystals. Reeti had slid the transparent bag across the table towards Malti Devi, who looked at it carefully.

'Where did you find this?'

'In Myra's room. Have you seen these before? They look like the stick-on variety.'

Malti Devi looked at the crystal flower in the bag, and then, before anyone could have stopped her, she had taken it out and held it in her palm. 'I don't know if we have clothes that have such a stick-on flower, but so what if we do? These are not even worth thinking about. If this is your investigation, I don't see much hope of finding Myra.' She had thrown it down on the table. 'Wait till I tell Prithvi about the harassment I have faced. He should have been here. What can one expect—always running away, coming home after midnight...' She started lamenting loudly, watching Charu.

Reeti switched off the recording. 'The rest is just her abusing us, showing us who is the boss. I'm just glad we realized that she had only thrown the bag on the table in time. Or it could have fallen on the floor when she slammed the bag down on the desk, as she claims.'

They had run after her. Charu had asked them to check her slipper. That's how Ravi had caught her.

'So, what do you think?' asked Reeti.

'She does seem to feel something for Anumita, but it is all twisted around in her self-interest. She truly believes she's acting in the best interest of her stepdaughter. She feels she knows how to secure Anumita's future and, in the long run, her own,' said Charu. 'She has probably lived through what she calls her beliefs about letting the husband do as he wishes. The three monkeys' analogy perhaps came from her own marriage. Money and power equal security.'

'Why did she go to the temple with Ram Vilas straight after her granddaughter was kidnapped? I can't digest it,' said Ravi. 'Reeti, please find out if there really was a *havan* performed at the ashram. I need all the details from when they started from here to when they got back. Schedule, time, luggage—everything. We know they left for Sirsa but stopped at the old ashram in Hisar for a while. The bags were left there, which is the usual practice, according to Prithvi.'

14. Prithvi

2:30 am, Thursday

'I need to think for a while. I'll be in Myra's room,' said Charu and left with a big lump in her throat. It was difficult when people like Malti Devi doubted her intentions. She wasn't the only one who had had an affair, and yet, she was always the only one being judged. She had barely reached the front door of the haveli when she heard it open. The smell of sex and alcohol bombarded her senses even as the cold night air made her shiver.

'Hey, what's wrong? Why are you roaming the house so late in the night?' asked Prithvi, crowding her as he came in.

'Nothing, I was just going up to. . .um. . .Myra's room. Why were you out so late? You did not tell us where you were either, Prithvi.' Charu took two steps back.

'I had. . .some work. And, Chumki, I am the one who called you to my house. Don't try to order me around. It is no one's business where I go or what I do with my time.' Prithvi was offended. He stared at her through the haze. She looked as soft and pure as she had in school. She was surer of herself now. He admired her grit, her strength to overcome her disability. It was hard not to compare her to Anumita, who was constantly needy and wanting. Myra's kidnapping had made her more unpredictable than ever.

'I needed some time away from the pressure, Chumki. You understand, right?' He lunged towards her, gripping her arms. She was immediately inundated with images of a rough coupling that made her feel sick to her stomach. She jerked out of his grasp.

'Chumki, dear, I was having sex, uninhibited sex bought with the taxpayers' money,' Prithvi whispered into her ear.

Charu smelt the liquor in his breath, the crude words laced with an intent to shock her. *He knew I would be able to see it. He did that on purpose. Prithvi is no more the troubled boy of my youth but a calculating and wily man who enjoys making people squirm.*

'Well, that is your business, and I hope you had a good time. Does Anumita know about your...indiscretions?'

'You are so innocent, Chumki. Sometimes I wish you weren't so...guileless. It would be so much fun to corrupt you,' he said, wistfully.

'You told everyone we had an affair in school. Why?' Charu was still smarting at Malti Devi's words.

'Listen, before I married Anu, I had to do a full disclosure. Swamiji told me the in-laws already knew, but it was a test to see if I would come clean. I did. Anu and I are different people. We married, in all fairness, for political gain—and I guess she saw me as a good enough candidate. Her father was difficult. So, we tried, had kids, one band-aid child after another. Nothing worked. And, as far as knowing about my—as you have very politely put it—indiscretions... I suppose so.' Prithvi smiled, leaning against the wall. 'Well, I am going to sleep now, Chumki. Every question is deferred until I am sober. Aren't you glad now I left, seeing me like this?' He hobbled up the stairs.

Charu stood in the quiet hall, listening to his tread until a door banged shut upstairs. *If Anumita knows about his escapades, could she be trying to get her husband to pay more attention to her through Myra's disappearance? Her anxiety and nervousness could be attributed to her complicity,* she thought, walking up the steps and into Myra's room. Even before she could draw a breath, she sensed a volatile presence reaching out for her.

'Where were you? Did you go out with him?' Anumita caught Charu's arms in a vice-like grip, knocking her white stick out of her hands. 'I saw you with him downstairs. I know how he leans towards you protectively. He smelt of sex, didn't he? Did you go with him to the house, as Mummy said? Tell me!' She shook Charu, unaware that she was hurting her. 'You call yourself professionals? Is this how you behave when a child is missing?'

Charu felt Anumita's nails draw blood from her arms, but she remained silent. 'Anumita, please calm down...' she whispered, placing her hands gently on her.

'Oh, don't you dare patronise me, you little bitch! You think you can fool me. But, he is mine! He's my husband whether you like it or not.'

Charu waited for her to calm down and then led her to the sofa. This time Anumita did not resist. 'Tell me what's wrong,' she said, quietly.

Anumita clutched her daughter's doll in her arms, holding it with all her might. She wanted to stop thinking of all the things she had done wrong. 'This is not what I wanted. I should have listened. I should have been satisfied with what I had,' she tried to put her fear into words, weeping. 'But, I wanted more than this lonely existence. I wanted respect and—I wanted to forget. I shouldn't have involved... It is all my fault.'

'Talk to me, Anumita. Listened to whom? Shouldn't have involved whom? What about? What did you want to forget?'

'Is it wrong to...move on after a horrible experience? Can one move on when the result is so...innocent and pure? When you love the result?' Anumita clutched at Charu's hands.

'What do you mean?' Charu instinctively moved closer, perplexed at her questions. *Why do I see this orange flame every time Anumita is distraught or scared?* Charu wondered. All she could catch from Anumita was a tangled mess of overwhelming grief and powerlessness. She wished she did not have to ask, but Myra was the one she had to save first.

'Anu, did something awful happen recently?'

'Myra...Myra...she left her doll, her pacifier, behind. How will she sleep?' Anumita cried helplessly.

'What are you doing?' Malti Devi's nasal voice asked before her bony fingers pulled at Charu's forearm. Charu's connection with Anumita snapped.

'It's nothing, Mummy. I just...' Anumita sprang up, agitated.

'What are you doing here, Anumita? You should be resting.'

'I...yes, Mummy. I just wanted to be with Myra. I just want to tell Charu...'

'Tell? Tell Charu what? What are you doing, you stupid girl? Your stupidity can ruin everything. Why don't you understand that?' Malti Devi said through clenched teeth. 'And you,' she turned to Charu. 'What do you want at this time of the night?' She turned to her daughter again. 'Come along, Anu, you need to sleep.' She led Anumita out of the room.

The room brimmed with unexpressed pain. Charu needed air. She walked to the open window, where she stood listening to the night. Her mind tried to decipher if Anumita's broken conversation had revealed anything new.

Why was she so regretful? Who did she not listen to? What did she want to tell me before Malti Devi interrupted her? And, what did Malti Devi mean when she said that Anumita would spoil everything with her stupidity? Charu took out a small notebook and drew the orange flame she saw whenever she was near Anumita. She lay down on the carpet, her hands by her side and allowed some time to pass to quiet her mind. She breathed deeply and let her body relax. The house was silent. The wind outside hushed. Charu's eyes grew heavy, her breathing slowed down as she felt herself floating down into a deep well. She let herself see the room as she had heard it described.

Candy-pink striped wallpaper, pictures of Myra, baby toys, the cot, her frocks hanging in the closet, frilly and fancy. Anumita smiled down at her child, rubbing her wet body with the towel; Prithvi said good night.

Charu felt her lips curve in a smile that imitated Myra's. Her fingers collided with something that had fallen on the floor. It was Myra's pacifier. *It must have fallen when Anumita left,* Charu thought, holding it. She stayed still. Another vision appeared. This time she could make out it was a different place. Charu realized this was where Myra was now.

It was late evening. The sun was just setting and the lights decorating the nearby temple were just coming on. Myra was sucking on the broken, purple pacifier. She fretted, and a woman lifted her and rocked her gently over her shoulder. She pointed at a sign on top of a nearby building. Myra looked up. She saw the letter V, but not the others. It didn't hold her attention for too long. The cap covering her head itched, and she tried to pull it off, unsuccessfully. The woman said sweetly to her, 'Do you want to go inside now?' It wasn't a voice Charu recognized.

The landline of the haveli began to ring shrilly, pulling Charu out of her trance. The extension somewhere outside was also ringing. She checked the watch. It was near dawn. She heard Ravi pounding up the stairs. Then she heard him knock on Anumita's door. Charu leapt to her feet.

'Anumita ma'am, is Prithvi sir back yet?' Ravi asked her when she opened her door. Instead of answering, Anumita stood staring at the ringing phone. 'He is sleeping…passed out drunk,' she said, woodenly.

'Anumita, you need to pick up the phone,' Charu said in a firm voice.

'I can't. I wouldn't know what to say.' Anumita pulled back from Ravi, who was leading her to the phone.

'It could be about Myra,' said Charu. 'Just pick it up and talk normally.'

'Hello. Hello?' Anumita's voice trembled as she held the receiver to her ear. 'Yes…I want to see. Where…who are you? My daughter…I am listening.'

Charu heard Anumita's side of the conversation and could easily fill in the blanks. She could feel Anumita struggle against her flight reflex with all her might.

'What! Please don't hurt my daughter… Let me…I will pay. Hello? Hello…?'

During the exchange that had lasted barely thirty seconds, Charu had felt a gamut of emotions in Anumita—from fear to confusion to relief, when the call was disconnected.

'Didi, *paani*,' Gita handed Anumita a glass of water.

'He…she…I couldn't make out if it was a man or a woman,' Anumita said, finally.

'It's all right. The kidnapper won't use their actual voice. It will either be a voice disguiser device, or they will distort their voice,' Ravi explained.

'Did you record the phone call?' Anumita asked Ravi.

'Yes, downstairs.'

'I think it was a woman, but I could be wrong. She said Myra is safe for now, but I would have to pay thirty lakh rupees if I wanted to see her again. Oh God, they are asking for a ransom. What does it mean?'

'*Tees lakh!* Have they lost their mind?' Malti Devi exclaimed. No one was aware she had been listening. She stood at a distance from her distressed daughter, studying the group of people surrounding her.

'What else? Anumita ma'am, please continue,' Ravi did not want Anumita to lose her train of thought.

'She said they would call and tell us the time and place.'

'They?' Ravi watched Anumita scratch her wrist mindlessly. The skin was already raw with her incessant scratching.

'She said, "We will call", so I assume there is more than one person involved.'

'Don't worry, at least now we know it was someone who did this primarily for money, and certainly not alone. We get Myra first, then we catch the culprits.'

'Could you hear anything else? Any noise in the background?' asked Charu.

'Not that I can recall right now,' Anumita answered, thoughtfully.

'Where is Prithvi? You should have let him pick up the phone.' Malti Devi walked up to Anumita.

'Your dear Prithvi was drunk and passed out,' Anumita replied. Her eyes were suddenly fiery. 'When his daughter needed him, he was, as usual, nowhere to be found. That is the man you tied me to. His daughter has been kidnapped, and he continues as if nothing has changed.'

'Shut up, you thankless wretch! Prithvi cares about you and his girls. He is doing all this for you! Stop complaining in front of other people. It doesn't behove a minister's wife,' Malti Devi cut her short.

'We don't matter. We never have, and we never will—in comparison to his own ambition and his Swamiji,' Anumita said bitterly before walking away.

Charu felt Malti Devi's eyes on her. When she left, Ravi and Charu walked back to the room where Reeti was waiting for them.

'Did we manage to trace the call?' Ravi asked her.

'No, it lasted less than thirty seconds, but I recorded it. Here, listen to this,' Reeti said, switching on the recorder. She replayed the conversation between Anumita and the kidnapper. The stranger's voice was neither distorted nor changed but seemed to come from a distance. It was hard to identify the person's gender.

'Well, it seems we received the ransom call I was worried about. If this is about money, we can narrow it down to people who are bound to benefit financially,' said Reeti, making a copy of the recording to send to the lab for analysis. 'You have your motive.'

'Thirty lakh is a substantial amount, but not insurmountable for Prithvi's family. The kidnappers, however, probably think it's exorbitant—or they need this particular amount for personal reasons. I mean, why would someone go through the trouble of kidnapping Prithvi's child for thirty lakh? It doesn't make sense,' said Charu.

'Thirty lakh is a huge sum for the lower-middle-class, or maybe the kidnapper is smart enough to know that Prithvi would consider this amount payable instead of making his daughter's kidnapping public knowledge. It could also be a way to flex one's muscles, show power, bring him to heel,' said Ravi.

'What I don't understand is—do the kidnappers already know we are in the house? They didn't ask Anumita not to inform the police or anything to that effect. So, either they are new to this, or they have an informant inside. But, the fact that they kept the call under thirty seconds, so it couldn't be traced, indicates knowledge of how this works,' Charu thought aloud.

'No one knew we had tapped the landlines in the house, so it could be chance,' said Ravi, as they played the recording a couple of times again, just to see if they could isolate any other noise in the background but could not hear anything.

'I had a vision while in Myra's room,' Charu suddenly remembered. 'I don't remember touching a pacifier in the morning, Ravi, but I found one on the floor just now. It triggered another trance and took me to a place that has a sign that begins with V. Myra is with a woman. Also, Myra has been kept in a room at some height. We should call the forensic artist again today. I also met Prithvi at the door when I was going up to Myra's room. It seems Anumita knows he has liaisons outside their marriage. She is very much on edge. She also believes Prithvi and I are having an affair. And, Malti Devi is fanning her misconception. I want to look into Anumita's past. She is trying to hide something. She has a deep feeling of guilt,' Charu finished.

'I will check Anumita and Malti Devi's past,' said Reeti. 'I studied the call logs again. One number does not match with anyone we know. It is a Hisar number, but the person to whom it is registered is dead. This number contacted Anumita a couple of times last month. It could be nothing, but I want to check it out. I found the same number on Prithvi's phone too. Same time period. No activity on the phone number recently.'

'Okay, let's get to work,' said Ravi.

Charu knew Reeti would find out everything through her network about Malti Devi and Anumita—as Ravi would about Ram Vilas's background. They all had their individual roles that helped solve the case. She could only hope that her contribution helped in some way.

15. Ram Vilas

7 am, Thursday

After the ransom call, Charu, Reeti, and Ravi decided to catch up on sleep in shifts. Ravi decided to take the first shift. Charu and Reeti shut off the lights and lay down on the mattresses that Anumita had provided. Charu heard Reeti's soft snores within a few minutes of lying down. Her mind in a constant state of turmoil, she found it difficult to fall asleep.

At 4 am, when Reeti woke up for her shift, Ravi noticed Charu's frown. 'Don't fret about dreaming, Charu. Whatever comes your way, I'm close,' Ravi's rumbling voice came to her from a distance.

'Can you hold my hand?' she whispered back. Ravi shifted his mattress next to hers and clasped her hand tightly. Charu turned towards Ravi, and with her nose buried in his chest she let herself gradually reach the precipice of deep sleep.

'Come on, don't be a spoilsport...' a grating voice in her ear woke her. She looked around at the foul, fear-laden shadows that filled the room. She knew she was dreaming but not about Myra.

The man prodded the girl with a stick, irritated when she kept silent.

His voice hardened. 'Do you know what I want to do to you? I want to take the butcher's skinning knife and gut you. If your father does not give me what is rightfully mine, I will kill you and send you back to him in small parts.' The girl heard him walk closer and steeled herself.

'Do you HEAR me?' he screamed next to her ear, making her jump and sob before laughing and launching at her shards of glass,

stones, darts, and all his treasures that he had been collecting. He enjoyed it when a piece of glass or dart embedded itself in her delicate skin, and she cried out.

Charu's eyes snapped open. She sat up short of breath. She clenched her fists, willing herself to balance out before she moved an inch. Charu tried to figure out how much time had passed, but she couldn't hear anything. Her nose was still raw with the putrid smell of the room with the man and the small girl. Her ears were still ringing with his rasping threats. A horrid fear was climbing up her spine, chilling her like a realization. The talons of panic were scratching at her neck.

Frantically, she started looking for her white stick, panting in abject terror. She needed to get out of this state of helplessness. That was how Ravi found her when he stepped out of the washroom, scrambling around on her knees, terrified.

'Charu...?' Ravi immediately handed her the stick, which she held on to tightly. He wrapped his arms around her, and she burrowed into him.

'I'm here,' he said, sitting next to her on the mattress, pulling her close.

'Ravi, I think...this time I heard the man clearly. I know the voice...'

'How...from where?'

'I mean, I don't know who he is, but I know that voice. It clicked today. It doesn't make any sense, but I don't know how else to explain it,' said Charu.

'Okay, anything concrete that would tell me the location?'

'No,' Charu murmured.

'So then, we wait,' Ravi said.

'I can't get the sound of the whimpering girl who wet her dress in fear out of my ears. The petrified mewling and the cackling insane laughter of the tormenter. I even heard the little girl's thoughts, as clearly, as if they were my own,' Charu told Ravi as he rubbed her arms slowly.

'She kept repeating—I have to find a way to survive this. Somehow, someway, I will do whatever is necessary. I will get out,' Charu said.

The words jolted Ravi. The words were the same ones Charu sometimes uttered when she was fast asleep.

Reeti entered the room with cups of tea that she had made for them and immediately evaluated the situation. Ravi's tormented eyes and Charu's curled trembling form was an oft-repeated scene. She knew what to do. Talk about the case and pretend nothing out of the ordinary had occurred. 'I can't get my head around the number of cameras there are in the house. I have gone through all the ones on the first floor. Later, I will start on the ground floor. But, we should primarily look at the nanny cam removed from Myra's room because it was faulty. I have sent a mail requesting the company to send us a full report on the kind of damage that occurred and also the status of the non-functioning cameras in the passages.

It shouldn't take too long to know if it was a mechanical failure or if someone fiddled with the nanny cam. And, you should check out the hospital where Gita's brother was admitted,' Reeti's voice was straightforward as if seeing two of her colleagues in an embrace was an everyday occurrence.

'I will have a word with Sia as soon as she is up,' said Charu, sitting up.

'I found out a bit about Ram Vilas. Everything that is available in the local papers, as of now. But, I've asked a couple of my contacts to get back to me about the stuff that isn't. Let us interview him after we've been through his history. Malti Devi's past is proving difficult to trace. Whatever has been written about her is from the time she joined her husband in the political circles,' Reeti widened her eyes at Ravi, who shook his head, telling her that this dream had nothing to do with Myra.

'Ravi, we should meet Ram Vilas in his office. It will make him feel more in control. And, you should dig into Malti Devi's youth. Why did her father get her married to a man twice her age?' said Charu.

'Ram Vilas is the son of a farmer. His formative years are sketchy. He started giving sermons in his youth. Gathered a following. He opened a small ashram in Hisar, where he came in contact with rich, influential people. There are some undocumented accounts that show him as a polarizing political organizer. Mobs, marches, speeches—but at the ground level, nothing major. After meeting Anumita's father, he aligned himself with the party and moved to Sirsa.

After that, there is a meteoric rise. Same things on a bigger stage. Prithvi came to him and, in him, Ram Vilas saw a young man with promise. Someone who could orate well and was willing to follow orders. He became Prithvi's mentor and guided him to where he is today.

Now, the problems between them started about six months ago, when Prithvi gave Ram Vilas a very public snub on a national stage. Prithvi had been introduced to Viswajit Majumdar, a highly sought-after campaign manager. He advised Prithvi to change his tact from divisive politics to developmental policies and adopt an anti-corruption stance. Prithvi started tilting towards this strategy and reaped benefits. Ram Vilas found his control slipping.

According to his peon, Ram Vilas and Prithvi have been at loggerheads for a few months. The manifesto being prepared for his nomination for the post of CM is the bone of contention. It seems Ram Vilas has been keeping tabs on Prithvi's vote bank. He feels Prithvi's followers are with him as long as he keeps the issue of religious superiority alive. And, Prithvi needs to be seen as a moderate. This clashes with his mentor's approach. The dwindling support from the old sponsors has led to several heated arguments. The driver said the sympathy-vote idea Prithvi was talking about was suggested by Ram Vilas.'

'But, if Prithvi is doing so well, why does Ram Vilas feel he needs a sympathy vote?' asked Charu.

'Ram Vilas feels he isn't the golden boy anymore. Therefore, he suggested they do something drastic to make people vote for him again. I will check Prithvi's numbers to see if he lied. Yesterday, Ram Vilas came into the house with Bilal Siddiqui.'

'We need to find out what their meeting was about,' said Reeti.

Ravi nodded. He picked up the phone and called the swami. 'Ram Vilas Ji, how are you this morning? Actually, we wanted to have a word with you, sir.'

'So, join me in the study, young man, and we can talk there,' Ram Vilas replied.

'We shall be there in a few minutes. Charu…'

'*Arrey*, this is not a job for her. What will she do? You come, and let's talk while I have my breakfast.'

'Sure,' Ravi agreed, after hesitating for a moment. He hung up and informed them that Ram Vilas didn't want Charu to accompany him.

'Go ahead, don't delay it on my account,' said Charu.

'Can you set up the system so that Charu can hear us in this room, Reeti?' Ravi was hopeful.

'Yes, no problem. A wire will work just fine. You will have to wear an audio recorder on you,' Reeti answered.

At 7:45 am, Ravi and Reeti sat opposite an empty chair, looking around the room. Each idol was sparkling clean, had a fresh *tilak*, which the Godman had probably applied during his morning puja. In his mentor's absence the day before, Prithvi had performed the rituals in the evening. It had surprised Charu enough to remark on it.

Ram Vilas entered his study, apologizing for the delay. Ravi surveyed the smiling man. The *tilak* was impressive, and his voice was consistently low-pitched and sweet. The soft smile seemed to say he could be trusted, and his eyes seemed to accept the person in front.

'Sorry, I had to take an urgent call. An important industrialist, a big donor from our party, has requested that I perform a puja for his friend in America. Some things can still surprise me,' Ram Vilas laughed politely.

'No worries, Ram Vilas Ji. We just have a few questions. Can you tell us why you left the house with Malti Devi when you knew Myra had been kidnapped?' asked Reeti, jumping straight to the matter at hand.

'Oh, I thought you would ask me about my journey into the big bad world of politics... And, you can call me Swamiji; Ram Vilas seems very impersonal. *Aur aap sab to ab ghar ke hi hain na,* like family.' His eyes twinkled.

'Of course, Swamiji.'

'Yes...yes, Malti Devi is a demanding mother. You see, Anu was having a lot of problems with her second pregnancy. I thought women were most comfortable with their mothers, so I called Malti Devi. But, how was I to know that she would coil up like a... I mean, that she would simply stay on?

Even after the child...Myra turned one; she wouldn't leave. But, then I told Prithvi *ki theek hai bhai;* it's okay. Since Anu was on the verge of a panic attack on most days, she needed a caregiver. I thought *ki* who'd be better than her mother, even if she was a stepmother?'

'Did you know Malti Devi before she married Anumita's father?'

'Not personally. Malti comes from a poor, low-caste family. She visited the ashram with her father sometimes. Her father asked me to look for a match, and I suggested her name to Anu's father's family, that's all. But, the decision was made between the two parties. I thought, what is a better *seva* than getting a poor girl married?

Anumita was still a young girl when they were married. Malti was a glorified governess, and Anu *beti's* father forbade her to have her own children. It was a hard decision, but he loved Anu over anyone else. Malti is bitter about that, but she was compensated for her sacrifice handsomely. My friend took her along for his rallies, she became the face of inter-caste marriage, her presence beside him gave us the edge we needed, and all the lower-caste votes were in the bag. The party won that year. Those were good days,' Ram Vilas's voice rang with nostalgia. 'But, now she does nothing except create more chaos,' he said and picked up his white handkerchief to wipe the corners of his mouth delicately.

'What a beautiful handkerchief,' Reeti commented, throwing a glance at Ravi. He saw it had the same crystal flowers as they had found in Myra's room. Three crystal flowers glittered at the edge of the hankie.

'They are called pocket squares, not handkerchiefs. Prithvi gifted them to me. I always wear them. These crystals are *sarvosky*...swaros...*kya kehte hein*?'

'Yes, they are so elegant. That is what I was admiring. Don't you fear the flowers will fall off?'

'Oh yes. I've lost a few of these flowers from one of the squares, even though I take such care. I suppose I can always ask Prithvi to get more. He has them too.'

'Prithvi sir got matching pocket squares. How nice of him,' confirmed Reeti.

'Hmm, anyway, when Malti called and told Prithvi that Myra was missing, he came home.'

'And you?' asked Ravi.

'Yes, I did too.'

'With Prithvi?'

'*Haan bhai*,' Ram Vilas snapped.

'Sir, you came back here in the middle of the day too, according to the security camera,' Reeti reminded him.

'Yes, right, I did. You see, I am an old man, I forget sometimes. Yes, I came around lunchtime to collect some files from the office here. Someone dropped me. We had a cup of tea, then he left. Later, I picked up some files and left too. Yes, I am sure.'

Ravi's pen stopped, and his muscles tensed. *Why has Ram Vilas not mentioned Bilal by name?*

'How long were you in the house, approximately?'

'*Hey Bhagwan*, how would I know?' Ram Vilas's irritation grew at the pointed questions.

'Sir, the time stamp on the security footage shows you were in your office for thirty minutes,' Ravi said, pointedly.

'So what? It must have taken me time to find the file. I cannot remember what I did during that time,' said Ram Vilas, leaning back. He was clearly peeved at the question. His phone rang. He looked at it and lowered the volume.

'We are talking about the day before yesterday, Swamiji,' said Reeti, trying to diffuse the situation. She nudged Ravi to back down.

'Okay, let me think.' Ram Vilas closed his eyes as if in meditation. 'I came into the house and had a cup of tea with a friend. I knew there was no need to rush back. Prithvi was in a meeting. So, I may have smoked at the window after he left. The cook came in to ask if I wanted lunch. I refused. She left, taking the tea tray with her. After picking up the file, I went out again. Yes, it must have taken me twenty to thirty minutes. Does that answer your questions?' Ram Vilas opened his eyes and stared at Ravi haughtily.

'Yes. We'll have a word with the cook.'

'Are you calling me a liar? Do you think I would harm the girl? I have spent my entire life in the service of people. I have built this family. Given up my dreams, my aspirations—for what? So that this boy can sit on the highest chair one day. But, rather than being thankful for all I have done, Prithvi now listens to professionals with MBAs to guide his political career. And, his mother-in-law wants to grab all she...I mean, did that woman accuse me of anything?' Ram Vilas's eyes were suddenly filled with suspicion.

'She had only good things to say about you, Swamiji. Why, is there something you would like to tell us?' Ravi asked, smiling.

'No...no, I am under a bit of stress, so I said all this. Malti Devi is all right. Look what you made me do. I lost my temper at these insinuations. But, trust me, I had no inkling about what was happening upstairs. I usually stay away from that part of the haveli. Mostly, the women are up there. It is best to stay away from young women in these times. One can never tell what goes on in their head. Anyone can stand up and accuse a man of anything now. And, Anumita is not completely well. They had to take her to the psychiatrist and all.'

'We aren't accusing you of anything, Swamiji; just collecting data,' Reeti tried to appease him again.

'So, you went back to the office. Then what happened?' Ravi continued.

'As I said, Prithvi got a call that Myra was missing. I came back here again with him. We reached home to find Anu *beti* behaving like a complete *paagal,* a madwoman. Then we looked around but found nothing. It was a futile attempt.' His phone vibrated on the glass table. He looked at the flashing number and disconnected the call.

'Who decided to keep the matter hidden from the police and the press?' asked Ravi.

'Dekho beta, this is how politics works. One has to understand that the opposition is like a *giddh. Giddh samjhte ho?* A vulture. They are just waiting to tear off your skin at the first opportunity they get. This scandal could be very bad for Prithvi's image. We just thought *ki ghar ki baat ghar mein reh jaye to achha hai na.* Best to keep things within the family.'

'So, it was you?'

'When Prithvi was about to call the police, I asked him to call Commissioner Bakshi. He suggested that Prithvi should call you people. He understands political games are perilous. If I am candid, I would say Prithvi is still very emotional by nature. You should look at his opponents. Those boys are goons. For them, all this kidnapping-*shidnapping* is child's play. They are so set on tarnishing Prithvi's name that they started a smear campaign a few months ago.' He leaned forward. 'Some woman came and claimed Prithvi had gotten her pregnant. I got him out of that mess. I mean, I proved that the woman was a liar and only wanted to extract money... You see, politics is like chess; you move only when you already know four moves that your opponent will be playing ahead.' Ram Vilas ran his fingers through his well-combed hair.

'Chess also lets you sacrifice your pawns,' Ravi said.

'Well, that is what they are there for, right?' Ram Vilas leaned back again with a chuckle.

'So, you are saying one of his political opponents may have taken Myra?'

'It's possible.' Ram Vilas relaxed and put his hands behind his head.

'But, to what end, Swamiji?'

'It could be showing clout, making an example of Prithvi for his quick rise...or just pushing him back. The old guard of any party does not like that a boy from a non-political family takes over what they consider their bastion, *baap dada ki jagir*. You have to be vigilant every second. But, Prithvi thinks I am paranoid. *Koi baat nahi,* never mind, soon he will realize his mistake.' Ram Vilas brushed away imaginary crumbs from his robe.

'Do you doubt any people within your party?'

'*Arrey bhai,* can you truly trust anyone in today's *kalyug*? I had thought there would be a ransom note, but whoever is doing this wants to dent his political career. How can a man who cannot keep his own house in order lead this country? That is going to be the spin they will put on this. You wait and see. Just find me some proof of this—and then it is war. *Beti,* can you get me a glass of water?' Ram Vilas said to Reeti, pointing to the copper jug at the far end of the room. Reeti stood up to do his bidding. He leaned towards Ravi as soon as she was out of earshot. 'One thing we men expect from women is to take care of the children. Even that they cannot do properly. They only want to work. I ask why. Why do they need to work? I want to put a stop to all this nonsense. Just you wait till Prithvi becomes...*arrey* thank you, Reeti *beta*. Young girls should work, *tabhi to desh badhega*.' Ram Vilas looked uncomfortable that he had let his mask slip.

'Did you never think of joining politics yourself?' Ravi asked him, not betraying any emotion.

'No, no, I am happier making kings than being one. It is easy to sit on the throne, but the decisions are made elsewhere.

As long as Prithvi listens to me, I will make sure he sits on the highest chair of this country one day.'

'And, if he doesn't?'

'Then he will reap the consequences of that. It won't affect me one way or the other. I have the ashram. I will go back to my *bhakti*.'

'You won't be able to devote much time to God when you are busy running the country…I mean, the state,' Reeti observed.

Ram Vilas laughed, his head thrown back, slapping his hands on the handles of his plush chair as if they had just shared a hilarious joke.

'Where is the blind one…um…Charu? She is a psychic, Prithvi says. Is she? Or is it all a big farce? You would be pulling her weight, I think. Does she really help in solving cases, or is she just a hook?' Ram Vilas asked with a grin.

'She helps where she can,' said Ravi. 'Ram Vilasji, do you smoke a bidi?'

'Yes, can you smell it here in this room? I will have to remember that. I try not to smoke inside the office. It has a special masala—a powder that I get from Sirsa. I try to quit, but it reminds me of the time when my life was simple. I never smoke it anywhere else. I don't tell anyone, but I don't want to hide anything from you,' he laughed.

'Did you often go and see Myra in her room?'

'No, not really. I don't get the time. Sometimes, I see Myra when we come home from work, and she is playing outside. I think I did go and see Myra with Prithvi at night a couple of days ago. Prithvi would remember the day more accurately. You could also check the security camera. *Sab naye ma baap ke chonchale*. We never had parents coming and saying good night to us, did we? And, we grew up perfectly fine,' he said with obvious disdain. His phone rang again. He smiled when he saw the number.

'Now look at this man, the friend I was talking about. He is a well-known industrialist, a Muslim. But, he is after me to do the puja for someone he knows. He is ready to fly me by chartered plane and all. He has been calling me continuously because I won't agree. Money makes this world go round, as they say. You can buy whatever you want, even politicians,' Ram Vilas chortled. He sat back, looking at Ravi and Reeti with a knowing smile.

Charu, who had been listening to the conversation in the back room, wondered at his remark about buying politicians.

Ram Vilas is not a man who would say anything in passing. What does he mean? Is he talking about Prithvi being bought, or is he saying something else? she thought.

'Who is this industrialist?' Charu heard Ravi ask.

'Bilal Siddiqui. He has lots of old money. I had tea with him that day; he came to drop me off. Initially, I thought, what's the point? Our ideas and views don't match. But, since I spoke to him yesterday, I think having him on my side would be a good idea. Appearances have to be maintained. You understand, right?' He spread his arms wide in a gesture of generosity.

'Can you tell us what you talked about?' Ravi asked.

'I met him when I was leaving the office to pick up the file Prithvi wanted. He gave me a lift. My own car followed behind his. We had a word in his car about the puja for his friend, and then I invited him inside for a cup of tea. It was a courtesy call,' Ram Vilas said. 'And now, if you'll excuse me, I have some work to do.' Ram Vilas stood up, suddenly eager to leave. Ravi stared at him, knowing he would get nothing from him for now. *He has an answer for everything*. Ravi stood up too. The old man accompanied Ravi and Reeti to the door.

'I hope you find Myra soon,' he said with his palms joined together. Ravi wondered if what he had seen was a challenge in his eyes.

16. Bilal Siddique

9 am, Thursday

Back in their den, Reeti played the recording from the camera at the gate from the day before. Silently, they watched as two cars turned inside from the gate. Arjun saluted. They could see a man smiling at him through the car window. He had a round face, a beard, and a Ray Ban over his eyes. Ram Vilas's car followed.

'The timestamp shows they entered Chauhan Haveli at 2:15 pm. Bilal left in twenty minutes, while Ram Vilas left at 2:40 pm,' Reeti read out from her notes for Charu's benefit.

'I can come with you to meet Bilal when you go,' Charu said to Ravi. 'It will ease your task and, since we want to keep this quiet, it will be better.'

'Okay, sure,' said Ravi.

'From what I understand, Ram Vilas has a tiff with Prithvi over his manifesto. That's what the peon told us. So, this is what we have. Prithvi asks Ram Vilas not to attend the meeting with the party president. Instead, he takes Viswajit along as his campaign manager. Ram Vilas leaves the office and bumps into Bilal Siddiqui, a rich donor to the party who also has a bone to pick with Prithvi. Bilal gives Ram Vilas a ride to Prithvi's house. Ram Vilas invites him to his office for tea. The cook has authenticated this bit. They leave one after the other. Ram Vilas returns to the haveli later with Prithvi when Malti Devi informs him that Myra is missing. Are we on the same page so far?' Charu summarized.

'Ram Vilas also hinted at "buying politicians" and the "power of money". He was reluctant to disclose what they spoke about in the car,' Ravi added.

'He and Bilal could be involved in the kidnapping together. Prithvi feels that Bilal holds a grudge against him.'

'He was angry and blamed Prithvi for his accident with a scary intensity. I was certainly taken aback when Prithvi told me he had affiliated himself to his political party. I don't really know if he ever resolved those feelings. According to this footage, they made no attempt to hide their meeting. I am sure Ram Vilas knew Prithvi would check the feed. Why didn't Prithvi mention it?' Ravi wondered.

'First things first. We should meet Bilal immediately. I have his office address,' said Charu. She made a quick call and fixed an appointment.

'Listen, both of you, go ahead. I will have a word with Gita. I am also waiting for the lab report on the nanny cam from Myra's room and the other faulty cameras. Manik will also come in today,' said Reeti.

It was still early in the day when Charu and Ravi reached Bilal's fancy office. The hidden lighting, the subtle flute music, and the elaborate flower arrangements were artfully placed. An enormous green Buddha, watching everyone through half-closed eyelids, was placed under a banyan tree that seemed to be growing in the middle of the building. It looked surreal. Even the koi fish looked at peace in the pond at Buddha's feet.

They heard a whirring sound. Ravi turned and saw Bilal on a high-end electronic wheelchair, making his way towards them. He was younger than Charu and had a confident look in his eyes that were focused on her. His broad smile was welcoming. The emaciated legs rested to one side as he operated his wheelchair with ease. Ravi remembered reading an article that expounded on how Bilal had worked tirelessly to make ramps mandatory in all public places. A philanthropist, Bilal was the son of a royal family that had given the country freedom fighters and politicians. According to Prithvi, Bilal opposed Prithvi's policies vehemently because he had caused the accident where Bilal had lost his ability to move his lower limbs.

Bilal had been present at Chauhan Haveli when Myra was kidnapped, making him a suspect, especially since he had a strong motive. Ram Vilas had referred to him as a friend, which was peculiar. Ravi watched the delight on Charu's face as Bilal came closer.

'Hello, my dear Chum...Charu. It is a joy to see you after so many years. You haven't changed a bit,' Bilal exclaimed happily, pulling her into a hug. Charu laughed, holding him.

'Always the charmer, Bilal, how are you?'

Bilal pulled at her hair in jest and let her swat at his fingers. Ravi watched the surprise on the receptionist's face as she saw her usually serious employer talk animatedly with the blind girl. Ravi cleared his throat wondering what more had Charu kept from him about Surat and her life there. She was obviously close to Bilal.

'Oh, sorry. This is Ravi Nair, my colleague. Bilal, my friend from Surat,' Charu introduced the two men. They shook hands.

'So, why are you here with your colleague, Charu? Am I under investigation for something? I don't remember murdering anyone in the last couple of months,' he sniggered.

'We just wanted to talk about...Prithvi.'

'Prithvi. Him again? Didn't you learn your lesson the first time, Charu, or is it back to Chumki?'

Ravi noticed the way Bilal assessed Charu's expression.

'I can hear the smile in your voice, but underneath that retort, I can also hear a warning,' Charu smiled.

'Just trying to look out for you, as you once did for me, dear friend,' he said.

'You don't need to worry about Charu, Mr Siddiqui. She knows how to take care of herself,' Ravi couldn't help saying.

'Hmm...a knight, are you? Well, we'll see. Now, Charu, I can't say I am not glad you came to see me but, truthfully, I was surprised to receive your call. I guess it's about the same thing?' Bilal turned his wheelchair and waited for Charu to place a hand on its handle. When he saw that she had, he moved forward to lead her at a comfortable pace.

Ravi followed behind them, observing the glass offices on either side of the passage they were walking through. He hurried to catch up with them, trying to take in the NGO Bilal ran.

'It was necessary and, though I wish it was a social call, it is about work, Bilal,' Charu said.

'Then I hope you have a warrant,' Bilal teased her.

'We just want to talk but, if you would like, we could get a warrant,' Ravi replied, thinking if Bilal did ask for it, how many hoops would he have to jump to get it.

'Oh...no, no, I was kidding. Come into my office, and we can talk in peace, unofficially, of course.' Bilal placed his thumb on the panel next to the door. They walked into the plush cabin, following Bilal's wheelchair.

'Do you know our history, Mr Nair?'

'Yes, she told us about her time in Surat,' Ravi replied.

'Did she now? Welcome to the inner circle. I thought I was the only man she trusted.' He took Charu's hand and put it gently at the back of an upholstered chair.

'Stop it, Bilal,' Charu snorted.

'I was her eyes in school once I was out of the hospital. We bonded over the fact that we had both been affected by that Prithvi.' Bilal invited Ravi to sit next to Charu. 'So, how can I help you?'

'Mr Siddiqui, we are sorry to barge in like this, but we need a little information regarding Mr Ram Vilas.'

'Why? What has he done that you are investigating him?'

'Sir, since at the moment our investigation is ongoing, we are not authorized to divulge the details. Would you be willing to share information with us voluntarily?'

'I have nothing to hide. Ask away,' Bilal agreed, cautiously.

'Charu called to ask you about your visit to Prithvi's house the day before yesterday. We wanted to know about the conversation you had with Ram Vilas, what you saw, how you happened to be there at that time and anything else you can tell us.'

'How do you know I was there?'

'Security cameras.'

'Ah, I didn't realize Prithvi was so paranoid. In the office, he thinks he is invincible.'

'Bilal, what were you doing at his house?' Charu emphasized.

'I was waiting for my car when I saw Ram Vilas stalk out of his office. He looked ready to kill someone. This was around 1:30 pm, I think. I had to catch a flight to Benares. He was livid about whatever fight he and Prithvi had recently had. Since that Viswajit has replaced him as Prithvi's campaign strategist, Ram Vilas has become persona non grata in Prithvi's meetings with the party president. Anyway, he was mumbling that Prithvi had let some opportunity pass. I asked him why he was so angry. I knew he was dying to talk, so I gave him a lift home.'

'Any special reason?'

'To find out what was going on behind closed doors. People usually say what is in their hearts when they are angry. I decided that my time would be better invested in finding out what was happening with Prithvi than having lunch.'

'Did you discuss anything in the car?'

'Um, the usual. My family, politics, his ashram—and how much he missed it—which, I know, was a blatant lie because, if that man likes anything, it is creating havoc. He is like a matchstick. Always ready to light a fire.'

'But, you didn't just drop him off; you went inside the house.'

'Yes, one—because he invited me for a cup of tea, and two—because Prithvi's wife had restored the haveli. I wanted to see it.'

'What did you see?' Charu asked with interest.

'No, I was only able to see the living room, actually. Ram Vilas wanted...um...to pick up a file he had to hand it over to Prithvi, which he did. We were there for about half an hour, and then we went our separate ways.'

'What did you talk about in the office?'

'This and that, just work stuff. Nothing specific.'

'Bilal, from what I understand, you and Prithvi follow different, rather completely opposite views on politics, but you seem to have spoken to Ram Vilas at length about it.'

'Yes, very much. The first rule of politics is: never burn your bridges with anyone. One never knows when one might need someone.'

'What does that mean?' Charu frowned. She wanted to ask him straight out if he had a hand in Myra's kidnapping. But, she knew she would have to let him lead the conversation to the point where he would admit it himself.'

'Why are you so interested in why I was at Prithvi's house the day before? Is there a problem?' Bilal enquired.

'Bilal, I'm really sorry, but we are not at liberty to say that for now,' replied Charu.

'Is this an official visit, or is it a favour? A missing warrant means you are fishing. But, for what? Charu, are you here at Prithvi's behest? I will never help the man who destroyed my life. I wish I could stand up and ask you to leave if that is the case but, as you know—and Ravi—you can see, I am forever stuck in this wheelchair all because of that rascal.'

'Bilal, it does have to do with Prithvi, but it is more important than his politics or yours. Please, lives can be saved,' Charu tried to coax him.

'Mr Nair, do you know Charu can convince a dying boy to come back and suffer through life because he is meant for bigger things?' Bilal laughed.

Charu picked up her white stick to leave.

'Sit down, Charu. I wasn't trying to ruffle your feathers. Prithvi and Ram Vilas have been at loggerheads with each other. Their coffers are drying out, and I wanted to see how much backing they have to contest this election. What I found was a mentor whose faith in his mentee has been shaken. Ram Vilas is not getting as much leverage as he has been used to until now. He was willing to trade.'

'Trade? Trade what?'

'His services for a favour.'

'What kind of favour?' asked Ravi.

'I will tell you my secret if you tell me yours.'

'What do you mean?' Charu was frustrated with Bilal's attempt to bargain.

'Why are you investigating him? For fraud, fund misappropriation? I checked you out, though—and you only take criminal cases. So, why are you here? Has something happened to Prithvi? But, how is that possible? He was in the office today but left early,' Bilal said, thoughtfully.

'For a person who doesn't like Prithvi, you are quite familiar with his schedule, Mr Siddiqui,' Ravi commented.

'Information is God. So, Charu, will you tell me the truth?'

'Will you use it against Prithvi or me?'

'Hmm, I can promise I won't...to the second option. To the first, I will answer once you tell me what it is about.' Bilal sounded firm.

Charu thought about what was at stake. Myra versus Prithvi. The choice was not that difficult for her. But, they were still working for Prithvi. He would have to be consulted.

'Can I call you or come and meet you once I have taken the go-ahead from my seniors?'

'Sure, sure, anytime...but remember, Charu, next time you will have to share information if you want information.'

'Of course.' Charu stood up and walked towards the door, feeling Bilal's eyes on her back. She knew him. He would keep twisting the information he had, until he had figured out the fastest way to win. Ravi, too, was thinking about Bilal. He had found out that Bilal was an astute man and dealt in the buying and selling of information.

'What do you think?' he asked a pensive Charu later. 'Is he really as clueless as he seems, or is he simply acting? Do you believe he doesn't know anything about the kidnapping?'

'Bilal hated Prithvi's guts in school. I know he doesn't look capable of carrying out a plan such as this, physically. But, appearances can be deceptive. Also, it would not be easy to carry a baby out without the guard knowing. But, he could have been party to the kidnapping. He has the money. And, his meeting with Ram Vilas is very unusual,' Charu said.

'Well, he has a strong motive.'

They were crossing the receptionist's desk. Charu stopped when she heard the receptionist finish her phone call. Changing direction, she went towards her.

'Hi. We just came from Mr Bilal's office. I am his school friend. I am planning a surprise for him with some friends. Please could you check if he has any meetings planned this Saturday?' Charu asked in a pleasant tone.

'I'm sorry, but I can't give you that information, ma'am,' the receptionist said, her voice full of pity.

'Oh, I was really hoping to give him a surprise reunion with old school friends. I am blind, and Bilal can't use his legs, so getting together is a problem. I just need to know if he is busy. But, I don't want you to get into trouble with your boss. No problem.'

'Please help my friend here; otherwise, she will drag me all over the town to find out his schedule. Or worse, she'll ask me to get it out of Bilal in a roundabout way. Please, help a man in need,' said Ravi with a pronounced drawl.

'Sir did look happy to see you.' The receptionist smiled back hesitantly. 'Yes, he is free on Saturday as of now.'

'Thank you so much. One more thing, since you have Bilal's schedule before you. He had to meet a friend of ours, the day before yesterday, in the morning. He had a meeting with him before he caught his flight to Benares. Can you check if the friend came?'

'Day before yesterday. . .no, there is nothing here. He came to the office, but he had no meeting in the morning. He also missed his flight but took the train to Benares.'

'Are you sure?' Ravi lost his relaxed pose.

'Yes, sir. He missed his flight, so we had to book a train ticket to Benares. He said it had to be a coupe. I was the one who booked it after much difficulty. He could have taken a later flight, but he insisted his luggage was now more than the permissible limit. He wanted to travel by train. Imagine booking a Tatkal ticket for a whole coupe. But, I guess he needs to be comfortable with the wheelchair.'

'What time did you book the ticket?'

'Around 3 pm.'

'Did he call you himself and ask you to book the ticket?'

'Yes, he was in the car.' Her voice was getting uncomfortable.

'And, he told you about the extra baggage?'

'The driver told me he had picked up an oversized bag from where they stopped. Bilal sir was handling it as if it was very fragile. He wouldn't let the driver touch it.'

'Did he say what was inside?'

'No, just that it was quite cumbersome for Sir to handle.'

'Do you know where they stopped?' Charu asked her.

'No, I didn't ask—but Sir's driver is standing outside, next to the Audi. He would know. Why are you asking me these questions? Who are you?' She sounded suspicious now.

'Thank you so much for your help. Please don't mention it to Bilal. We will include a train theme because he had to travel via a train, something he dislikes doing,' Charu offered with her warmest smile.

'Let me know if you want me to do some decorations,' she said.

'Yes, of course. Thanks. I will call you soon after confirming everyone's availability.' Charu hurried out with Ravi's hand upon her elbow. Waiting for the car to come around, Ravi asked, 'So, what do you make of this?'

'I thought there would be a simple explanation. I don't want to believe it of a friend, but Bilal is still extremely angry with Prithvi. He was in the haveli during the time Myra was kidnapped. The secretary says he carried a bag out of the building, that he was handling it gingerly. His name goes on the board.'

The next stop for Charu and Ravi was at the carpenter's workshop. They found him unlocking the shutter and introduced themselves as friends of Prithvi's.

'We came to ask a few questions about a trolley you brought from Prithviji's haveli. I am keen to have something similar made for myself,' Charu told the man looking at her quizzically.

'Ah yes, that's the one,' Ravi pointed it out to the carpenter.

'That is an excellent choice,' said the wiry young man. 'I restored this trolley for Anumitaji. It was left behind by the family that sold the haveli. She has an impressive eye. Only a true artist can spot a rough diamond. In fact, most of the pieces in her haveli were restored by me.' The demeanour of the carpenter changed as he spoke about his work.

'We are interested in this trolley. Can you make a similar one?' asked Charu.

'I can. And, if you want more shelves inside, that's possible too.'

'Does this have shelves inside for crockery?'

'It has a removable shelf, see?' The man opened the cupboard doors and turned it towards them. The empty space inside was enough to hold a small child.

'Hmm, it does have adequate space, honey. We thought it would be a good time to discuss how we could improve upon it,' Ravi said to the smiling man.

'Yes, sir. Their daughter's nanny, Gita, called me to pick it up. But, when I got there, she was already standing outside waiting for me. She saw me and, without helping me to load it on the rickshaw, went inside. I called after her to wait and give me a hand, but perhaps she didn't hear me. It is too heavy for one man to lift. I had to ask a passer-by to help.'

'What was the problem? How did you fix it? I hope I won't face problems later,' Charu sounded like a harried wife.

'No, madamji, not with my work. The panel on the side has swollen up. It happens if there's moisture in the air or if the trolley is left outside in the rain. Anyway, I will have to replace this panel, that's all.'

'Was there anything inside when you took it over from Gita?'

'No, madamji.'

Ravi clicked pictures of the trolley from all sides. Charu moved away with the carpenter to discuss other pieces for their fictitious house. A little later, Ravi told Charu that the space inside the trolley was adequate for a child to fit in, but it would be a very tight fit. Then he sent the pictures to Reeti for safekeeping.

On the way back, Ravi asked Charu, 'Do you want to talk about the dreams about the little girl and the man in the basement?'

'I just hope they are in no way connected to Prithvi's girls, Ravi. They are both younger than the girl I am seeing. Once we find Myra...I will warn Prithvi and Anumita before I leave.'

'Could it have anything to do with the others?'

'What do you mean?'

'Maybe Anumita...or even Malti Devi as a young girl. I'm just thinking aloud.'

'If this has already happened, it would mean the woman or girl has gone through a major traumatic experience. It's possible that it could lead to the individual living as detached and unencumbered as Malti Devi or as guarded and scattered as Anumita. Truthfully, one cannot really predict how someone will process or cope with childhood trauma. But, for now, let's keep our eyes only on Myra.'

'Hmm...' Ravi looked at Charu thoughtfully as the cab sped towards the hospital where Gita's brother had been admitted.

17. Reeti

9:15 am, Thursday

Back in the house, Reeti heard the door to the backroom open a few minutes after Charu and Ravi had left. Turning around, she saw Prithvi walk in.

'Where is Chumki?' he asked, looking around.

'Charu and Ravi have gone to the field to follow some leads.' Reeti watched him pick up Charu's stole and caress it. She found his attention to Charu bordering on obsessive.

'Hmm, Anu tells me we received a ransom call last night and that you recorded it. I want to listen to it.'

'Yes, of course.' Reeti turned to bring it.

'When will Chumki be back?' he demanded. Reeti noticed he did not bother with niceties when Charu was absent.

'I couldn't say, sir.' Reeti found the call recording and handed Prithvi a set of earphones. He listened to the small clip then removed the earphones in irritation.

'Thirty lakhs, is that all? All this for loose change? I want you to say yes to their demands when they call next. Just tell them to give Myra back. I will pay the money. I am going to make arrangements to take the cash out now. If you receive another call, just message me. I will go and drop off the money.'

Prithvi rushed out of the room. Reeti noticed he took Charu's stole with him. He was the kind of man she had learnt to be wary of, possessive and controlling. She hoped Ravi was aware of the dynamics of the relationship Charu had shared with him. Following a hunch, Reeti had copied Prithvi and Anumita's drives when they had swept the electronic devices in the house. She decided it would not be a waste of time to dive deep into Prithvi's folders.

Gita came in around lunchtime to hand her a tray. She asked when Charu and Ravi would be back. Reeti switched the recorder on and told her to sit with her as she had her lunch.

Gita threw a glance at the door, then sat down on the edge of the chair. 'Anu ma'am wanted me to tell you that Manik sir is here. You can tell me when you want to talk to him. Have you found out anything, Didi? Where is Myra? Is she all right? Do you think Prithvi sir will pay the amount the callers asked for yesterday?' She fidgeted. 'Thirty lakh is nothing for Prithvi sir, no? If he pays it, Myra can come back to us.'

Why is she asking about the ransom amount? Reeti wondered.

'Who are the people in your family, Gita?' she asked, diverting her.

'I have two younger brothers and a sister. They live in the village.'

'Oh, I thought you had some family here. Someone told me your brother lives here. I think it was...' Reeti pretended to think aloud.

'Ramu told you, didn't he? About my brother and the scene he created? Arjun Bhaiya told me he would...and that I should tell you about him myself,' Gita interrupted her.

'Why didn't you tell us earlier?'

'He is not a threat, Didi. Mavu is just misguided. He started drinking in the village. I brought him to Delhi the last time I went home. I found him a job at a taxi stand, but he found bad company again. He came here one day and fought with Arjun Bhaiya. Ramu beat him up because he broke some pots outside, but Anu ma'am helped us so much. She knows everything...even Prithvi sir does. She got him admitted to a hospital nearby. They allowed me to meet him every day. I was not trying to hide it; I just didn't think it was important.'

'Where is he now?'

'He is at the de-addiction centre. Anu ma'am got him admitted. You can ask her. He is locked up after all.'

'Gita, did you tell Malti Devi something you shouldn't have?'

Reeti saw Gita's eyes fill with tears. She began sniffling. 'I. . .I made a mistake. I know she doesn't like Anu ma'am. But, I was angry, and it just slipped out. I didn't mean to get her into trouble. Anu ma'am had taken us for a movie and, when we got back, Auntyji asked me where we had been wasting our time. Without thinking, I told her where we had been and that Manik sir had also accompanied us. Didi, she said such horrible things to Anu ma'am, I was shocked.'

'What were you angry about?'

'I don't even remember now. It was a few months ago.'

'From now on, don't keep anything to yourself, Gita, however small. Where is Manik? I should talk to him.'

'He is upstairs.'

Reeti's phone rang. It was the camera company. Charu and Ravi walked into the room while she was still talking to the company executive. They waited for her to finish the conversation. When done, she spun around on her chair. 'Good news. The spycam in the room wasn't functioning due to water damage. It's functional now.'

'Someone did that purposely,' Charu whispered.

'I agree. Only Gita or Anumita gave Myra her bath. Anyway, the camera's pictures should tell us what happened. I had someone pick up the cam from the company and take it to the IT lab to retrieve the images. But, it will take at least twenty-four hours. The teddy bear was an aesthetic inclusion, kept on the middle shelf of the changing table. I checked Myra's baby pictures. The toy was always there. The nanny cam was in the button eye. The most obvious place.'

'I spoke with the company that installed the cameras. They said that Anumita contacted them when the camera stopped recording. She asked them to change it immediately and check the original for defects later. She also said she would pay for the new camera if the insurance took time to come through. She wanted it done at the earliest.'

'I guess that takes her off the hook for tampering with the camera in Myra's room.' Charu slumped back into the couch.

'What about the other malfunctioning ones?' asked Ravi, studying the feed.

'They said it could be faulty wiring. The technicians will examine them when they come to install the new cameras.'

'I think I will ask our guys to check the wiring. This is a bit too convenient for my liking. Security cameras can't remain non-functional for three days.'

'That's what I said, to which they answered that the property has more than enough cameras to capture an intruder. Since I couldn't give them my details, I had to behave like a petulant house manager.' Reeti bemoaned her lack of freedom. Then she told them about her conversation with Gita.

'Yes, we found out Mavu was admitted to the hospital. Anumita paid the bill. The hospital, however, wouldn't tell us where he went after being discharged. I will have a word with Anumita and find out.' Charu closed her eyes, dreading dealing with Anumita and her baseless insecurities again. She knew she detested her, regardless of how politely she spoke.

'What happened with Bilal?' asked Reeti.

'Bilal was fishing for information from us, wanting to trade. Reeti, when Bilal walked out, was he carrying a bag with him?'

'In the security footage, we saw his driver carrying something.'

'He carried Bilal's office bag inside. We couldn't see what he was holding as he left. I could take another look.' Reeti played the clip where Bilal could be seen leaving the haveli through the front door. His wheelchair came into the field of view of the camera. The driver walked alongside, carrying something.

'We missed this,' Ravi uttered. 'If you look carefully, Bilal has the office bag on his lap while leaving the haveli. His driver is carrying another bag—obviously heavy. You can make out from his gait. Also, look at this.' Ravi paused the video and circled the edge of the black bag that was barely visible.

'What is the driver holding?' asked Charu.

'We have to go back to Bilal,' Ravi said, firmly. Charu nodded.

'Did he tell you what they spoke about in the car?'

'No, we didn't tell him why we were asking the questions. Later in the evening, I will try and meet Bilal's driver and Ram Vilas's.'

'Every time you mention Ram Vilas, I recall his striking *tilak*. My eyes get stuck on it whenever I come face to face with him. It is difficult to concentrate on anything with that thing shining like a beacon,' Reeti sniggered.

'What do you mean?' asked Charu.

'It's in the shape of a teardrop...like a vermillion flame.'

'What? Wait.' Charu rummaged around in her pocket for her notebook.

'What's the matter?' Ravi watched her frenzy as she flipped the pages.

'Does it look like this? Even sort of similar? I can't really draw.' Charu held up a sketch of the flame she had drawn the night before, after talking to Anumita.

Ravi looked at the irregular lines that Charu had drawn. She did this if she saw something in her trance, and no one was around to write it down. It was a rough sketch but quite close to the shape of the *tilak* on Ram Vilas's forehead, especially the dot in the centre. She had made the dot with her inked fingertip and drawn the flame around it.

'I keep seeing this whenever I am near Anumita, especially when she is agitated. It isn't there when she is composed.'

'It is close to what he puts on his forehead. Anumita does not like the control Ram Vilas has on Prithvi. It could be because of that. It probably shows her insecurity. Let's try to find out.' Ravi tightened his hand on Charu's shoulder. It was his way of saying, 'good work'.

Reeti removed her things from the desk to make space. 'Manik is here. I will bring him in for the interview. Gita mentioned the ransom amount. She was keen to know if Prithvi would pay it.'

'Did you ask her about the money Anumita refused to give her?'

'No, I thought we could ask Anumita,' she replied before going to get Manik.

Charu heard Manik's sonorous voice first and then encountered confusion and worry in his mind as he came closer to her. His thoughts were muddled, wondering how to behave, unsure about his place. She heard Ravi ask him to take a seat and explain what was going on and how they would proceed.

'Hello, I am Charu. How are you doing?'

'Fine, thanks. I am slightly worried about Sia. She is quieter than usual. Sorry, I couldn't make it yesterday, Ravi sir, but I was under the weather. I've had an upset stomach for the past couple of days.'

'No worries. I hope you are feeling better now.'

'Yes, yes, getting better.' He sounded nervous. Ravi watched as his eyes darted everywhere.

'Manik, there is no need to worry. We will simply ask a few questions. Answer them based on whatever you remember, all right?'

'Yes, sure.'

'Start with your name, and where you are from, how you came to Delhi. Basically, we need to know your background.'

'I am Manik Chauhan. I teach in a government school in Delhi. I am from Sirsa. My family is from there, I mean. I came to Delhi to look for a job after I finished my MA. It took me a year to find one. I live nearby and offer tuition to supplement my income. I am also a cricket coach at the local club.'

'So, how did you come to be here at Prithvi's haveli?'

'I am sure Prithvi must have told you. He is my first cousin. My father is a simple carpenter. Like my Chacha,

Prithvi's father, Prithvi has also done well by following in his footsteps—in politics. Watching me struggle to make ends meet, my father requested Chachaji to ask Prithvi to help me get a job. That was how I began working at the school.'

'When was this?'

'Around three years ago, when Anu Ji was still thinking of renovating this place.'

'Oh, so you were a part of that?' Reeti exclaimed.

'Not really. I lived close by, so I would bring Anu Ji here when she needed to oversee the renovations and then take her back.'

'And, Myra? You were there when she was born. You took Anumita to the hospital for her birth, Prithvi told me,' said Charu.

'Huh? Um, yes, she was alone at home, with no one to drive her, so I took her to the hospital. I am sure anyone in my place would have done the same.'

'Of course. I meant, since you've been part of Myra's life since her birth, you must be very close to her.'

'Myra is an angel, a gift. She was so tiny—I was always scared to pick her up. She fit into my hands like a gentle flower. I guess you could say I share a special bond with her. Myra is the most curious baby. She would...,' he sniffed, '...crawl over to us and want to sit in my lap. Sometimes she would fall asleep in my arms.' He remembered the little girl in tiny ponytails fondly.

'You care a lot for the girls,' Charu remarked.

'Can one stay immune to a child's warm, trusting heart?' Manik replied.

Charu turned her face away with a 'yes' on the tip of her tongue. She knew of people who did not think twice before breaking a child's trust. The result was always the same. A broken child.

'Have you found any change in Anumita recently, Manik?' Ravi changed the line of questioning, watching Charu's strained face.

'What do you mean? No, she hasn't changed. She was always quiet and reserved. She is worried about her daughter's safety. Not everyone is as strong as Prithvi, who can hide his feelings well and continue his life as if nothing has changed.'

'What do you think about Anumita?' asked Charu.

'Anu Ji is my *bhabhi*, my sister-in-law. I wish she were happier, but that is between Prithvi and her. Look, I don't interfere in their household affairs. I am a charity case. I am the one who supervises the decorations at the Diwali party but isn't invited to it. I have no hard feelings about that. I do my work, keep my head down, and hope I can make my dreams come true so that I can get out of here once and for all.'

'What about Malti Devi? Does she make her feelings for you fairly plain?'

'It is quite evident, I suppose. She feels I am feeding off Prithvi and does not like that I come from a poor background. She is right on both counts,' he shrugged.

Charu found Manik straightforward and practical. He spoke thoughtfully, weighing his words. His initial nervousness was no more palpable. But, she felt his thoughts flicker every time someone mentioned Prithvi.

'Have you found out anything at all? Who could have taken Myra? Prithvi asked me if I saw anything but, trust me, the door was open, and I didn't hear anything from Myra's room.'

'But, you went to the bathroom twice in the one hour you were there,' Ravi reminded Manik.

'Yes, well, I was suffering from an upset stomach. I agree someone could have slipped in, but the camera in Myra's room would have caught the person, right?'

Charu wondered how he knew about the nanny cam. The purpose of the device was to capture images without the knowledge of the staff. She found it strange that Manik and Gita both knew about it.

'Hmm...can you tell us about that day, Manik?'

'I came to the house around 1:40 pm and started my class with Sia in her room. Gita came and asked me if she should stay since Myra was sleeping. Since I had come at her lunchtime, I told her she could have her lunch in peace while I would keep an eye on Myra.' Manik went on to repeat the account everybody had already given them. 'Malti Devi called Prithvi and Anu Ji. I went down to the grounds to see if the guards had seen anyone or anything. We looked everywhere but found nothing. Since I was unwell, I left early. Prithvi didn't need me. I expected a call from the police in case they didn't find Myra, but I didn't expect Prithvi would call a friend of his from school instead.' Manik stared at Charu. She kept her eyes on him, not letting her uneasiness show on her face.

'You have been here since morning. I wonder where you were,' said Reeti.

'I just met Sia. She is fragile like her mother. And, Anu Ji is also devastated. So, I was talking to them, reassuring them as much as I could. I came over today because you called me, though I am still on antibiotics. It's been a whole day since Myra went missing. I have been worried.' He looked out of the window. 'It seems Prithvi is not around to do what is needed, as usual…I mean, since he is so caught up with work and all….'

Charu heard the sarcasm in his words.

Ravi looked at the man before him. 'Well, we may have more questions later. I came to know you used to play cricket at the district level.'

'In another life, it seems. My dream was to play for my country, but everyone cannot be lucky like Prithvi.'

'But, you could have asked Prithvi to help. Surely, he would have put in a word?' said Charu.

'Ma'am, do you think I came to Delhi to become a government school teacher? No, my cousin knew I wanted to play, but instead of using his clout to get me entry into a cricket academy, he got me this job. Now I teach little children to play cricket instead of playing myself. Dreams change.'

'What do you want to do now?'

'I have decided I will start my own cricket academy. I will find my way up.'

'It seems you blame Prithvi for not helping you rise. Is that true?'

'I...no, I don't blame him. I blame my luck that I was born to my father and not to Prithvi's. All my life, I have seen him receive whatever he desired on a platter, while I had to struggle even for the scraps off his table. I may sound ungrateful to you, but both of us know how we feel about each other. We stay out of the other's way for the most part. He did what his father asked by getting me not one but two jobs, and so did I, by accepting them,' Manik replied.

'Manik, I wish we had met under better circumstances. I would have asked you about the trellis you built from the wooden slates. I have to say you have a great aesthetic sense.' Ravi shook the young man's hand.

'You liked that? It was just some old wood. I got the kids and Anu Ji involved. We enjoyed the process. It feels wrong to smile at a time like this or even think about other things. Myra was, I mean, is the sweetest little girl.'

The landline started ringing. Everyone in the room stood listening to the sound for an instant. Ravi rushed to the phone attached to the recorder first. It flashed the same number the kidnappers had used the night before. Prithvi opened the door just as Ravi was about to call him. Anumita followed him inside. The sound echoed in the haveli as all expectant faces crowded around it.

18. Pradeep Driver

1:45 pm, Thursday

Ravi was the first to move. He motioned to Prithvi. 'Putting the call on the speaker, sir. Try and keep them on the line for a longer time. Keep your eyes on me. Everyone quiet, please.' He was relieved that the kidnappers had called for the ransom, which meant they were willing to negotiate.

'Hello,' Prithvi spoke into the receiver. His voice didn't sound hollow or troubled.

Charu closed her eyes, tuning herself into everyone present. She pushed Ravi and Reeti's razor-sharp focus aside to reach Prithvi's excitement. He wanted action. Anumita was terrified, and Manik determined. She wished she could ask Ravi to describe their body language.

'Do you have the money?' the voice asked. It was definitely a female voice today.

'Yes, I do. Tell me where to bring it. The locati…,' Prithvi replied. A child began to cry in the background. Everyone heard it and froze. Charu's heartbeat picked up pace. She closed her eyes and focused on the sound. Her hand sought out Ravi's and squeezed it. It was an acknowledgement that Myra was alive.

The caller paused. 'I will call again.' Then the phone was disconnected.

'Myra!' Anumita whispered. Charu felt the waves of fear and anguish in her. Ravi watched Anumita's face lose colour. She looked ready to faint.

'Damn. This time the conversation was even shorter,' Reeti said, frustrated.

'What...what happened? That was Myra crying, wasn't it?' Anumita turned towards the others for confirmation.

'Were we able to trace the call?' Prithvi wanted to know.

Ravi shook his head. He found Prithvi's missing concern for Myra disconcerting. 'No, the call needs to last longer for that.'

'It sounded like Myra had just woken up. She was restless but not in pain,' said Charu. 'Anumita...' She moved closer to the woman, with her arms outstretched.

'Don't touch me. Stay away from me, or I swear I will rip you apart.' Charu's hand was jerked away as Anumita uttered the bitter words.

'Anu, you crazy bitch! Chumki was trying to help!' Prithvi turned on his wife. Ravi noticed that Manik, standing silently at the back, took a step towards Prithvi.

'I don't want her help. But, you do, don't you?' Anumita yelled at her husband. She glared at Prithvi and rushed out.

'Sorry, Chumki, she can be crazy at times,' Prithvi apologized on behalf of his wife. As soon as he turned towards her, she could sense his anger against Anumita. It was so intense that it almost pushed her back. She collided with Ravi, who stood behind her. His hand on her shoulder steadied her. Anumita's animosity towards Charu was evident to everyone in the room, but Ravi knew Charu would continue to reach out to her regardless. Sometimes he wished she wasn't this sensitive to people's emotional needs.

'Prithvi, Anumita Ji is under stress. Charu Ji, I am sure it was the strain of the past couple of days along with the call just now. Hearing Myra's voice probably caused her to overreact,' Manik tried to diffuse the situation.

'Yes, I think so too. Thanks, Manik, I understand,' Charu replied, smiling thankfully at him.

'Why are you still here? I thought you were planning to go back to Sirsa. Isn't your father unwell?' Prithvi asked Manik.

Ravi watched the cousins look at each other directly for the first time since they had met. Their body language was clearly confrontational.

'Manik, you will not leave the city unless we give you the go-ahead. Sir, no one can leave for any reason,' Ravi interrupted Prithvi's attempt at stoking up an argument.

'Are you saying you suspect me?' Manik asked.

'As of now, everyone is a suspect.'

'But, why? I was there the whole time, and I am the last person who would think of harming Myra. She is...'

'Yes, do complete that sentence, Manik. I want to hear the end of that line,' Prithvi jeered at him. Charu wondered why Prithvi was baiting his cousin.

'There is no need to be rude. I am not here of my free will, Prithvi Bhai. I know you have no more use for me, so you would prefer that I leave forever. Myra is the sweetest kid; that is all I wanted to say. Ravi sir, if it's all right, I will wait outside, so my brother doesn't have to look at me anymore. Please, let me know when I can leave.' Manik left the room.

'Bloody bloodsucker. That idiot thinks I can't see how he wishes it was him instead of me.' Prithvi began to pace the room.

'What do you mean?' Charu turned towards him.

'He has always competed with me, Chumki. He wanted whatever I had. But, eventually, he had to come crawling back to me to ask for help. That hurt his ego. He feels I am always trying to pull him down. I have helped him—always—and this is the thanks I get. He is jealous of me. I sometimes wonder why I keep him around, but everyone has their use, I suppose.'

What did he use me for in school? And, he is still using me. 'You said Manik wants whatever you have. Do you think he could have kidnapped Myra for money?'

'What! Oh, no-no. Manik is engaged to be married to the daughter of a rich landlord from our village. Swamiji fixed the match. He will become so rich after marriage, he won't need to stay with us in Delhi. The bride's family has a lot of land in the village. He will be looking after that. That has got into his head. He can't wait to show off his wealth.'

'Why did Ram Vilas Ji fix his marriage?' Charu was perturbed at the manner in which Ram Vilas was pulling this family's strings.

'I asked him to find a wealthy family. You see, some six months ago, Manik came to me with a proposal. He wanted to start his own cricket academy. Now, if that is not a silly pipe dream, I don't know what is. He has played some cricket, but he is not a businessman. One needs to have more than love for the game to run a business. I told him the truth, and he was offended. Really offended. Lost his mind.

He blamed me for not letting him become a cricketer, for not allowing him to achieve the greatness he was destined for. Actually, he doesn't have enough talent to become a world-class player. That day I realized he was an ungrateful lout. But, family is family, so I asked Swamiji to find a rich family to marry him off. Let him waste his bride's family's money and start whatever he wants. Why should I bet on a losing horse?'

'He doesn't come across as an angry sort of man to me,' Reeti said.

'Exactly. Manik is quite the chameleon. He pulled my collar. Can you imagine, Chumki? Anumita had to hold him off. He was ready to punch me.'

'Was anyone else there at the time?' asked Ravi. He could not picture the docile looking Manik assaulting Prithvi physically.

'Gita saw, I think. Anyway, I just hope this woman calls and tells me where to take the money. I have got it in that bag. You can keep it here. I just want Myra back. Find my daughter, Chumki.' Prithvi walked out of the room.

Left to themselves, Ravi, Reeti, and Charu tried to process what they had learnt about Manik and Prithvi.

'Let me go and have a word with Anumita if she is willing to talk,' said Charu, walking towards the door. 'Let's do a round-up after that.'

There was so much to think about. Charu wanted some time alone. She decided to sit in Myra's room after she had spoken to Sia and her mother. She felt herself getting sucked into Prithvi's life. Anumita's revulsion grated on her nerves, even though she was trying her hardest to give her the benefit of the doubt. Charu felt like her mind had split into two. One half wanted to help Prithvi find his daughter and rebuild his shaky marriage. The other half rejoiced in his attention and was immediately repentant when she felt Ravi's eyes on her. She walked up the steps to look for Anumita.

Back in the room, Reeti waited for the door to close behind Charu and then whispered to Ravi, 'You need to see this.' She turned her laptop towards him. 'I know we should have sought permission, but I don't know why I did this. Call it a whim, or maybe Charu is rubbing off on me. The skeletons in this family, I tell you. I found these in a folder on Prithvi's laptop.'

Ravi scrolled through Charu's pictures. There were several and had been clicked at different times ever since she was in college. They were obviously taken by a long zoom lens, without her knowledge. Ravi was incensed to know that Prithvi had been stalking Charu.

'What does this man want?' he murmured. His eyes narrowed, and he exhaled sharply, telling himself to calm down. Every atom in his body wanted to storm out of the room and shake Prithvi for having Charu's pictures in his possession.

'You realize what this could mean, right? We could be on a wild goose chase if Prithvi is directly involved,' Reeti muttered. 'And, this is not all. Once I found the pictures, I went slightly overboard on his history, bookmarks, etcetera. The day Myra was kidnapped, he cleaned out his internet browser history and emails. I retrieved his searches, and now I am working on the deleted emails.'

'Reeti, take a printout of all of these. I don't want any wriggle-room for him when we hit him with this. This is crazy.'

Ravi stepped out to look for Charu, wondering how she would react to what they had found. His mind kept circling back to Prithvi's intentions regarding Charu and the past they shared.

As he neared the main door, he heard Manik ranting at someone agitatedly on the phone. Ravi stopped short, eavesdropping.

'I can't wait to get back. This has become unbearable now. He thinks I want his life. He can't be bothered to take care of his children—and talks about family! This whole drama of being a caring parent is for the benefit of his lady-friend. No, don't worry. I will see you soon. Yes, I just need to stay for a couple of days, then we can begin our lives.' He spotted Ravi and smiled apologetically. 'I am sorry, Ravi sir, but Prithvi and I just don't gel. He can't help lording his position over me, and I can't seem to stop reacting.'

'Who were you talking to?'

'My fiancée.'

'Oh.'

'After marriage, I will bring her to Delhi, or maybe I will be better off in my own village. We'll see. How long do you want me to stay here?'

'For another couple of days. Are you in a hurry?'

'Hurry? No, but after something like this, I would like to be with my family. My father is unwell,' Manik looked forlorn.

'I understand that. I will let you know soon.'

Manik nodded and looked towards the stairs. When Ravi remained where he was, he turned and went out. Then Ravi heard him driving away on his bike. He wondered about that look. Once or twice he had wondered if something was brewing between Anumita and Manik, but it looked like that angle would have to be closed. Manik seemed quite happy with his fiancée. In fact, he was in a hurry to be married.

Ravi walked out into the crisp air, looking at the late afternoon sun. It was a painted circle in the overcast sky. It had been two days since Myra had gone missing. He heard the tapping of Charu's white stick as she, too, stepped out. 'I thought you were going to have a word with Anumita?'

'She is taking a bath. I thought I'd take a breather. I didn't know you were outside.'

'Walk with me.' Ravi took her hand and placed it in the crook of his elbow.

They walked the perimeter of the boundary wall slowly, comfortable in their silence. Occupied by their own thoughts, both pondered how one could carry a child out of the haveli unnoticed.

They were still trying to figure it out when they heard Arjun scolding someone inside his cabin. They walked towards the two men.

'Look, tell me where you took Prithvi sir's car,' Arjun's voice was stern.

'But, Arjun *Bhaiya,* I did not take it out. Have I ever lied to you?' It was Rambir, Prithvi's driver.

'You are Prithvi sahib's official driver. His car goes to the office and comes back right here. Prithvi sir is very strict that he does not use this car for any other purpose. So, why are the readings not matching?'

'But...I am telling you, sir did not go anywhere else.'

'What's the matter, Arjun?' Ravi intervened.

'*Arrey,* Ravi sir? Namaste, Charu madam. This is Prithvi sahib's driver. He takes sahib to the office and back. I sign the travel slips, so he gets paid by the office. Prithvi sahib has asked me to keep a check. This time the reading is more than what it is normally. I am asking him where he took the car, but he refuses to tell me.' Arjun glared at the person in question.

Ravi had spoken to Rambir, Prithvi's driver, during the preliminary interview. The man looked aghast at the accusation Arjun had levelled at him. He joined his palms together, pleading his case. 'Sir, madam, I didn't take the car anywhere. You can check the slips. The car went from here to the office and back. The day before, sir took it out for some work himself. Sometimes he does that, but otherwise, it didn't go anywhere.'

'Where did he go?' Ravi asked.

'I don't know. Sir took the keys from me and asked me to wait for him at the office.'

'What time did he leave?' Charu stepped towards Rambir. His thoughts were scattered. He was frustrated that he was being doubted even after so many years of service.

'Around 1:45 pm, soon after Swamiji left.'

'How can you be sure?'

'Madam, all the drivers were standing there together. First, Swamiji's driver and Bilal sir's driver left, and then Prithvi sir came out asking about Swamiji. I told him they had left together. He asked me when they had left, for which place, and he looked furious when I told him. He asked me for the car keys, almost snatched them from my hand, and drove away in a hurry.'

'Rambir, when did Prithvi sir return?' Charu asked him, gently.

'He came back after more than an hour and went straight into the office building, just like Swamiji. Swamiji had returned before him. His face was thunderous. I know because I was waiting outside, thinking I was surely going to lose my job. Sir came out again, soon after, to hurry to the house. It was only when we reached there that I realized why, madam.'

'Do you know where he had gone?'

'No, madam, I wouldn't know that. Usually, if he goes to...' He looked at Arjun and then at his feet.

'You can tell her. Charu madam can be trusted,' said Arjun.

'Madam, when he goes to the other house, he calls me and takes me along even in the middle of the night. I am the one who drops him, parks the car outside, so Anumita madam does not hear the gate opening. But, I don't know why he didn't want to take me along this time,' he said.

'Give us this slip. And, Arjun, is there a caretaker for the other house?' asked Ravi.

'Ji, sir, I have his number here.' Arjun located the number on his phone and showed it to Ravi.

'You don't need to discuss this any further. I am sure it is nothing. Is that understood?'

'Yes, sir,' they said simultaneously.

'Where did Prithvi go, and why did he hide it?' Charu asked as they turned around the corner.

'It seems Prithvi has been keeping a lot to himself, Charu.'

Absorbed in their own thoughts, Charu and Ravi barely spoke to each other on their way to meet Ram Vilas's driver. Ravi texted Reeti the number of the caretaker along with some instructions. When the car finally stopped, Ravi asked around and found the slum where the driver, Pradeep, lived. The driver—a man with stooped shoulders and a weary manner—came out wearing a vest and a lungi. Recognizing Charu and Ravi, he invited them inside.

'Sahib...madam, you should have called me instead,' he said, flustered.

Charu smiled to ease his concern. 'We just wanted to have a word with you, Pradeep Ji. I hope we aren't disturbing you?' she asked.

'Is your duty over for today?' Ravi looked around the shanty, bereft of any idols. There wasn't even a single picture of any deity in sight.

'Yes, sahib.'

'Ram Vilas Ji lives close by, doesn't he?' asked Charu.

'Yes, madam. This is my daughter. *Namaste karo*. She is studying at a school nearby. Go make some tea.'

'Thank you. You didn't send your daughter to the ashram? I heard Ram Vilas Ji has a separate hostel for girls where they live for free.'

'Um...no, madam. I want her to grow up in front of my eyes,' he said, looking away. His distaste at the prospect of sending her to the ashram was evident.

'How long have you worked for him?' asked Ravi.

'It has been more than five years.'

'I know you told my colleague something, and so, instead of calling you to the station or talking to you at the haveli, we came to you. Look, Pradeep…' Ravi leaned forward and decided to be honest. In his experience, most people wanted to do the right thing if they could. 'You know Myra has been kidnapped.'

'Yes, we all were sad to hear it. But, sahib, I don't know anything about it. We are common folk, but our children mean everything to us. Prithvi sir and Swamiji's disregard for us is one thing, but doing something like this is unthinkable. Still, I am not comfortable around people like them. My mother used to say, someone who cannot be loyal to their family can never be loyal to anyone else. I have seen and heard too many things to trust them.'

'What do you mean?' Charu prompted him. Ravi took the cup from the offered tray and wrapped Charu's fingers around it. Charu heard the daughter's thoughts—*oh, he loves her*—before she hurried away. Pradeep and Ravi remained unaware of the girl's speculations. Charu struggled to pay attention to what the driver was saying.

'All that is the past, why rake it up? You have come here to ask what Swamiji and Prithvi sir were talking about, isn't it?'

Ravi nodded, sipping his milky tea.

'A few weeks ago, in the evening, when I went into Ram Vilas Ji's office to carry his bags to the car, I heard loud voices. He and Prithvi sir were arguing about Prithvi sir's ratings and changes in the manifesto. Then they came down, and Ram Vilas Ji urged a surly Prithvi sir to travel home with him. They spoke about Bilal Ji's growing clout in the party in the car, and some tender-related argument followed.

Anyway, Ram Vilas Ji kept hammering that point into him. Finally, fed up with his constant tongue-lashing, Prithvi sir asked him to offer a solution rather than add to the problem. It was then that Ram Vilas Ji suggested that they should play to people's sympathy to get him elected. Prithvi sir asked him what he meant. Ram Vilas Ji explained that the people of our country get swayed by a sob story. So, a tragedy in the family, such as a fatal accident with a family member, would help people overlook any perceived faults.

Madamji, Ravi sahib, I know Ram Vilas Ji has his faults, but this was just too much for me. I decided that day that I would eat one *chapati* less if I had to but find another job.'

'You are a righteous man, Pradeep Ji. Tell me, how did Prithvi react to what Ram Vilas Ji said?' Charu asked.

'Well, initially, he was agitated and upset, but slowly as Ram Vilas Ji explained the necessity, he grew silent. Ram Vilas Ji told sir that it would only be a pretence—to win the election. If someone did get hurt, would they not reap the benefits of Prithvi sir's position? *Bataiye*, what kind of logic is that? I may not be highly educated, but I would kill anyone who even suggested I harm my family. When I came to know Myra Baby had been kidnapped, I couldn't get the conversation out of my head.'

'You did the right thing, Pradeep Ji,' Charu said. 'You followed Bilal's car back to the haveli in the afternoon that day, didn't you?'

'Yes, madam. I was shocked to see Ram Vilas Ji sit in Bilal sir's car. According to the driver, they were very chatty. I don't know what Ram Vilas Ji was looking to do, inviting him into the haveli. After all, we all work for Prithvi sir. We have to be faithful to the person who pays us our salaries.'

'You are employed by Prithvi?'

'Yes, madam.'

'Just another question. Did Bilal leave the haveli with something—I mean, like a bag or a case?'

'Yes. It was a long bag, the kind you carry on your shoulder, rounded on the sides.'

'A duffle bag, the kind with a zipper on top?'

'Ji, ji, it was made of leather. Bilal sir's driver was carrying it when he came out. It was too heavy for him. Bilal sir constantly told him to be careful, to put it on the backseat next to him, though he barely had enough space. I held the door open while his driver folded the wheelchair, so I saw how careful he was with the bag. He checked it again and again.'

'What do you think was in it?'

'Money, what else? I have seen things like this all too often.'

Ravi wondered if Bilal could possibly have pulled off a kidnapping using the bag. It was improbable, but not impossible. Then another thought occurred to him.

'Pradeep, you drove Ram Vilas Ji and Malti Devi to the ashram in Sirsa that evening, right?'

'Yes, sir, but we went to the original ashram in Hisar first—on our way to Sirsa for the puja. It was closed for some time a long time ago. The Sirsa ashram was started when Ram Vilas Ji shifted there. The Hisar ashram is smaller, and it is also Malti Devi's *peehar*, her maternal home.'

'And, you took the bags she carried, filled with clothes, into the ashram to be distributed?' asked Ravi, pleased with Pradeep's honesty so far. Though he could not confirm the content of the bags, their presence meant Myra could have been carried out by either Bilal or Malti Devi.

'No, the caretaker of the ashram took the bags from the car. Arjun, the guard, put them in the car boot at the haveli.'

'You didn't touch them at all?'

'The bags were big, heavy. Since Malti Devi carries the bags every time she visits the place, I didn't think much about them. And, after driving for almost three hours, I was glad I didn't have to heft them up the stairs.'

'What happened when you reached the Sirsa ashram?' Charu probed further.

'I parked the car, and Ram Vilas Ji and Malti Devi went in. They met the caretaker of the ashram. I waited outside with Vakil sahib's driver. When they came out, we started back.'

'Who is this Vakil sahib, a lawyer?'

'Oh yes, he is the local man, a big devotee of Ram Vilas Ji. He is like a supervisor of the ashram in Sirsa.'

'Pradeep Ji, approximately how much time did they spend inside?'

'A few hours, maybe two or three.'

'Thank you, Pradeep Ji. You have been very helpful.' Charu stood up to take leave.

'Don't discuss this with anyone. This is my number. If you remember anything else, call me immediately.' Ravi stood up too. At the door, he asked, 'Pradeep, did you, by chance, see Prithvi while you were waiting at the haveli with Mr Bilal's driver?'

'No, sir, I didn't. We usually park our cars and sit inside the guard room.'

Ravi nodded, patted his shoulder, and made his exit. They then drove to the residence of Bilal's driver.

19. Sia

6 pm, Thursday

Late in the evening, when Charu and Ravi returned to Chauhan Haveli, Charu felt as though someone had stolen her breath. Her head was spinning. Everyone seemed to have a reason to kidnap Myra. Usually, she could rely on her instincts to guide her around the suspects. But, with Prithvi and Bilal on the list, her emotions were interfering with her ability to read them. She kept second-guessing herself, at odds with how she usually functioned.

'I need calm, space, distance. I will be in Myra's room,' she told Ravi and turned towards the steps. She walked up the stairs, aware that Ravi was watching her reach the landing safely.

Charu knew all the rooms arranged on either side of the wide corridor on the first floor. First, Myra's and Anumita's opposite each other, closest to the stairs. Prithvi's and Sia's bedrooms next. And, at the far end, were Malti Devi's room and a guest bedroom.

She heard Sia's voice through the door. *I haven't spoken to Sia yet,* she thought. She knocked on Sia's door, feeling guilty at the delay.

'Come in,' Sia called out.

Charu turned the doorknob. Ravi had described how Sia looked, so she had an image of her in her head. She smelt coconut oil in the room and sensed confusion and sadness. 'Hello, Sia. Is it all right if we talk for a little while?'

'Yes, sure,' came her soft answer.

'Didi, come and sit.' Gita took her hand to walk her to the sofa. Her hand was warm, and her thoughts were focused on

Sia. She seemed worried about how well Sia would manage to answer Charu's questions.

'Gita, do you always stay here when the class is going on?' asked Charu.

'Yes, Anu madam instructed me to stay here with Sia ever since Manik Bhaiya started teaching,' she said.

'But, not on the day of the kidnapping?'

'No, Didi. I told you, *na*, I went to have lunch. You see, Manik Bhaiya comes in the afternoon. There is no fixed time. So, some days he comes when I am having lunch, and some days he arrives after I've finished. That day he came early, and I hadn't had lunch, so he asked me to go. Didi, Manik Bhaiya keeps Anu madam updated on the girls' progress—and even spends time with all of them. He plays with them when he does not need to. Manik Bhaiya teaches them things, not like Prithvi sir...I mean, he is not someone who would do this kind of thing,' Gita said with a heavy voice.

'Why do you say—not like Prithvi sir?'

'She means Papa has no time for us. He is busy doing his work and barely makes it home before we sleep. Manik Chachu plays with Myra and me. He comes to my school to attend the functions,' Sia said.

'Have you found out anything, Didi?'

'Not yet, Gita.'

'Sia, talk to Charu Aunty, all right? I am just going to get your soup,' said Gita. 'I will be back in a minute.' The door closed behind her. In the silence that filled the room, Charu felt the little girl watching her.

'Sia, do you remember me?' asked Charu, thinking what a silly question it was.

'Of course, I do. I am not a baby,' Sia said with pride.

'And, do you know my name?'

'Yes, your name is Charu. You are here to look for Myra. Gita Didi told me, and Mummy told Papa she doesn't like you,' she said, quietly.

'Hmm...she is worried about Myra. Anyway, are you all right? Can you sit here beside me?' Charu patted the cushion next to her. She heard Sia take small steps towards her. 'Sia, don't be scared of me. I just want to try and find Myra at the earliest but, to do that, I need you to tell me what you remember about that day.' She held Sia's hand between her warm palms.

'I am not scared, and I knew you or the others would ask me questions. Mummy explained. I had hoped Ravi Uncle would be the one to ask, though.'

Charu smiled. 'Why?'

'He is nice.'

'Ah, I have to agree he is nice.' An unexpected laugh escaped Charu at this compliment to Ravi. She decided she would try to figure out the reason for this happiness at a later time.

'You like him too?' Sia asked.

'Yes, he is my partner. We work together. Would you rather speak to him?'

'No, it's all right. I know what I remember.' Sia repeated the story the others had already told them. '...We looked at the crib, and Myra really wasn't in it. Only her favourite doll was still there...' Sia stopped. 'I thought...she wouldn't be able to sleep without it. Why didn't she take it with her?'

Charu remembered the doll Sia was talking about. Anumita had grabbed it from Myra's room the night before, before the first ransom call.

'Manik Chachu asked Gita Didi to wake up Nani. My grandmother sleeps very soundly, you see. Then he checked the room and the bathroom quickly. Nani opened her door and scolded us. She scares me, just like Papa sometimes does. Then Chachu went to look for Myra around the house. When Papa came, Chachu asked him if Papa wanted him to stay, but Papa said he could go, so he went away.'

'He didn't come to meet you yesterday, did he?'

'No, but Mummy spoke to him. She was crying at first, then she stopped. He always makes her tears go away. He called to check on me later.'

'That was nice of him. Did he come to meet you today?'

'Mummy asked him to come.'

'Does Mummy sit with you during the class or when Manik Chachu comes to teach?'

'No. Gita Didi sits with me. Sometimes, Mummy comes home early and says hello. Sometimes, she watches us play from her bedroom window.'

'Do you like Manik Chachu?'

'Yes, he is very kind. I think he was not feeling well that day. He was all sweaty, and had to use the washroom twice. He said it was an upset stomach.'

'Did he ask you to keep any secrets?'

'No. Why would he do that? Mummy has told me anyone who asks me to keep secrets should never be trusted and that I should tell her immediately if anyone does that.'

'Yes, you should hide nothing from your mum. Your mummy is very sensible. You must miss Myra a lot, don't you, Sia? Do you wish she would come back?'

'Yes. I have been praying every night—that this is all a bad dream. Mummy says this sometimes. I feel like that now,' Sia whispered.

Charu frowned, wishing Anumita would not treat her young daughter as some kind of sounding board. Did she realize the type of damage she was causing to this child?

'Sia, if you saw anything or found something strange, you must tell Ravi Uncle or me. It could help bring your sister back,' Charu explained slowly. She pulled Sia closer and felt the little girl's head against her chest. A feeling like nothing she had experienced before unfurled in her heart. She sat with Sia silently, feeling her loneliness. The door opened, and Gita walked in. Charu could smell the warm vegetable broth. 'Sia, have your soup now. We will talk later. You are a very brave girl.' She kissed Sia on her head and stood up to leave. On her way out, she entered Myra's room, still thinking of Sia. She heard a sniffle, then the rustling of clothes.

'Anumita?'

'Yes, Charu. I am sorry I snapped at you earlier. I don't know what comes over me at times. My daughter...it is so difficult to do this. I shouldn't have said those things to you.'

Charu could utter platitudes to appease Anumita's guilt. They were on the tip of her tongue, but she swallowed them. Instead, she said, 'Yes, you shouldn't have. But, for the moment, let us focus on what is more important. We may be able to make the exchange with the kidnappers. Since they have called twice, it means they are after money. Hence, they're willing to return her. Hold on to that.'

'Yes, I should stop being such an embarrassment and help instead. How do people survive this feeling? You meet so many... How do they manage to live with this uncertainty?'

Charu walked towards her and sat down next to her, 'One day at a time, I guess.' She found Anumita's agony overwhelming, as though she would drown under the strong current. She relaxed her muscles and allowed herself to feel Anumita's feelings more fully. Some of the pain was directed towards Myra, but most of it seemed chronic. It was as though Anumita was used to living with it. Once again, she saw a flash of the orange flame—the *tilak* on the Swami's forehead.

'Anumita,' she said, hesitantly, 'Are you scared of Ram Vilas for some reason?'

'What! Why would you ask that?' Anumita turned away from her instantly.

'Sorry. It's just that...'

'No, I am not scared of him,' the woman said in a determined voice, 'Is that clear enough?'

'Yes, sorry.' Charu tried to do immediate damage control. 'You said you hired Gita yourself; your mother didn't. Why was that distinction important?'

Anumita relaxed at the sudden change of subject. 'Gita has been with me since Sia was born. I hired her way before my mother decided to come and stay with us. She wanted me to change Sia's nanny. She said it had been too long, and Gita was getting too full of herself. But, if I trust anyone after myself to take care of my children, it is Gita. She has been my support, and she loves the girls.'

'What about the incident with her brother who came here drunk?'

'Mavu? Yes, he came here and made quite a scene. He is a drunkard and a bully. That day when Ramu beat him up, I got him admitted to the nearest hospital. Gita was so sorry. I felt bad for her. So, I...we paid for his treatment. Once his injuries were taken care of, she wanted him to be admitted to the de-addiction centre.'

'And, did you do that too?'

'I knew how attached Gita was to her family, so I did. But, then she started asking for money every couple of months. She said she wanted to help him set up some business, a shop or something once he was cured. Then, when she started asking for an advance now and then, I refused. I told her she couldn't hold us to ransom like that. I told her I'd start looking for another nanny,' Anumita explained. 'But, why are you asking about Mavu? Do you think he...? No, no, Gita is indebted to me. She wouldn't dare to even think of something like this.'

Charu could make out Anumita's confidence was shaken. 'Why don't you tell me the name of the centre? I will find out and let you know,' she said.

'I don't remember the name, but I can look it up and tell you. It was several months ago.'

'Yes, do that. Another thing, your mother took old clothes to the ashram to donate. Did you help her pack them?'

'No. Since Myra had just gone missing, I was not in any state to hear her taunts about what a bad mother I was. When she said she was going, I was glad that I wouldn't have to deal with all the sanctimonious crap she spews all the time. I didn't bother to ask to help her.'

'Is it normal for her to rush to the Kul Devi mandir if such a crisis falls upon your family?'

'Frankly, I was surprised. She barely has any love to spare for the girls and me. All this religious pandering is for Prithvi's benefit.'

'You aren't all that religious, are you? But, Reeti tells me you were at one time. She saw some pictures of the time when you were newly married and when Sia was born. Was that also for the sake of Prithvi's public image?'

'No, I. . .one can lose their faith with time and. . .circumstances.' Anumita seemed quite distressed. 'And sometimes, you just need to take life into your own hands.'

Her stern voice left Charu puzzled. She tried to read Anumita's emotions but failed. 'What do you mean? What circumstances?'

'Never mind.' She stood up. 'Let me get that address of that de-addiction centre for you.'

Charu sat silently thinking about all the bits and pieces of information in her head. She felt drained and sleepy, now that the room was quiet and empty. Charu wondered if she had time to take a nap or at least close her eyes for a minute. As she did so, her hand happened to touch the cloth doll lying on the bed. Immediately, she could see Myra.

The child lay on the bed, nibbling at something. Anumita was playing peek-a-boo, smiling from behind the doll. Gita sat next to Myra as the sunlight filtered in through the billowing curtains.

In an instant, it was night. Sia looked down at her sleeping sister. She snatched the doll from her arms and ran away when the toddler woke up and started crying. She watched from the door as Gita woke up to Myra's cries, and her parents, whose argument had been escalating, rushed into her sister's room and tried to calm her down.

The scene changed again.

A soft lullaby came from someone next to Myra. A song emerged from a woman's lips painted a deep pink. She lay next to the child, coaxing her to sleep. Myra's eyes were drooping, her mind recalling what she had seen that day. A massive orange statue with long, strapping, muscular legs. A kind of cave stood between the feet with marigold garlands waving in the breeze.

A faded blue, large rectangular board appeared at a busy marketplace. It said 'WELCOME' *in red. A red and yellow building shone next to the sign.*

Charu tried hard to read the letters beneath. If she could only read the name of the place. But, she could only make out the first letter—G, and the last—R. She tried hard to read the word, but it was a grey haze.

'Here is the address. Sorry, were you asleep?' Anumita came in, jerking Charu out of her trance. She stopped when she realized her folly. 'God, I'm so sorry! I didn't mean to disturb... Did you see something? Where is she? Did you see the room or anything at all?' She clutched at Charu's hands.

'No, nothing. I'm sorry, I just fell asleep for a minute.' Charu stood up, careful not to give anything away. She was exhausted. 'Thank you for this.' She took the paper from Anumita and started walking towards the stairs.

Charu entered the backroom downstairs with the de-addiction centre pamphlet in her hand. It was empty. She heard the water running in the bathroom and tried to dislodge the image of Ravi standing under the shower from her mind. She fumbled with her phone and called the sketch artist requesting him to return to the haveli. Then, to keep herself busy, she dialled the number of the de-addiction centre she had asked Anumita to read aloud and memorized. After a few rings, a perky voice picked up.

'Hello.'

'Hi. I am sorry to call so late in the night. I would like to ask about a patient,' Charu began, hoping to find Mavu, Gita's brother.

'I am sorry, official hours are only till 6 pm. This number is only for emergencies. Also, we don't give information about patients over the phone; it's confidential. If you are planning to visit, please get a proper authority letter and an ID. Or, you can visit with the patient's guardian.'

'And, if I need the information for an investigation?'

'Please come with a warrant in that case. Client confidentiality is paramount to us. Is there anything else I can help with?'

'No, thank you.' Charu disconnected the call, discouraged. She pressed another number on her speed-dial list and was immediately connected to the IO, helping them.

'Hi Charu, I have what you needed from Nagaland.' The man at the other end came straight to the point.

'Good. Tell me. Anything that will help.'

'Gita's family has started living well, bought land, and is in the process of renovating their house here. It looks like they came into some money recently. Their neighbours say some uncle of her mother's bequeathed some money to her, hence the improvement projects. Apparently, the uncle lives in Delhi.'

'Ah, okay. Any word on the brother, Mavu?'

'As she said—her brother was a drunkard and troublemaker. She took him with her to keep him away from his friends, and no one has seen him since. The parents receive money every month, and everyone remembers Gita fondly.'

Charu was making audio notes of her conversation with the IO to share with Ravi and Reeti when she heard the door's handle being turned slowly. Sia entered the room.

'Hello, Sia.'

'Oh, hello, Charu Aunty. I came looking for my mother.' Sia had heard Gita talking about her gift. She didn't understand why her family and the helpers spoke about her in whispers. Charu was the first blind person she had met, and she was nothing like the people they showed on television.

'She isn't here, sorry,' Charu said. 'Was there something you wanted to say to her?'

'No, I was just looking...'

Charu waited for her to continue.

'These drawings...are they yours? This is Myra, that's her crib, this is me, and Gita Didi.'

'Sia, these are the pictures I see in my mind,' Charu explained, surprised the child had noticed.

'There is one of my room, and one of Myra's room, and the stairs, and the whole house. Do you really see all this in your mind?'

'Yes. Can you recognize everyone from the sketches?'

'Yes, all of us are here, even Swamiji,' she said.

'Does Swamiji ever come and say hello to you?'

'No, we sometimes meet when we are playing in the front garden. But, Mummy prefers that we stay in the back garden, so she can keep an eye on us from her room.'

'And, Myra? Does he ever come up and say goodnight to her?'

'No, he is not allowed. Mummy and Papa had a big fight when Myra was born. Papa had brought Swamiji upstairs to bless her. Mummy was very upset because she did not like anyone coming up to our rooms. Papa said she was making a big fuss over nothing. He has never come up since then. But, the day Myra went missing, I thought I heard…' she paused, unsure about whether she ought to say more.

'It's all right, Sia. What did you hear?'

'I am not sure if I really did. I thought I heard Swamiji's footsteps in the corridor—or maybe in Myra's room. But, he didn't come up to my room, so I may be mistaken.'

'How would you recognize his footsteps?'

'All of us have a different gait. Gita Didi drags her feet. Ravi Uncle walks with purpose. Mummy walks as if she is in a hurry. Papa has noisy shoes. Swamiji walks silently, but his strides are long, and his heels press hard against the floor.'

'You are very observant, Sia.'

'It is a game I play, guessing who is coming or going.'

'So, you heard Swamiji on the first floor? When was this? Around what time, do you remember? Was it while everyone was searching the grounds for Myra?'

'No, it was when we were doing writing practice after Manik Chachu came back from the bathroom.' Sia said thoughtfully, chewing her lip.

Charu recalled he had gone to the bathroom around 2 pm the first time. *Sia heard Ram Vilas on the first floor after Manik had come back, perhaps around 2:15 pm. That would explain the bidi smell and also the crystal flowers he lost from his pocket squares. He could have easily taken Myra,* she thought.

'I expected Swamiji to peep into my room and check on me, but no one came. I looked at Manik Chachu, but he didn't say anything, so I thought maybe I just imagined it.'

'Maybe. Did you hear him go down?'

'No, I didn't.'

Charu took a deep breath. 'Do you want me to look for your mother, Sia?'

'No, I will find her, thank you.' Sia closed the door as she left.

'You can come out now, Ravi,' Charu called out.

Ravi stepped out of the bathroom and began to dress quickly. 'I was waiting for both of you to finish. It looks like Ram Vilas went up to Myra's room after all. Let's recheck the first-floor security camera feed. A lot could be explained if we find Ram Vilas was upstairs just before Myra went missing from her crib.'

Reeti entered the room just as Ravi began fiddling with her system. 'Hey, don't mess with my system,' she called out. 'Tell me what you need.' She hurried to her laptop and stood protectively before it.

'Reeti, please check the feed from the first-floor security camera again—when Ram Vilas was in the haveli. See if you can spot him,' Charu requested her.

'Let me find the file, but why?'

Charu played the audio clip of herself and Sia that she had recorded on her phone. Ravi and Reeti listened to it and exchanged glances. Charu heard Reeti's fingers move furiously on the keyboard.

'Charu, the camera was not working. The one over the bathroom door got Manik walking in and then out. Nothing else.'

Charu felt deflated. She could feel the second day coming to an end as the sketch artist joined them. Sia's doubts about Ram Vilas visiting the first floor kept revolving in her mind. She put her thoughts aside and sat down with the sketch artist to describe the woman and everything else she had seen in her vision. She tried her best to explain the gigantic orange statue. Once they had put a face to the woman, they would be able to search for her. She could hear Reeti and Ravi discussing something in hushed tones. It felt like they were close to a breakthrough.

'It's done, Charu,' the sketch artist said, drawing everybody's attention. She heard the papers rustling as he handed the sketches to Ravi.

'Have you ever visited the big Hanuman Murti near Karol Bagh, Charu?' asked Ravi.

'Not that I can recall,' she replied. 'Why?'

'Because what you described just now sounds like the big statue of Lord Hanuman in Karol Bagh. It is a famous temple, and there's a metro station nearby.'

'There are others too,' said Reeti. 'I know the Gufa Mandir in Preet Vihar has a similar tall Hanuman statue and a metro nearby. How do you know that isn't the one? Or some other Hanuman temple in India?'

'I think it's in Delhi,' said Charu. 'I saw other landmarks fleetingly.'

Reeti ran a Google search. 'Let's start,' she read out from her laptop, 'There's one in Karmpura, Delhi; Loni, Ghaziabad; and Govindpuri in Delhi. There's a Virat Hanuman Mandir in Latur, Ichchapurti Hanuman Mandir in Jaunpur and, of course, the famous Sankat Mochan temple in Karol Bagh here.'

'I wish you had been able to read the board,' Ravi said to Charu.

'Well, the statue had its forearms against its chest...if that helps.'

'It does,' said Ravi. He turned around. 'Reeti, please put our trusted men on the job. We need to check out all the ones in Delhi. They need to match the details with whatever Charu saw. Ask them to look for a rectangular blue board spelling out the name of a market that begins with G and ends with R. The area Charu has described sounds like old Delhi but could be central or even east.'

'Let's check out Karol Bagh first and then widen out our search from there. Maybe, Myra is being kept there, or the kidnappers took that route. The Navaratri bhajans and the lights could be those at that famous temple. Also, there are lots of tenements around that area,' added Reeti.

'We also need the family to look at these sketches and tell us if they know this woman.'

When the sketch artist had left, Reeti said, 'Charu, while you were busy with the sketches, I told Ravi about that number from Hisar we couldn't trace. It is registered to a person who is no more, but both Prithvi and Anumita received calls from it. Obviously, someone has reactivated it.'

'Do we know who is using it?' Charu asked.

'No. But, the telephone exchange has traced the location to central Delhi. They have triangulated the area, and Karol Bagh falls squarely within the triangulated cellular towers. I told my contact at the exchange to trace the call and tell me if it is used again.' She waited and opened another window on her screen. 'I also wanted to tell you both that there are gaps in the family's schedules. They live a fairly routine life, but here and there are some unexplained absences. For Prithvi, I have been able to fill in those gaps. He is either at the "other house" or has some engagement that can be verified. Anumita's is more interesting. She has been missing or veering off course weekly. Not too many times to raise any suspicion, but it forms a pattern.

Look here. Her schedule here says "beauty salon" but, when I called to check her appointments, I realized she was away for much longer than the time the parlour would have taken. Our person spoke to the parlour she frequents. The parlour girl said Anumita is always in a rush. Last time she left the place within ten minutes, but her schedule shows she reached her meeting after an hour and a half.'

'What about the day Myra was kidnapped? Did Prithvi go to the other house?' asked Ravi.

'No, he went last night.'

'Where did he go from the office that day?' Ravi rubbed his chin. 'The car reading shows the same number of kilometres as the distance to the haveli. Could he have come back, unseen?

The drivers were waiting at the gate while Bilal and Ram Vilas were inside. But, none of them saw either the car or Prithvi.'

'He may have waited outside to see if Ram Vilas and Bilal were actually inside,' Charu suggested.

'Most likely. I don't like the fact that Prithvi is constantly hiding things from us.'

'We could simply ask him.' Something in Reeti's voice alerted Charu.

'Is there something I should know?' she asked.

The pause that followed was hurtful.

'Charu, Reeti found your pictures on Prithvi's computer, in hidden folders,' Ravi sighed.

'My pictures, from school?'

'No, college, I think. Someone used a telephoto lens. They were taken without your knowledge.'

'What! How is that possible? Why would he do that?' Charu was shocked. She recalled all their conversations since the time he had called the day before. It made no sense.

'Oh God, no. It can't be possible. I couldn't have been so wrong about him.'

'We need hard evidence before we can make it official.' Ravi turned around as the door opened, and Prithvi entered with Anumita.

20. Ram Vilas

8:45 pm, Thursday

'I saw the sketch artist leave. Did you see anything, Chumki?' inquired Prithvi.

Charu felt weighed down by guilt and disbelief. Her perception had been altered by Ravi's disclosure.

'What's the matter with you? You seem like you are about to faint.' Anumita leaned forward to steady Charu.

'No, I am all right. Yes, I did. Ravi, please show them the sketch of the woman.'

The couple studied the sketches quietly. Charu moved away from Prithvi.

'Did you ever take Myra to this statue?' Ravi asked him.

'No, Anumita is not comfortable taking the girls to crowded places. I don't think Myra has even been near this area. But, this woman looks familiar, isn't it, Anu?' He looked up at his wife.

'No, I don't forget a face. I have never met her. I can't speak for you, of course. She may be one of your special friends.' Anumita stared at the woman's face intently. Ravi saw Anumita clench her jaw and glare at Prithvi, who was frowning at Charu's back.

'Sir, we are planning to send these out to the police control room, so they can start looking for her,' said Ravi.

'No, once the police get a hold of it, this news will spread like wildfire. Can you try at your own level first? Chumki, what do you think?' said the minister.

'Prithvi, it has been two days. I don't think we should delay this any further. We can cover more distance with the help of the police,' Charu answered.

'So, we will have to go to the police ultimately, as I suggested. Had you listened to me in the first place…' Anumita trailed off.

'That's enough. Ravi, I want you to look for her on your own. Involve the rest of your team if you need to, but not the police. I don't want to hear another word on this, is that clear?' Prithvi said categorically, then stomped off, followed by a calm Anumita. Ravi allowed his anger to subside. Prithvi was behaving unreasonably selfish.

'She did that on purpose. She knew Prithvi would snap if he felt he was losing,' Charu commented.

'Well, it looks like the gloves are off. If marriage is anything like this, I am glad I have been able to keep away. Anyway, I will email this picture to the rest of the team,' Reeti shook her head.

'I think I will talk to Commissioner Bakshi,' said Charu, dialling his number. Ravi considered the sketches again. It made no sense not to send them out.

'I am planning to rattle Bilal again tomorrow,' said Ravi.

'Did you speak to Maitri, the cook?' Ravi threw a glance at Charu talking on the phone.

'Yes, I called her in while you were out. The interview is on tape. Would you like to hear it? She said she had been called to make tea for two people, which she did, and then took the tea service to Ram Vilas's office. The room was empty when she went in, but she saw Bilal in the garden as she crossed the living room.'

'Did she see Ram Vilas?'

'No, but he could have been standing further away. Maitri said she just glanced at Bilal and wondered if she should take the tea out. He waved her off to the office.' They turned towards Charu when they heard her walking back.

'Commissioner Bakshi says Prithvi has the final say, but he will try and convince him to do what is right.' Charu seemed crestfallen.

'There are too many loose threads. We need to start tying them now. Reeti, why don't you take on Anumita? Charu,

I am waiting for an email from Hisar. Please call me as soon as you get the notification.'

Charu nodded and swivelled her chair towards the door. Ram Vilas entered the room, followed closely by Malti Devi. They looked curious and sceptical at the same time.

'Namaste. I hope we are not disturbing you? Prithvi told me Charu Ji saw some woman in her vision. I thought we must see the picture for ourselves before I left for the day. Malti Devi insisted we do.' Ram Vilas stretched out his hand.

'Yes, of course.' Ravi handed them the sketches to peruse. Ram Vilas passed them over to the woman next to him without a flicker of interest. Malti Devi scrutinized the woman in the drawing before she looked away as if thinking. Ravi noticed her furrowed brows.

'Do you recognize her, Malti Devi?' he enquired.

'Hmm. . .no. She looks familiar, but I can't be certain.'

'It is such an ordinary face that everyone will think they know her. Nothing that stands out, nothing special. If you asked me to describe a woman—any woman—I would say this. Medium nose, bindi on the forehead, hair parted in the middle. Even the eyes are average, neither too large nor too small. Charu Ji, this is a good way to keep yourself relevant,' said Ram Vilas, glancing at his watch.

He hardly glanced at the sketch, thought Ravi. Charu remained silent. He was baiting her.

'Her hand has a mark under the thumb, near the wrist. That is specific, don't you think?' Reeti came to her defence.

'Now, that is interesting. You have something to go on with. Great work,' Ram Vilas said derisively, turning away. Malti Devi seemed preoccupied. She hurried out without another word.

'Ram Vilas Ji?' Ravi called out. 'I wanted to have a word with you. Why don't we talk here? It'll only take a moment.'

'Sure. I thought you had asked all your questions last time,' he replied, walking back towards the interview space.

He watched as Reeti and Charu took their place opposite him. Charu told herself to calm down. Every time she was near Ram Vilas, her instincts told her to run.

'This seems like an interrogation,' Ram Vilas laughed, but Charu heard the nervousness he was trying to hide.

Ravi began recording. 'Ram Vilas Ji, you brought Bilal Siddiqui into the haveli on the day Myra was kidnapped. Why?'

'I invited him in for tea. I already told you all this; why are you asking me again?' he said, irritably.

Charu started speaking and was surprised at the vehemence and force of her own voice. 'All right then, let's stop these silly games. We know you went up to Myra's room just before she was kidnapped. You came down with a heavy leather bag—large enough to carry a child—and gave it to Bilal.'

'What! Do you think you can put the blame for the kidnapping on me? What kind of game are you playing?' Ram Vilas seemed incredulous.

'Ram Vilas Ji, you may not have realized it, but someone heard you upstairs. We have a witness,' Charu clenched her teeth and looked straight ahead. Her chest rose and fell evenly. She sensed Ram Vilas's gaze on her.

Ravi held his breath at Charu's bluff. She was taking too big a risk. If Ram Vilas caught on that they were trying to trap him, they would lose all credibility or advantage with him. He just hoped she knew what she was doing. He watched as Ram Vilas squinted at her. The corners of his mouth turned down, and sweat ran down his sideburns.

Ram Vilas weighed his options carefully and answered slowly, 'I did not kidnap Myra,' he said. 'It wasn't Myra in the bag.'

'What then?' Ravi frowned.

'It was the jade cups—the precious ones Bilal's ancestors made, the ones for which Prithvi outbid him. I had no choice. He was willing to trade, and he wouldn't settle for anything less.'

'What!' Charu asked after an instant of stunned silence. 'Why?'

'To show him we could help each other. It was an olive branch. I knew he was upset about Prithvi's childish behaviour. It was my way of showing him he could trust us.'

'You haven't told Prithvi, have you? Imagine how he will react when he realizes that you gifted Bilal his most important, his most precious...'

'You cannot tell him. I will do so myself. It has to come from me,' Ram Vilas interrupted Charu. 'I did it for his sake. Yes, leaving Bilal in the garden, I went up to Myra's room. She was fast asleep in her crib,' he admitted, leaning back against his chair. 'I knew where Prithvi hid those jade cups. I took the bag out. He did not know I knew about the hidden panel under the window. I went downstairs and handed the bag to Bilal. We called his driver, and he carried it outside into the car.'

'So...you gave priceless artefacts to Prithvi's rival without his knowledge?' There was disbelief in Reeti's voice.

Ram Vilas stared at the team. The expression in his eyes changed from irritation to pity. 'I didn't kidnap Myra,' he repeated, 'I really didn't.'

They gulped down their dinner where they stood, eating out of necessity rather than hunger. Neither Charu nor Reeti could stop discussing what Ram Vilas's revelations meant. Reeti ran a search and confirmed the auction and the buyer of the cups.

'He admitted he saw Myra in the crib around 2:15 pm. That is, *if* he was telling the truth. It means Myra was still in the haveli until then. Bilal left with the bag at 2:35 pm. The time stamp on the security tape confirmed that part,' Reeti checked the printouts they had pasted on the board.

'He must've told us the truth. He's not a fool. Neither of them would have tried to pull off a stunt like that with the whole world watching,' said Charu. 'That means someone kidnapped Myra between 2:35 and 3 pm. Could Myra have been carried out later in the day? Or could she still be in the haveli?' She contemplated the possibility. It seemed too farfetched.

They heard the bell sound on Ravi's laptop. Charu wondered whose email he had been waiting for and sent an audio note to him immediately. He had stepped out of the room to instruct his team on ground.

Charu moved back as if something had just struck her. 'Listen,' she said, 'That also means Myra was not in the trolley Gita took out of the haveli at 2 pm because Ram Vilas saw her in the crib after that.'

'Three bags and a trolley went out of the house that day. They all had sufficient space to carry a child of eighteen months,' said Reeti. 'The first was the one Bilal carried out of here, or his driver did. And, two were Malti Devi's bags. However, Ram Vilas has brought in this new angle of the precious cups. We need to check that. If that's indeed the case, then it only leaves the ones Malti Devi carried out. Personally, I don't think he was lying. It seems the trolley's been ruled out.'

Charu looked at the door as it opened and Ravi came in. 'Ravi, what do you think?' She repeated their discussion for him.

'Yes, I think we need to verify the truth of Ram Vilas's claims ASAP,' Ravi concluded. 'I will have to speak to the forensic team. This is a huge lapse. The panel was where Ram Vilas said it would be. The crystal flowers we found probably fell from his pocket square when he was removing the bag. We will have to speak with Bilal to confirm all this, of course.'

Ravi rubbed his aching head. He lay on the couch. Charu placed her palm on his forehead and felt the painful throb in her own forehead as she absorbed his tension headache. Reeti turned her back to them, letting them have their moment.

'Charu, don't,' he said, feeling the warmth spread in his body.

'Shh. I can do this. Let me.' Ravi turned quiet. After a few minutes, he woke up to find Charu was no longer beside him. His headache was gone, and he felt revived.

'Ravi, regarding the email your friend sent, I found corresponding articles with some sources,' Reeti said.

'This is interesting. When I asked for some background checks on Ram Vilas or Malti Devi, I certainly didn't expect these from before Ram Vilas shifted to Sirsa. The gist is—Ram Vilas had a small but flourishing ashram in Hisar. There was a scandal that some girls had been kept in the ashram against their will. Ram Vilas had created a personal harem in the name of spiritual awakening. A couple of girls were found to be pregnant and brainwashed. Soon, he closed operations in that ashram to start the one in Sirsa but, this time, without any women's hostel and with political support.'

'He later started a hostel in Sirsa too, right?' said Charu.

'Yes. A complaint was filed by one of the girls, who named Malti Devi as the girl who pushed her to have sexual relations with Ram Vilas. The complaint was later retracted,' Ravi said, scanning the article.

'How is that helpful to the case?' asked Reeti.

'I feel Ram Vilas and Malti Devi have a deeper connection. Also, Ram Vilas isn't the clean, saintly soul he portrays himself to be. If you join the dots, Malti Devi obviously lived at the Hisar ashram and is his staunch follower or devotee, or whatever. She may have had a sexual relationship with him; I wouldn't be surprised.'

'Consider this. The scandal forces Ram Vilas to close the ashram and move bag and baggage to Sirsa. He gets Malti Devi married to a close friend and enters politics. Then Prithvi comes along, and Ram Vilas sees an ambitious boy in him. He mentors Prithvi and marries off Anumita, his friend's daughter, to him. Ram Vilas is now forever entrenched in this family setup. He has prestige and political clout at his fingertips,' said Charu.

'But, they still have no motive to kidnap Myra—unless there is a connection we don't know about. Even if they are lovers of some sort, it has no bearing on Myra's kidnapping,' Reeti reasoned.

'Money may have been a motive. They could have colluded together. Ravi, can you ask your friend to dig deeper? Find out more about their relationship?' Charu insisted.

'We could conduct a parallel investigation. But, even I am not sure what these two had to gain. Thirty lakh. I don't think so. As Prithvi said, Ram Vilas is financially better off than him. However, I will ask someone from the team to go and nose around the Hisar ashram personally.' Ravi stood up. 'Let's compile our findings.' He walked to the whiteboard. Charu and Reeti took their seats.

'Prithvi, Myra's father. Motive: garnering sympathy votes for the upcoming election and trying to pull Charu back into his life. If we consider his married life, political career, and actions in the recent past, he had enough motives.'

'What! But, he was the one who called us in and initiated the investigation,' Charu protested.

'And kept the regular police force out of it,' Ravi pointed out. 'He could be leading us a merry dance for nothing.'

'His alibi is solid, though. He was in a meeting at the office,' Reeti countered Ravi.

'No. Prithvi was very clever. He was at the meeting, but not all the time. At some point, he left it and took the car to go somewhere, all by himself. He didn't call his driver, remember? The time ties in with Myra's kidnapping. The kilometre-reading is double what it is on an average day, to be exact. It may suggest he travelled back to this haveli. And, he never told us he had left his office.'

'But, he could have gone somewhere else that was the same distance? In another direction?' Charu tried to defend Prithvi.

'So, we need to find out where Prithvi went alone in his car,' Reeti said.

'Anumita. Mother. Her unexplained absences, her anger towards Prithvi and his wayward ways, or his past relationship with Charu could have made her want to teach him a lesson.'

'But, wasn't she out for a meeting?' said Reeti.

'Yes, but Gita has just received a windfall and had easy access to Myra,' Charu explained. 'They may have planned something.'

'Gita. Nanny. Her brother Mavu is an alcoholic, which she didn't disclose when we spoke to her,' Ravi continued. 'She asked Anumita for money and was refused. The brother is a loose string we need to tie. Also, she took the trolley out in the absence of the guard and asked about the ransom amount. Both are suspicious actions, even though it seems the trolley is ruled out for now. She knew about the camera in the room and had access to the child.'

'Ram Vilas. Mentor. He has been insecure for some months—ever since he could see Prithvi slipping away from his grasp. He was in the haveli when the kidnapping took place, with Prithvi's opponent, Bilal. They were talking about trading services for favours. When confronted about his deal with Bilal, he admitted he wanted to get information from him. He has admitted that he gave precious jade cups to Bilal without Prithvi's knowledge. However, this fact needs to be verified.'

'The fact that Bilal left at 2:35 pm, and Gita found Myra missing at 3 pm, means the kidnapper had only 25 minutes to carry Myra out. It is, therefore, possible that Myra was still in the haveli when they were searching for her,' Charu said. 'Even if Ram Vilas was not in cahoots with Bilal, another two bags went out after a few hours—the ones Malti Devi carried to the ashram. They could have carried Myra out in them.'

'I, for one, don't buy this puja thing,' said Reeti.

'Bilal Siddiqui.' Ravi returned to the board. 'Prithvi caused his accident in school, leaving him paralyzed. He then became a big donor to the party where Prithvi is rising. He, however, acts as a roadblock for Prithvi, thwarting him at every turn. Recently, he had a public spat with Prithvi when he got the tender instead of Prithvi's guy, allegedly, with some inside information from Ram Vilas. He wants to bring Prithvi down. After this, we have to talk with him about the bag with the cups to confirm whatever Ram Vilas said.'

'Malti Devi. Stepmother to Anumita. She is definitely hiding something regarding Anumita and her connection with the ashram. The bag she carried to the ashram in Hisar is suspect, now more so than ever. She was on the same floor as Myra. She's only a few years older than Anumita—and quite fit physically. She says she was asleep. But, what if she wasn't? What if she was only pretending? She was physically capable of carrying the child out of the haveli.'

'But, what would kidnapping Myra for a few lakh rupees achieve? She is already well taken care of here. And, if she was caught, she would have lost much more than she gained. Surely, she knew that,' said Reeti.

'It could be her dislike for Anumita. Being only a couple of years older than her, without a child, and acting as a caretaker could have made her bitter and spiteful,' Charu replied.

Ravi nodded.

'Moving on, Manik, the tutor and uncle. He feels Prithvi has a life that rightfully should have been his. He considers himself wronged by Prithvi since he refused to help him fulfil his dream. He asked for money to invest in a cricket academy but was scoffed at. He may harbour feelings of jealousy and vengeance. He, too, had access to Myra, being on the same floor at that time. He used the bathroom twice. Money and vengeance can make a man do dangerous things.'

'He was at the haveli until Myra's parents came home. Then Prithvi told him to leave. He then drove out on his bike, in full view of Prithvi and several guards,' Reeti completed.

'What did you find in Myra's room?' Charu asked Ravi.

'I couldn't see any other way to get in beside the door. The window would be a long stretch. The room has a main door, a bathroom, and a window.'

Charu heard Ravi draw everything on the whiteboard. The odour of the marker and its squeak were audible in the silent room.

'The room is square—with only one entrance. The first floor overlooks the boundary wall on the left. A guard is stationed there, and he can see the window if he turns. We've discussed the other possibilities already. Now, if someone came in through the door into Myra's room, the camera in the lobby should have recorded their movement, but that camera was conveniently faulty—as was the nanny cam in Myra's room.' He thought for a while before speaking again. 'Another way could have been—to hide in the bathroom. But, for that, the person would've had to stay inside the bathroom since morning.'

'What about the window?' Charu asked.

'Charu, there is nothing outside the window. If someone had put a ladder there, the guard was bound to notice. He said no one came there that day. Only Gita, the children, and Manik.'

'The trellis?' Charu pressed him yet again.

'It's too flimsy. It would not support any weight. The vine is not strong enough either. I also checked the bathroom next to Myra's room, used by the staff. It does have a window, but the very narrow parapet, and a thorny vine, need to be tackled to reach Myra's room. No, not possible.'

'Let's also discuss the visions you have had so far, Charu,' said Reeti. 'I suspect that Myra is in the Karol Bagh area. She is being kept in a shabby room, most likely a *barsati* or roof-top room. She is with a woman whose photo we have circulated in the haveli and our trusted team members. There is heavy traffic and a metro line nearby. Our team in the field confirmed it's the same Hanuman Temple—from how you described the lights' placements, the flag on top, and the temple dome. We're yet to find signage with the letter V and a school made of red bricks with a blackboard outside.'

'Reeti, please run a search for all these things in Delhi. The Hanuman murti is our breakthrough, of course, and can be your starting point.'

'What about the ransom call? The kidnappers have not called us again to tell us where to drop the money,' Charu broke in.

'We can only wait,' Ravi replied. 'Maybe, they got cold feet. Maybe, they're waiting and watching too. It's a minister they're dealing with.'

They discussed and rearranged the information on the board according to the sequence of the interviews. The sky was still purple when Ravi said, 'Why don't you rest for a while? It's going to be a long day tomorrow.' His hand on Charu's shoulder felt reassuring. She nodded, feeling the warmth of his words. She slipped into sleep as he began writing an email to his friend in Hisar.

It was 4 am when Reeti shouted, 'Ravi, wake up!'

Ravi had fallen asleep on the chair and sat up, startled. Rubbing his eyes, he staggered to her desk. She was concentrating hard on her laptop. Charu, too, sat up tense. 'What is it?' she asked.

'The lab has sent Prithvi's search history that he deleted from his laptop. There are tons of articles here on how families died in car crashes, by fire, poison, kidnapping, perfect crimes, drowning...it goes on and on,' muttered Reeti. 'There is more. Prithvi was looking for ways to kidnap a young child and how to hurt someone and make it seem like an accident. Besides, he was reading about how serial killers have kidnapped women and children. He'd been doing it for a couple of months before Myra's kidnapping.'

'We don't know that. He is her father, he wouldn't...' Even as Charu tried to justify Prithvi, she couldn't help asking herself why he had searched for these criminal acts...for curiosity or inspiration. Charu was unable to deny anymore that Prithvi could have kidnapped his own daughter.

'We will figure it out. Reeti, please call the lab to hurry up with the feed from the faulty cameras. If we get pictures or a video from the nanny cam, it will help,' said Ravi.

21. Ravi

11:45 pm, Thursday

Having breakfast with a family where everyone was a suspect was a tense affair. The members sat around the table with their guests. The spread was lavish, but nobody was hungry. The team answered their questions in monosyllables.

'No school today, Sia?' asked Ravi. Sia shook her head moodily. He smiled and resumed his meal. He did not expect Prithvi's next words.

'Answer his question, Sia.' Prithvi scolded his daughter sternly. 'Is this what we have taught you? Don't become like your mother, always expecting everyone to cater to her needs and moods.'

'Sorry, Papa. Ravi Unc...Uncle, the sch...school has given the prim...primary classes a holi...holiday today.' Her little body trembled.

Ravi felt an overwhelming desire to strike Prithvi. He felt responsible for Sia's sudden transformation into a shaking, diffident child.

Charu jumped when Malti Devi asked her suddenly, 'So, did you have any more dreams?' She obviously wanted to draw their attention away from her granddaughter.

'No, we barely slept.' Ravi came to Charu's rescue.

'Oh. So, you did find something?' Prithvi looked up at him.

'We are working on it, sir. We should leave now, so we can follow some leads.'

'Today is your third day here,' Anumita reminded them.

'Prithvi, Gita's brother, Mavu, is in the de-addiction centre. I called them, but they will only tell us his details if his guardian is present,' said Charu.

'I am his guardian. I am paying for his treatment. I will come along with you,' said Anumita.

'I don't know why you keep giving in to her demands, Anu. We are paying her a salary.' Malti Devi scolded Anumita, who remained silent. Charu couldn't help the shiver of dislike she felt for Malti Devi. Charu tried to explain away her nastiness to her life experience, but she always sensed that the woman used her words to manipulate or deliberately hurt others. Malti Devi was conspicuously opposite to her own mother, Uma. *Thank God.*

Ravi, Charu, and Anumita left for the de-addiction centre after breakfast. Since Prithvi had already made the arrangements, the in-charge of the place, a heavyset, worried looking man, welcomed them into his office. The centre stretched over a large piece of land. Charu asked about Mavu and if they could meet him.

'Last month, Mavu hit the ward boy on his head and ran away at night,' he sighed. 'I tried to contact you on the number provided but received no response for a few days. Finally, a girl answered and told us that her brother had gone back home to Nagaland. When I insisted that she send Mavu back because he would likely seek alcohol again, she told me categorically that she would file a complaint against us—say that we had been torturing him. We can't afford to be involved in legal troubles at this time, so I left it at that.'

'But, I gave her the money for the quarter at the beginning of this month!' Anumita cried.

'Well, we have not received a penny of it. I suggest you trace the money, and you will find the boy.' The man washed his hands off Mavu.

When they were leaving, Ravi asked Anumita, 'How much did you give Gita?'

'One lakh and fifty thousand for this quarter,' Anumita told him.

'Enough to start a small business,' Charu conjectured.

'I can't believe Gita would lie to me. I have supported her, trusted her completely with my children. She is not... Maybe, she was forced into kidnapping Myra. Mavu could have threatened her; I saw how scared she was of him, especially when he was drunk. My daughter is not safe with him. You have to find him now.' Anumita started sniffling. Charu felt her distress and placed a hand on her shoulder.

A picture flashed in her mind as soon as she touched Anumita. *She was standing before Gita wagging her finger threateningly. Gita was crying.* Charu blinked, and the picture dissipated like mist. Ravi told Anumita that she could return home while he and Charu had more work to do. He hailed a cab for her. 'What did you see?' he asked when Anumita had left in the taxi.

'Ravi, I know she portrays herself as a caring employer, while Gita is the one taking advantage of her, but I keep seeing her be the aggressor. And, yet...'

'If Mavu does indeed have Myra, we are really short on time. I think I should involve the rest of the team in locating him. Gita hid the fact that her brother had run away. What did she do with the money meant for the centre? We will have to question her again. She looks guilty now.' He hailed another cab and climbed in after Charu.

'I agree, Ravi. Brother and sister had enough time to plan. She could have easily disabled the nanny cam herself. But, I can't believe she'll hurt the child.'

'Maybe, she never wanted to hurt Myra. The intent is to get the money and then return her safely.'

'Let's hope we get to Myra before they take her out of the city.'

'Are you sure she is still in Delhi...in Karol Bagh?'

'I think so.'

'Well, the field officers are on it. They are combing the area triangulated by the Hisar number too. Let's hope they find something,' said Ravi as the cab stopped in front of Bilal's office building.

Charu and Ravi walked into Bilal's office. There was a different receptionist today. Ravi walked up to her and introduced himself, flashing his ID card. She looked taken aback. Nervously, she asked them to wait and called Bilal.

'Where is the other front-office woman, the one we met here yesterday morning?' Charu asked her.

'She left. I am filling in until we get another one,' the woman said, timidly.

Charu turned around and stepped away from the girl. She hoped that the previous receptionist hadn't gotten into trouble because of them.

'Sit,' Ravi said to her. 'I think Bilal found out we got information out of his receptionist. He probably knows we know about his change of plans and the extra baggage he carried on the train.'

'Sir...ma'am, Bilal sir has called you into his office,' the girl at the desk called out.

They hurried to Bilal's cabin. After a cursory knock, they walked in.

'Good afternoon. Meeting you for two consecutive days feels like we are back in school, Charu. How can I help you?' Bilal came straight to the point. Charu found his demeanour colder towards her today.

'Mr Siddiqui, we would like to ask you...' Ravi began.

'I hope you have a warrant?' Bilal cut in.

'Bilal, you know we don't.' Charu stepped closer to his seat.

'Then I am not under any compulsion to tell you anything.'

'No, Bilal, except that I am asking a favour as a friend. Your political games have nothing to do with us. We only want to ask a few questions.' Charu knew what he was after. She knew he was a negotiator.

'That's very noble of you. But, tell me, why does the needle of suspicion—of some crime—point towards me? Does it have anything to do with my religion?'

'No, you know that's not the case. We are questioning several people.' She turned towards Ravi. 'Ravi, I will talk to Bilal alone. Would you wait outside, please?'

She felt Ravi stiffen beside her. 'No, this is not right. The procedure is that there should be at least two of us to interview someone. We cannot break protocol,' he replied.

'Mr Ravi, you can pretend that this is an official investigation all you want, but I know Prithvi has asked you to look into whatever has befallen him, away from the eyes of the media. Now, I admit I did contemplate the idea of leaking an anonymous tip to some friends of mine in the media. But, I didn't...out of respect for Charu. Just don't test the limits of my patience. Especially when I found out you were planning a reunion for me with old friends,' Bilal's voice rang with sarcasm.

'Then you should have told me the whole truth,' Charu returned evenly.

Ravi hesitated, weighing his options. Did Bilal really not know what was afoot, or was he simply a good actor? Had he really not kidnapped the child? Had Ram Vilas only given him Prithvi's precious cups, as he said? He knew there was only a one percent chance that the man would admit anything to Charu. But, if Bilal did, it might be the clinching point. Could he let that opportunity slip?

'I will wait outside. Call out if you need anything,' Ravi squeezed Charu's shoulder and left.

'He feels for you,' Bilal observed.

'He is my colleague. Obviously...'

'That's not what I am saying, Charu, and you know it. The man looks at you with a truckload of emotion.'

'Sad for him then that I can't see it,' Charu said, dismissively. 'Tell me what is going on, Bilal.'

'Put your phone on the desk, Charu.'

She switched off her phone and slid it on the desk in front of her. 'You went into Prithvi's house on Ram Vilas's insistence.'

'Well, he invited me inside, and I accepted his invitation,' Bilal replied.

'You said Ram Vilas gave you inside information on the tender Prithvi's man lost in the past.'

'Yes, and promised to continue to do the same in future.'

'To what gain?'

'Money, power. Nothing is for free, Charu. You give, and you get. Simple.'

Charu could feel Bilal's mistrust. He would not open up if he didn't trust her. And, he wanted to know the reason behind her questions. If he seriously hadn't kidnapped Myra, Charu didn't want him to find out.

'Bilal, you told me you went to Benares the first time we spoke.'

'I did. I didn't know you wanted to know which mode of transport I used.'

'And, the bag?'

'Aha. So, is it this bag you are after? Is that my so-called crime?'

She heard the glee behind his words. 'Bilal, what was inside it?'

'Are you confirming some theory, or do you really not know?'

'This is not a game. You don't know what kind of trouble you could be in. The best thing would be to come clean now. If you do, I promise to help.'

'Why should I get into trouble? Ram Vilas is the culprit; he will take the blame.'

'But, you were accessory to the crime, weren't you?' Charu thought she had him. Ram Vilas's lie was about to be exposed.

'Crime? What crime? It was a gift, Charu. How was I to know what was inside the bag?' Bilal laughed.

'A gift? Can you elaborate on that?' Charu felt deflated.

'Why couldn't you ask Ram Vilas? Why come to me? Or does he blame me now? I wouldn't put it past him. He is loyal only to himself.'

'He said he gave you something very precious,' Charu said. 'Something that belonged to Prithvi.'

'Does Prithvi know what he did? I wouldn't be surprised if he does, you know. They have quite a symbiotic relationship—Prithvi and Ram Vilas. When I saw the contents of the bag, my heart stopped for a minute. Only someone who had a lot at stake would have made this big a sacrifice. So, I got out as fast as these electric wheels would take me before he could change his mind.'

'You are talking about...?'

'The jade cups Prithvi outbid me for some years ago in Mumbai.'

Charu sighed.

'Why are you acting so surprised? Isn't that what you are here for? What did *you* think the bag had? Ransom money?' Bilal guffawed.

Charu rubbed her forehead. 'Bilal, you can call Ravi in now,' she said. Bilal pressed the buttons on the intercom. Ravi rushed in to find Bilal watching Charu with a frown. She asked him to sit down on his chair again.

'We were talking about the bag Bilal took from Ram Vilas. He says that Ram Vilas gave him Prithvi's precious jade cups.'

Ravi watched her face in silence.

She sensed his scepticism and turned towards Bilal again. 'Why don't you tell us why they were so important to you?'

Bilal relaxed in his chair, ready to tell the story. 'I traced my family back to the period of the Mughal Empire and earlier. We were a family of jewellers and craftsmen who attached semi-precious stones to sculptures and such. Some time ago, I got into a bidding war with Prithvi over a set of jade cups that had been made by my ancestors—in 1657—for Shah Jahan's use. These cups were taken by a British officer, most likely, after the mutiny in 1857, who then sold them further to someone else. The cups exchanged many hands until, after so many years, they resurfaced at an auction in Mumbai. I knew they were genuine and felt it my duty to bring them back into the family. Prithvi got to know about them somehow and outbid me with the help of a big industrialist. I decided I would make sure he regretted crossing my path that day.'

'He feels you have it in for him because of the accident at school,' Charu admitted.

'It was too long ago. Do I like Prithvi's politics and policies? No. But, I have my own legacy to build. I don't have time to get involved in other things. But, then he made the mistake of being juvenile and taking what rightfully belonged to my family. After that, I was determined to teach him a lesson. When I gave Ram Vilas a lift to Prithvi's house, I never expected he would invite me in for tea or hand me the cups to show his conviction towards my proposal.'

'Can you prove that the bag had jade cups?' asked Ravi, still not ready to believe this strange story at face value. 'Can you show us the cups, Mr Siddiqui?'

'They are at my family home in Benares. Let me try to end this speculation here. But, you have to understand, now that I have them, I am not giving them back.'

Bilal made a video call to his nephew at his house in Benares and asked him to pull out the bag he had carried from Delhi from a particular cupboard. He turned the phone towards Ravi, who watched as Bilal's nephew walked into a room with a state-of-the-art lock that only opened once it had scanned the young man's retina. Once inside, Bilal's nephew put the phone on one side and pulled the duffle bag out of its shelf to place it on a large table.

'That is our safe. Like Aladdin's cave,' Bilal said, proudly.

Ravi watched as the young nephew unzipped the duffle bag and took out a deep velvet rectangular box. Bringing the phone closer, he opened the box and removed the top protective layer. Then, he held up the phone, so they could see the cups closely. Ravi saw a small piece of history before him. He was spellbound.

'Describe them to me,' said Charu when he gasped.

'These are made of white nephrite jade in the shape of a paisley. The handle is like a ram's head, and the bottom, or the pedestal, has a lotus and acanthus leaves. They are exquisite, Charu. Imagine Shah Jahan drank wine from these. Can you blame me if I wanted them back?' Bilal took his phone back from Ravi and asked his nephew to lock his treasure in the safe again.

The three people in the room sat thinking about what they had seen and heard. Bilal seemed to be in the clear as far as the kidnapping of Myra was concerned.

'Now, it's your turn,' said Bilal. 'Obviously, you were not here for the cups. That means Prithvi has lost something else. What is it, Charu?'

'Money. He has lost a substantial amount of money, and we thought maybe Ram Vilas handed it over to you,' Ravi jumped in, so Charu wouldn't have to lie to her friend.

'Hmm...I don't think you are telling me the truth, Ravi. But, I will find out one way or another. I guess it is enough that Charu believes me, for now.'

'Thank you, Bilal.' Charu stood up.

'Charu, come again. This time...only as a friend. I missed you.'

'I will. See if you can bring back the receptionist you fired. She just wanted to make you happy.'

As they waited for a cab outside Bilal's office, Charu turned towards Ravi. 'This leaves us with Malti Devi's bags.'

While Ravi and Charu were speeding back to Chauhan Haveli, Reeti received another email from the IT lab with some pictures attached. She looked at them and smiled. She was still scrolling down the attached files when Anumita walked in.

'Reeti?' she called out.

Reeti minimized the open window on her screen and turned around. 'Hi, please come in.'

'Could you tell me what is happening? Prithvi is tight-lipped, and I don't want to keep asking Ravi Ji. It is the third day, and we are not even close to locating Myra. Is there something I can do to help?'

'I know the process is slow, but, Anumita, we have to follow the leads we find.'

'So, what have you found?'

Ravi and Charu walked in and heard Reeti's prevarications. Anumita's nervousness was palpable to Charu. 'Anumita, we will let you know the moment we find Myra. Before that, could you tell me a little about your mother? What do you remember about her from your childhood?'

'Why do you want to know about her? Do you think she is involved?'

'We are looking at everyone. Since there isn't much about her life in the papers from before she married your father, I just wanted to know. We have only found her school certificate. Do you know if she attended college?'

'No, she studied at the school at the ashram in Hisar. She is the eldest daughter of a lower-class family that was completely devoted to Ram Vilas. Since she was a teenager, she had stayed at the ashram because her family couldn't afford to support her. After the ashram was closed, she came with him to Sirsa. Ram Vilas got her married to my father. I was in my teens at the time.'

'And, she is only a couple of years older than you.' Charu noticed that Anumita had dropped the suffix 'ji' from Ram Vilas's name.

'Yes, I think my father wanted someone for me, as I was a lonely child. He used to travel a lot to be with the people of his constituency. He thought we could be companions. But, she wanted nothing to do with me. She wanted to gain visibility and power. She wanted to go on the campaign trails with my father. He tried to tell her to stay home but, when Ram Vilas insisted, he gave in. For a time, I thought she would try and join the party, but my father didn't allow it. My father made her promise they wouldn't have a child together. He felt she would only have me to exhaust her maternal feelings on. He was so wrong. She does not have it within her to feel that kind of love.'

'What do you mean?'

'She is not maternal. Even with my girls, she is not your typical grandmother. Her own needs and desires always take precedence over everything else.'

'What are those needs?' asked Charu.

'Power, status, money, comfortable life and, of course, her devotion to Swamiji. That has been a constant in her life. When Myra was born, she came over to stay here with the excuse that I needed her. I wanted to laugh. I hadn't needed anyone for the longest time, and she was the last person capable of taking care of my child or me.'

'What do you know about the Hisar ashram?' Ravi asked next.

'It was shut down because of some scandal. Ram Vilas approached my father, who pulled some strings and got him off. I don't remember the details now. He opened a new, larger ashram this time, with tighter political connections, in Sirsa. After a few years, they reopened the Hisar ashram again, when the bad publicity had died down.'

'Prithvi says you have changed in the last few years—that you are no more as religious as you used to be.'

'Prithvi can believe what he likes. He is blinder than you are, Charu. Is there anything else about my mother you want to know because otherwise, I need to go,' Anumita replied without malice.

Charu shook her head and heard Anumita walk away.

22. Charu

10:30 am, Friday

Charu checked the time on her Braille watch. The morning seemed to have gotten away from her. It was the third day at Prithvi's haveli, and they still had nothing much to show for it. They were yet to narrow down the kidnapper and figure out how Myra had been carried out of the place. Telling herself to relax, Charu concentrated on what Reeti and Ravi were discussing.

'Bilal did not carry Myra out in the bag,' said Ravi, striking off Bilal's name on the board. He quickly outlined what he and Charu had learnt from him regarding the jade cups.

'Ravi, I also double-checked with the ticket collector on the train that Bilal took to Benares. He remembered the man in the wheelchair and his bag. Since it was oversized, he had asked Bilal to open it and show him what was inside. He confirmed that there were just two deep saucers in a rectangular box,' Charu added.

'What else?'

'I retrieved the pictures from the nanny cam while you were with Bilal. Guess who tampered with it,' Reeti said.

'What! Who?' exclaimed Ravi.

'Anumita,' Charu and Reeti said simultaneously.

'You knew?' Reeti brought up the folder where she had saved the pictures.

'No. I just read your thoughts.'

'It never gets old, what you can do, Charu. Ever thought of hitting the casinos? We would make a bundle,' Reeti joked.

Charu smiled. She envied Reeti's ability to compartmentalize work and play effectively. This was just a case to Reeti. Charu, however, felt tied to Myra. Maybe because she had seen her, touched her thoughts, her confusion, the newness of her surroundings. She heard the sound of the scroll wheel on the mouse. Ravi went through the pictures Reeti had received from the lab. Charu waited for Ravi to tell her what he was looking at.

'The pictures show Anumita taking Myra for her bath. Next, she comes back into the room and takes down the teddy bear from the top shelf. Myra's face, as Anumita offers the teddy, is full of wonder in the next picture, which is from a close range. And, the last picture is of Myra reaching for her toy.'

'Was that not dangerous? I mean, water and electronic devices can cause shock, right?' Charu asked him.

'Myra is not in the water. She is standing beside a full bathtub,' Reeti said. 'What possible reason could Anumita have to damage the nanny cam—unless she was the instigator?'

'Money?' Charu offered.

'We checked their bank records. Compared to the assets Anumita has declared as a minister's wife, the ransom amount is peanuts.'

'To catch Prithvi's attention?'

'That is a possibility. She knows about Prithvi's philandering ways. People have committed graver crimes for lesser reasons, I agree, but does she have it in her?'

'It is probable. Prithvi and Anumita are spending more time together. He is working from home. He is more attentive. It isn't so far-fetched, actually. She kidnaps Myra. A small ransom amount is given, which Prithvi will not even miss. No publicity because she knows Prithvi and his obsession with maintaining his image. Myra is found after a couple of days, and Prithvi is a concerned husband and father again,' Charu built the likely scenario.

'Her unexplained absences could be due to this. Maybe, we need to confront her with these and ask her point-blank,' Reeti suggested.

'In time. Let us gather as much information as we can first. Prithvi's list checks out. I called the women he met at the house and the hotels this month. All of them were escorts and agreed that the liaison was consensual.'

'We haven't found anyone questionable in Anumita's life yet, but I agree there has to be a reason for her sudden absences,' said Charu. Before Reeti could answer, the phone rang. Ravi picked it up and spoke in monosyllables. His face was livid when he disconnected.

'What happened?' Reeti looked puzzled.

'I wanted to know if any of the servants, drivers, or guards came into some money recently, like Gita. Just to cover all bases. There is a discrepancy the bank flagged. It seems Ramu, the night guard, has been receiving an amount of Rs 49,000 every month from an account in Sirsa for more than a year. The amount is borderline, so it did not require any identification to be shown for its withdrawal. Reeti, the bank records are being sent by email.'

'Who is the account holder?' Charu asked.

'Ratan Lal Chowdhury,' Ravi said.

'What! Anumita's father? How is that possible? When did Ramu join the household as a guard?'

'A year ago.'

Reeti's phone started buzzing. Charu heard Reeti talking on it enthusiastically. 'I am telling you, Rajat, you are brilliant. If you were not my colleague, I would have hugged you. This is great news. Where did you dig it out from…? Great! No, Ravi and Charu are right here. I will tell them now, thanks. Bye.'

'What happened?' Charu asked her when she put the phone down. She had understood Ravi had put Rajat, one of their other colleagues from the office, at work.

'You won't believe what Rajat uncovered in Hisar,' Reeti chirped.

Ravi turned to Charu. 'I sent him to dig around for Malti Devi and Ram Vilas's past connection, as you suggested.' He turned back to Reeti. 'What did he find?'

'They have a child together.'

'Oh God! Malti Devi and Ram Vilas? Are you quite sure?' Charu exclaimed.

'Yes. He was born in Hisar before the scandal broke. In fact, he was brought up as an orphan at the ashram in Sirsa. He is now an adult, the caretaker of the Hisar ashram.'

'Oh my! Do we have any evidence of this? Does Anumita know? Did her father know?' Charu's mind was buzzing with questions.

'No, I don't think so. Rajat found the man's birth certificate. The names on the certificate are R. Vilas and M. Jatav. Malti Devi's maiden name is Jatav. Rajat said he went to the ashram to find out about the bags. But, when he saw the caretaker, he found his face very familiar. According to this picture he has sent, he is a carbon copy of Ram Vilas at twenty years of age.'

'Does the man know he is their son?' Ravi wondered.

'It doesn't seem so. He spoke about being abandoned at the ashram and how every child thought of Swamiji as their father. They all call Malti Devi Ma, by the way.'

'And the bags?

'He came across them in the hallway. Old clothes and sheets only. The bag was half empty, so we don't know if Myra had already been taken out. They could be in it together. They have certainly lied about their relationship, right?'

'But,' Charu mused, 'supposing all this is true, and they do have a child together, what motive could they possibly have for Myra's kidnapping?'

Reeti paused. 'I have no idea, Charu, but it seems anything is possible with this family.'

Prithvi entered the room and walked up to Charu. 'Sorry, Chumki, I haven't been around. There is too much work right now.'

'How come you are home today?'

'I have been unwell,' he said. 'My daughter is still out there, Chumki. I didn't expect you people would take so long to trace her. It's been three days.'

'We are trying our best, sir,' Ravi said, politely.

'What about Bilal?'

'Still on him,' Charu answered.

'Good, good. He should be looked into thoroughly. And, Chumki, I hope you will bring any wrongdoing on his part to my notice.'

Charu decided this was the moment to be plain with him. 'Prithvi, you knew he was at your house with Ram Vilas Ji that day, yet you never mentioned him. Why?'

'Chumki, Swamiji is trying to throw a tantrum. He does this when he feels I need to show him how important he is in my life. I saw him, yes, when I checked the security footage—just as he would have wanted me to. It was a power move, Chumki.'

'So, you didn't ask him about it?'

'No. He knows I know and what it means. He wanted to get the message across that he could join hands with my rival under my nose. He is waiting for my reaction. And, I am biding my time to show that reaction,' Prithvi smiled.

'And, what about us? Why didn't you tell me the truth when I asked you about the people who were in the haveli or had visited it that day?'

'Because he had left. Swamiji also left after collecting the file, so I didn't think it was important.'

'You also called a carpenter to pick up a tea trolley.'

'What? No. Actually, I gave the number to Gita to call the man to pick it up and forgot all about it. She'll do it when she gets the time. Anyway, that is the least of my worries right now.' Prithvi left the room.

Reeti's phone pinged. Charu knew she had been listening to their conversation.

'The mysterious number got activated again,' Reeti told her, looking up from her phone. 'This time, they were able to triangulate the area and the cell tower.'

'Where is it located?' Ravi's asked.

'They are sending us the coordinates now.' Reeti found a map of the city and began placing dots on the map as she received them. It was time-consuming and made Charu fidget. She wanted to help, but she knew she would be in the way. Leaving Reeti and Ravi to finish the job, she went to the garden.

Charu waited for Ravi to finish taking feedback from all the field heads, so they could leave to talk to the night guard, Ramu. She was mentally so focused on Prithvi and if he could have stooped low enough to kidnap his own daughter that she didn't realize someone was approaching. She felt Sia's presence only when she stood before her.

'Charu aunty, can I sit here with you?' Sia asked her.

'Yes, of course, Sia. Are you feeling all right?' Charu relaxed.

'Yes, I am. But, Mummy is not. Papa is angry with her again.'

They sat in silence as Charu heard something smash against a wall upstairs. She felt Sia cringe, then move closer to her. She wrapped her arm around the little girl, feeling her hurt, the fear in her little heart.

'Why does Papa drink?' Sia asked in a small voice.

'Are you scared of him, Sia?'

Sia shrugged her shoulders. Charu hugged her tighter.

'Can't you make him stop? Nani says it is natural for men to lose their temper, raise their hand, but Manik Chachu disagrees. He says no one should hurt others,' Sia said, softly.

'Sia, does your father raise his hand against your mother?' Charu asked her, scared of the answer.

'He doesn't mean to, but Mummy is clumsy around him. She always drops something or bangs into something. It is less often now, after he injured me badly once but, earlier, Mummy used to fall a lot.'

'He hit you?' Charu was heartbroken. Prithvi was not the man she had thought he would be. She realized she had been fooling herself since she had met him, refusing to trust in her instincts that had never let her down.

'Well, he pushed me. Last year, just before my birthday, Papa had come home late, and Mummy was angry. They started fighting loudly. I tried to press my hands over my ears to block the noise. When that didn't work, I put in my earphones.

Since my room is right opposite Papa's room, I can hear everything he says. I know all the words he uses for her. They aren't good words. But, then he started throwing things around, and I crept out. I saw he was shaking Mummy. I went to stop him. I was pulling at his arm when he pushed me away. I fell against the mirror. It shattered into small pieces. That's how got all these small scratches.'

'Were you badly hurt?'

'Well, there was some blood. Mummy and Gita Didi spent the whole night sitting beside me, pulling out glass from my hair. Mummy was so angry at Papa, she told me she would not live with a man who hits his own children.'

'Where was Myra?'

'She was here.'

'You must have been so scared.'

'I was...but then Papa was so sorry when he was sober again. He kept saying sorry again and again. He started coming home late...and he would go to his own room to sleep, which was better than them fighting.'

'They don't fight anymore?'

'Now they don't talk so much. But, since you came, they have started again. That is why I was scared and came here.'

'Where's Gita?'

'She has gone to call Manik Chachu. He will sort it out. I know he will.'

They heard footsteps and then a door banged shut.

'Doesn't your grandmother help?' asked Charu.

'She doesn't interfere. She says it is between my parents, and she has no right to meddle.'

Charu looked up when Gita entered, calling Sia. 'Sia, I have been looking everywhere for you. Let's go. I have some snacks for you.'

'You want to go, Sia?' asked Charu.

'Yes, I will go to my room, thank you. I think you will be able to find Myra,' Sia said before walking away.

Then she suddenly ran back and gave Charu an unexpected hug. The hope in Sia's voice, the quick hug, broke Charu.

Charu felt hollow, as though someone had scooped out all her optimism. She sat with her head in her hands, stuck in a time warp, her mind reliving all the moments with Prithvi. She cursed herself for turning a blind eye to what she had sensed even at school.

Ravi found her shredding the skin of her index finger raw in the garden. She told him haltingly about Prithvi's alcoholism and physical abuse towards Sia and Anumita. Ravi cursed Prithvi. Setting their collective anger aside and determined to find Myra, they headed out to Ramu's home.

Ramu lived in a room in the makeshift huts provided by the security company on the city's outskirts. Ravi asked Charu to wait in the car while he went inside the *basti*—the slum area—to find him. Ramu shared his room with two other men, who had also come to the city for employment from the neighbouring small towns.

The rooms were made of asbestos sheets joined together, with little space between them. Ravi entered the maze. A grey haze hung over the settlement. The orange and blue tarpaulin sheets didn't look effective enough to keep the cold at bay, Ravi observed as he walked through the slum. It was not yet evening, but small fires had been lit in anticipation of dinner already. Ravi asked around for Ramu and found he wasn't home. Someone mentioned he would be back in a couple of hours.

Ravi then drove to the nearest police station and requested a bit of help.

As they drove back to the slum, an unmarked van followed them. They parked the car a little distance away from the edge of the tenement. Ravi raised his hand to signal to the vehicle behind them. Checking to see if Charu was comfortable, he gave instructions to the men, who then alighted from the van. He strode back into the narrow sewage-strewn lanes with a policeman in plain clothes while the others waited with Charu.

Ravi yanked the curtain open, and found Ramu asleep on the cot in his room. Two other young men watched something on their phones. They scampered out, fearing Ravi's intimidating presence. Ravi shook Ramu awake and asked him to follow him out. A disgruntled Ramu followed Ravi to the edge of the slum. Ramu saw Charu step out of the car and became nervous. He had heard from the staff at the haveli that she could read people's minds.

'What happened, sir? Why have you brought me here? I have told you everything.' His eyes were trained on the policemen standing some distance away.

'Ramu, I will ask you a simple question...and I want a simple answer. You have been receiving Rs 49,000 from someone every month for the last two years. Who has been giving you the money and why?' He motioned to a burly policeman, who glowered at Ramu. Ramu stood silently, weighing his options. He gauged the distance between himself and the nearest exit.

'Don't even think about it, Ramu. You have been to the lock-up several times, so I don't have to tell you what these men are capable of doing.'

'Sir, it is my salar...'

'And, let me warn you—I am done with you lying to me. Be very careful about what you say because, in my opinion, *you* have kidnapped Myra. We have evidence to claim that you were paid for it.' Ravi grabbed Ramu by his smelly vest, twisting it.

'No. No, sir, I didn't. Why would I do that? Sir, I have been a petty thief, I admit, but, I swear, I have not taken Myra Baby. You are trying to pin this upon me,' Ramu whined accusingly, full of false bravado. His eyes shifted to Charu as she came forward to stand next to Ravi.

'Ramu, you have been hiding things from us,' she said.

'It seems until we give you special treatment in the lock-up, you will not come out with the truth,' said Ravi. He pushed Ramu towards the unmarked van. The burly men circled Ramu and Ravi, tapping their batons.

'Sir...Sir, please, I will tell you everything. Don't send me with them.' He fell down on his knees, wrapping his hands around Ravi's legs.

'Charu madam, please help me. I haven't done anything.'

Ravi pulled the frightened man to his feet. 'Get him some water,' he said to one of the men.

'Charu madam, I swear I have never kidnapped anyone. I, too, have a daughter in the village.' He gulped down the water from the bottle he had been handed. Ravi gestured to the men. Ramu watched them step back until Ravi and Charu stood alone with him near the van now.

'Ravi sir, I have to show you something, but it is hidden in my room. I promise I am not trying to trick you,' Ramu stammered.

'Come on then, but don't try anything stupid, Ramu.' He helped Charu back to the car and walked to Ramu's room along with two policemen. Ramu walked hurriedly into his room and waited for Ravi to enter. Then he closed the flimsy door. The policemen waited outside. Ravi watched as he slipped his fingers in between the two asbestos sheets that formed the wall of his room and pulled out a thread he had hung in between. At the end of the thin cable was a mobile phone wrapped painstakingly in plastic and tape.

'Sir, this is why I am being paid the money.' Ramu switched the phone on and handed it over to Ravi. There was a video clip on mute. Ravi's face blanched as he watched the clip. Switching it off, he placed it in the evidence bag and walked back silently to where Charu was waiting.

'What happened?' she asked.

'Ramu has recorded a video on his phone. Ramu, explain,' he said. Charu could hear the anger behind his words.

Ramu began his story. 'That day, Arjun was ill. At the time I was working at a restaurant as a cleaner. He requested me to fill in for him. I had done it earlier, too, so I didn't think much about it. According to the rules, it was not allowed because the security company did not have me on their roll. But, all the guards help each other out, so their salary is not deducted.

Ram Vilas came in his car late in the night. Prithvi sir had gone out for three days. Everyone else was asleep. Ram Vilas said he had to pick up some files from his office, so I let him in. I could smell the *ganja* on him, but I said nothing, of course. It wasn't my place to comment.

In summers, there is still some noise due to the ACs running, but it was winter, so everything was quiet. Sometime later, I heard noises coming from his office.'

'Noises? What kind of noises?' Charu felt the dread build in her gut.

'Distressed noises, madam. As if someone was in pain... the kind injured dogs make in the night.'

Charu gasped at what she knew was coming next.

'I thought of waking Rambir, his driver, who was sleeping in the car. Then I thought I should make sure everything was okay, myself. I didn't want to be caught snooping. I just wanted to make sure he hadn't fallen or hurt himself.'

'You told me you could look into his room from the guard's cabin,' Ravi remembered.

'Yes, but we couldn't see the whole room. So, I crept closer to peep in. Sir, what I saw shook me to the core. I don't know why I recorded it. At the time, I wasn't thinking. I just did it. Ram Vilas left after three or four hours. I waited for the morning guard, my brother Arjun, and left without saying a word. I thought of sharing what I had seen with him, but I knew he would go straight to Prithvi sir. As I watched the video again, I realized I didn't have to do anything. I was sure Prithvi sir would do what was necessary when he came back. Later, I asked Arjun, more than once, if something had happened at the haveli. But, he said nothing had changed. I asked if Prithvi sir was back, and he said Sahib had been back for a few days. I was perturbed by the fact that either he didn't know or he didn't care,' Ramu finished.

'But, then you got greedy?' said Charu, her voice tight. She found it difficult to remain polite to him in the face of his actions. 'You didn't think of raising the alarm, did you?'

'I...I thought of my brother. He would have been fired for sending me in his place. I thought surely Ram Vilas would be reported by Anumita madam. But, when nothing happened for weeks, I approached her at the haveli and showed her the clip. I had gone there seeking an explanation for her silence. She accused me of blackmail. I realized she hadn't told anyone what had happened. All these high-society ladies are more scared of people finding out about the skeletons in their cupboards than about the brutality they face. It was then that the idea to demand money for my silence came to me. She agreed, but she said she could only pay in instalments.

Since then, the amount is credited into an account I opened only for this every month. I am saving up for my daughter's dowry. But, sir, I swear I have no idea about Myra's kidnapping.' Ramu joined his palms again.

'Does Arjun know about this?'

'No, sir. Please don't tell him. He has no idea. I asked for the job, and Anu madam requested Prithvi sir to call the security agency and vouch for me. Arjun thinks it was due to his recommendation that the company gave me the job.'

'So, why is Malti Devi paying you?'

'No, sir, Malti Devi isn't paying me. It is Anumita madam.'

'Wait,' said Ravi, as a thought occurred to him. 'How long after the incident did you show her this clip?'

'About a month later, when I came to know she was pregnant again,' Ramu replied. He paused, and suddenly looked up at Ravi, open-mouthed, as he realized the implication of his words.

23. Anumita

2 pm, Friday

Charu and Ravi both had been quiet throughout the drive back to Chauhan Haveli. The information they had extracted from Ramu was too disturbing to be believed. It was even more harrowing that Prithvi did not know about the horrifying incident. How ironic that the very man he worshipped had violated his wife.

'Do you think we should tell Prithvi?' Reeti asked, shocked at what they had uncovered.

'Before that, we must talk to Anumita and find out what really happened,' Charu answered. She knew what sexual abuse could do to a person. She had seen her sister, Aruna, go through years of trauma at the hands of her first husband.

At that moment, Anumita walked inside to tell them their lunch would be ready in a while. She sat down, wondering why they looked so forlorn. She inquired about their day and was surprised when Reeti locked the door.

'What is the matter? Has something happened to Myra? No...you said she is safe. Charu?'

Charu felt Anumita's fear. There was anxiety in her voice, but also confusion and guilt. 'No, this is not about Myra,' she said. 'Anumita, we have something to show you. Trust me, we didn't go looking for this, but we need to know about this now that we have it. It could be linked to Myra's kidnapping.'

Ravi played the clip and took a few steps away from Anumita to allow her privacy. Charu could feel Anumita's heartbeat quicken, her body started to shake. The profound helplessness, sorrow, and self-blame slowly spilt over. Charu grabbed her hand when breathing became difficult for her.

'Ravi, take the phone away,' said Charu. Then she rubbed her palm on Anumita's back. 'Anumita, I am so sorry.'

It took some time for Prithvi's wife to control herself.

'Anumita, I am sorry, but we have to ask you about this. Is Myra Prithvi's daughter?' Charu began again, even more gently.

The Anumita in front of them now was very different from her usual self. 'I had to say she was...once I came to know I was pregnant,' she confessed. 'Prithvi and I had stopped being intimate after I came to know about his many women.' She shook her head.

'That means he does not know Ram Vilas assaulted you?'

'No, he...he doesn't know. I didn't think he would believe me, especially when it was his beloved Swamiji. I made the mistake of calling my mother, who, instead of encouraging me to report my abuser, pushed me to have sex with Prithvi so we could pass off Myra as his child. I realized later I shouldn't have listened to her. I was already in a depressive spiral. At the time, I thought she had come over to support me, but it was to keep me from opening my mouth. Once Myra was born, it was over. I was stuck.'

'Did it happen again?'

'No. I stayed away, got cameras installed. He apologized later, said it should never have happened—as if that was enough. But, why are you asking me about this now?'

'Does he know Myra is his daughter?' Reeti asked, softly.

Anumita fell silent. 'I guess so. He made her his nominee in all his properties. Or, that is what he told me.'

'Is that why you have been paying Ramu? To keep this from Prithvi?'

'Charu, you know him—how vicious he can be. I thought about telling him all, despite what my mother said. I thought, what man would not believe his wife? But, then my mother said something that made me stay silent. What if Prithvi refused to accept Myra as his daughter and asked me to give her up? He might get angry that I didn't tell him earlier and that I would be blamed somehow. He can be vindictive towards anyone he thinks has wronged him.

Oh my God, what if he's already found out? No, he couldn't have. No one else knew. Ramu would not have said anything. Ram Vilas and my mother wouldn't have either.'

Charu heard the doubt in her voice, the frustration behind her words. She could hear the acceptance of the wrong done to her in Anumita's voice. Charu hated this acceptance. It meant, like Aruna, Anumita too had chosen defeat.

'But, for how long would you have paid Ramu? Does Malti Devi know he was extracting money from you?'

'I would have thought of something. My mother knew. She was the one who sent the money every month. Prithvi and I have a joint account. He didn't allow me to have a separate one. He said it was because we are a family, but I know he wanted to track my expenses, to control me. When Ramu demanded money for his silence, she paid up.'

Anumita looked drained. When she left, the three of them sat contemplating the disclosures.

'Malti Devi made sure Anumita didn't report Ram Vilas. What an ode to motherhood that woman is turning out to be,' Reeti said, caustically.

'We didn't ask Anumita if she tampered with the nanny cam or about her absences.'

'We can ask her—once she is in a state to talk. Ravi, you said the driver told you Malti Devi's lawyer was also at the ashram when she went off with Ram Vilas on the day of the kidnapping. Why did the lawyer go for a puja no one knew was being conducted?' asked Charu.

Ravi called the ashram in Sirsa and put the phone on the speaker. Someone picked it up after the bell rang several times.

'Hello.'

'Namaskar.'

'I would like to speak to the caretaker of the ashram, please.'

'Speaking.'

'Sir, are you also a practising lawyer in Sirsa?'

'Yes. If you would like to consult me for legal help, please use the other number.' Ravi scribbled the number and address the man gave him. Next, he called up his colleague in Hisar and told him to go to Sirsa and question the gentleman.

Reeti tapped on the desk to draw Ravi's attention. 'Ravi, I found Gita's brother. He took a train when he ran away from the de-addiction centre. They found him at Dimapur railway station, working at one of the stalls. He said he was working to collect enough money to travel to his village by bus. Gita sent the quarterly payment she got from Anumita to her grandparents in Nagaland. We were checking Gita's account and her parents. Their bank records, and Anumita's transaction details, prove it.'

'Okay,' he nodded. 'Charu, what is happening with the search for the woman or the place where Myra is being held?'

'It is going slow because we aren't allowed to have more people on the ground. They are combing the areas for a *barsati* from where the Hanuman murti, and the temple, are visible, but no luck so far,' Charu answered.

'Reeti, do we have the cloth bag similar to the one Malti Devi took to the ashram?'

'Yes,' Reeti picked it up.

'So, if they carried Myra in this, covered her with old clothes, it could have been more than fourteen kilos. Someone would have noticed such a heavy bag. It does not make sense to me,' Charu murmured.

'Also, there is a number in Anumita's call records from a few months back. It is some property dealer's number in Karol Bagh. The area is suspect. We should go and check it out first thing tomorrow, once I can narrow down the location.'

Ravi looked at Charu, then nodded. 'Take Charu with you,' he said.

Ravi decided to step out for a bit of air. Arjun joined his palms in greeting when he spotted Ravi. They stood together companionably.

'You weren't relieved by another guard today, Arjun? Are you on double duty?' said Ravi.

'No, sir, my brother Ramu is unwell. He asked me to cover for him,' replied Arjun.

'Has Prithvi sir come back?'

'No, sir.'

'But, his car is here.'

'He goes to office in the official car, sir.'

While they were still talking, Prithvi's car turned inside the gate. Prithvi stepped out and asked the driver to leave.

'Is everything all right, Ravi?' he asked, walking into the corridor with him. 'Your face says "No Progress". You guys are starting to worry me. Anu will be proved right if it goes on like this, my man.'

'Let's talk in a bit, sir. Why don't you change and meet us in the back room?'

'Of course. Give me fifteen minutes.'

Ravi returned to the den and located the printout of Prithvi's search history.

'What is the matter, Ravi?' Charu enquired, stepping into the room. 'You are hassled.'

'I met Prithvi near the gate. He was acting as if he knew nothing. I am going to shove this list of crimes in his face.' He slammed it on his desk.

'And, what would that achieve?'

'Satisfaction.' Ravi sounded irate.

Charu smiled. 'Ravi, we haven't found any substantial proof yet that has been authorized. Reeti copied his hard drive without his knowledge'

'Yes, but we have found this curiosity for crime. And, if one is to couple it with all the other…'

'Hi.' Prithvi walked in.

'Sir, please take a seat.' Ravi switched on the recorder.

'Ah, all right. Why are you so agitated, Ravi? Were you offended by something I said?'

Charu heard the mocking note in Prithvi's voice. She kept her eyes averted.

'Sir, I would like you to explain this.' Ravi slid the printout of Prithvi's search history from his laptop across the desk and watched him pick it up.

'I'm not sure why you are showing me this. What is it?'

'This is your search history for the week before Myra was taken,' Ravi saw Prithvi's face pale at his words.

'What's the big deal?' Prithvi said, trying to look unconcerned.

'This doesn't look good for you. If one was to couple this search history that we retrieved from your laptop with what you told us your mentor suggested...this looks like research.'

'Rubbish! Why don't you admit you couldn't find my daughter? That you've failed!' Prithvi countered in a scathing voice.

'Then tell us why you were looking for ways to kidnap a child. Trying to find inspiration, were you?'

'That was just something I was investigating. This...this does not prove anything,' he wavered. Charu heard the panic he was trying to hide under the bluster.

'What about these?' Ravi put Charu's pictures Reeti had found on his laptop before him.

Charu sat opposite Prithvi, next to Ravi. She hadn't said a word since he had come in, hadn't even acknowledged him.

'Chumki, don't tell me you think I have kidnapped my own daughter! These are nothing. I cared about you. This is how I have always been. I went through a phase where I needed you, and...just having your pictures made me feel better. Ravi, you have seen how I keep Swamiji's cut out in his office. It keeps me grounded. Please say you believe me, Chumki.'

'Prithvi, why were you looking at ways to kidnap a child, ways to cause an accident, ways to hide a body?' Charu asked.

'Chumki, you can't believe this stupidity. Do you think I am capable of such a thing?'

'Then please answer the questions truthfully.'

Prithvi picked up the sheets before him and examined them thoughtfully. Then, straightening his shoulders, he began to talk. 'I know it seems as if I have committed this horrible crime, but I haven't. I told you Swamiji had suggested that my win was a given if there was a sympathy wave in my favour. I thought about it. I was even swayed for a little while but, I swear, it was just to see if I could pull it off. I wouldn't have followed up on it. No way.' The strain in Prithvi's voice was evident.

'What happened that day?'

'I had a disagreement with Swamiji on the proposed manifesto a few weeks back. He wanted me to fire Viswajit. Swamiji threatened to leave if I stuck to him. Fed up, I asked him not to attend the meetings if he couldn't agree with us. He left my office, angry and hurt. The president was also unhappy with the numbers from the party-sponsored poll. That was when Swamiji's words came back to me. I thought of just seeing if the idea had any merit. I really wasn't thinking. I checked it out, yes. Then, as if waking up from a dream, I realized I was thinking of kidnapping my own daughter, harming my own family. I was immediately contrite. On that day we again disagreed and he stormed off. I had never spoken to Swamiji in that way so I followed him, wanting to seek his forgiveness. I sat in the car a little distance from the haveli. I saw him with Bilal and knew he was retaliating by taking my enemy into my house.

When they had entered the haveli, I drove back to the office, my head pounding with anger. After a few minutes, I received a call that they couldn't find Myra. My heart stopped. I know it sounds crazy, but it is the truth. I didn't take Myra, you have to believe me.' He looked imploringly at Charu.

Charu felt his desperation.

'Prithvi sir, I will request you not to step out of this haveli. I hope I make myself clear,' Ravi said. They would have to confirm what he had just told them.

Prithvi seemed to be sleepwalking as he walked out of their den.

'If what Prithvi says is the truth, we are back to square one,' Ravi sighed.

Prithvi is telling the truth, Charu thought but refrained from saying so. Instead, she reminded Ravi, 'We still don't know how Myra was taken out of the haveli.'

'The trolley is a definite no, as is the bag Bilal carried out.' Ravi crossed the words on the board.

'Rajat called and said a sweeper at the ashram confirmed Malti Devi's bags were opened before him. He was given some clothes from them,' Reeti sat on the couch, sighing tiredly.

'So, just how in the world was she kidnapped?' Charu said out loud. All their theories seemed improbable. The three of them sat, building and rejecting scenarios, worried about what they could have possibly missed.

After Prithvi's admission about getting swayed by his mentor's words, Ravi decided to stay in Chauhan Haveli to keep an eye on him. He would also wait for the report from the forensic expert. Charu and Reeti set off to explore the address of the property dealer in Karol Bagh. Reeti led the driver to the address she had found, through the back roads of the city.

After spending two hours roaming the dirty, narrow streets and tenements in different pockets of the area, both the women were tired. It seemed like a pointless exercise. While they were on their way to the heart of Karol Bagh, their car stopped, stuck in a traffic jam. Suddenly, Reeti pulled Charu's elbow. 'Charu, I think I just located the blue rectangular board you saw in your vision—a grey-blue, with "WELCOME" dangling from the end of the red-and-yellow building at one end, as you said.'

Charu sat up straight.

'It's Ghaffar Market!' she cried, excitedly. 'Of course. The name begins with G and ends with R. We're on the right track.'

They halted before an almost deserted community hall, in a state of disrepair.

'Google is showing this location, but the exact address is not flagged. Let's walk around,' said Reeti, opening the door of the car. They slowly walked the deserted marketplace nearby. Reeti asked a few men loitering about if they knew any property dealer offices around. They looked at her with a smirk on their face that made her reach for her service revolver.

'Reeti, I think we should check if there are any offices in the community centre,' Charu suggested.

They entered the building. The mouldy walls, dark interior, and smelly shafts made the women feel unsafe. Reeti tried to locate the office number, careful to guide Charu over the wires that crisscrossed the floor, waiting for someone to trip over them. They finally came to the tinted-glass doors of an office. There was no board, but the light inside was on. Reeti opened the door and found a thin boy watching a small TV on the wall. She called the number she had, and the phone beside the boy began ringing. He, however, continued to watch TV.

'Why don't you pick up the phone?' she asked, irritated.

'I am on a break. Why are you asking?' the boy said in a confrontational tone.

'Is there someone we can talk to?'

'My father is not here. Can I help you?' The boy, the proprietor's son, stood up and studied the two women.

Charu nudged Reeti's elbow. Reeti softened her voice. 'We just wanted to ask him about the...flats. I mean, if any are available to rent.' She gazed at the pictures of apartments, flats, and houses on the wall.

'I think you misunderstood. We deal with rooms for the labour class, not flats for rich women,' the boy said, walking towards them.

'Someone told us you rent out flats, so we came. We need a cheap place for two weeks. We can pay upfront. Where do you have these rooms you are talking about?' Charu stepped forward.

'All over Delhi. You can pick a location, and we will have a room for you. Here, take this.' He handed them a brochure that had all the areas marked on a map of Delhi.

'Would you have some rooms near the Hanuman Murti—maybe a *barsati*, from where the Jhandewalan temple is visible?'

'Madam, the list is in your hand. You can choose and let me know. I can show you the rooms.' The boy lost interest and turned back to the TV. Reeti started scanning the list that was five pages long.

'About two months ago, a friend of mine came to take a room from you. Would you be able to recognize their face?' Charu asked the boy again.

'I think so. I am the one who shows renters the rooms. I'm good with faces.'

Reeti took out her phone, brought up Prithvi's family photo—with Malti Devi and Ram Vilas in the frame—and turned it towards the boy.

'No, ma'am, none of them have ever been here. Our clients are not so "hi-fi". We deal with poor immigrants who come to the city for work.'

Charu touched the boy's shoulder and knew immediately he was telling the truth.

Reeti turned around, disappointed. They made their exit and walked down the corridor towards the road. Suddenly, Charu stopped. 'Reeti, you had clicked the pictures of the sketches, right? Let's show them to the boy.'

They went back to the office. The young boy was surprised to see them again.

Reeti held out the phone once again, this time with the sketches. 'Did she come here?' she asked.

The boy recognized the picture immediately. 'Yes, ma'am, she did. She spoke like she was from a small town but didn't look like a labourer. I remember her. Since she paid the rent in advance, we didn't mind. We don't ask too many questions, you see.'

'Where is she? Can you tell us?' Charu asked the boy.

The boy took a step back. He realized they weren't really looking for a room. 'Is there a problem? Should I call my father?'

'No, there is no problem. We just need this woman's address.'

'Actually, ma'am, that is private information. We cannot...'

Reeti flashed her ID at him. 'This is an investigation, and I need you to cooperate,' she told the boy.

'Ma'am, we don't want any trouble. Let me check. Can you tell me her name?'

'Check if any rooms were rented out near Hanuman Murti in Karol Bagh, around this time,' Charu said, mentioning the date on which Anumita had withdrawn cash from her father's account.

The boy took out another folder. The women waited impatiently while he checked the entries. Then he came up with the receipts in the name of Seema, closest to the date Reeti had given him. Reeti read the address and, warning him not to alert the women, rushed out holding Charu's hand.

24. Myra

5 pm, Friday

Charu and Reeti climbed inside a cab and gave the driver directions. On the way to the location, Charu updated Ravi. He told them he would have an additional backup team ready nearby. 'Reeti, don't move in yet even if you find her. Only check if she is there. Report once you spot her—or them. Charu, stay in the car and call me when you reach there.'

As soon as Ravi disconnected, Charu's phone rang again. It was Rajat, their team member Ravi had sent to Hisar to find out about Ram Vilas and Malti Devi. He was now in Sirsa, trying to gather information.

'Hi, Charu. I have some news for you. So, the lawyer with Ram Vilas in Sirsa is a hard-ass who refused to discuss even the ashram with me. Anyway, I went around the court asking the clerks, the draftsmen, the stenos, and the notaries, if any papers had been drawn up in Ram Vilas's name. I hit the jackpot, thank God. I found a draftsman who drew up some papers for the lawyer—with Ram Vilas as the first party. He didn't remember the exact details but said it was a new will. Ram Vilas signed it the day Myra was kidnapped. The notary attested the papers the next day. Tell Ravi I am heading back to Hisar to see what more I can find out.'

'Thanks, Rajat. Be careful.' Charu disconnected and sent a message to Ravi, relaying Rajat's message.

Reeti was silent when she looked up at the big Hanuman Murti as they passed it. The sound of the metro was loud and close.

'Reeti, what's wrong?' Charu asked.

'Charu, we are crossing the Hanuman Murti you saw, or we think you saw. There is a temple with a garland shop in front of it.'

'Great, that does mean we are on the right track.'

They reached the address Reeti had noted down at the property dealer's office. Reeti informed Ravi. As they waited for the backup, Reeti looked around and was awed at what Charu could do. All the clues she had provided them with came together to form this reality in front of her.

'Reeti, can you describe whatever you see?' said Charu.

'Yes. We are near the main road, in the service lane. From here I can see the school building. It is, as you said, made of red bricks and has a black coloured board outside saying FA Model School. The houses are all four-storeyed, with barely any space to separate them. There are tangled electricity wires overhead. Can you hear the temple bell?'

Charu heard the clanging of the temple bell and knew they were in the right place. She hoped they would find Myra soon.

After walking some more, Reeti said, 'Charu, we are standing before the address that we got from that property dealer. It's an old construction, with a grey-and-white façade. But, from here, I can't see if it has a *barsati* on the roof, though there is a safety grille.'

'There should be a motel nearby, the name starting with the alphabet V,' Charu reminded her as Reeti went into the opposite building to check from a distance.

'V Motel, that is the name—V,' Reeti exclaimed when she returned after a few minutes. 'There is a row of rooms on the terrace, and a thin safety grille on the three sides. You were right about the colour too; it's green. And, I could see the top of the Hanuman idol and also the flag of the temple. They are all here, all the clues you saw!' She lowered her volume, realizing people were staring at her. 'The doors were closed. A few people were outside on the terrace. There were clothes on the clothesline. Among them were clothes for a small child, but they could belong to anyone. Until we see Myra or Seema for ourselves, we cannot confirm their presence.'

Charu called Ravi and apprised him. He found it hard to stay at the haveli. His team members were in the field while he was too far away to help in case of an eventuality. The backup team had still not reached. He knew Charu would want to go in and find Myra and asked her to stay back. He was not far from the truth.

'Ravi, at least allow us to do a door-to-door search. There are only six rooms to check,' she insisted.

Ravi refused and ordered them to return to the car. The extraction team was on its way.

'Reeti, let's at least see if Myra is here,' said Charu when he hung up. Reeti watched Charu thoughtfully, then grabbed her hand and entered the building. As they reached the terrace, they attracted the attention of the few young boys who were sitting on a cot, playing carom. Reeti shooed them away.

She knocked on the door nearest the entrance. A sleepy, bare-chested man, wearing a lungi, opened the door. She politely joined her palms and said, 'Sir, we are waiting to meet the property dealer to show us a room. He isn't here yet. May we use your phone?'

He stared at Charu, who was holding her white stick. 'Wait outside, I will get it,' he said after a moment. Reeti took the phone he brought out and stepped away. 'Do you both need a room?' he asked Charu. She sensed his suspicion. *'Yeh to baat theek nahi hai*—this is not right. We already have a single mother living here. Now, how will we keep a blind girl safe? Listen, this place is not for you. You should look for a room on the ground floor somewhere.'

'Oh, a single mother? Where does she live?' Charu asked.

'Why do you want to know?'

'We would like to ask her if it is a good place to rent.'

'Haan haan, why not? That door.' He pointed towards it, then realized she couldn't see. Instead, he showed it to Reeti, who had returned. 'That third door. She mostly keeps to

herself but, sometimes, when the child is fussy, I see her walk around outside.'

'She must have been living here for some time now if you know her routine?'

'Why are you asking all these questions?' He snatched his phone from her and went back into the room, glaring at them as he closed the door.

Reeti knocked on the door the surly man had pointed out. Charu stood beside her. Her heart beat with a staccato rhythm when she heard the tinkling sound of anklets walking towards the door.

'Who is it?'

'Hi. We are two women who've come to see the rooms on this terrace. We wanted to have a word with you regarding renting a room here. And, my friend is a bit tired. Could you spare a glass of water?' Reeti called out.

There was silence on the other side. Charu felt the woman peering through the peephole in the door. The latch was released, and the door opened slightly. Before them stood the woman in the sketch, the woman who had appeared in Charu's visions. She was dressed in a salwar kurta, and her hair was tied in a bun. She looked over their shoulder. 'Are you alone?' she sounded apprehensive.

'Yes, we came to find out if the rooms here were safe,' Charu answered, smiling.

'They are okay. For how long do you need one?' She became more comfortable as she chatted with them because she saw Charu was blind and hence harmless.

'We are here for a few weeks for a training programme. Have you been here long?'

'Umm...for a couple of days, but I shall be returning to my village soon. This place is completely safe, though I don't really step out that much. Nobody has troubled me much because I have a small chil...' She stopped short, biting her lip.

They heard a sound from the other room. Myra had probably woken up.

'Just a minute,' Seema mumbled and went inside.

Reeti squeezed Charu's hand. 'It's her, Charu. We found her.'

When the woman opened the door again, she had the glass of water in one hand, Myra in the other. The child was sucking on the old pacifier with the rubbed-off print and a broken ring.

'Oh, what a beautiful girl! Hello, baby,' Reeti exclaimed. 'She wants to come to you,' Reeti nudged Charu.

Charu's hand shook as she felt Myra reach towards her. They had hoped to find Myra, but they hadn't decided what they would do once they did find her.

Charu held out her hands to take Myra. She felt Seema's trepidation, and then her pity, towards her when she said, 'I rarely get to hold children.'

Seema leaned forward, and Charu felt Myra's arms wrap around her neck. Charu held on to Myra and took a step back. Reeti watched Seema's smile turn into a frown when Charu moved away. She blocked Seema when she tried to rush forward to grab Myra from Charu.

Reeti held her arm tightly and whispered, 'Seema, if that is really your name, you better not make a noise. You are under arrest for kidnapping Myra Chauhan. Now step inside.' She pushed Seema into the room behind.

Charu closed the door.

The room was a small cubbyhole—bare, with only a single bed and a temporary kitchen. There were two chairs and a few bags of groceries and milk lying on the floor. A large bucket of water and several bottles of mineral water also lay on one side. A single stove with a pot over it was where, Reeti assumed, Seema prepared the food.

'Who are you? Give her to me,' Seema yelled, rushing towards Charu again.

'The question is—who are *you*?' Reeti pushed her into a chair and bent over her threateningly. 'We are the police.' She flashed her ID. 'Now, you better start talking before the rest of the team arrives.'

'I will not say a word. You entered my room and took my child by force.'

'I don't think you understand how serious this is, Seema. You have Myra, a minister's kidnapped daughter. If you cooperate with us, we could help you,' Charu said.

Seema thought for a moment. Then, in a sulky voice, she said, 'What do you want to know?'

'Who are you? And, who are you working with?'

'I took Myra. It's all my fault,' Seema announced dramatically.

Charu sighed. 'Seema, the fact that Myra has been with you means you are going to prison. But, you were nowhere near Chauhan Haveli the day Myra was kidnapped. It would be better if you tell us the truth,' Reeti scowled at the thin woman. Her phone rang. It was Ravi.

'We've got Myra, Ravi,' she said to him, then winced when she heard him shout in her ear. 'Yes, we are at the location. Myra is with us. We are coming back. I'll send a location pin for the extraction team. Will talk once we reach.' Reeti disconnected the phone.

'No, no, don't take her back. Please, just let me talk to... I was told she had to be kept hidden from the people in the haveli,' Seema pleaded with them. 'It's for her own safety. Please believe me.'

Reeti was about to send the pin to Ravi when she felt Charu's hand on her shoulder. Charu handed over Myra to her and sat down beside Seema.

'Listen, Seema, we don't want Myra to be harmed in any way. If you tell us what you know, we will be in a better position to protect her. Who are you? Who do you want to talk to?'

'Manik,' the woman sobbed. 'I need to speak to Manik. I'm his fiancée.'

While Charu and Reeti were hurtling towards Chauhan Haveli, deciding what to do with Myra and Seema, Ravi had an unexpected visitor.

'Hello, sir. I thought I would ask if you found any lead on Myra. Are you alone today?' asked Manik. Ravi saw he was dressed in his cricket uniform.

'Yes. Did you come straight from the coaching centre?'

'Yes, I missed practice for a few days due to ill health, so I have to make up for it. I came to pick up my phone from Sia's room, so I thought I'd say hello. I will see you tomorrow. Bye, sir.'

Ravi nodded and turned away. A few minutes later, the door opened again. Ravi turned, irritated at the interruption. His glower turned into a smile when he saw Sia at the door.

'Has Manik Chachu left? I saw him run upstairs, but Gita Didi said I had to finish my food first. He didn't even meet me,' Sia sounded hurt.

'Don't worry, Sia. He forgot his phone here, he came to collect that. He will probably see you before he leaves.'

'No, no, not his phone. He must be looking for his bag,' Sia interjected.

'Bag? Which bag?' Ravi's was suddenly alert.

'His cricket kit. It's lying outside. I saw it and came here to remind him to take it, thinking he must be with you. Sometimes he forgets to take it with him—like he did the day Myra was kidnapped. Since it is a big bag, he usually leaves it in the broom cupboard upstairs. But, when Mummy and Papa came, he was already downstairs and, in the confusion, he forgot it here. Gita Didi had to run and give it to him later.'

Ravi remembered the slim storage cabinet between Myra's room and the washroom. He needed to see the bag.

'Gita Didi? How did she give it back to him? He must have covered quite a distance on his bike already by the time she discovered it,' Ravi said gently to not alarm Sia.

'No, no, Uncle. There's a shortcut from the back gate,' Sia answered.

'You saw this yourself?'

'Yes, from the window of my room. While Papa was talking to all the guards, we were waiting in my room. Manik Chachu phoned Gita Didi to tell her he had forgotten his cricket kit in the broom cupboard. The volume on her phone is quite loud. I heard his voice. He asked her to bring it to the back gate. He didn't have time enough to come to the main gate.'

'But, isn't that gate is always locked?

'Yes, but she just had to pass the bag to him. The vertical grille in the middle of the gate is spaced out enough that she could pass the bag through it. Papa sometimes just crouches down and slips in through the grille without bothering to unlock the gate.'

Ravi wondered how they had missed this fact. He thought back to all they had found out about Manik and realized that no one had mentioned the cricket bag. Neither Prithvi nor Anumita or Manik. 'Sia, don't tell anyone that you mentioned the bag to me. I just remembered I have to make an urgent call.'

'Okay, sure.' Sia agreed, running up to her room.

Ravi hurried out to check the broom closet. He bumped into a bag lying near the main door, the cricket kit. Ravi bent down and picked it up. He rummaged inside. His hands felt something that made him frown. He put the bag down and walked into the kitchen, where Manik was saying his goodbyes. Manik saw Ravi standing near the entrance.

'Is everything all right, sir?' he asked, approaching Ravi.

'Yes. Why don't you come with me? I have a few questions,' Ravi said.

Manik looked perplexed at the stoic man before him. 'Ravi sir, could we do this later? I should leave, or I will get really late. I shall come in tonight, and you can ask me questions then.'

'No, come with me now, Manik,' Ravi's voice and his grip on Manik's arm was firm. Ravi's phone rang. It was Charu. He spent a few minutes listening, answering her only in monosyllables, aware that Manik, who was walking beside him, was listening to his conversation. After disconnecting the phone, Ravi turned to the quiet man beside him.

'Manik, we found Myra and the woman with her. She is under arrest. They are getting her back to the haveli. I think you better start talking.' Manik froze, looking at Ravi wide-eyed.

'That's impossible...I mean, what does that have to do with me.'

'Guess what I just found in your cricket kit?'

'What? Why?' Manik's face had lost all colour.

'Myra's doll. Would you like to tell me why you have Myra's favourite toy?'

'What! I don't know how...I didn't put it there. Maybe, Sia put it in by mistake,' Manik stammered.

'Is Anumita involved?'

'She hasn't done anything. She is innocent,' Manik emphasized.

'Not so innocent. Here, look...proof that Anumita destroyed the camera in Myra's room. She put the teddy bear in the water when she knew the water would destroy the camera. There are also her unexplained absences. And, the money she paid the property dealer in cash for the room where we found Myra matches a withdrawal via ATM by Anumita from the joint account with Prithvi. We have the security footage of the ATM. You can't defend her, Manik. She is going to...'

'No, wait. I will take the blame. Completely.' Manik sat down. 'On one condition. Do you promise to help Anu?' he asked.

Ravi thought for a moment. 'Yes, I promise. Now...'

'I don't think you mean that.'

'Fine, let's wait for them here,' Ravi said as Manik started shaking his head.

'No, no...don't get Myra back to the haveli yet. Ravi sir, I am begging you. Yo...you people don't know everything. You have to trust me. Please, don't bring Myra back. It was for her own good. First, hear me out?'

'Why should I trust you?'

'I will tell you everything, please...,' he beseeched, joining his hands.

'What's going on here. Manik sir, I thought you had left. Why are you still...?' Anumita entered the room. She looked at Manik's joined hands and stopped.

'You found her,' Anumita's voice lacked all emotion.

'Yes, Charu and Reeti found Myra. They are bringing the woman, Seema, and Myra, back. Seema is in custody but not talking yet. Once she is sent to the police station, she will cooperate.' Ravi saw them exchange apprehensive glances. The door opened again, and Charu and Reeti came in with Seema. She saw Manik and Anumita and began to cry. Manik went to her side and apologized.

'Seema, I am so sorry for dragging you into my life. You should blame everything on me and leave before more people come to know of your involvement,' he requested her.

'I am so sorry, Manik, I had to tell them. They were going to bring Myra back here,' said Seema, looking distressed.

'It's okay, you did the right thing.' Manik mollified her.

'Nobody is going anywhere. Manik, you and Seema together kidnapped Myr...' Ravi announced.

'Where is she?' Anumita interrupted.

'At my house. Do you want me to send for her?' asked Charu. She found Anumita's reaction at odds with her expectation. Where was the happiness, the relief? Anumita sounded worried and unhappy.

She took a deep breath and said, 'Manik didn't do it, Charu. I did it. *I* kidnapped Myra.'

25. Manik

7:30 pm, Friday

'I think we should all sit down and start from the beginning,' said Charu.

Ravi switched on the recorder as everyone took their seat.

'I did it. Manik and Seema aren't at fault,' Anumita whispered.

'Why?' asked Reeti.

'Anu...,' Manik pleaded.

'Manik, it's over. I should have listened to you. But, I thought...' Anumita sounded tired and defeated. 'Ram Vilas arranged a match between Prithvi and me. I met Prithvi a few times before marriage and found him full of himself. But, he was courteous. I wanted to leave my father's house and my jealous stepmother, so I didn't object.

After our marriage, he became overbearing. The more he succeeded in his career, the worse he became. He started drinking heavily. He had no love for me. I found out about his obsession with Charu during one of his drunken rages.

It was like Prithvi was two very different people. He has a split personality. After Sia was born, I became depressed, and he started travelling. We stopped sharing a room. I knew he was sleeping with other women, but he kept Charu in his sights. He would look at her pictures at night, in his room.'

Charu felt uneasy about what Anumita had revealed about her husband and mourned the loss of the boy she had once loved.

'Last year, he started talking about buying this haveli. I thought it was for my interior decoration business. I thought he was trying to fix our marriage. Later, I realized he wanted to be close to you,' Anumita continued.

Ravi watched as Manik took her hand. They looked at each other lovingly. But, he let go of it quickly when Prithvi's heavy tread became audible in the corridor outside. In a minute, Prithvi was at the door.

'What's going on?' He stood stunned at the sight of Seema in the room.

'You are the woman from Chumki's sketch. How come you're here? Chumki, what's going on?' He turned towards Charu.

'Prithvi, your daughter is safe,' Charu informed him. 'Anumita did it…with Manik's help. She's explaining why.'

'Anu? Anu! What did you do? You wretch! What the hell did you do with my daughter?' Prithvi shouted, enraged. Then he turned towards Manik and punched him in the stomach. Manik fell back.

Ravi leapt to his feet and helped him up again. Then he stood between Prithvi and Manik and held his hand up in warning. 'No, sir, don't.'

'That punch was for trying to take my daughter away from me. Manik, my brother, I gave you a job to help my daughter. Anu would also benefit, free to test new waters, to indulge herself. But, you failed even in that.' Prithvi sat back, sneering at Manik.

'You knew about us, didn't you? You set this up?' Manik said, bitterly.

'Why did you think I let you into the house? Do you think anything happens here without my knowledge?' Prithvi leaned forward. 'Of course, I knew. I am not a fool, Manik.'

'And yet, *Mantri Ji*, you know and realize nothing. For an elected representative, you are pretty unaware of what goes on in your own house.'

'What the hell do you mean?'

'Did you never wonder why, suddenly, cameras were installed everywhere in your haveli?'

'Anu wanted added security for the girls.'

'When did she start getting the panic attacks? You never cared to think; you were too busy with your sycophants, your constituency, too busy to see what was happening under your roof.'

'What is it that you want to say? Just spit it out.'

'Your wife was raped by your mentor, your dear Swamiji. Myra is his daughter, Prithvi,' Manik said in a flat voice.

'No...that is not possible,' Prithvi shot up from his chair. 'Anu, what is he saying? Tell me it isn't true! You're making this up to torment me, aren't you?'

Anumita silently turned her eyes to the floor and began to weep.

He turned to Charu. 'Chumki, did you know about this? You, who always knows everything, *did you know*?' He was mad with rage.

'Prithvi...'

'Tell me, damn it, did you hide it from me?'

'Initially, I only sensed Anumita's misery. We came to know about the reason behind it only recently.'

'No, no...this is a conspiracy against Swamiji...and all of you are in it. Nothing you say can make it true.' He slowly shook his head, unwilling to believe what they were saying about the man who made him what he was.

'You still don't believe me—your wife? You don't believe anyone in the room. You are so blinded by your faith that you are willing to accept everyone else is wrong, but not your Swamiji. But, why am I surprised?' Anumita's resentment showed in her voice.

'Prithvi, there is a video,' Charu whispered. 'We have proof against Ram Vilas.' She looked towards Ravi. Ravi handed it to Prithvi. Then, as an afterthought, he gave him a pair of earphones. He watched as Prithvi's expression underwent a change from scepticism to shock, to fury—all carefully contained.

'Where did you get the video?' he asked, woodenly. 'Could it be doctored?'

Anumita laughed. 'Now, do you understand why I didn't tell him, Charu?'

'And, that's why I didn't want Myra back in this house,' said Manik. 'I don't trust him and his devotion to that crazy old man.' He stared at Prithvi distastefully.

'It makes no sense...' Prithvi continued, unconvinced.

'I wanted Anu to be free,' Manik took over from Anumita. 'When I began visiting Prithvi, Anumita would always look deeply troubled. I wondered why. I began to notice small things about her, how she cringed when Prithvi shouted at someone, the bruises she tried to hide. I tried to stay away, but we were constantly thrown together. We fell in love, but we had no future together. She was my *bhabhi*—a minister's wife.

Malti Devi came over to live here, and things took a turn for the worse. She overtook Anu's life, spying on her for Prithvi. Somehow, I convinced Anu to confide in me. That was when she told me that she was pregnant and Ram Vilas was the father. She was scared of Ram Vilas and scared of her husband. She wanted to break free.

Things were difficult when Myra was born. Prithvi even injured Sia during one of his fits. Anu wanted to leave with the girls immediately, but Prithvi's minions would have found them. I suggested that she send Myra out first, and then she and Sia could slip away after some time. She would have enough reason to walk out on him. We would start a life together... away from this city. I thought we could pull this off.'

'Prithvi, I decided to leave after you injured Sia. I had stayed on with you because of the girls, because I thought you loved your daughters. But, the day you pushed Sia, and she fell on the glass, it was the last straw for me,' said Anumita.

'But, I said I was sorry. I was drunk,' Prithvi reasoned.

'Did you plan to take Gita along when you left Prithvi?'

'No, it would have been difficult enough to survive in another city with two girls. Adding another person would not have been wise. I explained it to her. I knew she was sulking.'

Charu knew it was Gita who had told Malti Devi about Anumita's plan to divorce Prithvi. She wondered if it was a slip or if she had wanted Anumita's plan to fail. That's why she had been living with her guilt.

'We were ready to meet the lawyer when my mother cornered me in Myra's room. It was a weekend, and I had just given Myra her bath. She came in with Ram Vilas and closed the door. She held my arms and shook me. She said they knew all about our sleazy affair and my plan to divorce Prithvi. She said they would never let it happen. I pleaded with them that Prithvi would hurt the girls or me seriously someday, but she only scoffed at my fear. She said, sometimes men lose control. It was the woman's job to keep them satisfied and happy. So, if Prithvi hit me, it was my own fault, and I should change my ways.

I was deathly scared. Ram Vilas said I should continue to live in silence, like the good girl I was, or he had other ways to convince me. He said my daughters were growing to be as beautiful as I was, and he was glad to be in their lives. My blood froze at his threat. I asked for Manik's help.' Anumita sat trembling. 'I had no option but to flee. Prithvi would never change his ways, I knew that.'

'Can you both stop painting me as the villain?' said Prithvi. 'I have never hit Anu on purpose. Chumki, you know that, don't you? I am not one of those men who beat their wives.'

'Prithvi, you are another person when you are drunk. You don't remember anything in the morning. Like Jekyll and Hyde.' Anumita seethed at his unaffected manner, his need to be seen as a perfect man who could never be wrong.

'But, how did you carry her out?' Ravi asked Manik. 'We know Anumita tampered with the camera in Myra's room. You went to the bathroom twice. How did you escape with Myra, unseen?'

'I entered through the window,' Manik replied.

'The window on the first floor?' Ravi asked, incredulous.

Manik nodded.

'But, that trellis is too flimsy. I know. I checked,' Ravi muttered.

'My father is a carpenter. I replaced some of the slats with real wood to support my weight when we decided to do this—except the ones at the base—the ones you must have tested.'

'How did Myra stay quiet for so long?' asked Charu.

'When I went to the bathroom the first time, I climbed in through the window and gave her a cough syrup—the one Anu gives her to get her to sleep when she is restless at night. I almost got caught.'

'Why?'

'As I was entering Sia's room, I heard a sound. It was Ram Vilas climbing up the stairs. I thought he was coming to check up on us or talk to Malti Devi, but he never crossed Sia's door. At 3 pm, the second time, I put her inside the cricket kit, gave her another dose, and she slept again. I pulled the zipper halfway, put the bag in the bathtub and shut the door. It was a risk with Gita, who could easily have checked inside the bathroom, but there was no other place. I just hoped she wouldn't.

When Gita saw that the cot was empty, she ran into Sia's room. We went to check the cot, then I sent her with Sia to wake up Malti Devi. While they were banging on Malti Devi's door, I pulled out the bag and put it in the broom closet. No one ever thought of looking there. I left without my kit, to ward off suspicion. Later, I called Gita, and she handed it over to me through the back gate.'

'Couldn't Gita see that it was Myra when she went to collect the kit for you? Was she also involved?' asked Ravi.

'I had covered Myra with a sheet. She was placed in such a way that the zip closed over her covered feet. I don't know if Gita knew what we were doing, but I didn't tell her,' Manik confessed.

'So much security—and you took her out with barely a hitch—in a damn bag!' Prithvi shook his head, his fury visible in his clenched fists.

'And, the ransom call?'

'I heard you all discussing it, wondering about it. We had Seema call up and ask for a small amount,' Anumita divulged to them. Charu realized Seema had been sitting quietly.

'Seema, you said you were engaged with Manik. Why did you involve yourself in this plan?' Charu asked her.

'It was Ram Vilas's doing. He convinced my father...and I had no say in the matter. I have a boyfriend, a nice boy from another caste. My father was dead against it and forced the engagement upon me. When Manik confided in me, I saw it as an opportunity for both of us to flee. I agreed to help him. It looked like the perfect solution for both of us. If only it had worked...'

Charu wondered at how many lives Ram Vilas and his interfering ways had managed to ruin.

Seema continued with her story. 'Two months ago, Manik called and asked for my help. He was honest and told me his plan and the circumstances that had led to it. They were planning to send Myra out first, before Sia and Anu left. They would build a new life. As a woman, I understood Anu would take such big a step, only for the sake of her children.'

'You have been scheming to take my daughter away from me for months? What kind of a mother are you?' Prithvi yelled at Anumita.

Charu was about to jump to Anumita's defence but, before she could say a word, Anumita spoke up for herself. 'I am the kind of mother who will do what is necessary to save her children...from even their father.'

Prithvi grumbled but then fell silent. Charu smiled. 'Manik, you would never have been able to go back to your family,' Prithvi retorted.

'Yes, I know,' Manik said.

'And, later, how was Anumita going to...?'

'What is going on here?' Ram Vilas asked as he entered the room with Malti Devi. The two of them saw the roomful of people and realized they had missed out on something important. Ram Vilas was surprised that Prithvi hadn't considered it necessary to invite him over. Malti Devi was simply curious and offended at not having been included.

'What are all of you talking about?' she asked, suspiciously. 'Oh, good you are here, Ravi Ji. Arrest him.' She pointed to Manik and narrowed her eyes when she saw Seema.

'Why?' Ravi stared at her in surprise.

'You caught Manik's fiancée with Myra, didn't you? Isn't that right, Manik? They kidnapped her together. The face seemed familiar when I saw that sketch you circulated. I thought I had recognized the ring. It was troubling me. Then I remembered I had seen Prithvi's *tai,* his uncle's wife, wearing it at one of the functions. I called her up and asked her about Manik's marriage plans. She told me Manik had taken his fiancée to Delhi with him. She had given her, her ring.' She turned to Prithvi. 'I told you this man was trouble. As soon as I found out, I called Swamiji.'

Oblivious of his protégé's volatile mood, Ram Vilas said, 'Prithvi, why are you sitting like this? *Beta,* these things are in God's hands... You see, you and I, we are mere puppets. Even if this team hasn't found Myra, we will find her. Myra will come home.'

'Arrest this woman,' Malti Devi ordered Ravi, pointing at Seema.

'She has nothing to do with this. She is completely innocent. She did everything under my guidance. Ravi sir, I have confessed. Please, say you will let her go, unharmed. She was only taking care of Myra,' Manik appealed to him.

'Prithvi *beta,* what is the matter with you?' asked Ram Vilas, finally sensing something was wrong. He pulled at Prithvi's arm. Charu felt Prithvi tremble.

'What is the matter, you ask?' Prithvi tried hard to control his fury. 'The matter is...I have just been told that the man I held above everybody else, even my father; the one who has been my mentor and guide...raped my wife! And no, oh no...that is not all. He is the father, the goddamn *father* of my daughter!' he shouted, spittle flying out of his mouth, his face purple with a murderous rage.

Ram Vilas snatched his hand away as if stung. Wide-eyed and speechless, he looked at the enraged man before him.

'Yes, you were a snake then, and you are a snake now,' Anumita found the courage to speak up. 'You went behind my father's back doing all sorts of rubbish with her.' She glared at Malti Devi. 'You think I didn't know? I tried to warn my father but, like Prithvi, he didn't believe me.' She turned to

Malti Devi, 'Why did you marry my father at all? You should have married him!'

'You are lovers?' Prithvi asked, thunderstruck.

'What! No, Prithvi *beta*. Anu has lost her senses. I haven't done anything,' Ram Vilas said.

'Are you saying that the caretaker at the Hisar ashram is not your son?' Charu intervened.

Malti Devi and Ram Vilas stared at each other, nonplussed.

'What are you talking about?' Anumita looked up.

Charu heard Ravi place a document on the desk. She knew it was the birth certificate of the man, who had grown up as an orphan.

'You make me sick,' Anumita said to Malti Devi.

'Your son is the caretaker of the Hisar ashram. You met him the day Myra was kidnapped and went to Sirsa with him to sign a new will.'

'So, the puja was only a pretence?' Prithvi couldn't trust himself to speak.

'No, they did perform puja, but, along with that, Ram Vilas also changed his will. Isn't that right, Malti Devi?' Ravi continued. 'Why did you do it, Ram Vilas?'

'It is his will; he can change it anytime he wants.' Malti Devi's eyes darted to the swami, who stood unmoving.

'Because, I felt like it,' Ram Vilas said, defiantly.

'And, because Malti Devi blackmailed you. She told you that she would tell everyone the truth if you didn't include her child in the will. That is why you went to the Hisar ashram, picked up your son, and then went to Sirsa to sign the papers,' Charu finished.

Ram Vilas started sweating. He backed away from Charu. 'How...how do you know what I am...?'

'You shouldn't have dropped your guard, Ram Vilas.'

'Prithvi *beta*, it seems you have forgotten what I taught you. You have forgotten who you are and what I am to you. I don't think I should stay here a moment longer.' Ram Vilas tried to walk away.

Ravi's heavy hand on his shoulder stopped him. He pushed him towards a chair. 'Please sit down.'

'Prithvi,' Ram Vilas made a final attempt, 'you will be sitting in the high chair in a few years. You just have to do what I tell you. Family is like collateral damage when you have to do good in the world. Women and children only come in the way. They make us weak.'

Instead of answering him or even acknowledging that he had heard his mentor, Prithvi glared at Malti Devi. 'You lived in this house, well aware that your daughter had been raped by this person. And still, you followed him around like a...'

'And you, what kind of a husband are you?' Malti Devi wasn't going to back down. 'A pathetic drunk who hits his wife and daughters. You are one to talk? Yes, I knew. I took her to the doctor for an abortion, but she refused. She insisted that we should tell you, but what good would it have done? You wouldn't have believed her. She wanted to divorce you. We had to scare her to make her stay with you. I did my best to keep things quiet. This Manik was just a diversion. I have seen such diversions fizzle out with time.'

'Now, do you see the kind of people you have around you? What choice did Anu have?' said Manik.

'Prithvi, don't listen to them,' Ram Vilas tried to reach his protégé.

'She is my *wife*. You should not have touched my wife!' Prithvi bellowed. Ram Vilas fell back, shocked at the hate directed towards him.

Reeti, who had left earlier at Ravi's signal, walked in at that moment with Myra in her arms. Anumita cried and ran to her. She held her tight and kissed her repeatedly, apologizing. Malti Devi went up to Ram Vilas and helped him up. Prithvi looked at his daughter and waited for relief and happiness to overwhelm him—but felt only confusion.

'We should take them to the police station and interrogate them properly, now that Myra is home,' said Reeti.

'No, you can't take her to the police station, and now there is no need anyway,' Prithvi declared.

'Prithvi, we have to take their individual statements,' said Charu.

'No, no one is going to take any statement,' Prithvi reiterated. 'Myra has been found. The case is closed. I don't wish to file any report.'

'Prithvi, your wife was raped by this man. Don't you want her to get justice?'

Prithvi looked at Ram Vilas and then at his wife. 'Ram Vilas and Malti Devi must leave Chauhan Haveli immediately,' he said. 'I don't want to see or hear from either of them ever again.'

'But, Prithvi *beta*...' Ram Vilas mumbled.

Prithvi raised his hand to stop him. 'Immediately,' he repeated, 'or I will hand you both over to the police, as Ravi suggests.'

Ram Vilas backed off. He left the room with Malti Devi before Prithvi changed his mind.

'Prithvi, you have to...' Charu began.

'Anumita, we should check on Sia,' Prithvi interrupted her, walking towards his wife. They left the room together.

'Ravi, what the hell is this?' Reeti whispered as the door closed behind him.

'Let me talk to Commissioner Bakshi.' Ravi walked to a corner of the room. He rang and informed his superior that Myra had been found, the kidnapper had been apprehended—and had confessed. Ravi also told him about Ram Vilas and his sexual assault on Prithvi's wife. The police had, however, not yet been informed. But, they had the confessions on tape.

'Ravi, that is some good work. I will get back to you. Sit tight till then. I need to ask Prithvi what he wants to do.' Ravi heard the uncertainty in Commissioner Bakshi's voice.

'Sir, the law has to take its course. We have a godman who has confessed to rape,' Ravi frowned.

'But, has the woman filed a complaint? It's a minister's wife, Ravi. You brought the truth out. That is all you were asked to do.'

26. Charu

10:30 pm, Friday

Charu sat on her desk listening to Ravi amidst the overwhelming chaos screeching and pulling at her, and closed her eyes. They were echoes of all the heightened emotions that had unfolded in the past hours. She wanted to push everything away for some time. But, there was so much still to be done.

Ravi tried to convince his superior, but to no avail. When Charu could not take it anymore, she left her desk and walked out.

'Where are you going? Ravi asked.

'I am going to check on Anumita,' she said.

'How's Manik?' Anumita asked when Charu had shut the door to her room. Charu heard Myra's babble, as well as Sia's gentle voice, as they played nearby.

'He is all right, all things considered,' Charu assured Anumita.

'I...I wanted to talk to you. I don't think Prithvi will let Manik off so easily. But, if you tell him, he will,' she said. 'You have sway over Prithvi. He still considers you his woman. He does not care for anyone the way he does for you, Charu. I don't wish to stay on here anymore. I want a divorce. It's my final decision.'

Listening to Anumita, Charu felt glad she would always have Anwar Haveli and her family ready to welcome her with open arms. She would never have to remain in a difficult situation because there was nowhere else to go. 'Anumita, I want you to know that whatever you choose to do, you can count on me,' she said.

'Hi.' Reeti knocked and entered.

'All okay?' Charu asked.

'Are you done here? We...um...need you downstairs.'

'Yes, I am done.' Charu stood up and held out her hand to Anumita. After a moment, Anumita took it. 'Goodbye and take care, Anumita.' Charu walked away feeling something she hadn't for a long time. Hope.

Charu and Reeti entered the back room, which was abuzz with the process of wrapping up after the case was solved. Overwhelming exhaustion that had been dodging Charu until now made her stumble. Ravi caught her just in time.

'You are tired. Rest for a while,' Ravi said, helping her to the couch.

Charu thought about protesting, then simply lay down and immediately fell into a deep slumber.

Ravi covered her curled form with a thin blanket and stood looking at her drawn face. Prithvi walked into the room. He looked at Charu on the couch. Lowering his voice, he said, 'I just came to say that Ram Vilas is out of the picture. I know you wanted us to file a complaint. But, this is an unofficial favour. So, until Anumita does not feel confident and certain, we will keep this to ourselves.' Prithvi started walking around the room.

'I am sending my mother-in-law back to her village in Hisar. She is not someone I want near my daughters...yes, they are *mine*. I have to let Manik go too. He is family, after all, and he tried to save Myra... What is the matter?' Prithvi asked, perplexed at their silence.

Ravi frowned and looked away. His eyes fell on Charu, who was sitting, her eyes huge, her face blanched of colour. Ravi reached Charu in two strides and sat kneeling before her.

Ravi noted her unfocused eyes. She was still dreaming. The sounds emanating from her throat were pitiful. She sounded like a wounded animal who could do nothing more than whimper.

'Charu...Charu...wake up... You are here...with me...,' Ravi said, softly.

Charu just squinted her eyes as if she was looking at something.

'Charu...come back,' Ravi said as he touched her hands.

'What is she dreaming about now?' Prithvi asked.

'I don't know,' Ravi said.

Ravi jumped when Charu screamed. For a moment, he felt frozen. Then holding onto her shoulders, he snatched her up, shaking her.

'Come back...Chumki...find a way out...you can...,' Prithvi commanded loudly near her ear.

Charu, who had been twisting away from Ravi's hands, yelping as if he was beating her suddenly, slumped at Prithvi's command. Prithvi saw Ravi fold Charu in his arms and rock her, just as he had rocked Anumita when she had nightmares just after Myra had been born. His heart squeezed now that he knew the reason why. Prithvi leaned against the table and waited. He knew Charu had found a way out.

Charu blinked, then crumpled into Ravi to wheeze into his shoulder. Ravi tightened his arms around Charu.

'It took you longer to get out. What happened? Was it...?' Ravi asked.

Charu shook her head.

'They are not part of a dream, Ravi...they are memories. My memories.'

'What do you mean?' Ravi demanded.

'As soon as I lay down to rest on the sofa, I felt the tension dissipate. I heard you walking towards me and wanted to open my eyes, but they were too heavy. I felt you drape the blanket over me. I wanted to smile, reassure you when I sensed your concern, your worry for me, but I felt myself sliding,' Charu whispered.

'Somehow, I knew where I was going. I wanted to raise my arm and call out to you, Ravi. But, nothing came out. I felt paralyzed. Then I slid inside the musty room and saw the girl kneeling on the floor,' she gasped.

'I saw…' Charu recounted her dream.

Sunrays touched the girl's hair. A tear rolled down her cheek. The mice were making quick work of the grains of rice near her knees. She winced, shifting as the mice grew more courageous and drew closer to her bloody knees.

Somehow, she sensed the man was not around.

The man had taken her school ribbons. Her Ma had plaited them in her hair so meticulously this morning…was it this morning? She couldn't remember what day it was.

She knew her shirt was dirty and torn in most places; her shoulders were jutting out sharp and frail. She held her hands tight at her back as she had been told to do. They were grubby, the nails filthy.

Hearing footsteps, her eyes fluttered, but she kept them closed. She heard the sway of the switch that alternated the footsteps coming her way, slapping against the pant leg. A familiar smell filled her nostrils. The scent of roses. She wondered what the man would do with them.

'I got these for you. I hear you like roses. Your mother has grown a few bushes near your window so you can smell them, hasn't she?' the man asked.

The girl nodded. He walked closer, and she heard the scattering mice, the crunch of rice under his slippers.

She got to know intimately the thorny branches of a rose bush tied together to make a flexible but deadly switch. The cutting thorns made her legs buckle when it was used to test how long she could go without uttering a sound. The thorns drew blood; she felt it run down her skin.

When the man was tired, he threw the decimated stems. The girl heaved a sigh of relief. Then unexpectedly, a shower of soft petals rained down on her. Her tightly closed eyes burst open at the silky feel of the petals tumbling down on her. And, that was what broke her.

'I can still smell the roses. The little girl then tilted her head to the side as if to look straight at me. The girl looked at me, her brown eyes filled with accusations in the face that was mine as a child.' When Charu finished recounting her dream, she sensed the shock from all of them. She couldn't remember the last time they had a rose bush anywhere on the grounds of Anwar Haveli in the past so many years. She remembered smelling roses as a child. The small scars she had on her back and legs now made sense.

'Ravi, take me home,' she said before falling into his arms.

27. Ravi

1 am, Saturday

Ravi looked at Anwar Haveli as they turned into the circular driveway. It looked imposing, portentous, even as if blaming him for not taking care of its daughter. He looked away. He rang the bell several times before Arun opened it. One look at Charu lying quietly in Ravi's arms, and all hell broke loose.

'Uma, UMA,' Arun shouted for his wife as if he couldn't face what Ravi would tell him, alone.

'Is she all right?' Uma asked, rushing to Charu's room behind Ravi.

Ravi's stomach was in knots. Usually, even in a trance, Charu would fight back, moan, go rigid, lash out...it told him she was in there somewhere. But, right now, she was still as... death. Only her pupils danced under her closed eyelids, tears flowing unbidden from her eyes. Ravi tried his best to shake her awake.

This dream...trance...hypnosis...whatever she was in that had sucked her into a place where she seemed unreachable. He lay Charu on her bed, covering her legs with a sheet, then turned to her anxious family and explained as best he could.

'Call her grandmother, Ravi,' Arun suggested once Ravi told them everything that had occurred. Ravi dialled the number with unsteady hands. When he replaced the receiver, Arun asked him. 'What happened? What did she say?'

'She said that Charu will come out of this trance, but she should not be disturbed. We have to stand guard while Charu finds her way out of this abyss, on her own.'

Charu's heartbeat thundered as she saw herself, a small girl crouched in the back of a van.

'Please. . .please, no,' I begged. A cloth covered my face, smothering me.

'Charu. . .CHARU. . .I can't. . .where. . .CHARU,' I heard Bhavya calling my name loudly, looking for me. I wanted to answer back, but nothing came out except a squeak. Something pierced my skin from the side. I flinched.

'Keep quiet, or I will kill you, then I will kill your sister,' a man, whispered.

I pressed my lips together. There was no way I would put my sisters in danger. The car started, and my heart sank when we drove away.

I knew I was being kidnapped. I was old enough to know that much.

It took 300 heartbeats from my school for the car to stop. With two fingers on my wrist I counted. Hard hands pulled at my arm and led me down fifteen stairs. I fell down and scraped my knees. Scared, I sat on the cold ground, every puff of breath shallow. I wasn't sure I could remove the cover from my head. So, I waited. Pulling up my knees, I hugged them, missing my mother. I curled on my side, trembling. The heavy footsteps, laboured breathing, and deep voices woke me. The cloth was ripped off my face. When I heard the scrape of a chair, my belly dipped. I knew someone was watching me.

The man tied something around my neck. He wrapped the other end of the clinking chain around the brick pillar. I had been tied to the brick column with a dog chain.

Then I heard the sound that I would get familiar with in the days to come. The sound when the belt buckle is released. The clip had made a squeaking sound when the man pulled at it.

I could feel his excitement. He wanted to hear me cry out, to see the red welts on my skin.

In the hours that followed, I knew which side of the belt I would be feeling by the sound of it cutting through the air. The chain around my neck didn't allow me to escape the belt. When the fat man got tired, he sat puffing like a steam engine. My throat, raw from screaming, closed up.

'Water...please...' I coughed.

'Stop this ruckus right now, or I will beat you again,' he said, slapping me. He threw the belt on the floor and walked away.

I heard small, bare feet running down the stairs. Someone handed me a bottle that I grabbed and drank from quickly.

'That's enough. You will make yourself sick. I can't leave the bottle, but I will bring it again,' a boy whispered before snatching it from my hands and running away.

The thin man came later. He pulled at the leash suddenly, and I fell to the floor. He pulled it high, and I had to stand on my tiptoes, stretching my neck to be able to breathe. I gasped, clawing at the chain around my neck, my feet slipping.

'Stop...please...please...stop...,' I choked, crying loudly.

The heavy man came running down and scolded him.

'You are going to kill her on the first day only. We haven't even been paid yet. Are you mad?'

'And, what are you doing? She's bleeding. Sahib won't be happy,' they argued as they climbed up the fifteen steps. I kept count.

After their voices faded, I heard another set of steps. Lithe, fast, they rushed down.

'Hey, get up quick, eat something before they come back. Jaldi,' the boy said. 'If they come to know I gave you food, they will kill me too,' he said.

I sat up and ate what he handed me. Stiff roti with chutney. I sensed his fear and his need to help me.

'Please call my mother, please...help me,' I begged.

'I...I can't...I...I...he will kill me. You will learn to take it. If no one comes and they spare you, they might, you being a girl. You will bring money.' He snatched the half-eaten roti and fled when the man shouted, looking for him.

They will find me...they would be searching for me...but what if they are relieved I am no longer there? The thought was so scary I told myself not to think it.

When I am rescued, I would tell the police everything.

There were three people there. All men.

One was heavy. His chappals slapped against the ground when he walked. He was cruel and liked to use the belt on me. He would hit me. Take a break. Then start again. The hours passed in a haze of pain.

One was skinny, slimy. He was the dangerous one. He liked to play with me and talked a lot, like a child. He enjoyed throwing darts at me. Shards or sharp pebbles were what he liked best. He would tell me what he would hit.

My left eye...right cheek...nose...collar bone...it went on and on.

The third was the kind boy who brought food and water. Anwar, he told me his name. He never said anything. He, too, was scared and felt bad for me.

One more man came...I don't know when. His step was sure, like he was confident of his place. He came in, looked at me. A grey smog clung to him.

'Where is my money?' The fat one demanded.

I heard the hand hit his cheek. The chokehold that made him beg for mercy. His thoughts crashed into me.

I will kill her once I get my money, I will break her...grind her under my feet...she will be nothing...she is nothing, he thought, his hate vicious.

I knew it was night when the men locked the door and left. That meant no one else was coming in. The pain was constant. But, I knew that for the next few hours, no one was going to threaten my life or my family.

I heard the door opening. I scrambled back as far as the chain would let me go expecting more pain. He was angry, the fat man. Someone had informed the police... Who would have done that... he hadn't gotten his money...he would peel the skin away from my bones before the police got here...he would kill me...he would take everyone down with him..., he said.

I heard his arm rise. I sucked in my breath, knowing he would hit harder this time. I continued crying in agony as the pin of the buckle slashed at my skin. I felt it claw some of my skin away every time it stuck. I...I wanted to tell him I was already broken; he could stop.

'Bhaiyaji...jaldi,' the thin man came running, asking him to forget me and run. He pulled at his arm, but the heavy man was not satisfied. I knew I would die today. I accepted my fate...almost welcomed it.

The next moment, the buckle hit my head with such ferocity that I was unable to breathe. The sound of the metal hitting my skull rang in my head even as I passed out. A black scab formed over it, blotting it out of my reality.

I don't know for how long I was unconscious.

I woke up thinking I had left the window open. The rain would drench everything. The bedcover, my bedsheet...then I realized someone was sprinkling water on my face.

'Shhhh...,' the boy, Anwar, whispered. 'Keep your eyes closed. Pretend for a while longer.'

I stilled. That was when the sound of the sirens registered. Running booted feet. CHARU...someone called.

I closed my eyes, letting the darkness carry me where it would.

Ravi sat beside a comatose Charu. A witness to the suffering that she had hidden even from herself. He resolved to never leave her side. He held Charu as she whimpered her agony in his ears. He was willing to promise his soul in exchange for an end to this purgatory that Charu was enduring.

11 pm, Sunday

'It has been hours...Charu has not woken up. What should we do?' Uma asked, looking at Ravi's tired eyes.

'I don't know anymore, Uma Aunty,' he said.

'She looks so peaceful like she is sleeping,' Uma murmured, caressing Charu's hair.

'She talks in the night,' Ravi said.

'About what?' Uma asked.

'About what happened...to her...in those three days...with those men...,' Ravi said.

'Yes, I sat with her in the hospital when they put her in a coma,' Uma said.

'Put her in...why?'

'The doctors said she had suffered a concussion...when... when she was hit on her head. But, I thought it was because they didn't want her...to go through the...trauma again. They didn't know that she relived it every night.'

'And, you with her,' Ravi added.

Uma nodded.

'You could have asked Arun Uncle or Suresh Uncle to stay.'

'No, they can't bear to see her like this. Hearing about what she had undergone would have destroyed Arun. And, Suresh—he would have died or killed those men with his own hands. No...there was no one else. I was responsible. I am her mother, I got so busy looking after Dheeraj that I...had I...I failed both my children,' Uma said.

'When she woke up in the hospital, Charu was so...so... fragile, otherworldly. She has always been...more astute... more sensitive than all the other children. One always had to be careful around her...maybe, I was more careful than I needed to be. She knew what I was feeling much before I did at times,' Uma said.

'Aruna and Bhavya were close, so I think she felt left out. She built an imaginary world around herself. The haveli and the *kothris* and the service passages became her playground. But once the police found her in that basement, she...changed. She didn't even want me to touch her. She wouldn't come inside the haveli.' Uma said, wiping her eyes with her saree.

'Outside, she would cry if she smelt the roses. She...she kept asking me why we had planted roses. I uprooted all the bushes just so she could sit in peace for some time,' Uma sobbed.

'Who is Anwar? She keeps calling for him,' Ravi asked.

'Anwar was the one who informed the police. He helped Charu, gave her food, helped her survive. He protected her. At the time, she would whisper his name as if she was calling out to him. Later, when she woke up and didn't remember anything, she named the haveli, Anwar.'

'Her protector,' said Ravi. 'What happened to him?'

'He was another boy they had kidnapped some years before. The grandson of a rich political family. But, no one paid his ransom, or...something went wrong. I don't really remember now. They kept him as a helper. He was around fifteen when the police found him with Charu. The boy wanted to meet her, but I said no. Some things are best forgotten.'

'What happened to the men who had kidnapped her?'

'They went to prison. Life sentences. Sureshji made sure. They never came out. One was caught in a gang war, and the other committed suicide in prison,' Uma's voice held secrets Ravi was not sure he wanted to know.

'Did you find out why they took her? Her file said for ransom.'

'We had a court case with Arun's stepbrother, Varun, that dragged on for years when the girls were small. Charu was home from the hospital. And, Sureshji and Arun had gone to the court. I got a call that they had left some papers home. I went to the court to hand them over. When I was coming out of the court complex, I saw Varun. He...he took out her hair ribbons, from his pocket...the ribbons she wore to... sch...school. I didn't leave Charu's side for days. But I knew her safety meant more than anything else, even my need to be with her.'

'That's why you sent her away to Surat.'

'It shattered us both, I know, but we could not risk Charu being in danger again. When we won the case, and Varun moved out of town, we called Charu back, but she was never my...mine again. She had found a new family in Surat.'

Uma walked up to her daughter and clasped her hand in hers.

'I will get you some tea, Ravi,' she said to the silent sentinel who sat beside her daughter.

Charu felt soft lips on her forehead. A whispered plea to find her way back. She, realizing all she had needed was to believe that she had reached the centre of her maze. The price may have been heavy, but she finally knew her truth.

Ravi heard Charu's breath rasping. She tightened her fingers around Ravi's.

'Charu…CHARU?' he cried, then she jerked upright as her eyes snapped open.

She cried uncontrollably, her hands on her face only to slump onto Ravi's warm chest.

When her insides revolted, Ravi simply cradled her and, in giant strides, carried her to the bathroom just in time to empty her stomach. He held her hair, rubbing her back, pressing a cold cloth on her forehead.

'How long was I out?' she finally said, her voice croaky and her throat choked.

'Almost twenty-four hours.'

Ravi grabbed her and carried her to the bed. He held her in his lap, rocking her gently. He tightened his arms holding her close as loud, wet sobs racked her body, the sound echoing in the room.

Here it is…this is my home…mine to keep, Charu thought.

If this is my destiny, to love Charu with everything in me and not have her ready to accept that love, then so be it, Ravi thought as he held her.

Uma paused at the threshold, watching her daughter grieving. Her heart-wrenching sorrow was reflected on Ravi's face. *Would Charu want me here?* Uma thought.

'Charu, I am so…' Uma sobbed. She spread her arms and folded Charu into them. Mother and daughter sat holding each other. Uma knew Charu had taken the first step towards healing wounds she never knew she had.

'Ma, why…why did you never tell me?' Charu said, feeling empty. Everything seemed coloured by the knowledge of what she had undergone.

'Charu, my love, you were ten years old. What could I tell you? You were completely lost. I just wanted to carry you around, hold you tight, never let you out of my sight, but you...you wanted nothing to do with people. You would start weeping if anyone came close. It took weeks to just...sit with you in the same room.' Uma gripped Charu's hands tight.

'But you sent me away...I felt abandoned,' said Charu.

'I didn't want to send you. But I preferred that you live safely away rather than risk your safety. Charu, we were so scared. Please forgive me.'

'Charu, it is not your mother's fault but mine,' said Arun, who had been silently listening to them from the door.

'There should be no more secrets between us. When Uma told me what she suspected, I became more determined than ever to keep the haveli. When Uma suggested we send you to Surat for your safety, I agreed with her. Rather than saying that I would help out in your care, I...let you go. Uma was forced to make this decision because she was handling everything alone. I barely contributed. If you girls are strong and independent today, it is because of Uma,' Arun admitted.

'You are right to question our intentions. There is no excuse. I accept responsibility for your pain and suffering. I have berated myself every time I heard you scream in the night for not doing what was within my power to do. Ravi watched as Arun placed a loving hand on Charu's shoulder, linking the three of them together. Charu lifted her eyes, and he saw the beginnings of a smile at the edge of her mouth.

She will pull through this, Ravi knew.

28. Charu

4:30 am, a month later

Charu heard bird song as she woke up with a smile, stretching her arms above her head.

She felt happy these days. It was a different kind of happiness. The type that swells and flows just close to brimming over. She could smell the steeping tea from the kitchen, so she knew Ma was up. She turned, and her hand collided with a head of coarse hair. She sighed.

He didn't leave me, as he promised. Charu smiled.

'Hi,' he said, waking up and turning his face against her hand.

'Beard,' she said, running her fingers down his jaw.

'Gina says, I look like a pirate now.'

'What's up, Cap'n.'

He chuckled; the sound rusty.

'Ravi...'

She felt him pause...waiting.

'I don't want to be that person who is constantly eavesdropping. I want to have friends and a...uh...a relationship. And, you can't have either without letting people have their secrets.'

Ravi fell silent, processing her words. *Relationship...*

'You asked me a question the day we came here, do you remember?' Charu whispered.

'Are you proposing to me, Charu?' he teased.

'Uff! Forget I said anything,' she stood up.

'*Arrey, arrey,* don't be mad. Of course, I remember.' He wrapped his arms around her. 'Have...have you changed your mind about not wanting to get married?' Surprise and hope rang loudly in his voice.

'Let's take the long way to it,' Charu replied. Ravi was rendered speechless.

'Stop smiling,' she said.

'What? I am not.' His smile grew wider. 'Okay, maybe a little.'

'Shut up,' Charu laughed and entwined her fingers with his as Anwar Haveli began waking up to a new day.

The wind carried Charu's laughter to the small woman in the kitchen who smiled in gratitude at the sound.

Epilogue

And, that is the reason I shall always be in her debt.

She suffered hellfire because of me, battling demons that she should have never seen. More than her parents, I feel most responsible for her pain. Varun coveted me, and Charu got caught in his greed.

Is it good that Varun's role was never confirmed? I don't know. One can never know, as they say. But, maybe Charu will find out more now that there is knowledge.

I can already feel her mind churn. Ravi, too is resolved to check out Varun's whereabouts and keep his eyes trained on him. I know that boy will fight alongside Charu as she battles her memories.

I wish I could make her wishes come true. If only I had any sway over time, I would give her the world. Her weary heart deserves it the most.

How different these daughters are from each other. And, yet, the one thing that runs common in them is the need to be accepted for who they are.

Where Aruna will hint at what she wants, and Bee will take what she needs, Charu will wait for others to understand her desires. Charu finally recognizes her strength and its foundation within herself. She will conquer her insecurities and defeat the demons that haunt her with Ravi by her side. Once and for all.

Is there anything more a parent can ask for?

This end is also a beginning. A newness that springs unexpectedly, an old forgotten seed taking root. My namesake Anwar, the boy who protected Charu in that basement...I wonder if Charu will look for him. I feel renewed, revived with a child-like exuberance and joy. This joy is tinged with a nostalgic wistfulness, a remembered ache that fills me when I think of him, Anwar.

Like looking at an old photo.

About the Author

New Delhi-based Harshali Singh is a Member Judge in the Consumer Commission. She has written in several literary genres—poetry to fiction, columns to essays. She is the contributing author in several anthologies and regularly writes for e-magazines. She has written several books on women-centric issues like domestic violence, alienation, female foeticide, marital rape, and women empowerment. Her novels, *A Window to her Dreams* and *The Anatomy of Choice*, form part of an eight books series, called the *Haveli Series* published by Readomania. She has written several short stories in anthologies that traverse varied genres from Historical Fiction, mythology, horror, erotica, and many more.

Her poems are part of a woman-centric bilingual anthology of poems called *She the Shakti*. She has been on the organizing committee of Kavya Kumbh, an International Trilingual Poetry Fest where her poems feature in the anthology. She has won the prestigious Write India—Season 2, a short story contest organized by *The Times of India Group* on Chitra Banerjee Divakaruni's prompt. In 2020, Amitav Ghosh selected her short story in the Top 10 for his prompt. She has also chaired discussions and has been part of various panels with eminent personalities in their chosen fields of World Peace, meditation, infertility, and social causes and stalwarts in writing. As a painter, she expresses herself and her observations of her surroundings in oil paintings, which have been exhibited in solo and group shows in India Habitat Centre, New Delhi, and also in Gurugram.

Email: harshalisingh@gmail.com
Twitter: @harshalisingh
Instagram: @harshalisingh

Readomania

Readomania exists to nurture, curate, and bring to you content you love. We are a publishing house that takes pride in encouraging talent, new or old, and provide a wonderful platform for awesome stories.

We make this possible in multiple ways.

First, as an independent publishing house. Readomania boasts of multiple imprints across various categories—fiction, nonfiction, children, to name a few. An eclectic mix of content for its readers, when you read a Readomania title, you enter a world that's yours, supported by unique and quality narratives.

Second, as an online publishing platform for writers—a place to share stories, poems, opinions, travelogues, a way to explore your creative talent. Available as premium, as well as free-to-read content across multiple genres, the reader is spoilt for choice.

Join us in this journey, as we explore, develop, and present stories to our readers and audiences. Welcome to the world of Readomania, get ready to craft stories that enrich lives.

You can visit us at: www.readomania.com

